Did It All Before

Cynthia Hamill

A NineStar Press Publication

www.ninestarpress.com

Did It All Before

Edited by Elizabetta McKay

Printed in the USA

ISBN: 978-1-64890-320-5

First Edition, June, 2021

Also available in eBook, ISBN: 978-1-64890-319-9

WARNING:

This book contains sexually explicit content, which is only suitable for mature readers. Warnings for death of a close friend (past); discussion of death of a loved one (past); description of terrorist/war violence, gore (past), and scarring from injuries; medical procedures; alcohol abuse (brief mention); depiction of PTSD/ anxiety attack.

Award-winning photojournalist Scott Rowe is struggling with the physical injuries and emotional scars caused by the terrorist attack that killed his interpreter, Omran Saleh. A long succession of doctors and surgeons have put his body back together, but to Scott, his mind seems beyond repair. Panic attacks ambush his days, and nightmares haunt his fitful sleep. He can't bring himself to touch his broken camera, let alone consider returning to work. His only sanctuary is the darkroom, where he can escape the secret he carries surrounding Omran's death.

Dr Jason Andrews is determined to bring Scott back from the brink. His alternative healing methods are like nothing Scott has ever seen, and at first, Scott feels foolish lying on Jason's table with hot rocks in his hands or acupuncture needles in his skin. But one thing keeps Scott coming back: the detailed visions that appear like movies in his mind, of himself in other times, cultures, and continents, and Jason himself, whose relentless hope steers them through the storms of Scott's recovery.

As his health improves, Scott begins to wonder what his visions mean. Are they vivid daydreams, figments of his exhausted mind? And why does he only have these visions when he is with Jason?

Scott hopes the answers will give him a reason to make peace with Omran's death and begin to truly live again, instead of merely surviving. But what if they also give him a reason to love?

For all my sisters

Chapter One

Exposure (n.) An amount of light permitted to fall on light-sensitive material such as film or paper coated with emulsion; the act or process of taking a photograph; harmful effects of cold or other extreme environmental conditions; the revelation of private information.

Scott opens his eyes slowly as he steps out of the darkroom. The small lamp on his bedside cabinet provides only a shadowy glow over the flat, and he shuffles toward it with a yawn, finally ready for sleep.

When he'd started renting this place in Camden three years ago, it was meant to be somewhere to crash between jobs, a glorified storage locker with a shower. It's square and plain, his bed on one side and galley kitchen on the other, decorated only with photos and trinkets from his travels. After the accident, when it became clear he'd be grounded for a few months, he transformed the bathroom by draping a blackout curtain around the door and setting a plank over the bathtub for his chemical trays. There, he can flip on the fan and work for hours, just feet away physically but miles away mentally from his bed, where insomnia and nightmares crowd out any hope of sleep.

His darkroom habit is his only connection to photography these days. He hasn't picked up his camera since he left the hospital in January; it's in pieces, after all, his £3,200 digital Canon collecting dust in his cupboard. Scott never did find out who collected it from the scene and sent it along with him in the ambulance. They shouldn't have bothered. He can't bring himself to touch the thing, even to throw it out. Instead, he finds solace in the undeveloped film from his 35mm Leica.

Film is reserved for London, family, and home, where there are no publishing deadlines to meet or editors to please. He has compiled quite a collection of undeveloped rolls over the last few years. Being home only a day or two at a time had given him a chance to take pictures but not develop them before he'd be on his way again, so his desk drawer holds a grab bag of birthday parties, impromptu picnics, and London day trips. He never knows what will appear on the long strip of film, but he knows what won't. There will be no Ukraine, no Kabul, no Delhi; no plane crashes, no war zones, no children dying in poverty.

Last night, the roll he processed had turned out to be all Olivia and Thomas, two years ago at Christmas. Scott's heart clenched pleasantly when the images appeared, remembering how he and his sister had sprinkled jelly babies and crisps in the garden for reindeer food because Thomas thought that's what they'd like. Tonight, Scott picks out a few frames to print for Olivia, of their mum filling stockings and Thomas's astonished reaction to his new toy train. He spends time printing the images, making sure the contrast is perfect. His eyes finally get heavy as he places the last few photographs on the drying rack.

The sky is not yet lightening. Scott picks up his phone from the bedside cabinet to check the time. Thursday, the 19th of May, 4:07 a.m. An appointment reminder lights up, and *shit*, today is his first session with the new guy Dr Coulter wants him to see.

At least the appointment isn't until two.

After he crosses the day off his calendar with his black Sharpie (he's up to day one hundred fifty-nine) and sends a quick goodnight message on WhatsApp, Scott arranges himself in bed, flat on his back with his bad arm propped up on pillows. He'll get a few hours of sleep after all.

*

The first thing Scott notices when he opens the door marked Dr Jason Andrews is the welcoming light-herbal scent in the air, so different from the antiseptic smell of the other doctors' offices he's visited. He removes his sunglasses to a room that feels like the lobby of a spa, with warm tan walls decorated with Japanese prints and sisal rugs on the floors. There is music behind it all, a soft percussion of drum and flute. When he closes the door behind him, he feels far away from the noise and clamour of Stratford.

Behind the reception desk sits a woman, probably about his mum's age, with a soft apple face and kind eyes. She stands and extends her hand. "Scott?"

"Yes, hello." Scott offers his left hand instead of his right, and they both chuckle a little, looking down at his splinted arm under his jacket. Transparent moulded plastic holds his arm in an L-shape, and the elastic bandage he wears from his forearm to his shoulder is visible underneath it.

"My name is Monica. It's lovely to meet you." She looks him in the eye when she speaks, which catches Scott off guard. "Let's take you back. Follow me?"

They make their way to a room that is too brightly lit; Scott looks mostly at the floor until his eyes adjust, and Monica turns down the dimmer on the wall.

"Here is some paperwork for you. You'll see it's quite involved, but Dr Andrews would like as much detail as possible, so please be thorough. Drop it in the slot outside the door when you're finished, and he'll be right with you."

She leaves him with a pleasant smile, and it takes Scott a minute to get comfortable. The splint makes him take up more space in the chair than he'd thought, so he teeters on the edge, slanting the clipboard on his lap. *Fucking forms.* If Scott had a pound for every form he's filled out over the last five months, he could buy himself a bionic arm and be done with it.

The top part is easy, and he fills in his name, address, and contact information.

> *Referred by:* Dr Lance Coulter, Royal National Orthopaedic Hospital
>
> *Emergency contact:* Olivia Rowe
>
> *Relationship:* sister

He fills out her phone number, wondering what could happen to him in this quiet place that would warrant a call. At its very worst, it could only be an improvement over the last emergency call she'd received.

> *Occupation:* Photojournalist

The word comes easily by habit. But as he crosses his t's, Scott takes a beat, not sure if he can still properly call himself that. He's officially off roster at Getty and *The Times*. "Indefinite leave of absence" was what they'd termed it. But the alternative is to write "Unemployed," so he lets it lie.

Have you ever been under the care of a doctor of osteopathy? No

Have you ever had a professional massage? No

Do you have any particular goals for this session? (Scott considers writing "to get my doctor off my back" but changes his mind.) Recommended treatment by orthopaedic surgeon

Do you have any difficulty lying on your front, back, or side? Cannot lie on right side (temporarily).

Are you currently under the care of a traditional medical doctor? Yes

Scott lists his primary doctor, his orthopaedic surgeon, his dermatologist, his ophthalmologist, and his ear, nose, and throat doctor. He leaves the burn specialist off the list; she released him almost two months ago. After a moment of debate, he adds his physiotherapist, even though their visit a week ago ended with a shouting match and a slammed door. She'd been frustrated with him, and Scott had been stubborn. He's not sure he's going back.

List prescription medications you take currently. (He'd finished the last of the pain meds early on; over-the-counter scar-reducing gel doesn't count.) None

Are you a smoker? (The answer depends on the day, as well as the continent and the company.) Not often

Do you drink alcohol? (This one is tougher. Scott sighs and stares at the line, weighing his options. He considers leaving this one blank.) Sometimes

Take recreational drugs? No

Please indicate "Y" for "Yes" and "N" for "No" to indicate occurrence of the following conditions. Do you wear contact lenses? Hearing aids? Any known allergies or sensitivities to topical applications? High blood pressure? Diabetes? Epilepsy? Cancer? No, no, no, no, no, no, no. No Pregnancy, no Ulcer, no Abdominal pain or HIV virus.

The momentum takes him, and he almost blows by *Serious accident*. He scans down a bit further. Should he call it *Serious accident* or *Recent surgery*? Or maybe *Fractures*? He circles *Y* next to all three.

He hesitates next to *Insomnia* and *Headaches*, then circles *N* next to these as well. This doctor doesn't need to know everything.

If you are currently experiencing discomfort, tension, or injury, please indicate on the following diagram and describe in detail below.

Scott stares at the line drawing of a genderless human figure, a blank canvas waiting for embellishment. *This should be fun.* He can't resist drawing shoulder-length wavy hair on the person's head, along with his two tattoos, a heart on the shoulder and compass on the forearm. Then he gets down to business.

Scott doesn't catalogue the ruptured eardrums, the concussion, and the corneal perforation, since they've long since healed. The lacerations on his face and neck are gone, too, except for the long, angry line on his jaw. He concentrates on the arm, drawing a line through the upper right humerus. "Compound fracture." He circles the elbow. "Avulsed radial head." They'd required multiple surgeries, the last of which had been six weeks ago, to clean up the scar tissue at his elbow. But the contusions on his forearm and the minor wrist sprain have healed, so he draws an arrow toward them with the label "wrist and hand fine!" along with a smiley face. He draws *X*'s from the shoulder to the forearm and all over the right torso, front and back. "Second-degree burns (scarring)."

That should do it. Gorgeous.

Scott places the finished questionnaire in the slot outside the door, and sees no one in the hall.

Once back inside, he takes in the room. It's got the organised feel of a doctor's examination room, but instead of an exam table covered by a paper sheet, there is a massage table in the centre of the room made up with sheets and a blanket. There is a stainless-steel sink in the corner, with real towels instead of paper ones, and next to them, a tray of brown glass vials. A slow cooker is plugged in on the counter next to a jade plant and some crystals, gems, and rocks; in front of them a large white feather rests on a piece of red fabric. Soft music filters from the speakers on the ceiling.

He's about to read the framed certificates on the wall when there is a knock at the door.

"Hi, Scott. I'm Dr Andrews." He places a bottle of water on the counter and extends his left hand for Scott to shake as if it's completely normal. His hand is warm. "You can call me Jason."

"Hello."

"I feel like I know you after reading the information Lance sent over." Dr Andrews gestures down to the packet in his hand. There's the questionnaire Scott filled out, but there's a thick file underneath, too, labelled, Rowe, Scott.

A thrum ripples through Scott's stomach. *Shit.*

"So. You've been through a hell of a lot," Dr Andrews states, with direct eye contact, just as Monica had done. "I'm glad you decided to come see us."

"Well, I didn't think I had much of a choice, to be honest." Scott tries to lighten the sting with an unenthused chuckle, but that sounds harsh too.

"Understood." Dr Andrews gives him a nod, glancing down at Scott's splint, then flips the questionnaire over so Scott's drawing faces them. It seems strange now, like someone else's drawing of a person he doesn't recognise.

"Well, I've looked over all of this, and I'm happy to say you're an excellent candidate for this type of work. As you know, I'm not a traditional medical doctor. I'm an osteopathic physician, so I have a DO after my name instead of an MD. I did go to medical school, and I can write prescriptions like a traditional doctor does, though I'd really rather not. I have additional training in what some call alternative healing paradigms—acupuncture, Reiki, and massage therapy, among some others."

All this makes perfect sense to Scott because this man looks like no other doctor he's ever seen. He doesn't have a stethoscope, or a watch, or even a pen in his pocket like other doctors do. And instead of a white coat, Dr Andrews is dressed in blue trackies, a jumper with the sleeves rolled up, and trainers, like a uni athlete might be. A headband holds his longish hair off his forehead, and light stubble shades his face. Scott counts at least three tattoos on his right forearm: an ocean wave, a hand, and a tree.

"Do you have any questions about what I do?" Dr Andrews asks.

"No, I don't think so. Dr Coulter said you could help me prevent a frozen shoulder." *What the hell, he's got my file anyway.* "And maybe get my headaches down to a dull roar."

"Yes. I think we have a great shot at both. Osteopaths believe the body works as an entire system. We can't treat one area independently of the others. For instance, if you're in any kind of pain, physical or otherwise, you're not sleeping. If you're not sleeping, your immune system, digestion, brain function, they're all impaired. Not surprising that you'd have headaches and your recovery would suffer. And no sleep means no dreams, which is a whole other story. But there are simple treatments that can help with all of that."

Scott studies his splint. *So he knows about the insomnia. He must know about my eyes and ears too.* "All right. Except, I'd prefer no needles today if you don't mind."

"That's fine. No needles today."

"Brilliant."

"Now let's have a look at you." Dr Andrews reaches both hands under Scott's jaw. "The explosion happened, when? Last December?"

"Five months ago." Five months, one week, two days, and three hours, give or take, depending on the time zone; technically, Scott had gained five hours flying back to

London from Kabul, though he'd lost a day and a half being unconscious.

"And how would you say you're feeling right now?" Dr Andrews presses his fingertips under Scott's jawline, then rolls them down the sides of his neck. It tickles a little and makes Scott's shoulders tense. The doctor examines his skin intently, and Scott feels like a specimen in a Petri dish.

Scott searches for a truth he can tell. "I'm, uh, feeling all right."

"All right?"

"Yeah," Scott sighs. "But my surgeon and my physio think I should be making more progress."

Dr Andrews raises an eyebrow.

Scott picks his words carefully. "I mean, they think I should be using my arm more than...what I feel comfortable with right now. So."

"I see. Are you in any pain today?"

"No, it's more just uncomfortable. Everything feels stiff." And my skin is scarred. My ears ring, and my eyes don't always work right. There was a bomb.

"Can I look at your eyes for a minute?"

Scott nods, and the doctor places his thumb under Scott's eye and pulls down gently to examine the tissues inside.

"Look at that tree over there," Dr Andrews says, gesturing behind him to a watercolour cherry blossom.

Scott stares, trying to focus. But he can hardly keep his eye open, even in the dim light, and has to concentrate to keep from blinking. *It's a painting, damn it, just look at it*. His nose starts to burn and a lump grows in his throat.

"Now this side," the doctor says quietly, switching eyes while Scott presses his lips together with the effort of focusing across the room. Finally, Dr Andrews picks up the water bottle and unscrews the cap. "Drink some of that, please?"

Scott takes a sip. The doctor waits, and Scott takes a bigger gulp.

"Well done." Dr Andrews turns to his files on the counter. "Lance filled me in on the circumstances of the accident. I was very sorry to hear about your interpreter. His name was Omran?"

Dr Andrews says it with an "oh" at the beginning, the same way Scott had done before Omran taught him the proper pronunciation. But the fact that he mentions him at all takes Scott by surprise. People don't talk about it. Scott knows they're scared of the way he'll react, or avoiding a topic they're sure Scott would rather forget. As if he ever could.

"*Oom*-rahn," Scott replies. "Omran Saleh."

"*Oom*-rahn," Dr Andrews repeats. He considers Scott curiously. "That must be very difficult for you. That he's gone. I'm sorry."

Scott clears his throat. "Thank you." It's all he can come up with. His drawing stares up from the counter like a caricature. *I'm sorry*.

Dr Andrews gestures to the centre of the room. "So, a bit about how this will go. You'll be on this table, face down at first. Do you think you can handle having your face in this cradle?"

The U-shaped form is covered with a white flannel casing. Scott presses its soft surface. "Yeah, that should work."

"If it doesn't, we'll do something different. The table has an extension we'll use for your arm, so you'll be supported there. Only the part of you we're working on will be exposed. You'll feel my hands on you sometimes and not at others because some of the work we'll do doesn't require physical touch. It might feel like a massage at times, or like physiotherapy at other times. If you're uncomfortable or in pain, physically or otherwise, at any time, I want you to speak up, all right?"

Physically or otherwise. Scott clenches his jaw, thinking about what other kind of pain there may be. But the doctor looks him straight in the eye again, and it makes Scott feel like he's ready for this. Scott likes the way this doctor talks, too, crisp and confident, like he's going to take the wheel and steer them through a storm. He says, "Will do."

"All right. Now we've got to pick an oil for you." Dr Andrews turns to the tray on the counter and chooses one. "Here's a blend that might work. Lemon and mint have invigorating properties."

He twists open the cap on the small brown bottle and holds it under Scott's nose. It's bright and astringent, so fresh that it hurts Scott's brain, and he makes a face.

"Sorry, no," Scott says with a little chuckle.

"Understood. Let's try this one. It's got lavender, more for calming and relaxation."

This time, the scent is soft, but dusty, like antique perfume. It reminds Scott of his great-aunt Margie, who died when he was little; he was scared of her, and sniffing it makes him uneasy. He shrugs and turns his face away.

"Not that one either. We'll know it when we find it." Dr Andrews peruses the oils and chooses another. "Ah, this one might be better, called arnica." He puts it under Scott's nose. It's piney, but gentle, with a hint of orange or grapefruit underneath. It's like the woods in spring.

Scott makes a happy sound before he can catch himself.

"That's it," says Dr Andrews, smiling. "Thought so."

"Yes," Scott says. "That's definitely it." He wants to take a bath in it, right now, and every day until he's ninety.

"Now, please disrobe all the way and lie on the table face down, with your face in the cradle. Cover up as best you can. The table is heated, so we can adjust the temperature if we need to. Any questions?"

Scott looks at the table, with the extension right where it should be to support his arm. He takes a shallow breath. "Um, no, I think I'm good."

"All right. I'll leave you to it."

Once the door is shut, Scott kicks off his shoes and returns to the certificates on the wall as he unbuttons his shirt. Bachelor of Science, University of Sheffield. Doctor of Osteopathy, British College of Osteopathic Medicine. Reiki Master, UK Reiki Federation. He skims over several others, wondering how the doctor made the time for all of this schooling when he can't be much older than Scott.

The flannel sheets are warm when Scott slides between them. It takes an awkward minute to get his splinted arm situated on the table, and he rests his face in the cradle with a few seconds to spare before the soft knock at the door.

"Ready, Scott?"

"Yes, come in."

The door clicks shut, and there's the soft creak of the floorboards.

"Comfortable?"

"Yes, I think so." Scott fidgets as Dr Andrews walks around to his injured side.

"Nice colours on your splint. Your kids do that for you?"

Scott lifts his head to see the doctor pointing at the crooked words and bright faces, along with Iron Man and a blue T-Rex.

"Uh, no, that's my nephew. Thomas. He's eight."

Dr Andrews tucks the blanket carefully over Scott's arm and up to the nape of his neck. "Looks like you're his superhero."

"Yeah. When I got home, we explained to him about the accident, and that I was...well, that I caught fire for a bit. At first he was terrified, but then the gross factor won out because, you know, being eight. Anyway, he decided I'm fireproof, and I'm Tony Stark's British cousin or something. It's kind of a running joke with us now."

"Fireproof. I like it."

An arm slides under Scott's ankles, lifting them, while a pillow is fit underneath. Dr Andrews adjusts his legs so they rest farther apart, and *aaahhh, yes, that's better*, they sink into the table as if they weigh ten stone each.

Dr Andrews tucks the blanket around his feet. "Since you're face down, I'm going to turn the lights up, all right?"

"No problem."

"How's the temperature of the table?"

"It's good." Scott forgets about fire, splints, and scars for a minute, amazed at how those few small adjustments could make his body feel balanced and at ease.

"Good. If you're ready, we'll start."

"Ready." *As ever*.

Scott waits for some movement, but instead, there is stillness and silence, with Dr Andrews standing at the head of the table. *Should something be happening?*

After a long moment, Dr Andrews peels the blanket from Scott's back to rest at his waist. *Here it comes*. Scott braces for the doctor's reaction to the pits and streaks of his scars. But if Dr Andrews thinks anything of them, he doesn't say; there is only the swish of hands rubbing together and the lovely smell of pine and citrus. Scott's legs get jumpy for a second.

"I'd like you to take three breaths, deep as you can."

Easy. Scott inhales, and hands press into his back, close on either side of his spine. They are hot, as if he's been warming them in front of a fire, or holding a hot cup of tea, and they glide back up toward his neck as Scott exhales. They go again, pressing down a bit harder on the inhale and easing up on the exhale. It feels good, no bother to Scott's skin or shoulder. The third time is slower, the pressure deeper, and it makes Scott cough.

"Water?"

"Nope, sorry about that," Scott says.

"No apologies, just get that stuff out." The doctor kneads between Scott's shoulder blades with the heels of his hands.

"What stuff?"

"Whatever's in there that needs to come out."

Next, he feels a forearm slide over the width of his back. It rolls in long strokes like a steamroller forcing the air out, and although Scott tries to stifle the annoying tickle in his throat, he starts to cough again.

"Jeez, sorry." He cough-chuckles, embarrassed, as Dr Andrews brings him water. Scott shifts as best he can to his good side to take it.

"This is a good start," Dr Andrews says.

After a few sips the tickle calms down. "I'm not even sick. I don't get it."

"It's okay. When you're ready we'll do some more."

Scott hands him the bottle and gets resettled, taking a breath and clearing his throat.

"Ready?"

"Ready."

Scott's shoulders feel stiff under the pressure of Dr Andrews's arm, but he sinks slightly deeper into the table. He wonders if he's coming down with a cold, or if he's allergic to something in the room. He hopes it's not the arnica. The smell is comforting and familiar already; he breathes it in, and darkness welcomes him, rich and deep, a perfect place for him to escape to for a bit. A deep purple shape swirls next to another of forest-green. Scott watches them dance, and his face relaxes into the cradle. *Soft*, he thinks, and *free*, as they get smaller and bigger, closer, then farther away. Little dots of white light sparkle too. The scene is beautiful and gentle and calms his nerves a bit. He finds that concentrating on it helps his throat keep quiet.

It's Dr Andrews's voice that makes the colours drop away; Scott remembers where he is as the blanket is pulled up to cover his shoulders.

"Your hands are cold, Scott. Would you be all right with some warm stones?"

Scott tries not to seem lost. "Um, where?"

"In your hands. Want to feel them first to make sure?"

"Okay." *Warm stones?* Scott wonders if he misunderstood.

He hears the *clank* of the slow cooker lid bumping against the counter, then the rumble of rocks knocking together.

"First one." Dr Andrews flattens Scott's good hand gently and places the rock in it. It's smooth, hot, and exactly the size of his palm. "How does that feel?"

Weird. "Good? I guess?"

"Ok, I'll wrap it up." Dr Andrews winds a soft towel around Scott's hand, binding the stone inside.

"Other side now. Hot rock."

Heat seeps into Scott's cold fingers as the doctor wraps the second stone. Now both of his hands are weighted down, and he must look ridiculous, but he feels heavy and tired and warm and taken care of, so he lets go, for a second, of the protection and defence.

The shapes begin to move again in front of his closed eyes. It's fuzzy at first, like a photograph covered with fog, but colours and lines slowly take the form of a mountain, then a treeline. The sky is a midnight-blue bowl overhead with sparkling stars beginning to shine through. He's at home here, far away in this remote, wide-open place that shows no evidence of modern life. He's so tired suddenly, and comfortable in this warm cocoon of a room; he realises he must be falling asleep, that this must be a dream.

No, not now. He doesn't want to lose the thread of what's going on in this room. *But what happened to the doctor?* Scott doesn't feel his hands anywhere.

"Dr Andrews?"

"Did you go away for a minute?" Dr Andrews answers softly, and Scott is surprised at how close he is, right up next to him on his injured side. He's covered up to his neck by the blanket, and now there's a warm weight covering the length of his back.

"I guess I did. What are you doing?"

"Working on your shoulder." Scott doesn't feel a thing. No pressure, heat, or movement, but he can hear Dr Andrews's breathing, deep and regular right beside him. Scott tries to relax his shoulder and make his arm heavy so whatever the doctor is doing can find its way in.

*

Scott isn't sure how long he's been resting when he feels cool air on his hand. He makes a fist, trying to hold the heat in.

"Ok, Scott, it's time for you to turn over."

Shit.

He's not ready. He doesn't want them to be halfway done, doesn't want to face the room. If he can be dead to the world a little while longer, he can keep the vision of mountains, trees, and stars in his mind's eye.

"I'm going to lift the blanket, and you can turn toward me. Then I'll move your arm support around to this side."

Dr Andrews holds up the blanket like a curtain, but the turn is a rocky manoeuvre, and Scott shifts awkwardly to get into position.

"Ugh. They'll have to pay you extra," he jokes, still adjusting as the blanket covers him.

"For what?"

"Hazard pay." Scott's legs feel too long, his shoulders too wide, and his arm feels like a clumsy dead weight. He plays the same game he played as a child: Close your eyes. If you can't see anyone, maybe no one can see you either. At least you don't see them seeing you.

"Nah, I signed up for this, remember?" Dr Andrews tucks Scott's arm in. "Good?"

"I'll be good when this is over." Scott sounds like a spoiled child, and as soon as it's out, he regrets it. "I mean, I'll be good when I'm—" He clears his throat of a tickle. "—back to normal."

Dr Andrews moves the pillow from under Scott's ankles to under his knees. "I knew what you meant. I'll do my best to help you get there, okay? Now let's do some hip work." He moves to Scott's right side, then pulls the blanket off his leg and tucks it around his upper thigh.

"Lifting," he says, taking hold of Scott's leg under the calf and at the back of his knee. Scott tries to relax, but he's afraid Dr Andrews might drop it, or it might slip.

"I'll just move it back and forth, all right? Easy."

Scott concentrates on trying to let it go, just enough to feel it relax as the doctor begins to pull it away.

"That's better, but you can properly let it go. I won't let it fall."

They try again, but it's a stalemate, with Scott stiffening and the doctor unable to move it.

"Okay. You win that round. But I'm not done yet." He lays Scott's leg on the table and retucks the blanket around Scott's hip.

"Why do my legs matter anyway? I thought Dr Coulter sent me here for my shoulder."

Dr Andrews oils up his hands and starts at Scott's ankle, then slides up the outside of the leg and up the side of his thigh. "Your injury immobilised one of your limbs, right? The rest of the body compensates in ways you don't realise. Your legs work harder, and your spine isn't lined up straight, so your hips, neck, and shoulders are strained." He changes direction to slide back, then begins again at the ankle, a long smooth roll of warm pressure all the way up. "We're working the effect of these compensations out, and it will help."

After the third go, Dr Andrews places his hands on the blanket, feeling through it until he finds Scott's hip socket. He presses down on it, pushing him into the table. It turns Scott's lower body to jelly; like magic, the stiff, floundering leg is a docile, rested puddle of muscle and bone. Dr Andrews lifts it easily, and its limp weight moves loose and free.

"Your arm will figure out the body is back to normal, and over time—let's say a few weeks—it will go back to normal too. So. That worked nicely, don't you think?" There's a chipper note of satisfaction in his voice. He covers Scott's leg and moves to the other. Scott can't even be bothered at the doctor's gloating. For now, he's content with Dr Andrews's strange work, and he feels fine to lie here, unwound.

After Scott's other leg gets the same treatment, Dr Andrews walks to the counter and opens a drawer.

"I have a pillow for your eyes if that's all right."

Scott clears his throat. "Okay."

"It's got some herbs in it, and it's weighted, to give you a deeper rest." Dr Andrews places it slowly, the silk brushing Scott's eyelids. When he lets it go completely, the dark is heavy and absolute, and Scott clears his throat again.

It's okay, it's okay. Scott's arm twitches, and the pillow gains weight, pressing down on his eyes and crushing the lids. *It's okay*, but his throat is closing, and his ears are ringing *no can't no*; suddenly, *Jesus*, it's too heavy and too dark, and he can't stand it another second.

"Um, no, I can't..." Scott begins.

The pressure lifts, the darkness gone. Scott takes a breath through his nose, relieved. A hand rests on his shoulder.

"Better?"

"Yeah." Heat rises in Scott's face. He is so fucking sick to death of feeling like this. It's a hateful place to be. "Sorry. I didn't think it would bother me, but..."

"I'm glad you spoke up. Let's try something different."

Dr Andrews's hands make a soft sound as they rub together. His fingers lightly touch Scott's temples, then sweep over his forehead making overlapping circles. At first, Scott's eyes swim, trying to follow, but soon they settle as the pattern repeats. Out and back, circle, circle. Scott's knotted brows go slack, the gentle and predictable pressure making him sigh. *Better.*

With his next breath, the mountains slide into focus. They strike up in deep purple, with the silhouettes of tall evergreens against a sky that's lit with more stars than he's ever seen. The place is at once strange yet deeply familiar, and Scott inhales the cool air tinged with crushed leaves and burning wood. Somehow, he knows there is a warm fire glowing behind him. He turns to look, but Dr Andrews's voice draws him back, and the scene fades.

"I'm sorry?" Scott blinks his eyes open, embarrassed.

"I just asked if you had any questions."

Scott wishes he still had the hot rocks in his hands to steady himself. "I saw your feather on the counter. What's it for?"

"It's for sweeping away energy that's stuck."

"Stuck?"

Dr Andrews rubs small circles at Scott's temples. "Sometimes it gets loose but doesn't want to leave, so we have to help it go."

"What kind of energy?"

"Could be pain, could be fear. Could be anger. Sometimes we hold on to whatever it is for so long, it becomes part of us. Some people believe that's where disease comes from."

"Where does it go?"

"I'm not sure, exactly." A breath. "We tell it to go somewhere where it can do some good."

Scott thinks about this, the pain and guilt knitting itself into the newly thatched fibres of his bones, fear and confusion weaving through the smooth tissues of his muscles. He pictures a purplish-red blob of it dislodged with nowhere to go, evicted. Lost.

He closes his eyes again. His pain is a part of him now, as much as his scars are. "I don't...I don't think we should do that. On me."

"We won't." Dr Andrews's fingertips are warm, moving back over Scott's forehead to massage the tense spot between his eyebrows. "Not until you're ready."

*

"Okay, Scott, we're done." Dr Andrews's voice is gentle, and his hand rests on Scott's good shoulder. "Take your time getting up. There's more water on the counter. Finish it as you're getting dressed, all right?"

Scott nods, keeping his eyes closed. "Okay." He clears his throat, the little tickle making him swallow.

"If you want to rinse off, there's a shower in that bathroom. When you're ready, come to my office, the next room to the right. We'll talk about our next steps." With that, Dr Andrews's footsteps retreat, the dimmer on the wall clicks faintly, and the door is opened and shut.

Scott rolls slowly to his side but makes no move to get up. He knows he won't shower; he would have to take his splint and elastic bandage off, and the thought of washing away the soft sheen of oil from his skin seems wasteful and unkind. He knows he's got to shore up, gather himself, and stand up on his own feet.

He takes a few last moments of comfort in the softness and heat of Dr Andrews's table. Even without the doctor here, the room feels curiously charged, filled with strange tools, soft light, and quiet humming energy.

Just one more minute.

*

Dr Andrews's door is open. A bookshelf takes up the wall behind his desk, with what must be a hundred books, interspersed with framed photographs and unusual pieces of rock and stone. One photo shows a sleek grey cat with a red collar and bell; in another, a dressed-up, laughing Dr Andrews is embraced by a blond man kissing his cheek.

The doctor leans on his desk, tapping on a tablet, with Scott's file beside him. "Your colour's better," he says when Scott approaches. "And your posture. How do you feel?"

"I feel good. Better. I mean...I thought I felt all right when I came, but I feel better now. Like, loose."

Dr Andrews nods with a smile. "I thought so. Did you finish your water?"

"Yes."

"Good. Here's another." The doctor hands Scott a new bottle, his serious tone leaving no room for arguments. "Ready for a recap?" He gestures to the guest chair, but Scott doesn't feel like sitting. His legs feel strong under him.

"First, you're dehydrated. Priority number one is water." He begins to write on a prescription pad. "We stirred up toxins in your body, and water will help flush them out." He rips the sheet off the pad and hands it to Scott.

H20 Th 1L, Fr–Mo 3L

"That means another litre yet today, and three litres each day after. Understand? That means you'll have water with you at all times. For the next five days."

Scott doesn't know what "toxins" might mean, and is fine being spared the details. "If I drink all that, I'll be spending the next five days in the loo."

"Quite so."

"I thought you wanted me to sleep?"

"Rehydration first. Once your fluid levels are back, you'll have a better shot at sleep. Your body needs to know that it's not in the desert anymore."

At that, Scott's eyes prickle. He folds the paper and pinches the crease.

"Second is your diet." Dr Andrews lets him off easy, changing the subject. "I'd like you to try to eat mostly from this list, if you can, for the next few weeks."

The sheet is titled "Foods for Wellness: Anti-Inflammatory." Scott skims it and spots salmon, brown rice, and organic yoghurt. He also sees berries, whole grains, ginger, and turmeric. Right now, his pantry has tinned spaghetti hoops and baked beans, along with three or four eggs. He's out of practice making meals from scratch as he's found it's harder with one arm immobile, but the list looks simple enough. "I'll try."

"Good. Do your best with it. One more thing and I'll let you go. Do your hands and feet feel cold most of the time, or just today?"

"All the time, I'd say. Especially at night."

"Right. So that's a symptom of what I call a 'shock body.' Your blood is pulling in from your extremities to the core, where all your vital organs are. It's an old defence mechanism we haven't evolved out of yet, meant to keep us alive in times of stress. Do you have a heated blanket?"

Good lord. He's lucky he has clean sheets and a pillow. "Really? It's spring."

"It might be spring out there..." Dr Andrews gestures to the window. "But your body isn't getting that message. It's doing its own thing as best it can. Our job is to remind it that it's not in danger. For now, I'd like you to sleep on an electric underblanket set on medium, with socks on." Scott's doubtful expression doesn't go unnoticed by the doctor. "Should I write out a script for that too?"

Scott glances down at the desk where the prescription pad lies, and his eyes stop on a framed photo. A group of lads in football gear celebrate with trophies in hand, and a younger, smiling Dr Andrews is propped up on their shoulders.

"Um, no, I'll get one on the way home." Scott considers the doctor, trying to see the football hero underneath the stubble and serious talk.

"So, can we see you back on Monday?"

Scott's got an appointment with Dr Coulter on Monday morning, and he could come here after that. But. "Er, I...I suppose so."

Scott feels better, stronger on his feet than he has in a while. But all this about alignments. Energies. Shock. Feathers and stones and fiery-hot hands and, well... *It's all a bit woo-woo, now, isn't it? And what is it about this place that makes me cough?* There's an itchy, annoying lump in his throat that water doesn't fix.

Dr Andrews offers him an understanding smile. "Not sure?"

"Maybe I could see how I feel, you know? In a few days? And then let you know." Scott tries to slide out of this gracefully, in a way that won't offend.

"All right. I'll put you down, and we'll see what happens. Next Monday, same time."

Scott nods and raises his hand to cover a cough that starts small but grows bigger with each breath. A water bottle is placed in his hand, and Scott takes a swig. "Damn, am I going to cough up a lung or something?"

"Hope not. Then we'd have to add a pulmonologist to your list. You don't have one of those yet, right?"

Scott clears his throat and swallows. "Let's keep it that way."

Dr Andrews studies him a bit, then walks to the other side of the room where he opens a cupboard door.

"Here. I'll add this to your bill." He hands Scott a small brown vial. *Arnica.*

"Thank you." Scott slips it into his jacket pocket along with his papers, then pulls the jacket on, laying the front over his splint. "I'll let you know about next time."

"Remember your prescription, about the water."

They shake hands, lefties again, but Scott doesn't meet the doctor's eyes. "Got it."

Scott manages a wave at Monica as he walks through reception.

She says, "Have a good day, Scott" as he passes, but his jaw is clenched too tightly to answer.

He pulls on his sunglasses against the mid-afternoon light of Forest Lane. It's too bright, too noisy, and he pulls his jacket around him, hunkering down against a cool breeze that may as well be a wintry gale. In his pocket, he finds the hard vial of oil. He grasps it tightly and doesn't let go until he gets his wallet out for the tube.

*

"Dunno, Liv, it was sort of...weird?" Scott puts his phone on speaker as he pulls his seldom-used rice cooker down off the top cupboard shelf. He's making rice with ginger, the way he'd learned in Thailand. He'll poach an egg to go alongside it and, voila, supper.

"Okay, weird-good or weird-creepy?"

"No, not weird-creepy. Weird-new? Weird-different." Scott ponders a minute more. "It was weird-nice, I think." He takes a drink of water, his third glass since he returned home.

"Hmm, that's a switch," Olivia says, her voice bright. "What's nice about it?"

He put hot rocks in my hands. There was a pillow under my knees that made my back feel better. He said Omran's name. But all of that feels private, and anyway, so much of it seems a bit silly, now, looking back at it. A pillow for my eyes? A sweeping feather? After his tube ride home to Camden, Scott had emerged from the underground on autopilot, ducking into the store with his list in hand and the darkroom on his mind.

But the solid bullet of oil sits heavy in his pocket, like a relic from a lost civilization, or an artefact from across time.

"His place is nice, you know, comfortable." Scott clears his throat. "And he's different from the other doctors. He really listens." Scott realises he probably said all of four sentences to Dr Andrews. But still.

"I like him already. What did he say about how you're doing?"

Scott measures out the rice and pours it into the cooker. "He said we had a good start, but..." He cringes. "He wants me to take better care of myself." He eyes the giant Argos bag he'd dropped next to the bed. It holds a new heated blanket along with the set of flannel sheets he'd sprung for.

"Ah," Olivia says after a pause, the *I told you so* unspoken. "Are you going back?"

"Not sure. Might see how I feel, you know, after a few days? Dr Coulter wants me to go, so." *And he has this soft, warm table. I went somewhere while I was on it. Somewhere lovely.* Scott sees the night-time landscape in his memory: there was a valley, with a forest and a fire, under a sky of pinpoint stars. He'd like to slip back to that place, to lie on the cool grass and look up at the constellations that seem to see him too.

"Well, might as well make Dr Coulter happy, hmm?"

"Ha."

"Seriously, go. It's a win for you and a win for Dr Coulter. And I bet it's a win for the massage guy too."

"He's not a massage guy. He's a doctor. Very professional. Lots of fancy diplomas on the walls." Scott squints at the measuring line on the side of the rice cooker and turns on the tap.

"As it should be," Olivia says primly. "Doesn't mean he wouldn't enjoy seeing you in his doorway again. You're a tall drink of water, you know."

Scott bites his lip. "Right. More like damaged goods." The rice cooker's lid slams more loudly than he intended.

"God, don't say that! You're on the mend, on your way to good as new. Any man would give his right ball to be with you."

"We both know one that wouldn't."

Olivia's sigh is exasperated. "Patrick was a self-centred twat who couldn't see farther than the next pretty picture you took of him. And that was *before* you got hurt."

She's right, of course. With Patrick there were pretty pictures, witty texts, and friends-with-benefits sex, not necessarily in that order. Scott's quite sure the sex was real; apparently, the "friends" part was not. "Maybe. But he was *my* self-centred twat."

"Until it got rough, and he bailed. You know you deserve better than that, right?"

Scott looks up at the ceiling, saying nothing.

"Right," she answers for him. "He's out there, Scott. You just haven't found him yet. But when you do, he's going to be batshit mad over you, scars and all."

"Because dudes dig scars, you keep saying." He coughs and takes another drink, pushing the tickle down.

"Because it's the truth, damn it. I always tell you the truth. Mostly."

"I know you do." Scott plugs in the cooker and returns the phone to his ear. "Look, I've got to go. I've got stuff to chop. Give the T-man a hug for me?"

"Okay, babe. You have everything you need? You sound like you're getting sick."

"Nah, I'm doing good. Really."

"All right, you have a good night, and I'll talk to you soon."

"'Kay. Love you."

"Love you too. Bye."

Scott trades the phone for a vegetable peeler and the ginger root. It takes a few tries to get the angle right, but once he braces the root against the cutting board, he can pare the papery skin from the flesh with the peeler so he doesn't slice his fingers. He leans down to open the drawer for the grater when the ginger's sharp scent reaches his nose.

It's a smell he loves that brings to mind Bangkok's brightly flavoured food cart snacks washed down with cold beer; this time it catches him sideways and turns his stomach.

Okay, it's okay, but no, all at once it's not, and he turns away from the counter, a clammy sheen of sweat breaking out on his forehead.

"Ugh, shit," Scott mumbles, turning on the tap. He closes his eyes as he splashes water on his face, trying to take deep breaths in through his nose. Instead, he coughs dry barks that feel like straw in his throat. "No, don't be sick, don't be sick, don't be sick." He holds his forehead in his hand, spits once, and braces against the nauseous waves. A few more breaths get him over the worst of it, and minutes later, it's dissolved into something he can swallow down and shake out through the trembling in his hands.

The episode wears him out; he's suddenly so tired he can turn off the tap but can't pick up the ginger from the floor. In the far corner of the flat his unmade bed looks like salvation, and he makes his way over on unsteady legs. He needs to close his eyes and curl up for a bit, just long enough to get his strength back and stop shaking.

*

In Scott's dream, he's digging in the ground with his hands in the middle of a desert field. It's easy work at first, though he's thirsty and the sun is hot on his back. Soon the sand gives way to reddish clay that coats his fingers like mud. He starts to sweat.

Footsteps come closer, and Scott looks up to see a young Dr Andrews, looking like the picture at his office. He wears his footie kit and juggles a ball between his feet. "Let's play," he offers easily, flipping his longish fringe with a tilt of his head.

Scott's suddenly got a shovel in his hand, and he's standing in the hole three feet deep. "This isn't a game," he says, frustrated. "It's hard."

"Nah, it *is* just a game. But you have to stop digging."

The clay clods up like cement, and Scott can hardly lift the next shovelful. *Now what? I'll never get this done.*

The hole shifts underneath him, and he's swallowed so deep he can't see the surface. He might not be able to breathe much longer, and he's scared he might cry; once he starts, he'll have no idea how to stop.

"Put the shovel down!" Jason calls from above. "Stop digging!"

Scott looks up, searching sightlessly for him. "Can you see me, Jason? Can you—?" His right arm is stuck to his side somehow, stiff and shrunken, so he scrabbles at the dark walls with his left, but it's no use. He can't climb up.

"I'm coming, wait, I'm coming—"

*

Scott wakes up groggy in twisted sheets damp with sweat. The details of the dream evaporate as he sits up, trying to place himself. Through the window is the black sky of late night; his room is lit only by the kitchen lamp, and Scott smells the nutty aroma of cooked rice. He shakes off the last of that dark, suffocating place as he gets up with the nagging feeling of a puzzle left unfinished.

The cooker has turned itself off. He shovels up a sticky clump of rice and swallows it, distracted. Something is different here, but he's not sure what. His head feels heavy and his ears are ringing, but that's nothing new; he turns to look around the flat, but sees nothing that explains this unsettled feeling. He rubs his hand over his face as two thoughts tangle for his attention: a shower, then the darkroom.

Scott slips off his shirt and catches a whiff of his skin as it's exposed. It's at once so new and so familiar, his sweat mixed with pine and bergamot. *Amica? Arinca? Where is it, God, where did I put it?* He pats his pocket and brings out the little brown bottle with its black cap and green label. *Arnica.* A chuckle escapes him as he opens it, feeling the relief of a tiny treasure found. It brings him right back to that room across the city, where he let go of his body and mind for a time. The place where he'd found the night valley. This may be it, what he's forgotten, or at least this might help him remember it again.

The abandoned Argos bag, now half-buried at the foot of the bed, stares back at him with the heated blanket still inside. Making the bed has never been his favourite task, even when he had two healthy arms to do it with, but for now, his shower will have to wait. He sets the bottle on his bedside cabinet with care and begins to strip the sheets.

Chapter Two

> Shutter (n.) A device that allows light to pass for a determined period of time, exposing photographic film, plate, or light-sensitive electronic sensor to light in order to capture a permanent image of a scene. (v.) to furnish or close with shutters; to cease operations or shut down.

When Scott returns to Dr Andrews's office Monday afternoon, Monica greets him with a warm smile. She looks down at his injured arm, which is missing its bulky splint and actually fits inside his jacket sleeve.

"Congratulations! How do you feel?" she asks, beaming.

Scott's "great, thanks" falls flat in the face of her excitement. He considers moving his arm around to show her how mobile it is with the new flexible fabric brace he got at Dr Coulter's this morning. But he tucks it close to his body instead, his other arm protectively layered over it. He smiles for her as they walk to the treatment room, but it feels like he's slapping a happy-face sticker on, and he waits until she's gone to dim the lights a bit more.

He opens the slow cooker, curious about Dr Andrews's rocks. They're smooth and plain, black or dun-grey in three sizes, stacked up in hills. Somehow, he'd thought they'd be shiny, or marbled in pretty colours, and he replaces the lid, disappointed. He considers turning off the music, a festive guitar that feels insulting. A thought creeps in that coming back here may have been a mistake.

There are a few crisp knocks before Dr Andrews breezes in with his files and tablet, extending his left hand for Scott to shake. His whiskers are a bit longer today, but his hair is the same, pulled back off his forehead with a thin red headband.

"Monica said you have news?"

"Yeah, big news." Scott extends his arm. He remembers how it looked this morning, naked under Dr Coulter's bright office lights. Scott wasn't surprised by the lack of muscle tone and the scaly, discoloured skin; he sees it all, fleetingly, whenever he showers. It's streaked and weirdly shiny in places, but he'll get used to it in time. *After all, it is what's owed, isn't it?*

"Nice! That movement must feel good." Dr Andrews's smiling eyes look into Scott's expectantly.

Scott doesn't answer right away. He'd worn his splint like armour. It had protected him for so long with its hard, unyielding shape, and its colourful messages scrawled in permanent marker. Scott feels too light without it, exposed, and it feels wrong to be this mobile. He'd tried to tell Dr Coulter so, but his arguments had fallen on deaf ears.

He settles on something close to the truth. "I'm...still getting used to it, I guess. I'm supposed to wear this most of the day, with short breaks where I can take it off."

Dr Andrews nods. "And limited activity, yeah? No heavy lifting?"

"For a few more weeks. And I have an appointment with my new physio tomorrow, so."

"Excellent." Dr Andrews raises his eyebrows excitedly and rubs his hands together. "So it's up to you. Should we work with your brace on or off?"

The thought of taking it off and leaving his arm free for Dr Andrews to see and touch is unbearable. "I'll leave it on, thanks."

"All right." Dr Andrews nods as he rolls up the sleeves of his jumper. "And how are you feeling otherwise? Any pain?" He touches the skin at Scott's jawline, skimming over the slightly raised line of his scar, making it difficult for Scott to think.

"Um...no, no pain." Nothing an ibuprofen he'd popped on the way here couldn't fix.

"Drop your jaw open for me."

Scott's mouth shifts, only opening a crack.

"That feels tighter to me than last time. Can you do this?" Dr Andrews opens his own mouth and loosely moves his jaw from side to side.

Scott looks away to focus. After a breath, his jaw unlocks and he can stretch it out and down, but not without an ache in his cheeks. Dr Andrews winces as he continues to touch him there.

"Pain now?"

"Not bad," Scott replies.

"Side to side now," Dr Andrews directs, and Scott tries his best, feeling much like the Tin Man in need of an oil can. The doctor's fingers move to the hollow under Scott's ears. "And what about that cough?"

Scott hesitates. "Uh, it comes and goes." Just this morning, he'd had a bout of it at Dr Coulter's. "Better keep an eye on that," he'd said, offhand.

"Look at that tree for me. When do you notice it most?"

Scott stares across the room with a little breath to bolster him. He feels the prick of tears straight away when Dr Andrews studies the tissues in his eyes. "Hmm?"

"When's your cough the worst?"

"I guess it's bad when I wake up, and again at night?" Scott sniffs and clears his throat. The tree is getting blurry, and the exertion of his focus causes a tear to escape. *Seriously? Shit.*

"Right. Could be some congestion. Or something else, we'll see. Your eyes look much better." Dr Andrews offers him the tissue box. "You've been drinking your water. Well done."

"Ugh...sorry." Scott forces out a thick chuckle as he wipes his eyes.

"For what? Tears? Pssh." Dr Andrews shakes his head. "Never apologise for tears. They're a good sign."

Sign of what? But Scott doesn't ask; he presses his lips together and tosses the tissue into the bin.

Dr Andrews takes Scott's hands and squeezes his fingers from their bases to tips, then turns each one over to examine his palms. Scott had thought his hands felt fine, but now that they're held in the doctor's warm ones, it's clear he's just used to them being cold.

"And how about the heated blanket?"

"It's good. It helps." He has actually had two nights in a row of decent sleep, almost six hours each. His nightmares have turned into fuzzy movies of himself in cars that never arrive at a destination or planes that never touch down. His body might be rested, but the dreams leave his mind scattered and spent.

Dr Andrews lets him go with a little smile. "Still shocky, but better. Let's get ready for round two. Arnica again today?"

"Yeah, arnica's good."

The thing is, there's a place I went last time? I want to get back there. I thought I could on my own. But I don't know how.

Scott hasn't seen the dark valley with its sentry trees and kind firelight since he'd dropped into it here the other day, but it hasn't been for lack of trying. Perhaps it was a delusion, a side effect of his chronic lack of sleep and Dr Andrews's warm table. But it had been so *real.* He'd recognised it from the inside out. He was different there; he had felt curious again, like there was something to discover. There had been no guilt, no fear, no friends lost, or bodies gone wrong.

"I think today should be a deep shoulders day. We'll work on those first, and we'll see where that leaves your jaw. What do you think?"

The words "deep" and "shoulders" together make Scott's fingers tighten around his brace. He'd like to say no, they can't possibly, but when Dr Andrews looks at him, rubbing his hands together like he's ready to tackle it, Scott finds he can't disappoint him.

"All right," Scott says, beginning to unbutton his shirt.

Dr Andrews picks up Scott's files and heads for the door. "Start face down. I'll be back."

"Dr Andrews?"

"It's Jason." He spins, and Scott feels a flicker of recognition at that name, a comfort in it from somewhere that flashes by and then is gone.

"No needles." Scott is shocked at his tone, but the events of the day are starting to get the better of him, and he's got to draw a line.

"No needles," Dr Andrews agrees. "Just stones."

*

When Dr Andrews finally stands still at the head of the table and takes a breath, Scott is more comfortable than he's been in four days. He's warm under the flannel sheet, the pillow under his ankles lifting his feet so that his thighs feel heavy and his shoulders are relaxed. Even his arm is supported at an easy angle. But his eyes are jumpy in the face cradle, blinking and unable to rest.

"Something's still off," Dr Andrews says.

Scott looks down through the face cradle. That jangly guitar is about to drive him mad, too many notes that never hang together. *It's the music.*

"One sec." The doctor's feet disappear as he turns to the counter. A click and a hum and the plucky strings fade, taking with them the flurried energy of their preparations. A slow bass drumbeat begins, backed with long, low notes that swell subtly and overlap.

Harp? No, cello. Scott lets his eyes slip closed. His next breath is longer, and his hips sink deeper into the table.

"Better," Dr Andrews says.

He is close enough that Scott can hear his steady breathing. He wonders if Dr Andrews might consider doing nothing with him today. Maybe he could just stand there like a sentinel, watching over him as Scott's head gets heavier in the cradle and his heartbeat slows. Maybe today, the doctor could just let him be.

No such luck; Dr Andrews's voice is a low whisper when he speaks, as if he doesn't want to break in. "We'll warm you up first this time, all right?"

"All right."

The doctor folds the blanket down to Scott's waist and lays a towel over his back.

"Heat pack. Tell me if it's too hot."

A warm, weighted pad covers his back completely. Its heat is surprisingly pleasant; Scott's eyes go soft in their sockets when the blanket is tucked in around him. He clears his throat. "Is it okay if I start to sweat?"

"Sweating's good, burning's not. Need some water?" Dr Andrews walks away again, and the cooker's lid clatters against the counter.

"No, I'm good."

"Hot rock," Dr Andrews says as he places the stone in his palm. "Is that okay?"

"Mm hmm."

"Good. We'll do your feet this time too." Dr Andrews presses Scott's fingers around the rock and swaddles it tight. The lovely balsam scent of arnica wafts around them, green and round and welcoming; it wakes up the thought of the valley, and Scott follows it, searching behind his eyes. But nothing comes, even after both of his hands and feet are wrapped with rocks, and he lets the effort dissolve away.

"We'll let those work on you for a bit," Dr Andrews says, stepping away from the table.

With Dr Andrews gone, Scott feels unmoored, as though a rope's been cut, and he's floating on his own in the middle of the room. He figures this is one of those times Dr Andrews had mentioned, when Scott wouldn't feel his hands on him, though they'd be working just the same. It strikes him as absurd, suddenly, that three hours ago, he was in Dr Coulter's cold office filled with stainless-steel instruments and ultrasound imaging machines. Now he's gone round a hundred and eighty degrees, well wrapped up and baking like a mince pie, treated with nothing more than warm sheets, hot rocks, and a pair of hands. *But Dr Andrews has all those papers on his wall, so he's got to know what the hell he's doing, right?* Eight certificates from universities and societies, but not a doctor's instrument anywhere. And he doesn't even want to be called "doctor," it's "Jason."

When Scott thinks of the name, he doesn't see the doctor with his patient files and office crowded with books. He sees the young lad in the black-and-white photo, scooped up on his mates' shoulders, smiling into the sun.

Jason.

"Hmm?" The swish of Dr Andrews's trackies comes closer, and Scott opens his eyes; *shit, I said that out loud?*

"Uh, just...I'm ready to start if you are."

The doctor's hands settle on Scott's shoulders, one to a side. They don't move at first, just rest, letting the rise and fall of Scott's breathing lift and lower them.

"Right," Dr Andrews says, "let's give it a go."

He pushes down through the layers on Scott's back in a walking motion, enough for Scott to roll a bit from side to side. The heat of the pad seeps into his muscles, making his shoulders feel heavy, and he breathes comfortably in tandem with the pressure. His mind wanders to the valley again. He tries to build the place from the patches he remembers from last time: sky splashed with stars, mountains covered with tall trees in silhouette, the pinion smell of wood smoke, and the mellow glow of fire. There had been a bird flying around above, too, not one he could see with his eyes, but one he'd felt with...*with what?* He'd just known it was there. But now, all he sees is an empty expanse of black. He opens his eyes with a sigh.

"All right?"

"Mm hmm."

"Good. Let's see where we are." Dr Andrews peels off Scott's layers one by one, leaving his torso and arms uncovered. When the air hits his hot skin, the cool is a welcome relief.

"You need to tell me if anything hurts," Dr Andrews reminds him.

Scott hears the familiar swish of his fingers. The velvet, earthy sound of the cello seems suddenly alien and ominous, and Scott hums along with a low note in an attempt to tuck down a little stab of nerves. He grips his rocks a bit tighter.

Dr Andrews's hands cover his shoulder blades and push down in a long stroke all the way to the bottom of Scott's ribs. *Easy, just like last time.* Scott settles in, breathing smoothly. He loosens his grip on the stones as the movement repeats, his muscles feeling warm and pliant. It's nice, this give and take they fall into, and Scott catches a glimpse of why Dr Andrews uses the word "we" when he explains what work they'll do.

"A little deeper this time, left side first." Dr Andrews breathes smoothly too; Scott can hear the air against his throat. The pressure now feels more concentrated, as if he's using the heels of his hands rather than his fingers. "Now the right."

The stroke on Scott's injured side is milder than on the left. The doctor's hands lift after a few seconds of gentle pressure. They push back more deeply on the first side, forcing a huff out of Scott's lung, but barely register any pressure on the right. After the third time of this uneven back-and-forth, Scott feels strangely cheated.

His eyes pop open, alert with challenge. "You can do that harder if you want. It's all right."

"Yeah?"

"Yeah, the other side too. I'm not that fragile."

"Agreed. Here we go. Left side."

Scott inhales. He watches the doctor take a step back with one foot, as though he's trying to get leverage. *This is going to be good.*

Dr Andrews takes a breath, then pushes down on Scott's good shoulder. It's pleasant for a second, like the pressure of a friendly hug. But then it gets more forceful, as if the friend has morphed into an MMA fighter with the hug becoming a pin to the mat. Scott exhales with a grunt as the doctor's hands push down over his ribs in a steady, heavy stroke, and Scott hears a muffled pop from somewhere along his spine.

"You good?" Dr Andrews asks.

"Yeah." Scott is sweating for real now; it's hot, and he feels *here* all of a sudden, plugged in, alive in his body. A tingle buzzes over the surface of his skin, cool and hot at the same time, that chases away the drowsy fog in his mind.

"Other side now. Try not to let your thighs tense up, okay?"

Scott hadn't realised it, but his legs are stiff under the blanket, so he wriggles around to slacken them. "Okay, ready."

Dr Andrews shifts to the opposite front leg. He moves his outspread hand back and forth over Scott's shoulder blade with a gentle rubbing motion that lulls Scott into closing his eyes. A fluttering like a bird's wings breaks through the black as the movement stops, and after a beat, the whole right side of his torso presses into the table under the full force of the doctor's hands. They knead almost *through* his shoulder blade and down his back. There is another dull pop as the first points of light burn through the dark in front of Scott's eyes.

"Still good?"

Scott watches as the dots get brighter and the void of black turns a purplish-blue. The mountains take shape against the sky, and the tops of the trees come into focus. The whole valley materialises out of the darkness as if it's an image appearing on paper in the darkroom.

Oh my God, here I am. This is it.

"Mm hmm," Scott manages, though he can't remember the question because the constellations are pricking light in showy patterns across the dark. Soon the sky is full of them, close enough to touch. This isn't a still picture, like a photograph. It's a place. Or maybe a time. The fire is behind him, he knows, though he can't feel its heat or hear the crack and pop of its burn. It's like watching himself in a movie; he can't hear the night sounds or feel the cool grass underfoot, but he knows they are real just the same.

"Again?"

"Yeah, yes." *Not asleep, not dreaming, the doctor is talking to me, and I'm talking back.* Jason's hands are on Scott's shoulders, and Jason's voice is in his ears, but Scott is in the valley too. He looks out at the trees with their tallest branches profiled against the sky. Somewhere out there is an owl looking back at him, he is sure of it.

Jason works at his good side in a smooth, forceful movement that compresses Scott's ribs and draws out his spine while Scott watches the other world playing on the screen inside his mind. He's not sure he's breathing, not sure of much anymore, except that he's meant to be here. There is something here only for him, something calling out to be found.

He turns toward the fire.

"Now we're getting somewhere. Don't forget to breathe, okay?"

Yes, breathe into this. Jason's strong hands push on, and Scott's muscles are supple underneath them, as if accepting an invitation. The fire should terrify him, but it holds no threat. It is strikingly beautiful, glowing and alive in orange and yellow and feathery bits of green and blue that lick and climb. It's made of light. And power. And something else. Scott can't retreat from it, can't even look away. He steps closer and feels no heat, only hope. The winking stars seem to look down on him with wonder. The flames are so close now. He takes one last step.

"This might get uncomfortable, so tell me if I need to stop."

Jason's voice pulls Scott back, and he jolts on the table with a spasm in his legs. Scott coughs before he can stop it, the night valley receding into the darkness.

"Sorry, did I scare you?"

The cough is enough to send Jason for water, and Scott rolls to his side to drink it down.

"No, I was just..." *How am I meant to square this up?* "...really relaxed, I guess." The fire was glorious with its glowing colour and energy. He'd been drawn to it, which is truly mad, considering, and he'd been about to, well, fall in.

"Yeah, your traps and lats are nice and loose. Well done. I'll take your rocks, and you can turn over."

The usual ache in Scott's shoulder has mellowed, and he finds he can easily manage a half-graceful twist to get onto his back. As he goes, he notices that Jason has taken off his jumper, leaving him in a short-sleeved T-shirt. Scott's eyes fall to the doctor's forearm, where his simply designed tree tattoo spreads its delicate branches from a slim trunk.

"Let me know if you want more heat under your shoulders." Jason adjusts the pillow under Scott's knees and tucks him in.

Maybe it was the pressure or the heat, or maybe it was being on the receiving end of the doctor's real strength, but Scott feels his blood circulating with an almost audible buzz, pulsing everywhere through his veins in a new way.

His arm especially, encased in the fabric brace, feels full where it had been hollow. He remembers gripping it defensively before he lay down, grateful for the little bit of protection it gave him, but now the brace feels heavy and uncomfortably tight, and he can't stand it another minute.

He raises it like he's asking a question in class. "I want to take this off, okay?"

"Yeah, let's. Here, I'll do it. Just lie there." Jason holds Scott's forearm still as he separates each Velcro strip with a satisfying rip. The brace opens, and Scott's arm slides out, and he can't help but let out a little groan of relief.

"Want to sit up a minute? Move it around a bit?"

Whew, yes, it wants to bend, shake, roll, and flex; Scott sits up and does it all, letting the blankets fall to his lap while Jason puts his brace on the counter.

"Better?"

Scott runs his good hand through his hair as he straightens and twists the other arm. "Yeah. Felt like it was suffocating."

"We can unwrap it if you want. If it's too hot?"

"Nope, this is good."

Scott likes the lighter cover of the elastic bandage and the delicious heaviness in his muscles. He makes a fist with his hand and looks at it curiously, as if for the first time, studying the flat, square nails and the veins visible under the skin. He flexes and releases it a few times and gives his arm one last shake from the shoulder. It feels like it's part of him again, connected, after a long time gone.

The relief makes him brave enough to say it. "Feels like it's mine again, you know?"

"You up for working on it a bit? Your jaw was next, but it would help if we could get this in the mix."

Scott doesn't hesitate. "Yeah, let's do it."

*

"Hmm. Stubborn."

Scott almost missed it, Jason said it so softly. "What is?"

"In your file, it shows..." Jason begins, then trails off, frustrated. His hot hand presses the shoulder joint where the elastic bandage starts. He holds Scott's wrist with his other hand, like he's trying to make a loop circuit. He's been at it for a few minutes now, just holding Scott's arm at both ends. Scott doesn't think anything is happening; the knotted look on Jason's face says he doesn't think so either.

"They put pins in here, right? To stabilise the fracture?"

"Yeah, a couple of screws. Why?" Scott asks.

"Screws," Jason mumbles as if he's been personally insulted.

Scott chuckles and tries to restrain a smile.

"What?" Jason asks.

"Screws. My screws are screwing with you. It's funny."

Jason quirks his eyebrow without taking his eyes off Scott's arm. His profile is all irritated angles, but Scott can see the gentle curl of his eyelashes in relief. "Funny, huh?"

"Maybe I'm easily amused." Having his arm back gives Scott a floaty, easy feeling he hasn't had for months;

Jason's frustrated face makes Scott want to lighten him up too. "Who says sticks and stones may break my bones but words will never hurt me?"

"Pardon?" Jason says, still not looking his way.

"It's a joke. Who says sticks and stones may break my bones but words will never hurt me?"

Jason blows air through his lips. "Dunno. Who?"

"A guy who's never been hit with a dictionary."

It works; Jason shakes his head and smiles at him with a little snort. "Really."

Scott's heart thumps light and trippy. "Thomas told me that one. We have a thing going. Injury jokes."

"Well, there's a smile." Jason returns his attention to the task at hand. "Didn't know if I'd ever see it."

Jason changes tactics, lifting Scott's forearm away from his body. He supports the bicep with his other hand and rotates it from the shoulder, giving it a pull until Scott's body turns toward him.

Oh, that feels...brilliant. "Can you do that again?"

"Let's do," Jason agrees. Scott breathes smoothly as he feels the stretch, his shoulder offering no resistance. Jason gives his arm a gentle twist while holding it at the elbow, and Scott exhales with a little groan.

"I think your jaw unlocked just then. Let's take a look."

Jason presses his fingers against the hinge of Scott's jaw, then back toward his ears and under them. It's true, the ropy muscles on each side of Scott's face have loosened, but Scott still can't drop his jaw freely when Jason asks him to.

"Try something for me?" Jason's voice is low, like he's sharing a secret. "You know that lovely feeling when you're just waking up? On a day where there's no alarm and there's no hurry...when you're conscious, but not ready to move or talk yet?"

Jason's fingers find a notch in each of Scott's cheekbones and rub in the tiniest of circles. "Mm hmm." Scott knows what he means. A Sunday morning feeling. Something he would only find in his other life, his life before.

"See if you can remember a morning like that." The circles get bigger. A muscle in the right side of Scott's face resists with a dull ache; Scott's eyes squint with it, but Jason keeps on. "A place where you're relaxed and rested. Content. No place to go. Nothing to say."

Scott doesn't know if the doctor is talking to him or that stubborn muscle. Doesn't matter. He finds that if he lowers his jaw a little more and lets his mouth open it feels a bit better, and he can think.

"Hmm. I suppose world-travelling, award-winning photojournalists don't get many days off, do they?" Jason asks.

Cheeky. But it triggers a memory. "World-travelling photojournalists could book themselves an extra few days in, say, Barcelona." Scott's voice is deep in his chest and his words come slowly. "Especially if they don't have to be in Madrid until the weekend."

"Well then," Jason agrees. "Barcelona. What do you remember about it?" His hands move back toward Scott's ears and press a slow trail down his neck.

"I was there for an awards dinner. Lots of tuxedos and champagne. The hotel had these antique model sailing ships in the lobby. My boyfriend Patrick—well, I mean, my ex-boyfriend, now—he flew back to London the day after, for a job. But I stayed. I slept in every day, and they'd send me up these amazing fruit and cheese plates with blood orange juice." Scott sighs, remembering.

"Hmm. Sounds nice. What else?"

Scott's eyes flutter shut. "Blue and green–coloured tiles. A book of beautiful buildings. The sun would slant through these massive French doors." Scott is surprised at how much detail he can remember about that room. "There was a white railing on the balcony. And a little ceramic dog on the night table."

"You could go back there now."

On Jason's warm table, with music that isn't music, and the smell of sunrise and soft trees in the air, it isn't a stretch. He remembers the ease of that morning after they'd said their goodbyes and Patrick had slipped out for the airport. The white sheets had smelled like sex and almond shampoo, and the day had sat out in front of him like a present to unwrap. He can see his award on the night table, next to the empty wine glasses and that little boxer figurine. He thinks he might go to the Picasso Museum later, wander around until closing and then take a walk to find dinner. But for now, the bed feels deep and soft and the sun is coming through the shades just so. He nestles his face into the pillow and curls further under the covers.

"Now turn you head for me, toward the window."

Scott's head rolls to the side obediently. His body feels like a bag of sand. The stretch in his neck as he turns his head makes a soreness flame up, but it's a distant annoyance, as if a car alarm is sounding blocks away.

Jason's hand rests against Scott's neck, then moves his hair out of the way before he slides his palm down the taut skin to where it slopes into his shoulder. Behind Scott's eyes, the sun-dipped hotel room in Barcelona dissolves into an inky darkness pinpricked with diamond stars, and the French doors turn into his beautiful, rising fire. Scott gets up from the bed and walks into the flames.

*

He arrives on the other side to a shadowy room whose walls are cold, stone piled on stone. He sits at the head of a table that is cold, too, a slab of dark wood big enough for twelve. Everything is heavy here, thick and dark, lit only by candles scented with sandalwood and spice.

Scott has to sign something. It is a decree from the emperor himself, painted on a scroll in bold, graceful characters that belie their threatening message. The parchment lies in front of him, next to the red lacquer box that contains his ink block and brush, along with the candle and wax with which he's meant to seal it.

He feels confused. *No, worried.* A weight on his shoulders presses down on him, but it isn't a physical weight. It is a weight of duty, of responsibility.

Men sit on either side of him with their arms crossed, some stroking their neatly trimmed beards or murmuring in guarded tones. These are men who look to him for guidance and answers, though all have the guilty air of rebellious soldiers who have eaten the last of their rations out of spite. None will meet his eyes.

Scott can feel the pull of the masses on the other side of the stone window. They are earnest people with simple lives, out there in the rice paddies and on the sea, faceless thousands who love him. This decree that he is meant to sign will confuse them. It will anger them. It will shake their trust in him and the dynasty his father's father's father built.

They will never forgive him.

Scott studies his hands, perhaps to find some wisdom there, and sees the hands of an old man, the red and blue veins crisscrossing like tree roots under leathery skin. Bronze bracelets adorn his wrists under long embroidered silk sleeves. One bracelet takes the form of an anchor, the same anchor depicted at the top of the parchment; it is the sign of his family, his dynasty, now under siege.

"How am I meant to do this?"

The only answering voice comes from the man standing at the window, staring out to the sea.

"They will understand, my king." His words are wise and reassuring, the voice of a man Scott trusts with his life. "The alternative is war. Our people will know you are keeping them safe."

He has never lied to me. Scott knows beyond doubt that he can't say the same of the other men in the room.

The man who speaks is broad and strong, still imposing even at his age, his long, straight hair now more silver than black. When he turns to Scott, the jade and gold pin in the form of a ship on his collar glints in the dusky light. They are brothers. Not by blood, but Scott feels a bond as unshakeable as these stone walls.

"Our allies will come," the man says confidently, pointing out to the ocean. "But not for months. Until then, this is our path."

It is too long to wait. The men, women and children, farmers and fishermen are *his*. And they will be afraid. Worse, they will panic, and break into factions. They will turn on one another. "Our people, they need reassurances. Their loyalty will be...tested."

His brother approaches with an uneven, limping gait, earned long ago in a different battle when they were young and new to the ways of war between emperors and their kings. He lays his hands flat on the table on either side of the document.

Scott needs to see his eyes. He'll know for sure then; he'll read his brother's eyes plain as he can read the wind on the sea, and he will know what to do.

"We show them our unity. We show them patience. We show them who we are. Who they are. We hold fast."

His brother's words are the bolster Scott needs, as always, and his eyes are his truth. His strength. His resolve.

Scott reaches for the brush.

*

"Scott?"

There is a nudge to his shoulder and a tug on the sheet.

"You fell asleep."

Scott's forehead is damp with sweat, and he finds he can't turn his head. Jason has put a hot towel under his neck, holding him in a position where his cheeks are slack and his mouth has fallen open.

"Jesus, sorry. I forgot where I was." Long ago. An old man. A fortress at the edge of the sea.

"No worries. We're done for today. Good work. Take your time getting up. Water's on the counter. Finish it before you come see me."

Jason's footsteps recede, and it is the click of the door shutting behind him that brings Scott fully back to the treatment room on Forest Lane. For a moment, he checks in with his body, flexing his arms, rolling his jaw, and bending his knees up as Barcelona and the night valley and the stone-walled castle slide together in a blur. He turns over on his side, baffled that he can feel more rested after forty minutes with Dr Andrews than he does after five hours of sleep in his own flat.

He pushes himself up from the table, a little woozy at first but looking forward to getting dressed. He finishes his water in three gulps and slips into his shirt as a small but insistent thought grows louder.

I wasn't asleep.

*

Jason is typing on his tablet when Scott knocks on his office door and steps in, brace in hand.

"So? You feeling good?"

"Yeah, I feel great, actually."

Jason looks up at him with a smile. "Brilliant. A lot happened today. You're going to need your water. You'll stay on that, yeah?"

"Yeah. I will."

"And the work we did on your jaw today loosened it up quite a bit, which will help to alleviate your headaches. That visualisation exercise—"

"You mean when you hypnotised me?"

"What?" Jason looks simultaneously amused and insulted. "I didn't hypnotise you, I reminded you of something so you could relax. And it worked. You fell asleep."

Scott smiles, letting Jason win. He can't possibly tell him because he doesn't quite understand it himself. But Scott was *there*, awake on Jason's table but also in the castle by the sea, living inside the story of the king and his brother as it unfolded.

"Anyway, keeping that jaw loose is key. There are a few things you could do. Visualization, like what we did, that's one. Or you can pretend you're pissed, you know, proper drunk—where you slur your words and your face feels like it's going to fall off?"

Scott gives Jason a quizzical look, then watches, fascinated, as all of the doctor's crisp edges go curvy. His eyelids droop, and he starts to sway.

"Ya know, cuz whenya drinkin yer brain doooosnt sen infomation to yer muscles? Cuz thuh nurropathwayyyz don reac like theydooo when yer sobah. Soooooo. But pretenin to be pissd workz jussaz good azereal thin." Jason smiles and snaps back to his old, sharp self, dropping the bit like a mask. "The drunker the better." He points to the lower part of Scott's face. "Gets everything in there loose."

"Or you could practice that one shocked selfie face." Jason opens his mouth and makes his eyes big, faking surprise. He holds an imaginary phone at arm's length and taps the screen. "Though I suppose photojournalists don't take selfies."

"I'll do the drunk thing. Without, or maybe with, the drinking part." Scott's face gets hot.

"Eight or ten times a day, or whenever you feel your teeth clamping together, drinking *water*, yeah? Do you need me to write you a prescription?" He turns as if to pick up his pad.

"Nah, I can remember. Blotto, every hour on the hour. Got it."

"Good." Jason crosses his arms and leans back against his desk. "Now one more thing."

"Okay." Something you do to me gives me visions. That's one thing.

"It's major."

"Oh. Okay?" The doctor's change in tone makes Scott cross his arms too.

"You're presenting with indications of muscle strain consistent with someone who...has a construction job. Or moves furniture. Someone who's carrying something heavy, who has had for a while. Shoulder buildup, tension in your jaw, compression in the throat. People who lug stuff around have that."

"So, what's that mean?"

"Well, it means I'm confused. Because you're not supposed to be doing any lifting. Your splint wasn't heavy enough to be the reason. So, what is?"

Jason's direct gaze makes Scott's palms sweat, and he looks at the floor. "Well, I used to carry my gear, you know. Tripod, camera, computer, all of that?" The buoyancy Scott felt moments ago drains away, leaving him spinning.

"Is that lately? Or do you mean before?"

"No, not lately." Scott tries to clear his throat of a scratchy lump. "I don't take pictures anymore."

"Since the explosion."

"Yeah." One hundred sixty-three days exactly, according to the calendar he hash marks with his Sharpie in the early hours of each morning, after the darkroom spits him out. He looks past the doctor to the bookshelf. Blocky letters on colourful spines look back at him. *The Twelve Powers. Clinically Oriented Anatomy. Radical Forgiveness.*

There is a knock on the door, and Monica pokes her head in without waiting for Jason to answer. "Pardon, your half three cancelled. Chemo went badly, and she just...can't."

Jason picks up his tablet and slides it awake. "Did she reschedule?"

"She thought Thursday, early."

"Right, thank you." He nods at her, and she gives Scott a small smile before she turns to go.

Scott waits as Jason taps in some notes. He waits for the question, waits for the direct gaze that sees right down into him, no nonsense and no hesitation. *He'll know.*

"Just so happens my half three cancelled." Jason returns the tablet to his desk. "If you want to, let's talk about what you've been carrying around."

"I don't know. Nothing. I don't know what you mean." Scott didn't see this coming. He'd thought he could fly under the radar, just for a few appointments so he could get back to sleep. But now, Dr Andrews—Jason, whomever—with his warm hands and coaxing voice is going to try to pull him back into the land of the living from this jagged, bleeding edge he's balancing on. There'd been a taste of it today, that brilliant feeling of being put back together, whole again, and it's more than he deserves. Scott had forgotten that for a while, left Omran aside, hadn't he? He can't let that happen.

All at once Scott knows he can't come back here.

He leans down to gather up his brace. Jason isn't here; it's Dr Andrews who is looking at him plainly, standing between him and the door.

"Let me tell you something, Scott. It's the greatest irony of healing, the secret nobody tells you. You have to feel better before you can get better."

Feel better? He can't feel better, because that would mean his atonement is over, and it couldn't be, not yet. The thought makes Scott's eyes itch again, and he reaches into his pocket for his sunglasses. He has to make himself walk out of here.

"Thank you, Dr Andrews. I...I really..." Scott takes one last glance around the room as he steps toward the door.

"We can work through it, whatever it is. It's heavy, I get that. But I'll help you."

Work through it? Talk it out? No, no, there's no way he can talk about what happened in Afghanistan. Scott never went to the psychologist that had been recommended to him, precisely for that reason, and he's not going to start now. "I...I'll think about it. But I can't stay today." Scott's throat is closing, and his legs may not hold him up for much longer.

"Thursday. Come back on Thursday at two, yeah?"

"Thank you," Scott chokes out as they shake with right hands. Dr Andrews steps aside, and Scott is gone.

*

That night, Scott dreams he's standing at a rotary-style payphone in the French Quarter of New Orleans.

Although he's never been here before, he recognises the wrought-iron balcony railings and narrow, brightly coloured buildings. They'd studied the photographs and news coverage of Hurricane Katrina in journalism school. Here, in his dream, there is no one around, and he's standing in cold brown water up to his knees. The phone booth has a broken door that won't close and a cord that's been cut. He finds some rupees in the pocket of his jeans and slips them into the coin slot. Before he can say anything, an elderly woman's gravelly voice is on the other end, telling him there is nobody here by that name.

Chapter Three

Ghost Image (n.) In time exposure photography, an object that is only partially recorded on the film and therefore has a translucent, ghostlike appearance. Ghosting also occurs when using electronic flash at a slow shutter speed and a second image is captured on the film by ambient light.

You have two new messages. First message received Thursday, May 26th at 5:20 p.m.

"Hello Scott, it's Jason. Missed you today, something must have come up for you, so I thought I'd check in. Also wanted to mention that if your hands and feet are cold, you can fill up a sock with raw rice and pop it in the microwave for a bit? It'll get warm, and you can hold on to it or tuck that under your feet when you're, you know, on the couch or wherever. Do me a favour, please don't put rocks in the microwave. I had a patient once who thought he—" *beep*

Next message received Thursday, May 26th at 5:21 p.m.

> "Hi, Jason again, I got cut off, so I'll say quickly—tea counts for water, so heat up a cuppa and hold on to that too. Two birds, one stone and all that. Monica tells me you didn't reschedule when you called to cancel, so I'd like to put you down for next Monday the first at two. Hope to see you then. And remember, you can call me on my mobile if you need to, 078149667. Take care."

*

Good day, you have reached the office of Dr Jason Andrews. Our office hours are Monday through Friday, 8:00 a.m. until 5:00 p.m. If you need immediate assistance, please dial 078149667. Press one to leave a detailed message, and we will return your call during regular office hours.

> "Dr Andrews, it's Scott. I, um...I guess I'm doing well with the water, and I'm doing mostly well with the diet...though there was cake that couldn't be avoided yesterday. Also, ice cream. And there was some pizza before that. There was a thing my sister threw for, you know, getting my splint off. So, about Monday—I think I told you that I have a new physio now? She's pretty good, I guess. She's...well, she's kind of a very large drill sergeant in a tiny package. She's Irish, and I'm a little terrified of her if I'm honest? But she's really all right, so...anyway, I don't know if I need to see you anymore? So. But thank you, again, for checking on—" *beep*

*

You have one new message and two saved messages. New message received Friday, May 27th at 9:44 a.m.

"Scott, it's Jason. You decided to celebrate, hmm? Good. You didn't seem much in the mood when you left on Monday, so I'm glad to hear it. Pizza never hurts, I agree. Glad to hear you're continuing your physiotherapy. From the sound of it she's putting you through your paces. Any case, please call me back when you can so I can update your file with her name and contact information. Thank you. Talk to you soon. Take care."

*

You have two new messages and three saved messages. First new message received Friday, May 27th at 6:06 p.m.

"Hi Scott, it's Jason. So, I didn't get a return call from you, and...well. There's this thing I have about starting something and leaving it unfinished. You've seen enough doctors, so I don't need to tell you what we're like. Monstrously large egos and all that. And usually an acute aversion to failure. I like to think I'm not like the rest, but...there you have it. Also, I need to say that I am sorry if I overstepped. I thought talking about it would help, but if you don't want to, that's all right. But I'd like to keep working on your shoulder. I hope you'll reconsider. Monday, 2:00 p.m. if you're up for it. And if nothing else, please try to drink your water—" *beep*

Next message received Friday, May 27th at 6:08 p.m.

"Hi, me again. Please do the jaw exercises. Those are going to be your best remedy for your headaches and will help you sleep. And do exactly what the sergeant tells you to do—unless there's pain, in which case, well, don't. It would be lovely if you'd call to fill me in. Thanks."

*

Good day, you have reached the office of Dr Jason Andrews. Our office—beep

"Dr Andrews, hi. It's Scott. Um, I'm doing fine, I think, most of the time. The rice trick works, and I'm sleeping better now, so that's good, right? Having some weird dreams, but I've only had one headache since Tuesday, I guess because I'm pretending to be drunk an awful lot. I taught Thomas how, and he's excellent at it too. My sister Olivia thanks you very much for that, by the way. The sergeant said I'm looking good. The elbow and shoulder range of motion looks okay for now. She's making me do some stuff for my knees too. You know, I think you two would agree on a lot of things, but her methods are, hmm, how should I say? A bit...I mean, she's more...ugh. I guess she's not as gentle. As you."

*

You have one new message and five saved messages. New message received Saturday, May 28th at 10:12 a.m.

"So, you're sleeping well. Excellent! I waited to call hoping I wouldn't wake you. Call me back and tell me one of your dreams. Or you can tell me Monday at two. This is Jason. I'm home."

*

Good day, you have reached the office of—beep

"Hi, it's Scott here. You wanted a dream report, which is weird, but all right, here you go. I had this one where I was back at uni, in my documentary photography class, but we were outside Saint Patrick's Cathedral, you know, in New York? I went there once to shoot a cop's funeral, and in the dream, it was like that, all draped in black with flowers and a hearse. Anyway, we were all there, waiting outside, and it's time to get our cameras out, and I don't have mine. And the professor is going on and on about composition and light, and I'm thinking, *Shit, how am I gonna do this?* Then I start to panic because I'm gonna fail the assignment. And then I remember. My camera is smashed to pieces in my cupboard, in London. How am I meant to tell my professor that my camera broke—" *beep* "—while I was working...in Afghanistan?"

Good day, you've reached the—beep

"So, another one. This was from a couple nights ago. I'm at uni again, Golds, in the studio presenting my photo essay final. Except there's nobody else in the classroom but me, and it's the middle of the night. Then I feel this tapping on my shoulder, and sitting behind me is Omran. He's saying, 'We're going to be late.' And I'm like, 'I've got to do an exam,' and he's bugging me, 'Come on, we've got to go. We're gonna miss it,' shaking my shoulder. Then some professor lady I've never seen before comes in, points this stupid laser pointer at me and says, 'Do you have something to share?' And I turn around to tell him to wait for me—" *beep* "—until after the exam, but he's already gone."

Good day, you've re—beep

"Okay, one more. I'm walking down this narrow street in New Delhi, right, near Chawri Bazaar? It's dusk, and there're so many beautiful colours—the saris and the canopies of the booths...it's gorgeous, you know? So I'm about to take some pictures, and then this bike comes toward me, weaving through all these people, with a big basket of purple and pink and yellow flowers in the front. And it's...it's Omran, driving this amazing, rickety old red bike. So he...he stops right next to me. And...I'm so...relieved to see him, you know? I mean he's...right there and he...and...*sorry—*" *beep*

Good day—beep

"Um, sorry. So...so he looks really happy, you know, just...radiating. I say, 'Omran, I thought you were in Kabul!' And...he shakes his head, and then he asks me to take a picture of him. And I'm thinking, *Yes, yes, let me get a picture of you before you go!* But my camera's hot suddenly. It's burning my hands, and I can't hold it. So I drop it, and the case cracks against the pavement and...he smiles at me, and waves, and he rides away. And I feel bad because I didn't get his picture, and...I know I won't get another chance. I reach down—" *beep* "—to get it, and I see your feet. In your trainers. You're standing there. And. You're young, you know, wearing your footie kit, and you're smiling at me, like you're happy to see me or something. And that's when I woke up.

"So. You're trying, I know, you're gonna try your best to help me, I see that.

"But. You know...what if I do get better? I mean...Omran's dead. He's gone. And if I'm back to normal, well then...that's not fair, is it? Won't I be leaving him behind? I never got his picture. It's wrong of me to...I don't want to...forget him. When I'm at yours, I feel like I do forget, and it's like I'm walking away from him, you know? And I can't let that happen. So."

*

You have two new messages and six saved messages. New message received Saturday, May 28th at 3:50 p.m.

"Hi Scott. I've been thinking about your dreams. I actually played them back a few times, and...you know, what happened to you is...it's massive, and I meant it when I told you that I would help you work through it. I still want to. If you don't, that's really okay. But I'll just put this out there. I think that maybe you don't have to give up that heavy thing you're carrying. Maybe, for now, we could work on you putting it down every once in a while. Maybe that's enough. Just consider it. Talk to you soon. I mean, I hope to hear from you soon."

Next message received Saturday, May 28th at 3:55 p.m.

"Hey, I forgot, I wanted to run something else by you. Why did the banana go to the doctor? Hmm? Because he wasn't peeling well. Tell Thomas that one. Just let me know if you're coming Monday or not, yeah? If you want, you could call me on my mobile? 078149667. I'll be here.

*

Good day, you have reached the office of Dr Jason Andrews. Our office hours are Monday through Friday, 8:00—beep

"I have bad news. Thomas didn't even laugh at your joke. Like, not even a snigger. I thought it was a decent try, but he said you're gonna have to work on it. Sorry. He has high standards for an eight-year-old. Anyway, um...so this is going to sound weird. Well, *I* think it's weird, you probably won't. So, there's this...way that I am, or I mean, way that I used to be that I can get back to when I'm at yours. It's really like...being *awake*, you know? And my sister said she misses that part. Of me. But I can't get there anywhere else. I've tried, and...well. I promised her I'd keep trying. So, I'll come tomorrow if you still have me down. Okay. Thanks. Again. Right. Uh, g'night."

*

You have one new message and eight saved messages. New message received Sunday, May 29th at 8:27 p.m.

"Hi. Thanks for calling. You're right. I don't think it's weird. I think it's brave. I'll see you tomorrow."

Chapter Four

> Sensitivity (n.) Expression of the nature of a photographic emulsion's response to light. Can be concerned with degree of sensitivity as expressed by film speed or response to light of various colours (spectral sensitivity); care and understanding of needs and requirements; capacity for physical sensation or response, such as to heat or other environmental factors.

The herringbone blanket is folded on the table in Dr Andrews's office just as Scott remembers. The slow cooker and crystals are in their usual places. The music of low strings and drum is "his," and the white feather rests on the scarlet cloth, right next to the little jade plant in its porcelain pot. The last time Scott was here, he thought he'd never be back; hell, just yesterday he thought he'd never be back. But everything fits and is warm and familiar, and it all comforts his anxious mood.

All except this new tool on the counter. *A stethoscope?*

Its stainless-steel shine makes it look menacing somehow, and out of place. This room had been a sanctuary from tools like this, and Scott realises how much he wants to keep it that way, keep himself from feeling like a patient here. He backs away from it and turns to the window.

Although he's fully dressed, he feels more naked than he's ever been on the exam table; everything he said to the doctor's answerphone is out there, and he can't take it back. He's got no brace today, no sunglasses, no splint to hide behind. Dr Andrews is going to be here in a minute and look at him the way he does, seeing into everything Scott's about, and see that he's not brave. *Not brave at all.*

He fiddles with the rubber band around his wrist and puts his hair up in a bun to distract himself, finishing it just before he feels the soft buzz of his phone. It's probably Olivia checking in, not so subtly making sure he's keeping his promise. He opens his messages, and the name he sees makes him sway on his feet.

It's his boss from the Associated Press.

Ken Browning here, how are you mate?

Any idea when you're back on roster?

Have a job in two weeks in DC.

Let me know.

The ringing in Scott's ears gets louder, and the phone is suddenly heavy and hard to hold. *For fuck's sake.*

His shoulders jump at Dr Andrews's quiet knock, and he fumbles to close the message. He slides the phone back into his pocket as the door opens, revealing a Dr Andrews that looks different; he's still sporting his trackies and trainers, but he is clean-shaven, and his hair covers his forehead in a long fringe. It makes him look younger, softer in the face.

It's Jason. From the football photo.

"Scott. Good to see you," he says, holding out his hand. As they shake his expression changes to concern. "Are you all right? You look pale. Need to sit down?" He doesn't take his eyes off Scott as he puts a tony leather holdall on the counter between them.

"No, I'm...good," Scott replies, watching him loop the stethoscope around his neck. "I didn't know you had one of those."

Jason pretends to be insulted. "'Course I do. I dust it off every few months so I don't get rusty." He gestures at Scott's arm with a little smile. "No brace today. Good on ya." He looks over Scott's cheek, eyes stopping for a moment on his scar, and a perplexed look crosses his face. "Your hair is different."

"So's yours."

Jason flips his hand up and smooths the ends of his fringe over his brow. "Ah, yeah. Kind of a different routine this morning." A quick look passes between them that says something Scott can't quite define before he changes the subject. "I got a call from Brenna Donovan. She sounds lovely, not like a drill sergeant at all. She sent over a report."

Brenna, Scott's new physio, is the direct sort who calls it as she sees it without any tiptoeing. She's all of four foot nine with black hair and a sweet, freckled face that contradicts her commanding tone. Scott likes her and her take-no-prisoners attitude, the way she manages to be compassionate but at the same time entirely without mercy. Mostly he likes the pain. It helps him pay.

"Yeah, she said she was going to do that, right before she said, 'Drop and give me fifty.'"

Jason puts a hand on his hip, his bright eyes looking out from under his fringe. “Oh, now you’re just making stuff up. You’re doing a post-op shoulder protocol with some elbow precautions. The only press-ups you did were standing against a wall. Like press-outs. Or press-sideways.”

“All right, fine,” Scott allows. “But she counted them. Loudly, in my ear.” Scott chuckles when he sees Jason smile. “Very drill-sergeanty.” He makes a face as Jason brings his hand up to feel the underside of his jaw.

“She’s good, very thorough. You should keep seeing her.”

“I will.”

Jason’s fingers press into the sides of Scott’s throat, then move up to the front of his ears and down his jawline. “That doesn’t feel quite as tight. Pain?”

“No.”

“That’s what you said last time. I think you weren’t telling me the whole truth.”

Scott swallows. “Well, pain is kind of...relative, isn’t it?”

“Um, no. Either it hurts, or it doesn’t.”

“Okay, well, then yeah. But it’s the kind of pain that hardly counts.”

Jason cocks his head. “How bad does it have to be before it counts?”

Shit. “I just meant...it’s not bad.” Scott’s back-pedalling is clumsy. “Not worth making a big deal out of, I guess.”

Jason's side-eye softens. "Do you think I can't tell? When you're in pain?"

Scott shrugs his shoulders, a bit wary of all that Jason knows.

"Sometimes, when I ask you a question?" Jason grasps one of Scott's hands, rubbing the fingers between his warm palms and examining the nails. His voice lowers to a stage whisper, but it has a smile in it. "I already know the answer."

"Then why do you ask me?" Scott stage whispers back.

Jason switches to the other hand, massaging Scott's fingers briskly from palm to fingertips. "Your body is easy to read. But this"—he taps his own temple—"and this"—he gives his heart a pat—"are harder. They all work together, so I want to know about them too."

No. Trust me. You don't.

Scott scrambles to change the subject. "What's the bag for?"

"You'll see." Jason pulls the stethoscope from around his neck. "So, Brenna mentioned your cough in her report. Should we have a listen?"

Scott's cheeks flush. He'd been unable to finish the easy bench presses this morning. Lying flat with even the slightest weight in his hand had tightened up his chest so much he'd struggled for breath, wheezing and coughing until Brenna had called it. "What'd she say?"

Jason steps to Scott's side and places the stethoscope to his chest. "Just noted it, nothing major. We'll see."

Scott breathes smoothly in and out, the cough that had pestered him this morning now nowhere to be found.

Jason removes the stethoscope from his ears. “Clear as a bell.”

“So? That’s good, right?” He watches Jason open a drawer and toss the instrument in, then bring out one that looks like a pen.

Jason shrugs. “Helps us know what it’s not. Congrats, you don’t have pneumonia, bronchitis, asthma, or whooping cough.” He clicks the penlight and a bright beam appears at its tip. “When’s the next time you see your ear nose and throat guy?”

Drop your jaw, drop your jaw. “Friday, I think?”

“Right. Let’s have a look then.”

Scott doesn’t know where to put his eyes as he’s told to open his mouth, stick out his tongue, and say *ahhh.* He settles on the red foiled seal on one of Jason’s diplomas. It reminds him of something, but he can’t place what.

“No drainage either. Doesn’t look like allergies or cold, but there’s some inflammation from...something.” Jason looks at Scott’s neck with squinted eyes. “We’ll see what ENT says,” he mumbles to himself as he backs up to the counter and returns the penlight to the drawer. He fishes out a notebook, then taps the holdall.

“It’s a lovely bag, yeah?”

“Yeah,” Scott agrees, glad they are changing the subject. It’s a nice bag, sporty, but all dressed up for the city with leather handles and two shiny buckles.

“Posh, innit? It’s my favourite. Good for carrying stuff. Or holding things for a while.” Jason opens it, the zipper making an expensive sound.

“What’s it for?”

"It's for you to put something in."

Scott stares blankly at him, then back to the bag. There is a bumpy flutter in his chest. "Like what?"

"What you're carrying, that heavy thing. You can just put it in here. Temporarily. Only if you want to."

Scott shakes his head with a little noise in his throat. He grips his injured arm, pinching at the elastic bandage through his sleeve. "I don't know what you mean."

"Here, it's easy. First, I leave, right? Then it's up to you how you want to do it. You could say it, out loud, into there." He taps the notebook with the pencil. "Or you could write it down and put it in. Or you could..." He makes a grabbing gesture with his hands in front of Scott's torso, shaping air into a ball. "Gather it up." He mimes chucking it into the bag, slides the zipper closed, and gives it a pat. "For safekeeping. You can take it back when you're ready to leave. Or not. So. Get it in there, zip it up, done." Jason puts a hand on his hip as if what he's just said makes perfect sense.

Only it doesn't. At all.

What kind of insanity? Scott takes a step back and squints at the bag. *This is a fucking game now?* Confusion and frustration sharpen into anger in a hot second. God help Jason if he's saying that Scott is meant to play at this, poking fun at this thing that's brought him to his knees.

"You're serious?" Scott's eyes and mouth feel flinty as the words come out.

Jason's voice is grave, his eyes unsmiling. "I'm serious."

Unfuckingbelievable.

"Fucking right it's serious," Scott bites out as he turns to the window, cold hands clenched into fists. Jason can't think his posh bag can hope to hold what Scott's got.

He silently, furiously rattles off the possibilities. *How about a fire so hot it's invisible? How about a car, melted and inside out? Noise so loud it can split eardrums, broken glass like slicing razors. A bloody shoe. Screams that choke. "I'm afraid he didn't make it." Nightmare, scalpel, scar. "We call it blood-blindness." Needle. Scorch. Blister. Widow. Sorry.*

These are the very lightest of the dark places, and Scott chuckles ruefully, barely masking the shake in his breath. Scott crosses his arms tight and lets out a harsh sigh that wants to be a growl. Sweat has broken out everywhere, but his mouth is dry.

He spins and levels his eyes at Jason. "Just one problem."

"What?"

Anger gives way to something that feels like futility welling up in his eyes, and it threatens to pool over. The words come out like he's spitting them. "This lovely, posh bag of yours? It isn't fucking big enough."

Jason grips the tan leather handles as he nods. "I thought you might feel that way. But I bet you'd be surprised what it can hold. Give it a try. Just one thing. Not all of it. Just one."

THERE. IS. NO. ONE. THING. I CAN'T. UNTANGLE. IT ALL.

Scott could hate Jason for this; he wants to tear that bag apart with his hands. "You really think I can..." Scott trails off with a contemptuous shake of his head. "Fucking drop it in there and zip it up and that'll help?"

Jason stands steady, bigger than his slight frame, his jaw set. "I do."

Scott blows air out of his cheeks and waves his hand as if to push Jason out. "All right. Go then." Scott's vision goes blurry with rage.

"I'll give you some extra time. Before I come back, I mean."

"Don't. I'll be ready in two."

*

Face down means Scott doesn't have to look at the bag. It's right where Jason left it, open and waiting on the counter, the notebook untouched.

If he wasn't still fuming, Scott might feel like a poor sport; Jason invited him to play a game, and Scott refused. Vehemently. *But Jesus, come the fuck on.* The anger has energised him. His veins rush with adrenaline, and it's impossible to sink into the table like he should because his legs can't get comfortable for twitching and his hands won't stay still.

Jason does what Scott asked, slipping into the room just after Scott tucks into the face cradle. He doesn't say a word as he smooths the blanket over Scott's legs and adjusts the pillow under his feet.

"Is the heat okay?" Jason finally asks, hovering around Scott's head. If he's angry, Scott doesn't hear it. He presses the blanket firmly across Scott's shoulders, tucking it in at the sides. That makes Scott feel worse. He squints his eyes shut with a twinge of guilt.

"Yeah, it's fine." *But I'm still mad at you.*

Now, Jason pulls Scott's hand from under the blanket, and his fingers graze over Scott's balled-up fist.

"All warmed up already. But we'll do stones anyway, yeah?"

Why? Scott thinks belligerently. He hadn't noticed, but now that Jason mentioned it, his hands throb with a hot pulse. He watches through the face cradle as Jason's feet step away. Then the bag slides to the end of the counter and the lid of the slow cooker clatters open.

"Okay." *Normal. Just be normal.* Scott concentrates on the ringing in his ears and the gentle drum music behind it.

Jason should be saying "hot rock" so Scott will know when it's coming, but there are no words, just Jason pulling against his fingers, using his thumbs to open them. Scott wants them to uncurl, he truly does, but they are frozen, and Jason has to knead Scott's fingers away from the palm with both hands.

"Oh, um, sorry," Scott offers.

"Don't be," comes the answer, and Scott isn't sure if they are talking about his hand or all the rest. But soon it doesn't matter because the scent of arnica is wafting over him, making his teeth slip apart. A locked-in breath is let loose with a sigh.

"Hot rock."

Scott grasps it tight as if finding the anchor he's been waiting for. Jason wraps his hand with a warm towel, and the gesture is enough to quiet the last of Scott's anger. It's like waking from a bad dream, finding himself truly back on the table, mind growing calm with thoughts like *thank you. I can't. I'm sorry.* Jason moves the blanket over his hand and gives it a quick squeeze before he moves back to the counter, as if he has understood, as if everything will be all right.

The door is open; now Scott just has to walk through it. He wants them to be on proper footing again, where they lob and volley and push and pull and work together from the same side. The heat of the rock and the scent of the night valley make him brave enough to take a risk.

"So, uh...what do people usually put in the bag?"

"Sorry?"

Scott pulls up from the face cradle so he can rest his cheek on its warm flannel cover. "Your bag. What do people put in it? I mean, if you're allowed to tell me."

"Hot rock."

This hand is quicker to cooperate. When it's tucked in, Scott feels balanced and squared up, ready for whatever might happen.

Jason moves to Scott's feet and lifts the blanket. "Well, I don't always know. Sometimes people tell me, and sometimes they don't. I don't need to know the details for it to work, does that make sense?"

"I think so."

Scott likes listening to Jason talk. His voice has a hard line in it, an insistent rat-tat-tat rhythm when he's in doctor mode, but Scott has heard a different tone, too, where it's milder, with long vowels and tender edges. He's talking that way now, as if he is telling a bedtime story to a very young, very tired child, which Scott supposes fits just fine.

"For instance, I know cancer's been in there. And addictions. Let's see...there's been some depression. Hot rock. And some guilt, I think. Things said or done that can't be fixed that just...weigh on people."

Scott hums, a swell of heat rippling in his chest.

"And there are all sorts of wrongs and hurts too. Grudges. Jealousy, abuse." A pause. "Infidelity." The way Jason clips off the word tells Scott they may have crept into some delicate territory. He recalls a photograph on Jason's bookshelf of a happy Jason hugged tight. *Shit.* Scott thinks of a question, to keep Jason talking.

"How do they, I mean, do they ever put, like, a real thing in there?"

"Sometimes. Symbolic things. Photos, jewellery. One patient put an ultrasound picture in there once. She'd had a miscarriage."

The heft of it silences them both for a minute. Scott's shoulders let go a bit, and his arms feel heavy on the table, like he might not be able to lift them if he tried. He's sort of crushed by the idea, that there is a sadness a woman out there is carrying around that no one can see, that she put into Jason's bag for a while. *Maybe that's why the bag is so posh. To hold precious things.*

"Oh, and someone put her wedding ring in there once. Said she didn't want it back either. Hot rock."

"Jesus," Scott whispers, horrified. "What did you do with it?"

Jason lets out a little sigh. "I really didn't know what to do with it, to be honest. I called one of my mentors about it. She suggested I give it back to the world somehow. So I took it to Forest Lane Park and hooked it on a tree."

"Holy shit, you did not."

"Holy shit, I did." Jason covers Scott's feet and rests his hands on Scott's heels for a moment. "That was back in...March? It's probably decorating some bird's nest by now."

Scott can see it, a little brown house sparrow picking the ring off a branch and flying home with it. It makes him smile. "Lucky bird. And lucky bird's lucky spouse."

Jason chuckles too. "Quite."

They are silent while Jason pulls the blanket down to Scott's waist and tucks it in.

I really didn't know what to do with it. Scott has trouble picturing Jason confused about anything, but can easily tick off a few things he himself doesn't know what to do with. Actually, it's just one thing, sitting on the high shelf of his cupboard.

Scott takes another step, feeling like he's out on a tightrope, walking away from the platform into the wind. "So...how would I know what to put in there? If I was going to do that?"

"Your body will tell you if you ask it."

What now? Good Lord.

Jason rests his hand on Scott's shoulder where bare skin meets the elastic bandage. "I'd start here. Or some other place where your body is tight. Jaw, hands...if we have to work to get them open, there's something they don't want to let go of. Only you know what it is."

Scott does know. It's there, massive and lurking, buried deep under the scars and rubble. He's been paying for it every day, and keeping score on his calendar every night.

"Know what? I think I owe you a dream," Jason says.

Scott is glad for the pivot, and the relief makes him sigh out loud. "Actually, you owe me three."

"Hey, I only asked you for one. You volunteered three."

Damn. "Okay, compromise. Two."

"Oh, all right. Three." Jason places a heat pack over Scott's back. "Let's see. There was one where I was flying down a ski slope. Not on skis, mind you. I was in this clear bubble, high off the ground, and I could steer it with my mind. It was cold, but it was beautiful from up there, and easy, you know? I got going faster and faster, but then I got scared, I guess, and lost control. I crashed into a tree, and that woke me up. But get this. When I woke up, I was actually outside on my front stoop, shivering because I had nothing but pants on."

"Oh shit," Scott says, chuckling. "I used to have flying dreams all the time. Except in mine, I was like Superman. No cape, but I could just think about it and take off."

"Sounds like fun. You could try to have a flying dream tonight if you want. See what happens?"

When Jason says it, it seems completely possible. "Okay. I will."

Jason presses down on Scott's shoulders through the layer of heat. "Okay, number two. This is one I have a lot. I'm in a fancy lift, all dressed up in a suit, going someplace important. So I press the button for the lobby, but I go up. Then I press Roof, and I go down. People keep on getting on and off, but no matter which button I try, I keep getting farther from where I need to go."

Scott finds it strange that Jason would have the sort of dream that leaves him alone in a lift, sharp in a jacket and tie, bewildered. It reminds him of a dream he had years ago, when he first started travelling for work. "I've got one like that. I'm in Grand Central Station in New York, all set with my cameras and luggage and my passport, waiting at the right track. But my ticket says *London Waterloo*, and the conductors won't let me board."

Jason begins to work a knot under Scott's shoulder blade. "And everyone else is going about their business, right?"

"Yeah."

"I hate those."

Scott inhales deeply, feeling a twinge of pain where Jason presses on a tight knot, but also a bit of sadness. "What happens with the lift?" he asks quietly. "Do you ever get there?"

"Haven't yet. But I'm hoping to, one of these days."

"Yeah," Scott says after a long moment. *One of these days*.

"All right, best for last. It's a sunny day, and I'm walking on a rocky beach, all alone. It's the most gorgeous place I've ever seen. There's a warm breeze, sunlight sparkling on the water, and the sky's as blue as can be."

"And what happens?"

Jason's voice grows wistful, his hands gentle. "Actually, nothing. I walk. Breathe. Take my time, wading in the shoreline. I pick up a rock, put it in my pocket. That's it. It's like I'm the only person left on earth. But it's not lonely. Or scary. Just peaceful."

"That's lovely."

"It really was. I had that dream so long ago, but I still think about it. The way I felt when I was there. Maybe I'll get back there someday too."

The last deep press of Jason's hand on Scott's back feels like understanding, and he doesn't mind when Jason tells him it's time to turn over. Scott can tell the two of them are back on the same side, their vicious scrap over and done, and he's ready to open up to the room again.

*

Jason lifts Scott's injured arm and dangles it by the wrist. It's stiff and heavy, and it wants to curve in tight across Scott's body in the position it rested in for months while it healed.

"It's all right," Jason says. "Don't try so hard. Remember what we did before? Think about something else."

Scott tries to envision the black silhouette of trees against the starry sky of the night valley, but the picture won't come. "We did this last time, and it was fine. Why can't I control it?"

"You've been protecting yourself for a long time now. We can't expect that you're going to have two sessions and everything's going to magically loosen up." He places Scott's arm on the table and tucks it in. "No matter how exceptionally skilled I am."

"It's frustrating," Scott mutters, and clears his throat of a little itch.

"There's something I'd like you to try. Has to do with your breathing."

Scott feels like he's used up his refusals for the day, and they've just returned to solid ground. "Okay," he says, trying to keep the doubt from his voice.

"Don't worry. This is an easy one." Jason tents his hand so his fingertips touch Scott's breastbone through the blanket. "See, your breathing is shallow, all up in here?" Jason places his hand down flat underneath Scott's ribs. "It'll help if we can get it down into here."

"Down there?"

"You're trying to fill this up, like a balloon. See if you can make my hand move."

It strikes Scott suddenly just how intimate this is, how close Jason is standing, and how clearly he can see and feel how well Scott's body works or doesn't. A prickle of goosebumps rises on his thighs.

"Now?"

"Go."

Scott takes his first breath and sees his chest rise, but Jason's hand hasn't moved by the time he has to let it out. A flutter in his throat makes him cough before he tries again, and by the third try, he has to roll to his side while Jason gets his water.

"My throat's closing up." He takes a few gulps. "I can't get enough air."

"Try slowing it down. Breathe in and out for the same count. One, two, three, four—" Jason inhales and lets it out. "—one, two, three, four. Just there, where you are."

Scott is propped up on his elbow with the bottle still in his hand. He counts in his head. *One, two, three*, but his chest feels tight. *Jesus, why can't all my parts work right at the same time?* He tries again, but this time only gets halfway through before he has to stop. Sweat breaks out on his upper lip.

"I can't—I can't breathe," he wheezes out, handing his bottle back to Jason. His easy relaxation is gone, replaced by dread.

"Okay, let's do it backward. Lie down, like you were. It's easier that way." Jason sounds like a coach now, animated, and his eyes are bright with the idea. "This time, do the exhale first. Empty it all out, pause for a bit, then inhale."

Scott rolls to his back, covering up again. "But that's the same thing."

"Nope, it isn't. I know you can do this. Show me." Jason's hand lands against Scott's abdomen again, and Scott can feel its heat even through the sheet and blanket. That heat makes him want to try.

"Okay, ready?" Scott asks. They exchange a nod, and Scott breathes the air out unevenly.

"Pause a bit," Jason whispers quickly, and Scott does, hovering in the space between out and in, and he actually feels his lungs flip open. His eyes get wide, turning to Jason with a shock, and he breathes in slowly for what feels like ages, and...*oh shit I forgot to count*, and that's enough to break his stride, landing under the kind, dark night sprinkled with stars.

Jesus. It worked.

"Perfect. Do it again."

Scott's already a step ahead, closing his eyes and pushing the air out until he's completely drained of it, then staying there for a few moments. He waits for the tiny shift in his chest, and when it comes, he's opened up and can let it all in for days. He forgets to look down at Jason's hand, but this is a feeling he's not sure he's ever had, and he doesn't much care if he's passing the test. He can breathe in and in and in, and when he can't anymore, that gentle turn inside flows the air out. It's...easy; he's not controlling it, or guiding it. *It* is guiding *him*. His head rolls back slightly, opening his throat, and it feels like he's riding on a wave, coasting effortlessly through the crests and the troughs.

Jason lifts Scott's hand and brings it down to rest next to his, rising and falling as Scott breathes. Scott can't feel his arm anymore, can't really feel anything but the depth of his lungs and the hot edge where their hands meet. There are stars and trees and mountains, pulling him away from this room and into the valley, to see the fire. A voice from the far corner of his mind says he can use Jason's hand as an anchor to bring him back, and that's all the permission he needs.

"Keep going," Jason says, but his voice sounds far away, and it's too much effort for Scott to make his mouth move to answer.

He's already gone.

*

When he gets to the other side, she's running. Or is it more like racing?

No. This is escaping.

Again, Scott can see a new world in sharp focus and feel it from the inside. She's been dropped right into the centre of it, this time outdoors, in a forest. And again, she is not alone.

Someone or something is chasing her for what she carries in the pack that rides high across her shoulders. They are her enemy, and though she has had half a day's head start, she doesn't turn to look for them; that will only slow her down. Her people have entrusted her to take the priceless contents of her pack and go, far out of the enemy's reach, away to safety.

She is a messenger and scout, no stranger to the long run. Painted feathers on her tunic and falcon colours on the trim of her leggings are the badges of agility and speed. Her feet in her soft hide shoes propel her over the forest floor as if she's dipping and diving through the air instead of bound to the earth. This path is as familiar as her mother's braid, the trees as comforting as her brothers' faces. She's been running since the sun was high in the sky, an easy momentum carrying her, the rhythm of her footsteps melding with the beating heart of the woods. Her legs feel strong and awake, and instinct tells her there is a speed in reserve just beyond this, waiting for her to kick into if she needs it. But for now, if she can keep this pace until dark, they will be able to stop to eat and rest for a short while. The enemy won't find them if she can get to the caves by the Great River.

The sheltering cover of the woods gives way to open prairie, and she stops for a moment before heading out into the sea of it. She swings the pack from her back and sets it on the ground to check on the child.

Scott pushes aside the red fox pelt and regards the little one's face, she who is the youngest of the story-keepers. The baby girl has dark hair that falls over her forehead in wispy down. Her cheeks are rosy, and a sepia triangle marks her tiny chin. Scott looks into the child's dark, curious eyes and feels the weight of their journey, not for the first time. She will take this little one all the way to Four Streams, where the next scout waits to take her further so the stories of their clan will not die.

"We are almost there, Littlest Fox. We will rest soon." The river is a short way beyond this stretch of open land, so close now. She lifts the pack to her shoulders once more.

She's gone only as many strides as she can count on her hands when she sees them. The feather fans of their war helmets are bright in the dusky sunlight, and their horses' black heads loom eerily still above the tall prairie grass. The sight crushes her, sucks all the air out of her lungs as she turns back in a frantic dash to the trees. Their whoop pierces her ears, and fear is ice in her chest.

She has never seen horses so big. She knows she is no match for them.

She calls to the Falcon. "See me! Lift us, carry us on the wind, away from here!" But her plea is choked off. She can't get her breath, can't open to the pulsing energy of the ground underfoot. She lets out a desperate wail as she darts blindly through the grass that has grown sharp, cutting her hands. How can she find the speed she needs when she cannot breathe? Where is the well-worn path? Where are the shielding brother trees?

The timber looms ahead, blurry and dark, closing the way to her because she misread this task somehow, misjudged the distance or the rhythm or the way out, and now she can't ever return. She has failed this little girl and her people, and the Falcon will no longer claim her.

The warrior hoofbeats are gaining, beating out their message. All her world will hear what she has done.

*

Scott feels the familiar pressure of a knot being worked in his thigh. His face is hot; his nose is running, and he sniffles. The blanket shifts over his leg, and a tissue is pressed to the side of his face.

"Jason, I was...ugh, I'm..." he gasps weakly, "crying again." He opens his eyes long enough to spot Jason and take the tissue from him.

"You know"—the crisp edges of Jason's voice have gone soft again—"you can let go of things in all sorts of ways. Crying's one of them."

Holy shit, wait. Scott's eyes snap open, and he's fully back. *This is what he meant.* His heart thumps with a hot skip.

"Is it too late to put something in the bag?" He scrambles to sit up. He's headachy, and his eyes hurt, but he is alert with urgency. Scott makes a quick writing gesture with his hands because Jason doesn't understand. "I have to...paper?"

"Oh. Yeah, just a sec." Jason rushes to the counter to get the notepad. Scott's eyes are bleary and leaking, but when Jason thrusts the paper at him, he wipes them clear and hones them into focus.

At first, the writing is choppy, starting and stopping as he tries to wrap his mind around it. The circuit between his brain and his hand is rusty, but soon the pencil slides swiftly across the paper. Images like movie clips flash one after the next, and he tries to get it all out of himself onto the page. The sentences start off complete and in straight lines, but soon they go messy; sights and sounds flood through until a page is filled. He rips it off, crushes it into a ball, and throws it over, quick to pick up the pencil again because his thoughts are coming faster than his hand will write. Sentences turn into phrases and then half words like shorthand, scrawled into the book so roughly he almost tears it.

He pulls off the second page and throws it to the ground without bothering to see where it lands. "You can have this. I don't want it back. Ever." Scott says the words without looking away from his work and without stopping. He doesn't hear Jason answer, but he knows he's been heard. *This is for the bag. And this and this and this. Take it, take it away. I want it gone.*

His gaspy breaths sound loud, but he doesn't care; he's hot, and he wants water, but he can't stop. Every last word needs to come out until there is nothing left to haunt him or ambush him in his sleep. He's not even sure he's writing in English now, strange adjectives, verbs, and pronouns biting and scraping at the paper. The writing looks nothing like his, crude letters crowding and spiking, so now he's adding pictures, and there is another page full, ripped to the floor again, and again, more and more, still running racing away, away, away, and the next page is one huge word that he rips off with a growl, and then the tears come again, dropping onto the lined paper. The next sketch is primitive like a cave drawing, but it condenses the wave of information precisely, so much so that Scott can't look at it, can't ever think of it again.

After that, the flood that had burst through slows to a trickle. One more page is partly filled, and finally, there isn't anything left.

Scott rolls his shoulders and looks over the side of the table as if in a rowboat looking down at the water. Pages litter the floor, some crumpled, some ripped. He looks up to see Jason with his arms crossed, leaning against the wall in the far corner near the loo.

Scott knows only one thing to do. "Can you burn it?"

Jason makes an impressed face, eyebrows rising with a quick nod. "Let's."

Jason takes three quick strides and bends over to gather all the pages. He crumples them, not looking at their contents.

"You coming?" Jason asks, turning his head as he continues on toward the sink.

"What, now?"

"Hell yes, now."

Scott grabs the blanket and wraps it around his waist like a bath towel as he makes his way over. Jason dumps the papers into the sink, then opens a drawer and fishes out a lighter. He holds it out for Scott to take.

Scott's eyes hurt. His face feels swollen, and his nose is running. He feels like shit, if he's honest. But something that had been clamping down on his chest has broken loose. A slight tremble in his fingers makes it difficult to work the lighter's wheel, but on the third try, the flame catches, and he touches it to the closest ball of paper. For long moments they watch as the glow eats the story, dissolving it, each piece catching on the next. When it threatens to go out, Scott blows on it gently and the flames grow with a hiss.

Jason speaks softly. "We could be done for today if you want. Or not."

There are only curly black shapes in the sink now, and Jason gestures to Scott to turn on the tap. The last pieces break up and slide down the drain with Jason and Scott standing shoulder to shoulder watching them go.

"Do you still have that eye pillow?" *And there's something you did to my forehead.* "Can we do that? Then we can be done."

*

This time, when Jason places the pillow over Scott's eyes, the darkness comforts him. There isn't any panic or fear, just a soft void that smells like cloves. Scott's eyes fold under the weight like they've been tucked in, and the pounding in his head quiets to a dull murmur.

"Are we late?" Surely he's used up all their time.

"We still have a few minutes." Jason's thumbs start their gentle strokes right above the bridge of Scott's nose, fan out to his hairline, then return over his eyebrows. They coax Scott to let his jaw go. He finds himself breathing in that pattern again, with the exhale first. He can pause in between for a second or two, waiting for that moment his lungs open up and breathing feels like the only thing he's meant to do.

The connection to the valley is tapped out; Scott is solidly here with Jason with no glimpse of stars or the world before. He thinks about the girls in the forest with flat curiosity, objectively, the way he would think about a maths problem or a hand of cards. The charge of it has faded from vibrant, breathing colour to a still frame black-and-white. Yet he has no doubt he was awake inside that world. He had known the terrain. He had felt the danger. He'd even known the outcome before it happened, but he'd had no power to change it. *So what was it then?* Like the king in the stone fortress, the girl in the forest is more than a character in a story. She is a memory. A detailed, familiar, brand-new-yet-impossibly-old memory.

From this calm resting place, his theory seems only mildly irrational. Scott considers telling Jason about it, but truly, he doesn't have any idea how to explain it if he did. He tucks the mystery away for now because Jason is ironing the tension from his forehead, which makes it hard to think.

"You okay?" Jason asks. "I bet you have a headache."

"A little. It's a lot better than it was." I wonder if we'll ever stop talking about my pain.

"It was...rough today. But really good, I think?"

"Yeah, it was. Good. And I guess rough too." Scott clears his throat and remembers their row with a cringe. He had felt desperate to hurt something, hating the adrenaline shake in his hands and the blur in his eyes. It frightened him, all that fury he didn't know he had, lashing out to protect the tender spots underneath. He's glad he can't see Jason right now.

"I'm...I'm sorry about getting arsey before. I didn't mean for it to come out like that."

"Pssh, I think it came out just the way it needed to. Sometimes getting mad is what it takes to bring things up and let them go. That's what we want."

Let it go.

People have been telling Scott to let it go ever since he'd arrived back in London and opened his eyes. "It's not your fault," Olivia had told him earnestly, over and over, with the best intentions. "It was just the wrong place, wrong time" had been Patrick's brilliant insight before he left.

But they hadn't walked on that street, and hadn't seen that car. They hadn't lived through that day while the man standing beside them died. It's Scott's responsibility to hold on to that, isn't it? He's the only one who can. But Jason says he can put it down, or maybe give it up completely. It's as if Jason is beckoning him, calling him down from the ledge. From this quiet place, a new thought wakes up in Scott's mind.

I feel good.

Last week, Jason had said it like he was letting Scott in on a secret: *You have to feel better before you can get better*. But Scott had blown right past him, the thought so impossible he couldn't stay in the same room with it. But he *had* felt better. He'd almost cried with relief when Jason ripped off his brace. It had felt like stepping out of a heavy, dark fog; Scott had actually laughed that day and teased Jason about hypnotising him. He'd felt so alive in his body and so clear and quick in his mind. He felt that again today when he stood at the sink, exhausted but standing strong and breathing easy as the ashes went down the drain. And right now, he feels it too. Even at rest, every system and muscle and cell in his body is queued up and humming.

Put the shovel down, Scott. Stop digging.

Scott is suddenly fidgety, his legs moving under the blanket and his shoulders lifting. The runner in his memory couldn't change her fate, but Scott can change it now. He's not going to stay lost and helpless in the dark woods. Not this time, not ever again.

He twists up so quickly that the eye pillow lands with a plop on the table, and Jason's shoulders jump. "I want to get better."

The simple declaration clearly takes Jason by surprise. He opens his mouth and closes it again, which gives way to a nod. "Okay. Good."

Scott goes on. "And Dr Coulter didn't send me here just for my shoulder, did he? I mean, he knew there was more." Scott grunts over a lump growing in his throat. "More that you would help me fix."

Jason picks up the eye pillow and runs his thumbs over the soft material. "Yes, he did."

Scott takes a deep breath, satisfied with this answer after everything else. They are going to do this; he's going to get himself back. And of all his doctors, it's going to be Jason, with his trackies and rolled-up sleeves and roomful of strange, simple tools who will help him get there. "Well. We have a lot of work to do then."

Jason stands up straighter, his chin rising. "Yes, we do."

"No, I mean..." Scott pauses. How will he tell Jason about the camera on the shelf? The scorecard calendar? The shake in his hands, or the nausea that cripples him? How will Scott tell him about that one heavy thing? It feels to Scott as if they are making a pact here, and Jason had better be well aware what he's getting into. "I'm telling you, it's...*massive*."

"I know," Jason assures him, his hands flexing and his eyes bright, looking ever so much to Scott like a fresh-faced, dashing young knight ready to slay the dragon. "I'm ready. Are you?"

*

Scott remembers the message from the AP only when he feels his phone heavy in the pocket of his jeans. *Was that just an hour ago?* It feels like a different week, a different continent. A different Scott.

He pulls out the phone and mumbles a curse; it takes so long to power on. His heart thuds as he opens the message, his fingers shaking with the itch to answer. He hits the reply arrow and types quickly.

Cheers, mate.

Not cleared for work yet.

A few weeks, tops.

Will let you know.

It's true, he hasn't been cleared for work. Not that he's asked, specifically. But he's on his way forward now. He as much as promised.

He bites his lip, then smiles. Jason is counting on him.

Chapter Five

> Juxtapose (v.) To place two objects close together or side by side for comparison or contrast, or to show scale in an image; also used to suggest a link between objects or people, or emphasise distance or contrast between them.

Scott climbs the stairs in a dormitory that smells like socks and new paint. An official-looking form in his hand has his room number on it, and a holdall is slung over his shoulder. He's starting a new semester at uni, but because it's one of *those* dreams, he has arrived to campus after all the other students are settled in.

He opens the door to his room to find Jason inside, arranging furniture in the dark.

"Oh, hi," Jason says. "I'd like to have this side, all right?" He moves a desk to butt up against the foot of his bed.

"Jason, can you see? Why don't I turn on the light?"

"No, it's better for you if it's dark, right? Better for developing pictures?"

"Um, I guess. But I don't know how to do that yet." Scott hears Jason's footsteps. "Where are you?"

"Over here. Let's get some light in then. Watch your eyes."

Though Scott tries to stop him, Jason grabs the heavy blackout curtain and throws it back with a flourish. The room is flooded with stinging blue-white light, and Scott is thrown back by the shock of it; he can't cover his eyes before he's blinded by the flash.

*

Scott wakes with a shudder, his heart pounding in his chest. It takes a minute for the furniture and fixtures of his flat to make sense. He rubs his eyes with a mixture of disappointment and relief, and checks his phone for the time. Quarter to ten. He's been asleep almost six hours.

The timeline rolls backward in his mind, like a DVD speeding through the scenes in reverse: he sways across the flat from the bathroom, clammy and pale, and lands on the bed in a heap; he's bent over the toilet, heaving, though nothing is coming up; he lurches to the bathroom with his keys still in his shaking, sweaty hands. He fumbles to open the lock on his flat door, taking three tries to slide the key in the hole. He tears across the street midblock, a car swerving to avoid him; his ears roar so loudly he has to grimace against the sound, and he breaks into a jog and then a run, *home, home, got to get home*; the shop window with all its shiny new cameras, lenses, and tripods looks blurry, as if the focus has gone wonky; Paul waves at him from inside the store, beckoning him to come in, though they haven't seen each other since November; he walks up to the familiar white awning of

Camden Camera, a little dodge in his step but his chin up and Jason's confident voice in his head: *"I know you can do this. I know you can do this."*

Scott groans out loud as he remembers. The plan had seemed brilliant in his imagination when he'd dreamed it up the other day after his appointment with Jason. Simple, foolproof, what could go wrong? *Walk to camera shop. Choose camera. Purchase camera. Walk home with camera. Take camera to osteo appointment. Show Jason you're ready to go back to work.*

But he had failed. Epically.

Tomorrow was going to be the day. Jason would be impressed and say, "Good on you" with his proud smile, and together, they would slay the dragon. But Scott hadn't even made it inside the shop before the panic had snuck up on him and sent him running.

Everything that had seemed possible when he'd left Jason's the other day is gone. The fight he'd found again, that electric feeling that made Scott's hands fist and his body hum had lasted only a few hours. If he's honest, it had begun to fade as soon as he stepped out onto the street, alone. He can't even catch a glimpse of it now, with his memories zipped up in a camera case lurking in the cupboard. He rakes his hands through his hair and recalls the message he sent to the AP when he was full of hope and Jason's strength. At the time, "a few weeks" felt completely realistic. The thought makes him curse. At this rate, he'll be lucky to get back to work by the end of the year.

*

Scott avoids his reflection in the bathroom mirror as he turns on the shower, unbuttons his shirt, and loosens the clips on the elastic bandage. Jason had said, "Call me if you need anything, all right?" The tan cloth slips from his shoulder, revealing the tender skin underneath, and the fresh air feels crisp against it. What exactly would Scott say? *Remember when you asked me if I was ready and I said I was? Maybe I lied.*

It was the look Jason had had in his eye, like he couldn't wait to dig in and wrestle this thing to the ground. Scott couldn't be scared in the face of that. Jason was too...compelling, and Scott had felt like maybe he wasn't sick anymore; they could unhook that dark, heavy thing and set it aside for a bit.

I thought I could. But now I'm not sure.

The biggest of his scars is a raised scarlet *S* that webs into four smaller lines snaking around his bicep. The skin surrounding it looks pitted, even chewed up in some places, or streaked as though it's been painted in varying shades of rose and coral. Strangely, there isn't any pain at all. Or maybe what Scott now defines as an annoying tingle really is pain, but he's just become used to it. He lifts his arm to study the underside, also rough and discoloured. There is a fresher, straight scar from his last surgery on the outside of his elbow, and a dip right above it, crater-like, that looks as if someone took a melon baller and scooped out some muscle. "It will even out," Dr Coulter had said. "Give it time."

Scott finally stares at his reflection, focused on the fading, rust-coloured line from his ear to down along his jaw. *Time*, thinks Scott ironically. *I've got my whole life.*

My whole life.

Scott spins to turn off the shower tap and strides across the flat to the bedside cabinet, where he finds the calendar propped up behind his lamp.

He picks up the Sharpie and crosses off today's square. Day one hundred seventy-three.

One hundred seventy-three days since he woke up and Omran didn't, forming an unbroken chain on this calendar he'd nicked from the hospital. Scott has no idea whether he's counting up or counting down, all he knows is there's an *X* for every day he has lived since then. The chain keeps him tethered to that day, bound to it. But now it seems Scott has to choose, before tomorrow. He has to figure out a way to show up at Jason's ready like he said he'd be while keeping Omran close too.

Scott pinches his lip, then picks up his phone. This will be more than his usual, simple "Goodnight."

He taps the conversation at the top of WhatsApp, and begins to type.

Salaam alaikum.

His thumbs hover over letters that can't possibly spell out all he wants to say. And ask.

Ta sanga ye?

Scott shakes his head at himself. *Dr Coulter was right. I really have lost it.* There won't be a response. There can't be. He's messaging a person who is not actually alive, after all. But.

I'm

He's what? Okay? Still here? Getting better?

I'm doing all right

Mostly

It's been a month or so since the last time Scott has sent this much; sometimes he'll write simply "bad dream tonight" or "I'm sorry." There was one time when he'd got drunk and written stream-of-consciousness ramblings about pain and guilt and responsibility. That night had ended badly, with broken glass, a vomit-stained bath mat, and Scott passing out in the tub.

I got my splint off last week

Nope. Scott deletes the words, then tries again.

I have a question for you.

He stares at the screen's white glow, clean and full of possibilities, trying to piece this together.

I'm not sure if I should

The cursor blinks the seconds by, waiting for him to continue. He's in no position to ask, is he? For forgiveness? Or Omran's blessing? Scott deletes this too.

How is he meant to make Omran understand when he doesn't understand it himself? How is he supposed to win this tug of war when he's pulling for both sides—his debt to Omran on one, and his family, his job, the rest of his life on the other? Jason is on that side, too, pulling hard, and Scott is getting the distinct impression Jason doesn't ever lose.

But now, it's Thomas's face Scott sees, asking him to jump with him on his new trampoline, or explaining how his Lego set works over pizza and cupcakes. And then Olivia, who told him she misses him even though he's still here.

I don't know what to do.

About you. About what happened. About getting better.

I have this doctor.

Something like pride makes the edge of his mouth turn up a bit, remembering that first day in Jason's office.

Dr Andrews.

Jason.

He knew your name.

He's

Scott hesitates, the fleshy part of his lip folding between his teeth. If he types it, it will be out there in black-and-white, blinking back at him. Scott backspaces again to get rid of it. He takes a deep breath and coughs over the lump in his throat, which is getting bigger.

Jason thinks it would be all right if I

Scott eyes his calendar again. He picks out the letters gently, as if it will soften the blow.

let go of some things.

But I don't know.

He wouldn't let it go forever, of course; he could bring it to Jason's, slip it in the bag, and Jason wouldn't even have to know. Maybe that's enough.

He's smart. And a bit strange?

I think you'd like him.

Scott sees the long white feather resting on its red cloth. Oils stand in neat rows on a tray, and hot stones lay in a pile in their pot. Jason stares suspiciously at Scott's throat and coaches him to breathe, then keeps watch over him as Scott enters the night valley to find the fire and the stories beyond it. Together, they watch over the flames in the sink as that other lifetime burns.

The next words come before his brain even thinks them, and Scott taps away at the phone, mouthing the words after they appear.

I trust him.

*

An hour later, after he has showered and eaten some tinned soup, Scott dims the light and climbs into bed. He's drowsy and can't help yawning, though his heart drums lightly with nerves. He has a mission to get back to the night valley, to walk through the fire and see what, and who, is on the other side.

The last two times he's seen it, he's ended up somewhere else; the other day, he ended up running for his life, and lost. Still, he is drawn to the valley's canopy of stars and beckoning fire. It's absolutely mad, but in spite of the danger and violence he's found there, he feels peace and safety too. Then there are the questions that have no logical answer: If the stories he finds are just his mind running away with him, then how can they feel so real? How can he know the things he does, like the signature of a king, or the map of a forest he's never seen? How can he feel the king's confusion, or the girl's desperate, paralysing fear? And if they are memories, not dreams, then what is he doing there? Why is he reliving them?

Scott closes his eyes. He tries to breathe slow and deep, concentrating on the exhale first. He searches the darkness for a hint of starlight, or the silhouette of the treeline, but finds nothing. His eyes snap open, remembering that the table is warm at Jason's, so he turns on the electric underblanket. While it warms, he opens his bottle of arnica and rubs some between his palms. He reclines again with the light pine smell rising around him. At first, it helps; his cheeks relax and his breath gets deeper. But the darkness feels flat behind his eyes, with no swirls of colour or pinpricks of light.

He can hear Jason's voice and see his curious expression. *I know you can do this.* But the harder Scott tries, the shallower his breathing becomes, and the more restless his mind feels. He even calls to the valley out loud, "Where are you?" thinking that perhaps he can pull it to him through sheer force of will. But in the end, his shoulders are tense and his jaw is tight, and he gives up with a groan.

He turns over and switches off the light, thinking about another question. What is it at Jason's that breaks open the door?

*

When sleep finally comes, Scott dreams.

He's driving his stepdad's old white Volkswagen on a long country road. The midday sun beats through the open window, and the breeze feels lovely on his arm. Jason's in the passenger seat, studying a map. Up ahead, the road curves broadly, and they have to slow down, but when Scott steps on the brake pedal there's nothing there, just a hole in the baseboard exposing the road going by underneath. *We'll coast*, Scott thinks, and Jason looks at him with an easy smile, asking if he's ever been to Land's End.

*

Returning to Jason's office on Thursday is like finally finding a clear channel after three days of static.

Scott swipes his hand along the surface of the counter. Those rocks, that bag, that sink where they set a fire, and that hum that is almost alive underneath it all, they are all here. He has missed them desperately.

He puts his messenger bag down on the chair, then opens it once more to check its contents the way he checks for his boarding pass eight times while he waits for a plane. He should be a bit scared, given what they'll be doing today, but the fear won't come. When Jason walks in with his headband and his long-sleeved T-shirt, Scott can't help but smile because the last piece fits into place.

Scott knows their routine and can anticipate where Jason is going to go next. He always feels Scott's jaw and neck first, then looks at his eyes and tests his hands. It's like a dance they do, where Jason has taught him the steps and Scott catches on to the rhythm. Jason glances at Scott's messenger bag in between, but doesn't ask about it. Instead, he mentions that Scott's neck is tight and asks him to turn around and look straight ahead.

"Now look down slowly, please. How's physio going?" Jason feels for how Scott's neck bones line up, with his thumbs on either side.

"Good. Oh, Brenna said, 'Tell 'im to mind 'iz manners,' whatever that means."

"Ha. Now tuck your chin into your chest as far as it'll go." As Scott does, Jason presses down, and Scott hears tiny popping sounds from the inside.

"Oh, no. What did you do?" Scott asks.

"I called her a couple of times, asking for another page on you. I guess I was bugging her."

Scott gasps. "Give her a minute, why don't you?"

"I emailed her too," Jason offers cheekily, starting at the top of Scott's neck again.

"God, no wonder she's irked. You're being a menace." But inside, Scott feels a warm pang of appreciation.

"Nah, just persistent. Now bring your head up slowly, all the way back."

Scott feels about a stone lighter, and his shoulders drop away from his ears.

"Slower. Keep going."

The red waxy seal on Jason's biggest diploma catches Scott's eyes on their way up to the ceiling. "I don't want you two fighting about me. Be nice, all right?"

"Who said we're fighting? She's excellent, and she knows I think so. I just wanted an update, sooner rather than later." Jason sounds pleased. "That looks better. Down again, please."

"What's the big rush?"

Jason holds pressure on the sides of his neck, and this time there is no sound.

"Just impatient I guess." Jason gives Scott a light pat on the shoulder to indicate they are done. "The more information I have, the better job I can do, the sooner you feel better. You can get back to your life, you know?" Jason walks around to face him, studying him with that open, curious look. "Get you back to taking pictures again. Right?"

Surely Jason can hear the thudding of Scott's heart; here it is, the moment of truth, and Jason doesn't even know it. Or maybe he does, and that's why he's staring, waiting for Scott to say something. *Something real.*

"About that," Scott begins. A wave of heat rushes down his arms, pooling in his hands. He swipes the palms against his jeans. "I don't think that's going to happen."

Jason's curious expression doesn't change as he folds his arms. "And why is that?"

Excellent question. Scott stifles a cough. "Well. I'm having trouble with my eyes, you know?"

"Your eyes?" Jason turns to place a hand on his files. His voice is gentle, but matter-of-fact. "Doctor, um,

Osborne, is it? I thought...he gave you the all-clear back at the first of May? Or am I mistaken?"

Scott remembers the day. How an ophthalmologist can complete an entire eye exam without ever once properly looking the patient in the eye, Scott doesn't know. But, yes, the doctor had signed off, with a clap on the shoulder and a "good luck to you" as he backed out the door, already handing Scott's file off to the nurse and taking up the next one.

"Right, he did, but it's more like..." Scott looks across the room, and his eyes land on the framed tree painting. "It's a focus thing. Like, I can't hold my eyes still long enough to...see. The way I need to."

Jason's mouth opens slightly as if he's about to say something, but Scott doesn't want to stop. It feels good to finally tell someone. It feels bloody excellent that that someone is Jason.

"They slip, you know? I'll be looking at something, but I can't keep focused. I have to look away, like my eyes are...nervous or something. It's hard to make them settle down." His hands feel prickly now, and his voice is getting stronger. "It's not all the time. It doesn't happen when I'm here. But when I'm out, walking on the street mostly. The light's too bright, and there's too much going on, so I can't focus. Almost like I've got to be watching everything at once. But I can't really *see* anything the way I used to. Everything blends together."

The way Jason is looking at him draws out the pieces of his story Scott thought would go away if he could ignore them long enough. Now he can look at it objectively, the way he did when he was working and there was a story to be told. This time, the story is his, and he can tell Jason all of it. *Well. Almost all of it.*

"But...it's also because of the cameras." Scott waves his hand dismissively. "One is, well, destroyed, and the other is right out there on my desk, and I can't pick it up. I walk by it every day, and I ...can't. You know, now I can't even step foot in the camera shop? I've tried, and this last time, yesterday? This feeling comes over me like..." *Like I'm going to die.* "I can't breathe because my chest is so tight it hurts, and I think I'm gonna be sick. Dr Coulter said they're panic attacks. It probably says in my file I don't have them anymore. It was easier to tell them I didn't. But I do. And when they happen, I'm down for hours after, you know? And I need to sleep it off. So yeah, the photography thing is...over."

That's more words than Scott's ever said in a row to Jason, who's waiting for more with his eyes fixed on him and his tablet in his hand. But there is nothing more to say, and Scott takes a deep breath.

Jason taps on his tablet. "Dr Osborne's file says your eye injury was caused by blunt trauma, as well as penetrating debris. You got hit with something."

Scott nods. "I don't remember, but they think so." Scott can still see Omran jogging toward the embassy building, calling out to a security guard. Suddenly all the heads in the frame turn at once toward a shiny silver sedan at the curb whose horn blares.

"You lost sight in your right eye temporarily."

"Yes, until the swelling and drainage went down."

"And your panic attacks. About how often?" Jason types without looking up.

"Once a week, maybe. Sometimes twice."

"Do you have a bad headache after? Chest pains, or numbness in your hands?"

"No, I just get massively tired."

Jason puts the tablet down on the counter after sliding it closed. "What you're describing isn't a physical problem, though it might feel like it. It's physiological, but I think it's caused by anxiety. You can take meds for them, but I have another idea about what we can do. Not sure you're going to like it."

Scott looks over to the counter, where the white feather and colourful crystals lie in front of the slow cooker. A bristle rushes up his neck. "Let me guess. Needles."

"Yes. There's a great success rate for treating anxiety and panic attacks with acupuncture. Even military personnel with PTSD are feeling a good measure of relief right away. What do you think?"

Well, sharp things cut. "How many needles?" Scott doesn't know whether they're talking two or twenty or two hundred.

"I think...six? Maybe eight, depending."

"Near my eyes?" No matter how confident Jason is about this, Scott may have to draw the line. By reflex, he crosses his arms, building a barrier against it. But Jason wouldn't hurt him; Scott knows that for sure.

Jason shakes his head and takes a step closer, extending his hand. "May I?" Scott finds himself offering his good arm. Jason turns it over, flipping the palm to face the ceiling, and rolls up Scott's sleeve. "Say we start with six. First one goes here." He presses his finger into the underside of Scott's forearm, below the elbow. "Then three in here." He draws a circle over the thin skin on the inside of his wrist. "We'll need one near the knee, and on your foot too. Then maybe, if you can, the last one right here." He touches his middle finger lightly on a spot between Scott's eyebrows, which furrow with concern.

"They're small, right?" Scott asks.

"Hair's width. Some patients say they don't feel them at all, but usually, there's some tingling, or heat." He tilts his head down toward the compass on Scott's arm, then looks up with a smirk. "If you can get tattooed, Scott, this'll be cake."

With that, the table turns. Scott suddenly wants to show Jason what he's made of, that he's not delicate, that he can level up.

"Okay. Let's do it."

"Ah, that's it," Jason says, rubbing his palms together. "All right. So get ready like you normally do, just start face up instead. Unless...there was something else you wanted to do?" Jason gestures to Scott's messenger bag with a questioning look.

"Oh, right. I brought this for you." It was supposed to be his calendar, to put in Jason's bag, but this morning, he'd lost his nerve at the last second. Scott folds back the leather flap and pulls out a large hardbound notebook. "I pretty much destroyed yours the other day, so."

Jason takes it from him with a priceless look of surprise. "You didn't have to do that. I've got more."

Scott shrugs. "I went through tons of those notebooks back at school, in Studio I and all through Drafting and Design, before I switched my major."

Jason runs his hand over the matte black cover. "Oh, you're an artist?"

"Nah, not really," Scott says, shrugging. "I'm much better with a camera. Or, *was*, I mean. Anyway, it's more like a sketchbook, you know? No lines. The paper is thicker too. I thought it would be good for people to draw on, or write, whichever."

"Yeah, I see. That's a great idea." Jason flips through the pages, nodding appreciatively. "It's perfect. Thank you."

Scott hasn't seen Jason like this before, taken pleasantly by surprise. Maybe it's Scott's nerves, or maybe it's the thrill of making Jason smile, but a giddy thought occurs to him, and he says it before he can think the better of it. "And that paper would make a cracking fire too. If there was to be, you know, a fire." He makes a whooshing sound, his arms rising with exaggerated jazz hands. "Burn, baby, burn, disco inferno!" Scott whisper-sings, a smile breaking over his face, and it's lovely because it's completely goofy, but he can't help it.

"Oh my God," Jason mutters, but a laugh bubbles out of his cheeks. "You sing too?"

"Burn, baby, burn, burn that mother down!" Scott sings louder, and he swears he can see Jason lighting up. He steps toward the door, and Scott catches him when he looks back fondly and shakes his head with a giggly sigh, a shine he's never seen before glinting out of his eyes.

"Goodbye," Jason laughs.

"I'll be ready in two," Scott calls after him, just before the door shuts. This time when he says it, it sounds like affection. *I don't want you to go, I'm more myself when I'm with you, please don't be long.*

*

Scott tries not to be nervous as he gets situated on the table, adjusting the pillow under his knees and straightening the covers. It feels strange to start on his back, facing the room. It's like waiting for a CAT scan, or the dentist. *Seven needles. Wait till I tell Thomas about this.* There is the beginning of a tickle in his throat, but he clears it away as he hears Jason's knock.

"Did you change your mind?"

"No, I'm ready. Bring it on."

"Good. You don't have anywhere to go after this, do you? I mean, it would be best if you go home and rest." Scott hears the opening and closing of drawers and the tearing of paper wrappers. The light fixture in the centre of the ceiling fan looks like an eyeball gazing down at him, kind and unblinking.

"I can do that."

"Perfect. We'll put the needles in, leave them for a while, then see where we are, okay? We might not do much more after that."

"That's all right." He closes his eyes as Jason walks around him, making sure his knees are in the right place and the blanket is tucked around his feet. For a second, an orange pinprick of light dances against the darkness, but as Scott's eyes try to follow it, it recedes far into the distance until it disappears. It makes his throat itchy, and he wants to cough. He swallows over it instead, trying to relax into the mellow tones of the cello music.

Jason slides a warm towel under Scott's neck. When his head settles back, his chin is raised just enough to open up his throat, and that helps; when Jason asks if it feels all right, all he can do is hum. Then Jason stands quietly for a few moments. His slow and even breathing steadies Scott's nerves a bit, and his thoughts turn to the night valley. He wonders what it will show him today.

He's brought back when Jason pulls the blanket from his leg, from the knee down. "We'll start here, all right? Just a little prick."

Scott snorts before he can help it.

"Oh, Jesus, I forgot. Easily amused." Jason deadpans without looking up.

Scott giggles for real now, even as Jason inserts the needle into the top of his foot, right above the arch. "Sorry. Can't help it."

"Is that okay?"

"Yeah, it's fine." It feels like a baby mosquito that hasn't quite learned how to bite.

"And here's the second." Jason taps the firm muscle just under and on the outside of Scott's knee. "A tap and a pinch."

The second one goes in smoothly, and Scott realises he doesn't feel the first one anymore.

"All right so far?"

"Yeah. I don't really feel...anything."

"Okay. Wrist next."

Scott's hand feels heavy as Jason pulls his arm out from under the blanket. He lays it palm up and kneads the forearm gently to relax it. Three needles go in quickly at Scott's wrist. These do bite, and Scott opens his eyes to study them. He is amused to find they look like little antennae sticking up out of his skin.

"This is weird," Scott says, genuinely fascinated.

"Maybe. But if it is, it's three-thousand-year-old weird. And it works, so, why not?" Jason looks up from Scott's arm, and for a moment, they share a smile.

Just as quickly, Jason's face turns serious, back to the task at hand. "One more here." He finds the right spot under Scott's elbow, then places the needle guide and gives it a gentle tap. It's tingly and hot.

"Did you heat that one up?"

Jason grins. "Nope, same as the others. Does it burn?"

It actually feels kind of...pleasant. "No, it's okay."

"Good. Now for the last one."

Scott's heart pumps a hot beat because Jason is half sitting on the table for balance, and this is truly about to happen.

"Yes, go."

Jason's face comes so close Scott can see the fine whiskers on his cheek and a few tiny wrinkles at the corner of his eye. His lips part a bit as he focuses on the spot between Scott's eyes where the needle has to go. Jason smells a bit like cinnamon. *And the ocean.*

"Relax your forehead, okay?" Jason's thumb gently presses over the spot to smooth it out.

Oops. Scott tries to concentrate on something else, but Jason is everywhere. The tender cello music seems to guide Scott's eyes over the smooth skin of his neck as it disappears under his collar, the hair over his ear swept under his headband, and his eyelashes, dark over his focused blue eyes.

Jesus. Scott's free hand stirs under the blanket, looking for something to grasp onto.

"Okay, last one."

The needle goes in with a tiny nip between his eyebrows. Jason rises up and away, leaving Scott feeling slightly dizzy.

"That's it, good job."

"Now we wait?"

"Wait, relax, breathe. You can close your eyes if you want."

"Do you stay?"

"Yep. Have to watch for side effects. Let me know if you feel any numbness or pain."

Scott feels like a science experiment, with Jason waiting for a reaction. But there are worse things than being pinned to a table with orders to do...nothing. He settles in and closes his eyes.

His mind picks through the possibilities of what he might do instead of photography. He might be able to work at a magazine; maybe he can talk to one of his contacts at *The Times* to see about openings. He could be a scheduler, or maybe a layout editor. That would mean sitting at a computer every day, on a phone, in a cubicle, inside a building. He couldn't ever picture himself doing something like that when he was in school, and still can't, even given what's happened. But maybe it's time to make friends with the idea.

A question nags at him: what happens if *Jason* is actually the one who's right? What if they can get the old Scott back? Could that Scott even exist again? That Scott had membership cards for every airline lounge, and stopped at home only long enough to do the washing and pack up again. That Scott's passport had been so tattered from use that the customs officer in Prague had broken protocol to mend it with duct tape. That Scott was the photojournalist the industry said was "one to watch." That Scott travelled, he created things, and he liked to think his work made a difference.

The thought lodges in his throat and makes him cough.

"Water?"

"Please. Can I move?" Scott asks, coughing harder.

"Slowly."

His water bottle appears, and Scott takes a drink, which smooths things over. Jason looks concerned.

"When's the next time you see your ENT?"

Scott mentally searches his calendar. He tries to schedule his ear, nose, and throat appointments on Fridays. "Tomorrow, I think?"

"Yes! Someone else I can pester."

Scott rolls his eyes as he hands the bottle back. "You are...an annoying person."

Jason shrugs. "I suppose that's fair. Why don't you try that breathing again? You were getting good at it."

Scott starts to lie back with Jason's hand already poised over the lower part of his ribs.

"Exhale first, pause, then breathe in."

The first one goes wrong; Scott's practice at home had been rough, and his confidence is shot.

"That's okay. It'll come." Jason rests his hand on Scott's abdomen, and the warmth makes the muscles there loosen. Scott closes his eyes and tries again, and this time it's closer. "There, you got it." Jason places Scott's hand where his own had been.

Even with his eyes closed, Scott can picture Jason's hand hovering over his body. It would make an interesting composition. The mid-afternoon light behind Jason streams in from the window, streaking across his arm and putting his tree tattoo in a kind of spotlight. The ink is an interesting contradiction in the room full of gentle colours and soft textures; its graceful black lines could be the striking focal point of the frame. All the details are visible in Scott's mind, down to the colours in Jason's veins and the shadows between his fingers.

But when Scott remembers that he doesn't take pictures anymore, the vision breaks apart, and behind it is a tall pine tree silhouetted against a dark sky. He tries to keep his breath steady, but it quickens. Maybe there's another story hidden in the stars up there, meant to show him another piece of his past.

Where is the fire?

Today, it is a warm orange glow off in the distance. He begins to walk toward it, telling himself he can find his way back because Jason is watching over him.

*

The country air smells like rosemary, and when it mingles with the scent of linseed and walnut oils, Scott thinks he may have arrived somewhere close to paradise.

This, the smaller of the two receiving rooms of the villa, is the best room for painting. It boasts a large north-facing window that gives them long hours of light, but it is private as well; they are all but isolated on the quiet side of the residence, too far away to be bothered by staff or family. Their work is too important, and they are under a fixed deadline.

Scott must create a portrait of Lorenzo, the duke's middle son. The work must be worthy of the nobility it represents, but must also depict Lorenzo in the finest light: educated of mind, vibrant of health, and fair of face and form. It is to Scott's advantage that Lorenzo is all of these things, so the work hasn't been difficult. Until now.

The only portion yet unfinished is Lorenzo's face, which has only been roughed in with flesh-coloured shades. Scott has kept it for last, partially because it is the most difficult to render, but more because Lorenzo finds this whole exercise a farce, and can't manage to hold an expression worthy of his noble station. When they began three weeks ago, his face conveyed only disdain. As the days passed, Scott began to see hints of wry cleverness, some curiosity, and most recently, his arch humour.

This afternoon, though, Lorenzo's expression has changed into something else entirely.

Scott watches helplessly as Lorenzo draws his hand up to adjust the embroidered collar of his own jacket, eyebrows rising in an unspoken proposition. Then there is a slant of his head and a suggestive lick of his lip. Scott turns his eyes away, feeling his face flush. He's been trying to see Lorenzo objectively, like a tree in a landscape or a bowl of pears, but it's no use; too much has passed between them, and now they can't go back.

This cannot go on. We will run out of time.

"Renzo, please. You're meant to look *noble*. How will I finish if you cannot behave?"

"Do not finish. It will be what it is. Or better, paint little Sandro from the stables. Isabel can marry him instead."

"Come, this is important. You are an upstanding citizen of Firenze. Just look dignified, please, for the time it takes for me to render it, will you?"

"Why don't you come out from behind your easel, Matteo, and see what part of me is *upstanding*?" Lorenzo counters, looking down to his own lap with a crooked smile.

Incorrigible, Scott thinks. *But also, irresistible.*

Lorenzo's short, curly hair sweeps over his forehead. He wears his black silk waistcoat with billowed, slit sleeves, while his legs in silk hose cut a shape of youth and privilege. He is nineteen years old, one half of a smart match brokered by those in charge of such things. But underneath, Scott can see the mischievous boy who began venturing into his sleeping quarters a week ago to tuck into his bed with him. Scott had tried to resist at first; he is under the duke's employ, after all. But Lorenzo is persistent, and gentle in his way, and very used to getting what he wants. His murmured, persuasive "Let me hold you, Matti" had cracked Scott's resolve like an eggshell.

Lorenzo takes Scott on middle-of-the-night escapades to the kitchens, where they share cold meats and cheeses and make off with bottles of wine. He shows Scott the custom commissioned artworks in the chapel, generations old, and they talk about patronage and martyrs and the nature of miracles. After, they creep back to Scott's room, whispering secretly, finally unable to keep their hands from each other's skin. Their loving is by turns desperately quick or deliciously unhurried, always ending with Lorenzo reluctantly stealing away to his private apartments before dawn, the promise of seeing Scott in the daylight in his kiss.

"Lord help us, Renzo. If I don't get this finished in time, the duke will dismiss me."

"The plague is taking people by the hundreds in the city. Surely the Lord has more pressing matters at the moment. And as for my father...he may dictate who I marry." A pause. "But not who I love."

Scott turns back to his paints, shy now, and makes a show of examining his brushes.

"You don't like it when I use that word." Lorenzo's voice has softened, but Scott doesn't look up.

"Don't speak that way. You are highborn. I am a painter. A labourer." He is no different than the craftsmen who replace the terracotta tiles on the roof, or the stonemasons who lay brick for the walkways snaking around the vast gardens of the palazzo. They are invisible worker bees that repair the hive. When one dies, there are dozens in line behind to take its place.

Scott hears the confident click of Lorenzo's heels against the cold marble floor as he approaches.

"Don't look. It's not finished." Scott moves to pull the heavy burlap sheet over the work, but Lorenzo catches his arm. Their hands join for a moment before Lorenzo steps behind him to look over his shoulder.

At first, his expression is pleased. Lorenzo's black waistcoat shines with richness. The gold of his ring and the delicate embroidery of his collar and cuffs mark wealth and refined taste. The books on the table denote intellect, and the model ship on the shelf behind him illustrates that he is well travelled. Scott watches as Lorenzo takes in the line of his leg, the glowing warmth of the wooden table, and the fine silk fabric of his sleeves.

"Your skill...is...it's *marvellous.*" Lorenzo's voice is a song in Scott's ear. He rests his hand on the back of Scott's neck.

Scott's heart quickens. Any moment now, he'll see it.

Lorenzo's eyes lock on the black-on-black embellishment of the brocade. His face is puzzled, then bright with understanding. His delicate finger reaches out to the canvas.

"Matteo...what did you do?"

"I..." Scott begins hesitantly, "I put a bit of myself in as well."

Hiding in the jacket's decorative texture are dozens of intertwining letters. The subtle brushstrokes curve and bend seamlessly, easily mistaken for the common textile pattern of flower petals and butterfly wings, but each is an *M* or an *L*, twisted through each other to form the decoration. This is not a signature or a maker's mark. It is a declaration that shines through the layers of paint, visible only to those who make it their purpose to see. Just as in life, Scott will hide in plain sight.

"Your eye is true," Lorenzo says softly. "But it is your heart I treasure more." His slender arms fold around Scott's wider ones, and they study the painting together, the weight of its purpose unspoken but heavy on their minds.

"We have five more days, Matti. Do you know what I want to do with all that time?"

Scott doesn't answer. Lorenzo is going to marry. Scott feels it as surely as a deed already done. It will be a strategic alliance; the couple will set up house in a stately palazzo in Firenze proper and have children, as expected. And years from now, Lorenzo will send for him to return to the country villa to paint their portraits. Scott will have to, because he will not be able to say no to Lorenzo, not ever.

Lorenzo slides his hand under the scratchy cotton of Scott's work shirt, grazing his palm over his heart. "I want to sit for you. I want to watch you looking at me. I want all of your attention." Kisses light on Scott's ear. "I want to sleep in your bed and wake up in the sunlight. I want to show you every bit of me, and I want you to paint the truth. Let them see how much I want you." It is the most beautiful and treacherous of dares, and surely Lorenzo doesn't mean it, that Scott should capture that direct gaze full of longing and desire. But Scott can't make himself argue, not with Lorenzo's lips on his brow.

Scott's stained hands feel crude against the delicate buttons of Lorenzo's waistcoat. So many, many buttons. He could tear them away just to get to the real beating heart underneath, the fair skin that smells of clove and citrus blossoms.

They crumple to the floor, bumping the easel and chair noisily on the way down. Scott hates this, their coming together just as they must let go. But the vivid rose in Lorenzo's cheeks rises, coaxing Scott to forget all the rest. *Lord in heaven, who wouldn't want to marry him?*

Lorenzo's hands grasp the hair at the nape of Scott's

neck and hold him there, their eyes finally locked together. “I want to make love,” he whispers boldly, with Scott on top of him and their legs tangling. “Love. Do you hear me? Love, love, and more love.”

*

Scott’s eyes crack open to the gentle colours of Jason’s room. The villa slips away as if sinking underwater, or maybe it’s Scott that is rising to the surface. He’s back now, relaxing on Jason’s table with little needles standing up from his skin.

His breathing has slowed to an effortless crawl, where he can stop in between breaths for several seconds before he has to inhale. His head feels strangely disconnected from his body, and he wiggles his fingers to make sure everything is still attached. A peaceful feeling surrounds him, of being no more than a cog in the wheel, humming along just where and when and how he should be. A man, breathing. It is enough.

Part of him wants to tell Jason how good he feels. But it can wait. He wants to hover here in this simple place, where inhaling and exhaling are the sum total of his life’s purpose, resting with the memory of a brave love letter painted with his own stained hands.

*

Jason removes the last needle and places the blanket over Scott’s foot.

“So? Everything feeling good?”

“Mm hmm, excellent.”

Jason walks around behind his head. "Good. Give me a second to check your shoulders, then you can go."

Scott closes his eyes as Jason reaches under his back and lifts Scott's torso off the table an inch or so, stretching his spine up and out while his lower body stays heavy and dense on the table.

The silence and slow movement give Scott time to think. Where he'd failed to find the valley at home, three times now at Jason's, he's found the fire door, opened it, and walked right through. It's no mistake, no coincidence, not an accident. How many stories might there be, ten? Twenty? A hundred? How far back do they go? Will there be an end to whatever this is? Will he lie here next time and find the fire burned out, or worse, the night valley nowhere to be found?

Scott tries to gather everything he is questioning into something that makes sense.

"Do people ever say they see things when you work on them?"

"See things? Like, in the room? Or..."

"No, I mean...more like visions, I guess. Or dreams?"

"Could be. I see things sometimes when people work on me."

"Yeah? What do you see?" Scott feels an odd twinge when he thinks about Jason being touched the way Jason touches him. Not that Jason *touches* him, really, it's just...work. But still, there is a kind of intimacy in what they do; they take up the same space, breathe the same air. On Mondays and Thursdays, Scott's world is this room and the progress they make together. The thought of someone having that with Jason makes Scott's mouth tight.

"All sorts of stuff. At chiropractic adjustments, I see colours mostly," Jason says, pulling Scott's shoulder blades back and sideways to widen them. Scott's upper body slumps like a ragdoll, shoulders caving in a little and his head drooping to the side. Jason is strong enough to support him completely, and Scott lets him. "When I go for a massage, it's more like memories resurfacing. I'll think of a person I haven't thought about in ages. Or an answer to a problem will come to me."

Hmm. So nothing like, oh, past lives or some such.

"Where does all that come from?"

"Sometimes it's just physiology, you know? Nerves firing, circulation increasing, waking up different parts of the brain." Jason settles Scott down on the table, gently cradling his head at the last minute so it lands softly on the surface. "But one school of thought says we store events in our bodies, actually within the cell structures. When we loosen them up and get them out, the brain 'sees' them. So. Make of that what you will." Jason pulls the blanket up to cover Scott's chest. "Why do you ask?"

Scott can't possibly tell him. The old king in the castle, the runner in the woods, and now the painter with a secret. Either he's holding these lives in his body or they are figments of his imagination. But either way, it feels like speaking about them out loud would...betray them somehow. And if he did, Jason might figure out that Scott has completely lost it, worse off than either of them thought, and Scott can't stand the idea of Jason looking at him with disappointment. *Or pity*. He veers off into safer territory.

"Hey, do you think acupuncture would work on the ringing in my ears?"

Jason leans on the table, his hands on either side of Scott's head. His face is above Scott's again, this time upside down. "Brilliant idea. Next time?"

Scott picks a freckle on Jason's forehead to focus on, so he doesn't get distracted by all the rest. "Yeah. Next time."

*

Jason is searching his shelves for a book when Scott knocks on his open office door.

"Come in, I want to show you something before you go."

"What are you looking for?" Scott asks, putting his messenger bag down. A fat Buddha smiles at him from one of the shelves, and on another sits an expensive-looking metal singing bowl with a mallet beside it. A sphere-shaped turquoise crystal rests on the next shelf, along with the picture of Jason and his boyfriend. Some book titles pop out at him: *Cranial Osteopathy. Human Anatomy and Physiology, Edition 10. Eastern Body, Western Mind.*

"An acupuncture book. So we can look at the plan for next time."

Scott's eyes fall to Jason's desk, which holds a date blotter, a vertical file, and a laptop, along with the picture of Jason with his football team. Scott takes a closer look and sees details he missed on that first day. Jason is so young, with his hair cropped shorter and cheeks clean-shaven. He balances on his teammates' shoulders, and though Scott can almost hear the crowd roaring for him now, it's clear that Jason's smile looks more like a wince.

"You played?" Scott asks, gesturing to the frame.

"Yeah, back in the day. Ah, here it is."

"Looks like you did well."

Jason comes closer. "I suppose. That's the day I hurt my knee. I was stupid, played the last half on it injured."

"Ugh, sorry."

"No, it's all right. To be honest, it's what got me interested in medicine. I looked at everything, no matter how mad it sounded. Acupuncture. Chiropractic. Yoga. Float tanks, guided meditation, Reiki. Of course there was some surgery and pharmaceuticals, too, but...that other stuff wasn't mad at all."

Scott tries to picture this footie Jason on crutches, putting on a brave face over pain. He tries to picture Jason needing help.

"Did you get to play again?"

"Nah, I tried. But that was my last game. You know, I'll pick up with the lads on a Sunday here and there, but...that was it." Jason stares down at the picture, stroking over it with his thumb, and Scott feels like a twat for bringing it up.

"I'm sorry, I shouldn't have asked. It must be hard for you to look at."

Jason tilts his head and chuckles. "Well, it might be a shit picture, but they can't all be award winners, like yours."

"No, I mean, doesn't it make you...sad?"

"What? No. It is what it is," Jason says simply. "I actually love this photo. It captures something, you know? That's why I keep it here. It's the end of one thing, the beginning of something else."

"That's very..." Scott tries to think of the word. "Zen? Of you."

"Yeah, I suppose. It took me a while to get there. Some days, I think I'm still trying to get there."

Scott wonders if Jason had someone special back then. Someone who might have carried his books at school, or propped his leg up on ice at home, and made sure he didn't chuck his crutches too soon. Someone who might have dried his tears and kissed the pain away. He looks at the other picture, on the bookshelf, of Jason and his boyfriend. There is comfort there, and intimacy; with their heads slanting together and their arms overlapping, he and Jason are more than boyfriends. They're partners. Scott wonders what kind of man he must be for Jason to be in love with him.

He shifts his eyes just in time so Jason doesn't catch him staring.

"Let me show you this." Jason has flipped the book open to a diagram of a human head, with colourful, snaking lines drawn over it that look very much like a map of the London underground.

"The ringing in your ears is both an ear issue and a jaw issue, so let's do these three"—Jason draws a circle on the human's ear—"and then these, and the one between your eyes too." He drags his finger down to the drawing's cheek, where three large dots mark the jaw.

"Seven," Scott states.

Jason cringes. "No, we'd have to do both sides. So that's twice six, plus one. Thirteen altogether. Upside is, you can stay dressed."

"Thirteen's okay. Let's do it."

"Perfect. We'll plan on it. Now, let me look at you."

Jason holds Scott's wrist with two fingers over his pulse and looks into Scott's eyes. Scott stares back directly, blinking easily with no itching or welling up. His jaw feels like it's hanging comfortably loose, his teeth not even touching. He notices that his neck feels long and open, and his shoulders rest lower on his body. He feels... tall. And bloody famished.

"Stick out your tongue, please?"

Scott complies without missing a beat, and Jason nods. He reaches for Scott's other hand and flips it over, examines the nails. He studies Scott's face again, the edge of his mouth turning up.

"You feel good, don't you?"

Scott smiles. *I want to watch you looking at me.* "Yeah. I do."

"Good. Lots of water today, and lots of rest. And keep up the heat. It's paying off."

"Will do." Scott swings his messenger bag over his shoulder, wishing there was a reason for him to stay. He doesn't want to lose this feeling of being healthy, being trusted, not needing to be coddled or fussed over. Strong. He has to figure out a way to stay connected to this place and this feeling, to tide him over the days when he's not here.

Scott may not be hiding his worry as well as he thinks because Jason says, "Call me, yeah? If you need anything? I always check my messages."

"Yes. I will."

*

Scott drops his jacket and bag to the floor when he gets into his flat and heads straight for the cupboard. He doesn't look up to the shelf but swims through jackets and coats to get to the six large portfolios propped up against the inside wall. He wrestles the whole pile out and spills them on the floor.

He hasn't seen the photo in years, but it came to mind on the bus ride home, and he knows it's the key. It's a print from his very first photography class, the one with the older-than-Moses professor who kept insisting wistfully, "Mistakes are wonderful!" It will be the bridge Scott needs to stay connected to Jason's office from across the city.

He unzips the largest portfolio and flips the leathery cover open to reveal a pile of prints in plastic sleeves. At first, he feels like a criminal, snooping around in someone else's things, but soon he begins to recognise the familiar curves, lines, and colours of his early work. But the one he wants isn't here, and he slides the portfolio aside.

His hands are hot again, and he flexes them before he opens the next one. These are the first prints he ever made for class, simple compositions with basic themes. He flips quickly through the prints he did for "candid and formal portraits," "focus analysis," and "motion studies." Scott regards them with fondness, smiling at his younger self's newly developing eye.

He passes over "self-portrait as a shoe" and "extreme close-ups," then finds what he's looking for.

It's the tree at Richmond Park, for the "outdoor lighting" assignment. It was during the golden hour, and

Scott had taken two thirty-six exposure rolls to make sure he got something to present. He'd finally settled on a composition with the tree off to the right of the frame, its curving branches arching down like arms in mid-embrace, with the weakening sunlight tilting through the leaves.

Look at that tree for me.

Scott slides it out of the plastic sleeve and holds it up. It's perfect, actually better than he remembered. Of course it's a beginner's print, and a bit generic, like a picture on a sympathy card or an inspirational poster in a middle manager's office. But no matter. For him, it's just right.

Tomorrow, he'll go to Bushey's for a matte and frame, and he knows where he'll hang it. It belongs right over his desk, where he'll be able to see it from the edge of his bed.

*

That night, Scott stands with Jason at the edge of a grassy cliff overlooking the ocean. His heart pounds with adrenaline, and he rubs his hands together the way Jason does. He can't wait to start.

"Are you sure you don't want to? It's easy, I promise," he tells Jason with a hopeful smile.

"Nah, man, I'll be here when you get back." Jason smiles, too, and squints against the sun. Scott almost doesn't want to leave him.

"Okay. I won't be long."

One last nod and Scott turns to the edge. He sets himself as if he's running track and waiting for the gun, but there is none, just Jason's encouraging "go," and so he does, taking off at a sprint toward the open ocean. His last stride is a leap, and up he flies, straight into the air with his arms behind him, steering by thinking of where he wants to go. The ocean is huge and green, and Scott makes a wide shape over it, curving away from the shore. He dips and climbs easily. When he turns back toward the cliff, Jason waves at him with both arms over his head, then cups his hands over his mouth and howls happily. Scott waves back to him before turning to the horizon, soaring toward the dusk with sunlight on his face.

Chapter Six

Balance (n.) Compositional harmony of a scene based on the placement of elements of different sizes, shapes, and colours, either through symmetry or placement of visual weight; a state in which a body or object remains reasonably steady in a particular position while resting on a base that is narrow or small relative to its other dimensions. For human beings, this most commonly involves remaining upright and steady on the feet.

Scott hates being late.

He closes Jason's heavy front door behind him with a satisfying *thwump*, leaving the drizzly Monday afternoon on the other side. He's been looking forward to this all morning, but the bus couldn't get him here on time, what with the rain and all the construction on Romford. The high-pitched hissing in his ears rises a little without the street noise to compete with, but he folds up his umbrella and lets out a comfortable sigh.

Something is different here though. It's *too* quiet, and he's surprised to see Jason standing at the reception desk with his head bowed toward Monica over the counter. His shape looks strange; it's the deep slope of his shoulders, or the way he's holding his forehead in his hand.

Scott's about to take the nearest seat when Monica peeks around to him with an apologetic smile.

"We'll be right with you, Scott."

"Sure," he answers, sitting with his bag at his feet. Jason hasn't turned, and Scott watches him pull out his phone and thumb through a few screens while Monica takes notes. Their voices are serious and low.

Scott busies himself, reaching for his bag. He'd snatched his calendar clean from the bedside cabinet on his way out the door before he could second guess it, and had ridden with it on his lap all the way here, protecting it like some precious contraband. He was going to put it in Jason's holdall, but maybe this is a sign, the powers that be telling him no, not so fast, not today.

When Jason speaks, Scott can pick out "family" and "services"; Monica nods and clicks through some screens, then replies something to do with flower delivery, to which Jason's only response is a curt nod. Scott's mind filters back to a patient who had cancelled a week or so ago, something about trouble with chemotherapy. *Shit.*

Moments later Jason turns to him, looking equal parts sad and exhausted. He's swimming in the T-shirt that hangs from his shoulders, and his face is an odd, pale colour. Scott realises now that he was wrong. Jason does lose sometimes.

He offers Scott a small smile. "Hi."

Scott rises to his feet, resisting the fleeting impulse to hug him. "Hi."

The stark planes of Jason's face soften a bit as he looks Scott over. "I'm glad you're here. I'll walk you back."

*

Scott places his messenger bag on the counter softly as Jason checks the temperature on the slow cooker.

"How are you feeling today? Any pain?" Jason asks. From up-close, Jason's eyes are heavy and dim, the lines under them a bit more pronounced.

Scott shrugs. "I'm all right." He wants to say something wise that will bring back the Jason he knows. "It seems you've had a tougher morning than me."

Jason considers him with a little sigh. "It happens every so often in this line of work. But it's never easy. To lose someone."

"I know...I'm sorry," Scott begins, at a loss. This is so *big*, and honestly, he's the last person who could steer anyone through grief. He looks around at the room and its contents, taking in the soothing colours and textures. He didn't know this person at all, and it is meagre comfort, but he is sure about one thing. He reaches down to stroke the soft blanket that covers the table. "I bet they really liked spending time here."

They don't look at each other, and it's a long moment before Jason answers. "Yes. I think she did."

They fall quiet and begin Scott's exam in a companionable silence, alongside the patter of rain against the window.

Jason's warm hands move over Scott's jaw with their usual gentle precision. There won't be any jokes or disco songs today; for now, they'll speak the language they've perfected over these last weeks, the one Scott only speaks with Jason, made up of touching and studying, feeling and reacting. Scott wants to be the strong one this time, steady enough for Jason to lean on if he needs to, and if Jason needs quiet, Scott can hold their space in silence too.

Scott's mind moves over all the things he could say that might make Jason smile. He recalls what Brenna said at his last appointment, that his range of motion was near normal and he would graduate from the wall to the countertop for press-ups next time. He could tell Jason how well he's been sleeping, that he hasn't had a panic attack in three days. He could mention he has his very own tree picture, now, that looks at him across the flat and keeps him calm. He could report how he'd had no trouble when he'd walked past Camden Camera to get to the framer's. Sure, he'd picked up the pace and walked on the opposite side of the street, but Jason would count that as a fair victory. The thought makes Scott stand up a little straighter, tall on his feet with his shoulders back. He notices Jason's small nod to himself after he finishes examining the places that are usually tight through his cheeks. When Jason examines his eyes, Scott breathes easy. Tears make Scott's vision blur, but his throat is fine, and he can hold his stare across the room with control.

He holds his hands out before Jason asks for them. They are warm and steady today, and as Jason turns them over, Scott thinks of his flying dream. He remembers how Jason had been right there with him when he took that running leap off the cliff and shot out for the horizon, and how the two of them grinned broadly at each other when he hovered like a dragonfly over the water. Jason had welcomed him back to land with outstretched arms and a look of both wonder and pride, actually quite the same as the look on his face right now.

"Well, Scott. I'd say we're getting you there, aren't we?"

Scott is mesmerised for a moment. *I did it.* The confident, buoyant Jason who wrestles demons is here in front of him, properly *seeing* him again. *And I didn't have to say a word to bring him back.*

"Yeah, we are," Scott answers. "Oh wait, I brought something."

He reaches for his bag and opens the flap. When he pulls his calendar out it seems strangely small, not taking up as much space in this room as it does at home.

Jason holds his hand out. "May I see?"

Scott nips at his lip, handing it over. Jason studies it curiously, carefully leafing over almost six months of days crossed through with thick black lines. Scott itches to take the calendar back, *careful, careful,* and it's all he can do not to grab it from Jason and put it away, telling him to forget it, he was mistaken.

"Want to tell me about it?"

All the good news Scott had—the flying and freedom and effortless sleep—is gone. With this between them, the only words he can find are "atonement" and "amends," words he can't make his mouth say out loud.

"Um, no, I don't...I don't think so." His throat suddenly feels scratchy and hot, threatening to close up on him, and he reaches for his water.

Jason holds the calendar carefully with both hands. "You don't have to put it in there, you know, if you're not ready to."

Two minutes ago, it was a done deal. When it was tucked in Scott's bag, it was just a curious artefact from a strange land all the way across town that he could use for show-and-tell. But now that it's out in the open, it feels like evidence from a crime scene. He presses his teeth together, trying to decide.

"It's okay. I want it back though. After."

"Absolutely," Jason agrees, holding the calendar out. Scott takes it with relief.

The zipper glides easily, and Scott smells the supple leather of the holdall as it yawns open. He places his calendar inside, making sure it rests flat in the darkness. It seems to look up at him with dismay, and Scott zips it closed quickly with a pang of remorse. *Just for a little while.*

"Well done. So now you have a decision to make."

"Hmm?" Scott turns back to Jason with the uneasy feeling that decisions may not be his strong suit.

"It's an easy one. Chair or table?"

*

It takes some time to get the table adjusted so that the head end is raised slightly, like a deck chair. By the time Scott is comfortable, with small pillows under his elbows, a bolster under his knees, and warmth seeping through his clothes, he wonders if he should have picked the chair after all. But Jason said it was no trouble, and that reclining was better for meridians and spinal alignment. Scott has another reason, one that he keeps secret—he's only ever been able to get to the night valley while he's lying down.

“Settled?” Jason asks from his side.

It suddenly seems quite ridiculous, all of this preparation just to stick needles into his face. But “settled” is truly the right word because Scott feels a puzzling but brilliant sensation of being heavy and weightless at the same time. “I’m ready.”

“Good. Let’s start.”

Jason has one hand on the table behind Scott’s head and the other on the blanket next to his hip. He should be moving, opening up the little paper envelopes that have the needles inside, but he stands very still, taking one long breath after another. Scott sneaks a glance at him and shifts quickly back when he sees that Jason’s eyes are closed. *What’s happening? Should I be doing something?* Scott thinks it’s rude to ask, so he waits, the sound of Jason’s soft breathing layering over the rain against the window and the deep hum of the string music. Scott’s eyes close, too, and they are together, peaceful. Too soon, Jason turns away, back to the counter.

“We said thirteen, right?” he asks lightly, putting the box of needles down on Scott’s thigh. He rips the first one open but looks quizzically at the side of Scott’s face.

“Yeah. What’s the matter?”

“I forgot about your hair.”

“Oh, I can put it up. I have a hairband in my pocket,” Scott answers, probably too quickly because his arms feel so dense that he may not be able to lift them.

Jason hesitates for a moment. “Nah, it’s okay. I’ll tuck it...back like this.” Jason sweeps his finger over Scott’s temple and hooks the hair behind his ear. “That okay?” Jason is close enough for Scott to smell his light cinnamon scent. It makes him want to lean into it a bit, but then he catches himself, answering Jason with a hum while he tries to keep his thighs still.

"We'll need six here," Jason explains, tracing a half-moon shape on Scott's cheek. "What's it sounding like in there today?"

Scott closes his eyes to listen as Jason feels for the right spot. His ear, nose, and throat doctor always asks him the same thing, and Scott has never come up with an apt description. "Right now, it's a hiss, like a hole in a balloon."

"High-pitched? Little pinch." Tap, tap, bite.

"Yeah, it goes up and down, but mostly it's high."

"A few in a row now," Jason says quietly, his breath warm over Scott's ear.

"Does it ever go away completely?" Tap, tap, bite. This one feels sharper, and Scott winces when it goes in.

"Sometimes. A couple weeks ago, I had a whole morning without it, and a few times, I've been here and it's been really quiet, almost gone. Sometimes it's in one ear and not the other." Tap, tap, bite.

"Well, you might find it changes with the needles in. Might sound more like bubbling or clicking. And it might get louder, so let me know, all right? Last one on this side."

It goes in with an actual popping sound, and Scott flinches.

"Well done. We're about halfway there." Jason gives him a little squeeze to his shoulder, then backs away to walk around the table.

"Scott, could you straighten up?"

"What do you mean?"

"I mean you're lopsided."

Scott has no idea how it happened, but his left side is drooping, and he can't pull himself up again. "Help?"

Jason giggles softly. "It's an inner-ear thing." He takes Scott by the shoulders and shifts him upright, then cups his hand under his jaw to straighten it too. "It'll go away in a minute."

"So glad I can amuse you," Scott mumbles, waiting for his stomach to roll back into place. "This reminds me of a helicopter ride I took over the coast of the Philippines. I walked crooked for twenty minutes after we landed." He groans, remembering. "Just wait until I'll throw up all over your lovely T-shirt. That'll be *hilarious*."

"Wouldn't be the first time. It'll get better when we get the other side in."

Scott takes a few breaths, and the seas calm a bit. He thinks there might be a sheen of sweat on his brow now, since he's nauseated, and the table has grown toasty, but Jason doesn't mention it. He gives Scott's forehead a few light sweeps to tuck his hair back on the other side.

"Ready?"

"As ever."

"Six more, plus one. Easy."

They are. Jason isn't any more gentle than usual, but thankfully, these feel like friendly ladybugs nipping on him instead of bees stinging. Even so, they make his eyes well up, and Scott can't stop the tears from leaking out of his closed lids. He feels the light pressure of a tissue dabbing at his cheek.

"Almost done. Does it hurt?"

"No, it really doesn't." Scott sniffs and clears his throat. "Don't know why I'm..." *Crying. Again. Fuck.*

"Physiology," Jason says simply. "Or something else. Either way, it's just fine."

Scott's eyes are still closed when the hot pad of Jason's thumb touches between his eyebrows, then, nothing.

"I'm ready, do it," Scott says, trying to keep the edge out of his voice.

"It's already done. How's it feel? Or sound?"

Scott's stomach has magically settled down. His neck is long and straight, there is no tension in his shoulders, and his breath comes slow and easy. He listens.

"The same, I think?"

"No pain?"

"No, none," he says sincerely.

"Perfect. So just relax for a while like that, yeah?"

"Yeah."

Scott hopes that the days of Jason pushing and pulling on him aren't over. He misses the feeling of his muscles being worked, the blood finding its way back through the dark places. He misses watching Jason lift and pull and think and puzzle him out. He misses the hot rocks in his hands that soothe their shake, and he misses the smell of arnica that lingered on his skin for the rest of the day and into the night. He misses how that smell would make him smile to himself when he'd remember, hours later, how it got there. Maybe missing all of that is why he had the dream last night, the dream that was a dream but wasn't.

*

Scott had fallen asleep with his bandaged arm propped up on a pillow as usual. He'd been drifting in that darkly veiled place between awake and asleep when he'd felt the mattress dip and heard Jason's voice asking if he was ready. He felt himself smile then; questions about how Jason got into the flat and why he didn't turn on the light seemed foolish and completely beside the point because *Jason is here.* The soothing smell of pine and orange filled the room. Scott turned over to his stomach, knowing he should start that way.

When the metal clips released, the bandage slipped away so his arm was deliciously free. Soon Scott felt the comforter lifting away from his back, and he broadened his shoulders in anticipation of Jason's touch. It was Jason's forearm Scott felt first, rolling over his back through his clothes, then Jason's hot fingertips searching out the little knots, this time not having to knead them free but only giving them a little tap to melt them.

Magic, some unquestioning part of Scott's brain said as he felt another set of hands, too, down by his feet. Those hands were colder and more delicate, like a woman's.

Jason asked him to turn over, and Scott did, twisting in a languid roll to his back. Jason began to speak then, all about eyes and cameras, and how they really are the same thing, lenses that focus and reflect light into pictures. He used words like retina and lens, iris and shutter, cornea and aperture, and the words were medicines that fell and lodged into the impressions Jason had made in Scott's body with his hands. It all made sense for a vivid split second, and Scott had to repeat it so it wouldn't slip away: *They both need light, they both need light, they both need light.*

"I got it, Jason, they both need light, right? Jason? They both need light! I got it!" Except the blanket had been pulled up over Scott's chest, and he was tucked in with a little pat on his arm. *Wait Jason, we're not done, please don't leave yet, you didn't tell me the rest, I didn't hear you, come back.*

The message had scrambled like fever dreams do, and Scott had woken up to the drizzly morning feeling well rested but left to wonder how his elastic bandage had come to be under the bed.

*

"How long has it been?"

"Seven minutes. Why, are you uncomfortable?"

"No, I just lose track of time when I'm here sometimes." Scott opens his eyes and turns his head toward the sound of Jason's voice at the window. The noise in his ears is now just a low rustle, like tall grass waving in a breeze. His arms sink even further into the pillows, and his legs may as well be dipped in concrete, but his head feels light and wide awake.

Jason walks to the table and half sits on it. "Can I try a pressure point on your foot? It should help your ears."

"Sure."

He slips off Scott's sock and rubs the ball end of the arch with his thumb. "This feel okay?"

“Yeah, that feels good.”

Jason presses a hot path across his foot to his pinky toe. “Do you want to talk?”

Maybe he should be wary, but Scott can’t muster the energy. Jason could ask him anything, and he’d spill. “Okay.”

“Good. Because I’d like to ask you something so I’m aware of the full story. It’s about Omran.”

Jason’s voice saying Omran’s name is music, and it wafts over Scott like a cloud. It makes perfect sense that Jason should be talking about him, that Omran should be here with them now.

“What was he like?”

Scott hums a little, remembering. His words come slowly.

“He was...twenty-nine, I think? *Proper* smart. His dad was a diplomat of some sort—I mean, *is* a diplomat, so they travelled a lot. When he was young, I mean. He knew six languages, I think? He spoke Pashto, Dari, and Farsi, and perfect English, of course, and French, and somehow he got Italian in there too.”

In his mind, Scott sees the two of them sitting at the hotel restaurant that morning. Omran is reminding him how to say “Here are my credentials” in Pashto over the sweetest tea Scott has ever had. Omran’s low voice repeats the phrase patiently, using his hands to punctuate the guttural consonants that Scott can’t get.

“I used to tease him because he spoke English with a Pashto accent, but he spoke French with an English accent, you know? And he said I spoke Pashto like a four-year-old with a lisp.” Scott didn’t remember that until just now, and he is fascinated that he can recall their exact conversation, the clothes the waitress was wearing, the smell of ginger and cardamom in the air. The way Omran smiled and snapped his fingers when Scott finally got the words right.

The heat of Jason's hand radiates over Scott's toes pleasantly.

"He could be quite funny, you know? And he had an amazing voice, really full and clear. He did some narration work for films and audiobooks and things, when he wasn't translating. I used to really like...talking to him. Well, listening." Scott remembers how they would spend their long downtimes telling stories; they'd be stuck in traffic or waiting in a conference room, and Omran would not only narrate but do impressions of each character as if he were putting on a play.

Scott shakes his head ruefully as Jason rotates his foot by the ankle, then gives the arch a light stretch. "Sometimes I can remember his voice better than I can remember his face." *And even that is starting to fade.*

"So, were you and Omran...together? Like a couple?"

What? "Oh God, no," Scott says quickly. His forehead crunches up with confusion. "Oh, no, you thought he was my *boyfriend*?" Scott rolls his eyes good-naturedly at the thought. "No. He was straight. He used to joke all the time about how Tasmin Lucia-Khan was going to call him up and he'd drop my arse so he could travel around with her instead."

He laughs a little at the memory, and Jason smiles, too, but then Omran sits beside him in his heavy green coat in the backseat of the taxi, showing Scott a picture of Rabia on his phone. She's a dark-haired, brown-eyed beauty with an endearing space between her two front teeth and an open book on her lap.

"And anyway..." Scott has to swallow. "He was married."

Scott turns his face to the window so he doesn't have to see Omran anymore, only the clear trails of rain slipping down the panes.

"So you were friends."

"Yeah. We were. We'd worked together a few times before, for the demonstration at Mazar-e-Sharif and then for the peace talks." Scott is treading dangerously close to that dark place he's holding on to, tiptoeing around it like a landmine. "We got on really well together, so I had...requested him. The last time." The back of Scott's throat burns, and he tries to cough it away.

"You asked for him to go with you?" Their eyes finally meet. Jason looks like he's about to say something more, but Scott doesn't let him. There's something here he wants Jason to understand.

"You get tight, you know?" Scott is unable to hide the note of weariness that is creeping in. How can he explain Omran's reassuring presence, the way Scott always felt safe with him no matter where in the world they were? "Yes, we were friends, but more than that. I mean, when you work together in these situations, you're a team. You're responsible for each other. It's just understood. You're going to watch each other's backs."

"And so?"

Jason's expression is calm concern. He's trying to steer them right into the thick of it, but Scott won't follow. Putting it down in the bag is enough.

He is exhausted suddenly, with the weight of the calendar and the conversation and the memories trying to drag him down. He wants to stay, truly; he has to be strong for Jason today, doesn't he? But still, his eyes close. He sees the first swirl of stars that light up the valley and breathes deeply with relief.

"I'm sorry, but I can't...talk about that...right now." He wants to say goodbye to Jason, and thank you; *thank you so much, but I can't stay.* His mouth forms the words in slow motion, and it feels good to let them out. "There is somewhere else, it's calling, I'll be back, I promise. I have to find the fire."

"It's all right, go," Jason says, his voice floating gently from the foot of the bed. What Scott hears clearly in his ear is "It's behind you." He smiles and turns to meet it.

*

Scott's first breath on the other side smells like hay and cow manure with a whiff of unwashed men and damp wool underneath. *Is this...Friday?* He peels open his eyes and stares up at the high barn ceiling, trying to piece it together. He had fallen asleep after post watch, which was after he'd checked on the radio, which was after chopping wood, so yes, it must be Friday afternoon.

He shrugs out from under his greatcoat and props up on his elbow to check on the soldier lying next to him. It's Royer, sleeping soundly, though his cheeks are flaming red and his hair is damp. The shoulder hit he had taken in the fray was easy for Scott to treat on the march because the bullet had shot clean through. But yesterday, Royer had turned up feverish, and when they'd peeled back the dressing, the wound was inflamed and had begun to weep.

Scott has done his best to keep it clean, rewashing dressings with water he heats in the cast-iron tub, but with limited supplies, there is little more to be done. Although the barn floor is certainly not the most sanitary, Scott is grateful for the roof over their heads and dry straw to keep them warm. It is comfortable compared to sleeping outside, and when they get their little fire going, it is downright luxurious compared to that goddamn trench.

The squad is just a shell of themselves. They still have the radio, thank Christ, but the horses with their riders had run off with the medic cart when the German mortars had blown a crater into their line. It had fallen to hell after that, the platoon sent scattering in all directions. Their bedraggled crew of only twelve had come upon the farmhouse at the edge of the timber when they had run out of road in the middle of the night. Their ranking officer, only a sergeant, had promised the stern, salt-and-pepper-haired woman who answered the door in her nightdress that they would be little bother. They would stay long enough to regroup and fix the radio, contact their company, and get a bead on where in God's creation they are supposed to be.

"Two days," Sergeant Joffre told her, straightening his glasses. "Three at the most."

"You'll earn your stay," the woman responded in a surprisingly bold tone, given the situation and the late hour. "I'll do with a cord of wood a day. You'll find what you need in the barn."

Out of respect for his elders, or just plain fatigue of fighting, Joffre hadn't told her that it was actually her civic duty to house members of her own country's army free of charge. He'd agreed with a polite handshake as two soldiers pushed past to sweep her house for anything suspicious. She'd retrieved two small lanterns, then pointed the men to the large white outbuilding that would become their temporary barracks.

For two days now, Perrault has been trying to fix the radio, which only sputters and crackles with static. They take shifts on woodcutting and watch. The woman, Mme Samuel, appears daily at four, hurried and unsmiling, with a loaf of fresh bread and a dozen eggs. But the blows keep coming. They have no gas masks. Scott is sorely low on clean dressings and has dispensed the last of the morphine to Gillet for trench foot. No one is coming for them; by now their platoon surely believes they are dead, or worse, has court martialled them for desertion.

"Gents, on your feet," Sergeant Joffre barks. "Incoming!"

Royer doesn't rouse, but Scott and his comrades scramble to their feet and line up in a thin formation. Joffre slides the big barn door open, revealing Mme Samuel walking briskly across the field, her arms crossed against the chill. Scott thinks it odd that she carries nothing. As she gets closer, he can see her usually tidy white apron is stained with rusty streaks of blood. *Perhaps she's been butchering chickens.*

"Your medic?" she asks Joffre with no preamble.

"Lavoie! Up front! Bring your kit!"

Scott gathers his backpack and medic box and weaves his way to the door. Madame doesn't wait for him but turns swiftly to start back for the house. He feels a clap on his shoulder and hears the sniggers and whistles of his comrades as he follows quickly behind her.

"Boots," she commands when they enter the little foyer of the farmhouse. He kicks them off as she takes his jacket. She then shows him to the sink. "Wash your hands, quickly."

It smells heavenly in here, distinctly feminine, like buttermilk soap and fresh thyme. He could close his eyes and fall back to sleep leaning against this warm wooden countertop that reminds him of home, but she's bustling around him, loosening the buckles on his box.

"You are a surgeon?" she asks, more of a demand than a question.

The water pump squeaks as he works the handle, but Scott hears a noise behind it, a long low note like the wail of an irritated cat. He looks at Madame, who is rifling through his box, glass bottles tinkling as she digs down into its pockets. "Yes, but I'm—"

"You have instruments, yes? To operate with? Where are they?"

The streaks on her apron alarm him suddenly. He grasps her wrists in his wet hands to stop her rummaging. The sound comes again, rising a bit. It is more fragile sounding this time, more afraid. It is no cat.

He turns to follow the sound, taking the box with him.

The sweet aroma in the kitchen gives way to the smell of field hospital as he moves through the small dining room. It's a smell that Scott knows well, made up of bodies and their by-products, blood and excrement and vomit. A thin groan comes through the open bedroom door. Madame is on his heels as he crosses the threshold.

It's a young woman.

She's balled up on her side in the middle of the bed, her face hidden under long brown hair. The mattress is wet with bloody mucus and littered with white feathers from a pillow she hugs to her very pregnant belly.

"My granddaughter, Hélène. Her pains started at three this morning, all fine, then, nothing," Madame explains tersely. "Something is wrong."

Christ almighty.

Frantic thoughts about the mysteries of female anatomy, his oath of "do no harm," and *where the hell had she been hiding the other night* collide in his mind for a long few seconds as the girl rocks herself, clad in nothing but a cotton shift. Scott knows no more about birthing than what he learned the few times he watched over whelping dogs at home. His legs are frozen in place, and his thoughts move to the surgery kit in his box: tweezers and clamps, bullet forceps and a bone saw, along with scalpels in three sizes, rolled in burlap and tied with string. He swallows.

"Hélène," Madame calls out. "I've brought someone to help." She bumps past him to lean down and grasp the girl by the shoulder. "Open your eyes now."

Hélène burrows in tighter. Scott looks at Madame as if to protest, but she is looking back at him with desperation, her face saying *now, you see?* So Scott crouches beside the bed, leaving the box beside him. He doesn't want to scare the girl, so he searches for his softest voice, the one he might use to speak to his little sister and her friends. When he finds it, he sounds like someone else.

"Hélène. That's a pretty name." He puts his hand on her forehead, sweeping away her hair so he can feel for fever. Her breath comes in short gasps, and she is shaking.

Scott wants to see her pupils, but her eyes are shut tight, and her skin feels strangely cool. "My name is Émile. I'm a medic. I want to help, all right?" Hélène flinches with a grunt, gripping the pillow harder. Scott reaches for her wrist and feels her pulse race before she brushes him away. "Okay, okay, in a minute then," he assures quickly, pulling back.

She is going to be in shock soon. Scott's mind filters over the symptoms, which look no different on her than he's seen on dozens of his comrades: ashen skin, racing heart rate, vomiting, trembling. And she shouldn't be so cold. *Keep her with you, get her talking, keep her here.*

"How old are you, Hélène? Are you seventeen? My sister is seventeen. Her name is Gabrielle." Her breathing begins to slow, and she loosens her grip on her pillow. "She's far away, at home in Bourges. I think she's still there anyway. It's been a while." *Sixteen months, give or take.* "Oh, wait, she's eighteen now."

Her head turns up to him slightly. She is terribly pale. Even her lips are white, though they are chapped and bleeding. Her puffy eyes search for him.

"Hello," he offers delicately.

"Hello." Her voice is weak, but he takes it as a step in the right direction. Now Scott can see into her bloodshot eyes. Her pupils are wide and sleepy inside a thin ring of glassy blue. *Shit.*

He reaches down to his box and lifts the top section out, revealing a compartment underneath that holds his field surgery kit. It is heavy in his hands, the steel instruments inside shifting and clinking. Scott has come to hate that sound. He tilts his head toward her. *Forgive me.*

"Boil these," he says, handing the package to Madame, who starts away without meeting his eyes. The Émile voice inside him says he can't cut her, no matter what Madame says, because he has no morphine. The Corporal Lavoie voice says never say never. Both sides agree on one thing: *God damn every fucking piece of this fucking war to hell.*

"What was that?" the girl asks.

Scott reaches for the quilt at the foot of the bed and pulls it over her, then rubs her arms as if he's just brought her in from a storm. "Let's get you warmed up, all right? Are you thirsty?"

She doesn't answer, but blinks in confusion. "What *was* that?"

"Some things from my kit."

Her face crumples. "I can do this myself," she contends, pushing herself up on her arms. "It's just—" She looks down at her body in bewilderment as if she has just found herself in the middle of someone else's dreadful mistake. Her chin trembles. "I'm so *tired*."

Scott finds that voice now, settling into it like an old pair of slippers. "I know you are. Your grandmother will be right back, and then we'll show her how strong you are, all right?"

Hélène nods quickly before her eyes widen, and her breath hitches in sudden pain. She bites her lip as the wave rises, then she begins to wail. Scott feels utterly useless, offering his hand, but Hélène hugs her knees instead. He thinks back to standing at the kitchen pump. That couldn't have been three minutes ago. They are running out of time.

When the contraction lifts, she seems to come back to the tiny room, unfolding her body and opening her eyes. They have a window before the next one comes, and he has to move fast. Her teeth are chattering, and the pitiful sound makes Scott's heart sink.

"Hélène, let's try to sit up now, hmm?" Scott slides an arm under her torso and lifts, embracing her, quilt and all. If she's upright, he thinks, gravity will at least be on their side. Hélène moves cautiously, just as Madame appears in the doorway with torn grain sack rags and a pitcher of water. Her eyes brighten when she sees Hélène sitting up.

"Yes, yes, Lèni, sit up for *mémère*. Both of you, come, right here, yes."

She directs them, arranging Scott like a warm armchair Hélène can recline in. He sits at the foot of the bed with his stocking feet wide apart, and Madame steers Hélène in front of him. As she stands, the thin quilt falls away, and Scott is struck by her body's graceful strength. Where his sister is fine-boned and narrow, Hélène is more widely muscled. She might spend hours on end outside, he thinks, on a summer day. She is rosy-cheeked and riding high in the saddle of a chestnut horse, or standing with a single braid down her back and nails between her teeth, fixing a fence with a hammer. She might carry heavy bales of hay to animals, or tear potatoes out of the ground with her hands.

Hélène takes the measure of him before she consents to sit; she is drained to exhaustion, but still, she is wary, reading his intentions. Scott squares his shoulders and broadens his back, letting himself be scrutinised. It is all he can do. He can't tell her this is their last chance, can't think of the scalpels on the stove. *We have to try. Right now.*

The moment is cut short as her knees buckle.

"It's coming, it's coming again." Her voice has a panicky tremor of dread in it, and her breath comes in shallow puffs as they guide her to sitting on the edge of the mattress with Scott's legs on either side. Her back rests against his chest, and he loops his arms under hers to support her. She grips him tightly as her groan lowers into a guttural growl.

"Lower, Lèni, squat down lower," her grandmother says, stooping down in front of her on the floor.

Hélène's arms tangle with Scott's as her legs splay apart. "I don't..." she pants, "I can't..."

"You can let go. I'll hold you." It's a promise, and Scott's arms lock in place under hers as she slides down, using his thighs for balance. Madame's arms move between her legs, and Hélène pushes her shoulder back into Scott's stomach.

"Lèni, I can feel it. Another push, hard, Lèni."

Hélène takes a big breath in and curls down over herself, grunting, the power of it shifting Scott, too, but she can't get enough air to try again before the contraction dies away. Scott gathers her up and leans back so she can take the weight off her feet.

"The baby's head is coming," Madame tells her, her face shining. "Strong, Lèni. Push as hard as you can."

Hélène sighs heavily, and her cold body goes slack in his arms. "I can't breathe." Her words are just a whisper. "I don't...I won't be able to..." She is trembling uncontrollably now. This work is getting the best of her, and Scott can't abide it.

"You can, Hélène," he says. "I know you can. You're strong. Breathe now, nice and deep, all right? Rest." He looks down at her face, and then to Madame. His comrades in the barn are forgotten, a vague memory, far away. All that matters is here in front of him, the balance of his world tipping on what happens in this room, with this girl he met only minutes ago.

"Brave, Hélène, you are so brave," he whispers.

"I'm not."

"You are." Scott thinks of the baby's father, off somewhere fighting in a tank or a trench, or maybe dead. He considers the dark forest behind the house, the distant sounds of war, and the dozen men, growly and lost, stranded in the barn. "So brave."

Her head rolls against his chest. "I'm scared," she says through chattering teeth.

"I know." *I'm scared too. Every day.* "But you only have to be brave for a minute, all right? Just for a minute." It's the same thing he had told Moreau, after he had twisted the tourniquet under his knee. It was Scott's first field amputation, and he had said it as much for himself as for the wounded soldier. Moreau had passed out, which had been a blessing for the both of them. But he needs Hélène conscious for this. *Please, Hélène, just a minute more.*

She stirs, pulling away from him, squatting low to the ground. She feels solid this time, and when the pain comes, she is ready for it, breathing deeply, facing it head-on.

"Yes, just breathe, let the baby come," Madame whispers.

Hélène gasps, "Here, it's here." She takes one last breath and pushes down hard as she and Scott brace together against the surge. Her pain is soundless, and time stops for a horrible, quiet moment where no one breathes. Scott sees Madame's expression change, and there is the wet, slippery sound of liquid splattering against skin.

"It was the cord, Lèni!" Madame exclaims. "Push, push now!"

The adrenaline shifts when they hear the words, and it is enough to raise Hélène up on her arms, away from him to find her own leverage. He feels the breath fill her and then hears her furious growl. Scott and Madame start talking at once, filling the air with eager, hopeful sound. The words he says might be "brave girl," or "please God," but it is no matter. When she leans back against him, she is wide-eyed and sweating.

"The head is out!" Madame exclaims, grabbing for her rags. Her voice is thick with tears and relief. "Almost done now, *bichette*, almost done."

Scott tucks his head down to Hélène, his vision blurry. "I want to see that pretty girl, don't you?" Scott knows it's a girl; he can feel it. This world has seen its fill of boys and men.

She reaches up then, turning her smiling face to Scott's, and it takes his breath away. Her cold hand—

*

—suddenly turns warm.

Scott turns his face toward it, tilting his head against her fingers, marvelling at the heat radiating from them.

The smell of blood and sweat turns into a clean, outdoorsy scent he knows from somewhere wonderful.

"We'll get the last of these out, then we'll check your neck and shoulders. Does that sound all right? Scott?"

Fingers hover near his ear, then move to his arm and give him a little shake. Jason is bringing him back as he does, and Hélène's face fades like a dissolve, down into the black of his eyelids.

"Scott?"

"I'm here, I heard you." *I heard you.*

Scott takes a slow breath. He needs a minute before he opens his eyes to the room, his favourite room filled with clean, soft things, so far away from where or when he's just been.

"Feeling all right?"

"Mm hmm." But then he's not, because they are Hélène's eyes he meets, pretty and crystal-blue under curving lashes. They are tired, but curious and kind.

Scott squeezes his eyes shut for a long second, then looks up again, and this time, it's Jason. Scott can see the edges of his teeth between his lips and the stubble on his chin that looks reddish up-close. It's Jason's eyes that trip him up again, a bit darker than Hélène's, yet the same. Scott presses his feet into the table, getting his bearings.

"You left, I think. Did you find the fire?" Jason asks as he pulls the needles out one by one. Scott can only study him, trying to shake away the blip that crossed his lives over one another for an instant. Maybe it was a side effect, or a trick of light. He's been having trouble with his eyes.

"Um, yeah. I did."

"Good." Jason tilts Scott's jaw to reach the other side of his face. "Do you want to tell me about it?"

"Uh..." Scott hesitates. Maybe he actually could. He wants to memorise it all, from the farmhouse, the road, and the barn to the pattern on Hélène's quilt and the shape of her strong, square hands. He wants to take notes and make sketches. A nagging feeling tells him there is a message somewhere inside it all, but he is too close to see it. It could be, given their conversations about the two friends they've lost, finally time to ask Jason about it. About all of it.

"Why don't you sit up while you think it over? I need to make the table flat." Jason offers his arm for Scott to pull up on, then moves behind the head of the table, out of sight.

"So...I've been thinking about something," Scott begins, half looking over his shoulder.

The table lowers with a soft *clunk*. "Hmm?"

Here we go. "Do you believe in reincarnation?"

Jason makes a surprised, interested sound, then motions for Scott to lie down. "Yeah, I do." He sits on his rolling stool.

"How come?"

"Well, everything that we can see was something else once, right?" Jason slides his hands under Scott's shoulder blades, then tugs and lifts him a bit. "Our fuel was dinosaurs once. Our dirt was trees and plants. All the water we have is the same water we ever had, it just keeps evaporating and raining and evaporating and raining... why should we be the exception? It doesn't make sense that we're the one thing that doesn't recycle, you know?"

Scott likes the analogy. He focuses on the eye of the ceiling fan, thinking. "Yeah. But don't you like the idea of having a soul? I mean...a soul that's just you, that goes to Heaven for all eternity or something?"

"Well, yes, I am particularly fond of my soul, actually. Doesn't mean I have only one shot at this. What's to say my soul can't go to Heaven, or Nirvana, or Elysium, or the stars or wherever, and come back here again for another go round when it's ready for more? It's energy, and energy can't be created or destroyed."

They are quiet. The music has gone silent somewhere along the way, and it isn't raining anymore. The only sound is their even breathing. Scott feels himself filling up his body again; he wiggles his toes because it feels good.

"Why, do you?"

"Recycle?" Scott asks, trying to deflect the question with a little smile.

"Ha-ha," Jason deadpans. "Seriously, what do you think?"

Scott takes a deep breath to steady his thoughts. "All right, um, the reason I ask is because I think...I think I do. And it's because of something that's happening here."

"At our appointments?"

"Right. Remember last time? When we talked about what people see, the colours and memories?" Scott's heart beats faster, and he has to clear his throat. "Well, you're going to think I'm crazy. Shit, I sure do. But...it's happened a few times now. When I'm here, on the table, I see a place where I can..." He blows air out of his cheeks. "Get visions. I guess. Or memories. Or dreams, or something, I don't really know. You think I'm asleep, but

I'm not. I'm...ugh, this is totally mad, but...it's like I'm somewhere else."

Jason's hands stop their motion at Scott's neck. "So *that's* where you go."

"Uh, yeah," Scott says, searching Jason's upside-down face for a reaction. "And it's not only another place, but it's another...time. In the past, I guess. I mean, I'm not me, in them. But I am. I don't know how to explain it."

"Interesting," Jason says, sliding his hands under Scott's neck again. "So you're not this Scott while you're there?"

Scott considers the runner in the woods who made a deadly mistake. Then, the lost soldier who helped a young woman in a farmhouse. "No, but...I guess I'm someone else but still me? I mean, I'm inside a person, not just observing, but really living it. At first, it was kind of hazy, but now that it's happened a few times, they're getting clearer? I know things, details, of completely different lives." The words sound insane, even as he says them, and he groans. "There. I've totally lost it, haven't I?"

"No, no, I don't think you have. In fact, there's a name for what you're experiencing."

"Wait. What?"

Jason nods. "It's called past life regression therapy."

"Past life regression? It's a therapy?" Regression sounds like a bad thing to Scott, but therapy doesn't.

"I'm not certified in it, so I'm no expert, but it's a real thing people do, on purpose. Patients retrieve their past life memories and process them to heal emotional blockages. Some people believe it can heal physical issues too. But it's usually under hypnosis. I'm surprised you can get there without directed help."

Jason presses along the base of Scott's skull, probing carefully until a notch is found. It feels good; it all feels good, suddenly, to have this mystery out in the open. "It's easy, to be honest. When I'm here, I mean. I can't get there when I'm at home by myself."

"Get there...to the fire, you mean?" Jason shifts his fingers until Scott's skull sits on the fulcrum, where his fingertips press gently and give a little pull. It makes Scott sigh, and a tingly burn crawls across his forehead.

"Yes. That's where they are. The...past lives. I can just walk through it."

"Huh. Ironic."

"I know, right?" Scott's fire isn't dangerous or destructive. It's warm, but it doesn't burn. It feels kind and inviting. And powerful. "What do you think it means?"

"I don't know, but it seems to be some sort of symbol for you. Something you can learn from."

"That's just it. I mean, what's this all about? What am I supposed to learn?"

"Well, again, I'm no expert, but I think it depends on what experiences you're having in those lives. How what you've done in the past may be shaping your present." Jason's fingers move again, rocking Scott's head back and forth gently, which makes a tingle ripple through Scott's body.

"Ooh," Scott gasps out before he can stop it. "Um," he chuckles. "Sorry, that went all the way down my legs."

Scott files away Jason's answer, letting Jason coax him into a place where only two things matter: here, and now.

*

They stand at the counter, finishing the last of the follow-up.

"So what's a float tank?" Scott asks as Jason reaches for his wrist to check his pulse.

Jason's eyes get wide. "Ah, one of my favourites. Where did you hear about float tanks?"

"From you. When you told me about your knee."

"Right, my laundry list of healing remedies. A float tank is a pool filled with salt water. You get in it and float with no sound or light. Very therapeutic."

Scott's hands are warm and pliant, and Jason makes loose circles with his wrists. "So it's like swimming."

"No, you can't swim. It's too shallow, and the pod's too small. But it's impossible for you to sink. You don't have to expend any energy at all. You just...float. There's a whole science behind it—sensory deprivation, theta waves in the brain, zero gravity physics and such. But the point is, the body can get more relaxed in a float tank than just about anywhere else."

"In the dark?"

"Mm hmm."

"And quiet."

"Mm hmm. Turn around, please."

"Why would I want to deprive my senses?" Scott asks as Jason checks the alignment of his neck. The thought is both terrifying and intriguing, like some exotic form of torture. "I mean, why does it have to be dark?"

"It's so the mind doesn't have any distractions. Every little thing we hear, touch, smell, see, even the clothes against our skin—it all gives the brain something to work on. When we take all that away, there's freedom to...just *be.*"

"Did it help you?"

"Yeah. Still does."

Scott wonders what Jason needs to float for, but it would be too intrusive to ask. In any case, Jason floats, so it must be useful, and it must not hurt. "I could do that."

The movement of Jason's hands skips a bit on its track. "Yes. You could."

"You sound like I can't."

Jason gives his neck one last swipe from nape to shoulders. "You could. I think it would be really good for you, actually, if you're interested."

"But."

"But." Jason sighs. "It can be rough when a person has had trauma."

No shit. Everything's rough when a person's had trauma. Going to Tesco is rough. Making an egg on toast. Walking through a parking lot. Meeting a kind person's eyes.

"Everyone's had trauma, though, right?"

Jason comes around to face him. "Scott. Not everyone's lived through a terrorist attack."

Quite so. "But it's a healing thing."

"Absolutely."

"And you can't drown."

"Right."

"Okay, then I want to. There's a float tank in London?" He wants to try it, today if he can.

"Several."

"Okay. I'll go."

"Wait, hold on. Let me show you some information on it before you make up your mind."

Scott can't understand why Jason is being so cautious about this when he usually can't wait to push them forward, straight into the action. And why does he need Jason's blessing, anyway? "Too late. I want to go."

"It's ninety minutes, usually."

That pulls Scott up short. Ninety minutes. Scott's appointments with Jason are forty-five, tops, and there's music. And light. And Jason to talk to.

"If you go, I think someone should go with you, for support. In case."

"In case I freak out, you mean?" Scott sighs and looks at the ceiling. It's a possibility, he supposes.

"Well." Jason purses his lips in a tight shape, then meets Scott's eyes. "Yeah, actually, in case you freak out. Do you think your sister would go?"

Olivia. She would, of course. But she's got her job, and Thomas after school.

Scott takes a stab. "I'd feel better if... Why don't you come? You know all about this stuff. You could help me if I need it. While I'm depriving my senses. And freaking out. In the dark. For ninety fucking minutes."

Jason chuckles a bit and considers it. "I'd feel better if I went along too." Jason rubs his palms together. "I can't float with you, but I can go, help you get situated, and wait for you."

"Okay. Let's do it. When?"

Jason thinks a minute. "We might try for next Monday? I don't think I have anyone after you."

A week away. "Yeah, that's fine. You'll let me know?"

"Definitely. Oh wait, before you go, I wanted to give you something. I'll be right back." Jason turns toward the door but looks backward as he goes through. "Don't forget your calendar."

Scott hasn't forgotten. In fact, he's been eying the bag the whole time they've been talking. He unzips the holdall, noticing again how good it smells, like leather and aftershave. He lifts the calendar out with mixed feelings. He's glad to see it, relieved that it didn't somehow disappear like a magic trick, but he's *not* glad to see it; to hold it again feels a lot like putting his brace back on after spending hours without it. Constricting. Suffocating.

Scott slips the calendar into his bag and tucks the flap over it. When he looks up, Jason is back, holding a thick paperback book with curled edges and clouds on the cover.

"You can borrow this if you like."

Scott takes the book and squints. He can't pronounce the title.

"It's Ah-KASH-ick," Jason says. "Akashic Records. I like it because it's not based on a hierarchical understanding of past lives, you know? Like we're going up a ladder, trying to get to the top or outsmart karma?

It's more like each life is a story, and all of them put together make up a...sort of database. Or library. I thought you might find it helpful."

The clouds make it seem like heaven. *But really? A database of my lives?* That makes Scott think of the research department at *The Times*, and how he could walk right up to the computer and type "Rowe, Scott, past lives," with an intern looking over his shoulder. No, that doesn't feel right. He much prefers the idea of a library. He pictures a gothic cathedral like Westminster Abbey, with flying buttresses and a rose window, filled to the top with books and framed artworks and people milling around, browsing through the stacks for their histories. There are at least four books there with his name on them.

Scott puts the book into his bag alongside the calendar, telling Jason he'll bring it back next time.

"Still quiet?"

Scott listens and only hears a whispery rush. "Yeah. How long will it last?"

"Could be a few hours, could be the rest of the day or more. We should have some follow-up treatments, but those will be shorter. We could tack one on the end of your next appointment if you want."

"Okay. Not for the whole time?"

"Nah—I think we should get back to your shoulders, and there's more arm work to do. But we can do both. What do you think?"

"Sure, that's fine." Scott thinks it's better than fine, actually. It's *brilliant*.

*

It's half eight before Scott steps away from his desk, unable to ignore the rumbling in his stomach. As he heads for the kitchen, he makes a list of things to get when he goes out tomorrow: coloured pencils, printer ink, glue, and a new pair of scissors.

He leaves behind his new black sketchbook. He'd arranged it like a diary, writing his appointment date at the top of each page so he can organise his lives, as he now refers to them. He is rusty at note-taking and sketching, but for his first try, it isn't terrible. He managed to capture the rustic feel of the two-storey farmhouse with its steeply pitched roof and fat bushes dropping their leaves by the front door. He remembered the chicken coop and the crumbling stone fence along the edge of the garden, and he'd sketched those roughly as well. Words are scattered on the pages too; he wrote "calendar day," "promise," and "Lèni," as well as "morphine," "hands," and "brave."

The first page was titled "Monday, 23 May 2016," and under it, he'd written what he can remember about the fortress by the sea. There was a man there, standing by the window, who had a kind voice and a ship pin. Scott was to sign something, like a contract, or a deed. He can still feel the terrible weight of responsibility that rested in that signet ring, and his position at the head of that dark, heavy table. But the man who had felt like his brother had reassured him, even in the face of all his crippling doubt. The words Scott wrote on this page were "allies," "ocean," "stone," and "trust."

"Monday, 30 May 2016" will be a collage. Scott bookmarked a photograph of a Native girl with a cradleboard on her back that he'd found on the American Museum of Natural History's web archives. He also searched for "falcon" and "fox" and bookmarked several pictures of both. He even found some photographs of the wild prairie grasses from the field where she'd been caught. Their names are soothing, and he listed them as he read them aloud: "Green needlegrass, big bluestem, switchgrass, and giant wildrye." This had been the day of his fight with Jason, the day of the fire in the sink. He wrote "horses" in scrawling letters at the bottom of the page and drew a triangle next to it, to remind him of the mark on the child's chin. He also wrote "fear" and "mistake." Tomorrow, he will print out the pictures and paste them here, to fill out the world of the girl he has come to know as Wings-on-the-Wind.

The next one, "Thursday, 2 June 2016," started out as a stream of consciousness poem but quickly turned into a letter to Lorenzo. In the margin, he drew a looping *L* intertwined with an elaborate italic *M*, as best he could remember from the canvas he'd painted. He is curious about the paints Matti might have used, and he might try to learn a bit about the plague. But that is for another day; for now, the lost love makes him sad, and he wants to leave it as it is. Eventually, he'll try to find a painted portrait of a young man in a black, slit-sleeved waistcoat, as well as a photograph of an Italian palazzo, perhaps with a terracotta tiled roof. Words on this page are: secrets, love, comfort, and risk.

That has brought him up to the present, "Monday, 6 June 2016," the French farmhouse. As he leans against the counter sipping his tea, he decides he'll take a stab at sketching the inside of the little bedroom as well. It makes him think of Hélène wrapped in her quilt, looking up at him with her blue eyes. Brave.

He hears the notification ding on his phone. It's a text from Olivia.

EastEnders! Tell me you're watching??

Nope, sorry. Scott lets out an ironic snort and thinks, I'm cataloguing my past lives right now, no time for soaps.

Don't forget Thomas's play on Wednesday night. You're still coming?

Absolutely. What time?

When no response comes, he turns to the croque-monsieur heating on the hob. He figures he might flip through the book Jason gave him while he eats.

His phone chimes again as he slides his sandwich onto a plate, and he picks it up, expecting Olivia. But it's Jason. His finger shakes a bit as he swipes the phone open.

Still quiet?

Scott chuckles softly and listens.

Hi. Yes, still quiet.

Scott picks at the sandwich crust, poised over the phone.

You're drinking your water?

Tea. You?

Same. How is your cough tonight?

Nowhere. You do house calls now?

Just curious. Didn't want to wait till Thursday to find out.

Before Scott can think of what to say next, another text appears.

Also realised I never filled you in on my convo with Dr Wareing.

Scott had forgotten; his appointment with the ear, nose, and throat doctor had been stellar regarding his hearing, inconclusive regarding his cough. But Jason probably already knows that.

You could call. We could have a conversation. Like normal people.

Scott's heart bumps hotly as he hits the send button.

You'll answer?

Cheeky, he thinks to himself. The cursor blinks in the response window, counting the seconds as Scott thinks. Only three flash by before he replies.

Yes.

Possibilities crowd Scott's mind: Maybe he could tell Jason everything he didn't say today, not about the farmhouse, not yet, but about Brenna, about sleeping, about flying. He could tell him thanks again for the book, and that he'd planned on looking it over at supper. He could ask him how he's holding up, make sure he's not taking blame for what he could or couldn't do for his patient who passed away. Maybe he could ask Jason what he goes floating for, and thank him again for offering to go with him because he thinks something big might happen there.

Scott's phone rings, and its trill is a gorgeous sound.

"Hello?"

"Hi, it's me."

Although Scott has heard Jason's voice on his answerphone, it's still a strange sound to get used to. Familiar, but different, close, but far away.

"I know," Scott says. "Uh, thanks for calling. I had... something I forgot to tell you too."

"Oh? About what?"

Dreams, somehow, have become a currency between them. Scott smiles, and a tingle buzzes through his hands as he starts to speak.

"Do you remember last week, you told me to have a flying dream? Well, I did. It worked."

"Yeah? Hey, good on you. How'd it feel?"

"It was...incredible. I just ran to the edge of this cliff and took off over the ocean. And you..." *You were there too.* Scott stumbles, realising that letting Jason know that isn't the best idea. The oddness of it strikes Scott suddenly, that Jason is the only one of his doctors he's dreamt about, and he scrambles to cover his slip. "You, uh, you would've been impressed. With my skills."

Jason laughs. “I bet. You didn’t crash, did you?”

“Nope. Soft landing. Perfect.” Scott leans against the counter and folds his arms, getting comfortable.

“Excellent. So you must be sleeping well if you’re dreaming. Oh wait, does this mean I owe you one?”

Chapter Seven

> Retouch (v.) To make small finishing, correcting, or improving changes to something. (n.) something that has been retouched, especially a photograph.

It should have been an easy trip up to Hampstead on Wednesday evening for Thomas's play.

The June night was fair and cool, perfect for walking to the tube, and Scott had made his way to the station with plenty of time to spare. He slipped into an empty seat as the train doors closed and smiled to himself, recalling the rehearsal video Olivia had sent of Thomas the dragonfly, singing in his best showtune voice among his frog and squirrel classmates.

The little dark-haired girl who was seated next to Scott looked up when he made a happy noise. She was younger than Thomas; her feet swung freely off the bench as she braided her doll's long hair. Scott glanced at her mum, who sat on the girl's other side. She gave him a little smile.

"She's got pretty hair, that one," Scott said to the girl in a gentle voice after a while of companionable silence.

She moved the doll a bit toward him and went on braiding, grabbing sections of hair and crossing them in no particular order.

He pulled a hair tie from around his wrist. "Want to see what I can do with mine?" She watched, rapt, as he gathered his hair in a ponytail, then pulled it through the tie twice to make a bun. Scott smiled at her. "Easy."

But her mouth made a confused shape, and he watched her eyes trace his scar from his ear all the way down his jawline. She seemed transfixed by it, as if she wanted to ask a question but hadn't picked one out yet. She caught his eye for a moment, then stared at his scar again plainly, as only children and Jason were bold enough to do. He let her, without turning away. *It's all right*, he told himself. *It's only fair. What I did should be written all over my face.*

"Now approaching Hampstead Station. Next station is Golders Green."

"This one's mine," he told her and smiled one last time. "Good evening." He looked down at her doll. "And good evening to you too." She didn't look away from him as he rose from the seat.

He turned and reached for the hold bar and promptly bumped into a man in a green coat whose short black hair resembled Omran's. A hot flush curled up Scott's neck. He must have looked stunned because the man asked if he was all right. Scott turned away to get his bearings, saying, "Yes, thank you, mistook you for someone else." He pushed out the door trying to recall Omran's face, now hopelessly mixed up with the features of a stranger.

Then there was the fire truck with its siren that screamed past outside the tube station. A few minutes later, cars screeched away from the curb when the light turned green, making Scott startle and curse, and then he had trouble navigating the full car park and the small but brisk crowd of people trotting along the pavement toward the school. Scott pulled his arm in as they bumped by, folding it close to his body to protect it.

All of it together is too much. As Scott steps inside the colourfully decorated lobby, his heart starts its erratic drumming and cold sweat breaks out over his lip. He searches the space for Olivia. She'd said they would meet at the double doors, but those are on the other side of the rotunda, and people are milling in a heavy current he can't make his way across. Their excited voices echo and bounce in his ears, making him unsteady. He shuffles toward a wall he can lean against so he won't fall over.

He presses his forehead against the cool tile as he reaches for his phone, the two sides of his brain arguing. Pull it together! You're fine, straighten up now versus You're not going to make it. You can't stay here. What made you think you could do this? He tries to take steadying breaths through his nose, but the ringing gets louder with the echoes overlapping. He shakes his head at himself as he texts Olivia that he's got to go home, so sorry, not feeling well. His mind reaches for the sanctuary of the darkroom, where he can be alone, where the amber light is warm and gentle on his eyes.

> *You're here? Where are you? I'm at the auditorium*

Scott's hands are trembling, and it takes him four tries to spell out the next sentence.

Yes I'm here but can't stay. Pls call me when it's over?

I will. But text me when you get home, OK?

Will do. want to talk to Thomas later. call me, serious

I will. I'm worried.

I'm OK just knackerd. Talk later. X

I'm sorry.

Scott detests that. There is only one person who should be sorry here, and that's himself.

Don't b. Tell T break a leg from me

The deep breaths of cool air outside help a bit, and so does the bottle of water he gets from the machine at the tube station. He even considers turning around and giving it another go for Thomas's sake, but the thought of having to cross the busy street again puts a stop to it, and the draw of the darkroom wins out. He wants to close the door against noise and light, hear the crack of the film canister as he breaks the seal and steps into a different time, the time before.

He pushes through the turnstile, shaky and ashamed, hoping there will be at least one roll left in his desk drawer.

*

There are four film canisters in all, and when his phone rings an hour and a half later, he's just finished developing one—of the day he'd gone with Olivia and Thomas to the fair in Brompton last spring. There were kites and balloons and a butterfly house; Thomas had wanted to stay all day, to see the kites fly in the afternoon and the coloured lanterns at night.

The smell of darkroom chemicals still fills Scott's nose as he sits on the edge of the bed. Although it's early, his eyes burn when he shuts them, and he rubs one to ease it. Olivia's voice is worried, asking if he needs anything.

"I'm good now, Liv. Seriously. I..." There's no point in telling her anything but the truth. "Something about all the people, and the noise. It's...hard sometimes." He tries to stifle a cough, but it escapes, sounding raspy and weak.

"Babe, I'm sorry. I didn't think about the crowd."

Scott says nothing for a bit. If it's not the crowd, then it's the traffic. If not the traffic, then it's a siren, or heavy heels on the pavement behind him, or a little girl who may have been frightened of him, or a man that still haunts him, with dark hair and a green coat. This isn't up to Olivia to fix.

Scott clears his throat. "Is Thomas there?"

"Yeah, he's right here. Love you."

"Love you too."

"Uncle Scott?" Thomas sounds breathless, still excited from the night's energy. It makes Scott get up from the bed and pace to match it.

"Hey! How did it go tonight, T-man?"

"It was great! Everybody said my costume was the best one! Where'd you go?"

Scott cringes and shuts his eyes. “I’m sorry, tiger. I wanted to hear you sing, but I had to come home.”

“Well, Mummy said you can watch it on your phone.”

“Perfect. I can’t wait to see it.” Scott is back in the bathroom, the clipped length of film hanging on the line with a clothes peg to dry. The negatives look eerie with their reverse colour; what is light will be dark, and what is dark will eventually be light.

“Mum said it’s bedtime now, because it’s late.”

“How about one joke, then bed?” Scott’s eyes catch on a sweet image of Olivia crossing her eyes at a butterfly that had landed on her shoulder.

“Okay. I went to the doctor and told him I broke my arm in two places. Do you know what he said?”

Scott smiles. Thomas had told him this same one last week, but he’d used “leg” instead of arm and had bumbled the punchline. “No, what’d he say?”

“He said, ‘Stay away from those places.’ Get it?”

“Oh yeah, I do! That’s a good one.” Scott tries to make his voice into a hug that will reach right through the phone. Thomas should have been hugged tonight.

“Is your arm still broken, Uncle Scott?”

Another negative on the strip shows an exotic-looking swallowtail resting on a leaf with its wings spread wide, Thomas’s thin finger in the corner of the frame. “No, T, it’s not. It feels much better now.”

“But you’re still sick?” Thomas’s clear, earnest voice is a sweet gut punch.

Scott’s eyes fill, and he has to stay silent for a minute so Thomas won’t hear his voice get thick and uneven. He turns from the strip of ghostly images and walks slowly across the room. "I um...sometimes, I am, yeah. But I'll be better soon."

"Okay."

"All right T, I'm proud of you, okay? And I'll talk to you later."

"Bye," Thomas says, and before Scott can answer, the call is disconnected.

Fuck. Scott swipes the call away and flops backward on the bed with a groan. He's got the itch to turn on the heated underblanket, to put this day to bed and himself with it. But he's not tired, just frustrated and small, and he's got two hours before the film dries hard enough to make a contact sheet. He could wrap his arm up for the night, brush his teeth, and treat his scars. He could make a cup of tea since his throat hurts and he's been coughing a bit.

Before he does, his eyes catch on the photograph on the adjacent wall. Its colours are muted in the dim light, but he can make out the curved shape of the tree branch and the dark fence behind it.

Look at that tree for me.

Scott stands up quickly, the phone forgotten, and closes the distance between himself and his desk where he'd left Jason's reincarnation book. He flips it open to a dog-eared page that had confused him, with a diagram of the physical and astral planes colliding. He takes it with him to the kitchen and fills the kettle.

*

The next afternoon, Scott puts his water bottle down on the counter next to the newest addition to Jason's office—a bowl of small, multicoloured crystal discs.

At first, he thinks they are fruit gums in a sweets dish, but when he looks more closely, he sees their hard, rounded shapes and polished shine. There are blues, greens, purples, and oranges, solid or marbled with pearly white-and-grey veins, and one is coal-black. Some are cold to the touch, while others are warm and soft. He holds a pink one up toward the sunny window, trying to see through it. He likes the way they feel, and likes the pretty clinking noise they make when he drops them back into the bowl. Scott wonders how Jason uses them.

He moves on to the feather, snowy-white with a leather cord wrapped around its quill. This he won't touch. It's smaller than he remembers, but seems powerful, and its fine edge looks more suited for cutting than for sweeping. The thought makes him uneasy, and he turns away from it.

Scott has been coughing all morning, and his jaw is tight. His eyes feel puffy from too little sleep, and his mind is foggy and slow like a hangover, all on top of the high ringing in his ears. It's far from where he'd been Monday night when Jason called. He'd felt warm and at ease then, sharp and truly awake. The back-and-forth of his recovery these days is maddening, like being trapped in a revolving door that spins him from darkness to sunlight and back again in an endless loop.

Maybe today will be the day Jason won't look too closely. Maybe he'll skim over the rough parts and let Scott off easy, with no mention of the dark circles under his eyes or the chill in his hands. Scott knows it's impossible, but he can wish; he's disappointed, and he can't stand the thought of Jason being disappointed too.

Jason opens the door after a soft knock, and Scott knows instantly that today is not that day.

"Hi, Scott." Jason's usual smile fades after a few moments. "What happened?" He puts his files down and reaches his hand out for Scott to shake.

"Is it that obvious?"

Jason rubs Scott's hand between his palms to warm them. "Well, sorry, but...yeah. Rough morning?"

"Rough night." Scott clears his throat, willing himself not to cough. His throat is a tricky thing. Sometimes what's inside is a tickle or a scratch, and sometimes it's raw like the beginning of a cold. But sometimes, like now, it's heavy and hot and hard to swallow over.

Jason's eyebrows furrow. "You're cold. What's going on?" He hands Scott his water, tipping his chin as if to tell him to take a drink.

"One step forward, two steps back, I guess," Scott says, trying to be glib but sounding just like he feels, frustrated and sorry. He takes a drink. Had he really told Jason about the flying dream? Yes, he had, and Jason had been tickled. But now Scott's feet feel hopelessly grounded, maybe forever.

"Want to tell me about it?"

The thought of unpacking last night's events is crushing. Snapshots will do. "Panic attack before my nephew's play, which I then missed. Darkroom. Not much sleep." He raises his elbow up to his face and turns away. The cough can't be helped. "Oh. And I might choke at any moment."

"Hmm, I see that," Jason says, his hands coming up under Scott's jaw. They feel the soft muscles of his neck, then the joint at his ear, where the tendons get harder. "Drop this open, and we'll have a look inside."

Dr Wareing had found no issues with his throat, but surely there is *something* there. When his chin drops, Scott feels as if his cheeks are stretching past their limit, and his molars feel achy in their sockets. He closes his eyes when Jason brings an instrument up to look inside. *Please, don't give up on me.*

"Say aaahhh."

Scott lets out a sound for a long breath. It is clear at the beginning but weakens to a hoarse whisper.

"All right, you can close up. I don't see anything, Scott. No drainage, no swelling or nodules, nothing strange at all."

"Just like Dr Wareing said," Scott grumbles, rubbing his neck. "There's something in there. I'm not imagining it." *Ugh.* He knows how insufferable he sounds. *But come on.*

"Wait, Scott. I said I didn't see it. That doesn't mean I don't think it's real," Jason says quietly. "We'll take care of it. Hang in there with me a little longer, yeah? I have some ideas. New things we can try."

Scott wonders if the new things have to do with a white feather or a dish of shiny crystals.

"So, your panic attack, you had those same symptoms, the racing heartbeat and the nausea?" Jason has moved on to his eyes, so Scott looks across the room and tries to focus on the tree.

"Yeah, same as always."

"But it doesn't sound like you went right to sleep after."

Scott should have realised this before, but he hadn't made the connection. Every other time he's had an attack, it's followed by crippling exhaustion, where he's had to sleep the rest of the day. But this one was different, a baby in comparison to some of those he's had. Hell, he'd even considered turning around at the tube station. But he'd returned to his flat and gone straight to work in the darkroom.

"No, I didn't have to. I wasn't tired. I worked a while in my darkroom, and then I read."

"Working in the darkroom? I'd say that's an improvement." Jason thinks a moment, then lifts his eyebrow. "Let's do a short acupuncture follow-up with those same anxiety points after our other work today, okay? To reinforce them?"

"Okay, yeah."

Jason nods, and Scott is relieved. Jason will drive them through like always. It will be all right now that they've got a plan. It makes Scott lift his chin and take a deep breath.

"What's going on with your arm? You're holding it funny."

"Hmm?" Scott hadn't realised, but his arm is bent close to his body, and his hand makes a fist.

Now, Jason focuses on his collar, looking at the skin that shows under the open button. "You don't have your bandage on."

"Oh, right. Brenna gave me a compression sleeve to wear instead."

Jason's face lights up as if he's won something. "Well, this keeps getting better! May I see?"

"Um, yeah, sure." This is the moment. Scott has pictured it dozens of times—lying down on Jason's table with some foreboding minor-key music in the background, then Jason peeling the blanket back and recoiling in horror. But as it is, they stand face to face with daylight streaming in, and Jason's bright eyes are curious. Scott takes off his shirt and pulls down the compression sleeve before he can overthink it, then places them in a pile on the counter.

"Jesus, mate, that's...that's *gorgeous.*" Jason tilts his head and leans in to get a better look. "May I?" He gestures as if he wants to touch it.

"'Course," Scott says with a shrug, but his lips press together, and he looks down at the edge of the carpet.

"This looks *really* good." Jason turns Scott's arm gently, looking at its underside, then studies the S-shaped scar that starts at the shoulder and ends just above Scott's elbow. "I love it. Don't you?"

Scott glances at it, then turns away quickly. It looks ugly here in this room full of clean linens and smooth surfaces. "Um. I'm not quite at the love stage. I'd say we're still getting to know each other. Like...an awkward blind date."

Jason shakes his head, his smile growing. "There's some contracture here, but this colour will flatten and fade a bit." He steps around to see the back, touching Scott's elbow gently. "Nah, mate. I think she's the one. You've got a beautiful relationship ahead of you if you treat her right."

Scott doesn't follow. "Why is it a she?"

Jason is following the largest scar with the tips of his fingers. "You know, 'she.' Like a boat. Or an aeroplane. She's going to take you places."

She already has. Scott clears his throat. *But.* "Sometimes I don't think she's enough."

The words surprise him; he hadn't planned on saying anything about that, but it's true. Sometimes he thinks he should have been paralysed, or made deaf so he can't listen to music anymore or hear the voices of the people he loves, or blind so he can't see beautiful colours, or places, or people. That would be better payment. It would be poetic justice.

"Oh, she's plenty." Jason nods, impressed. "You had a talented team."

Scott can only shrug.

"They proper saved it, didn't they? Incredible, with the extent of the trauma as it was."

"How do you know what the extent of the trauma was?"

Their eyes meet. "From the report and the pictures in your file."

Scott swallows. "Pictures?"

"From the ambulance, and the...oh shit." Jason trails off. His face drops, the brightness gone. He bites his lip. "You didn't see the pictures."

Scott's chest feels like it's caving in. "No. By the time I woke up, it was all over and done. They told me what they did, and I saw loads of X-rays, but no one said there were pictures." He looks down at the files. Rowe, Scott,

Ortho. Rowe, Scott, Ophthal. Rowe, Scott, Physio. He shifts them around without asking, and a quick glance shows files also labelled *ENT*, *Derm*, and *Osteo*. "They're in here somewhere?"

Jason makes a grab for them, bumping Scott's hand away. "Yeah. But wait, they're...um..." He sweeps the whole pile aside, shaking his head.

"They're what? I want to see them."

Jason raises a hand. "Hold on. They're case photos, you know, for documentation." Now it's his turn to swallow hard. "They're graphic, yeah? Rough."

"I've seen rough." Scott turns on Jason as if he's ready to fight. There are pictures someone took of him in that missing, in-between time when he was gone and woke up different. He'll be able to see what happened, what's real, against what he's conjured up in his imagination. "Anyway, they're mine, aren't they?"

Scott waits for Jason to argue because he's standing with his hand on his hip and his chin up like he's going to make a case. But then his eyes change, looking into Scott's as if he can read something there.

"Prints or digital?" Jason asks. "I have both."

Scott holds his gaze. "Prints."

Jason turns to his files and picks out *Rowe, Scott, Osteo*. He flips it open to the back, to a stack of photographs.

"Right. There are a few from the ambulance, some from both hospitals, and two or three post-op." Jason taps the pile on their edge to line them up, and Scott gets the feeling he's stalling. "You're sure?"

Scott holds his hand out.

"All right. Do you want me to go?"

Scott's jaw hardens. "No, stay."

There's not much to see in the first one. He's inside the ambulance on the stretcher, though it looks like a pile of brown fabric and green blankets, with some dark-brown hair showing at the edge.

The next one is out of focus, but he can make out the remnants of his shirt and his balled-up brown coat streaked black and red. The blankets are gone, exposing a large scarlet puddle on the white mattress. The blurry face, swollen and bloody, is covered with a clear plastic mask. Two sets of hands work in the foreground with scissors and a line of tubing.

The third is a close-up. Scott's heart begins to tap erratically, and he takes a breath. "What is that?" Scott mumbles to himself, tilting it up to get a different angle. He brings it in closer to his face and squints. The wound is grisly, and the surrounding fabric resembles the curls of the burned papers from the sink.

"What *is* that?" he repeats, louder this time. Because it couldn't be. *It's impossible.* That's his chest and his neck, so that must be his arm, bent at a terrible angle on the blood-soaked table. His skin is tan but also pink and red in places, and concave in the middle. Someone has placed a measuring tape along its side, giving the photograph the look of crime scene evidence from a cop show. The familiar sick feeling rears up in Scott's throat, and he pinches his lip with his thumb and forefinger so Jason won't see the quiver in his chin.

Jason is close enough that his body heat warms Scott, and his voice is calm. He speaks in short sentences, a bit of information at a time.

"This part is your shoulder," he says, circling the murky mess of brownish-red. "This part"—he traces the grey section showing through—"that's this bone here, your humerus." He touches Scott's upper arm along the bumpy trail of scar tissue. "This"—he circles another pale shape in the centre—"is here." Jason touches Scott's elbow. He points at an irregular mass of bloody tissue. "And that's your bicep muscle."

All the words Scott's doctors had used flood back in blur. Compound fracture vascular contusion limb viability you are very lucky penetrating trauma extensive tissue damage it cleaned up nicely you'll be just fine.

They go through the rest with Jason navigating, showing Scott what's skin and what's bone and how the team worked from the inside out to pull it all back together. The cramped, bloody ambulance turns into the stainless-steel sheen of an operating room, the broken mess getting progressively less gruesome in each picture until the one where Scott recognises the familiar trail of stitches and staples. On that first day, the lines were bold, and thick with black sutures, where now, they've faded into trails of purplish-red. He looks startlingly exposed among the sleek surgical blues and whites, and then childlike, bandaged and sleeping in the muted pastels of the recovery room.

After Scott puts the last picture down and they share a moment of silence to digest it, Jason speaks quietly.

"They did a proper good job, didn't they?"

Scott is afraid his voice won't come if he tries to say something, but *yes, yes, my God, they really did.*

"Listen, Scott. Are you listening?"

Scott's eyes pull away from the pile to look at Jason. He nods, blinking back tears that almost spill over.

Jason turns to pull the tissue box closer to them, and Scott takes one. "This is where you are now. It is what it is. And I think it's...lovely." When Jason uses the word it isn't a compliment, nor is it patronising. He speaks it as a fact, with conviction. "It's what you've come out the other side of. What you've survived. It *is* enough, isn't it?"

Scott looks down at his arm that hangs between them. Jason's hand is still on it, resting on the forearm, covering the pitted scars. It feels protected, important.

"Maybe." Scott sniffs. He recalls Jason's footie picture—the look in his eye, the pain behind the smile. "The end of one thing, and the beginning of something else?"

It's enough to bring a bit of brightness back into Jason's eyes, and Scott almost can't bear to look at the kindness there. That's Jason, behind him in the revolving door, pushing Scott out of the dark into the light. "That's up to you, isn't it?"

They stand like that for a few moments more with the story of Scott's brokenness spread out before them. Scott reaches out for the first picture and then the last, and holds them side by side. Maybe he can carry Omran around on his body, and that will be enough.

Scott nods at the photos, then sweeps them up with a final clear of his throat. He swipes the tissue over his cheek. "Thank you. For showing me these. Now let's get to it, yeah?"

*

Scott is face down, and Jason adjusts the pillow under his feet. He is comfortable and warm, and his eyes are quick to close. He likes this part, when all of what they do is still out in front of them.

"Question," Scott says softly.

"Hmm?"

"What are you doing before we start, when you're standing there?"

Jason doesn't answer for a minute and adjusts the blanket around Scott's feet instead. Scott wonders if he shouldn't have asked.

"Um, tuning in, mostly, to where you are."

It isn't the answer Scott was expecting. He pulls his face up from the cradle and lays his cheek on its edge. "How do you do that?"

Jason walks along the side of the table, tucking and smoothing as he goes. "I get quiet. Stop thinking. Try to let go of my own expectations, I guess?"

The idea that Jason has expectations for him scares Scott a bit. *What do they look like? Am I meeting them?* He takes a small, worried breath.

"And I pray too."

"For me?"

"No, not just for you. For both of us." Jason rests his hands near Scott's shoulders. "It goes something like, 'Show me what you need me to see. Let me hear what needs to be heard. May the highest part of me serve the highest part of you.'"

That sounds familiar, and Scott takes a minute to figure out where he's heard it. *Namaste.* The word in his mouth stirs a memory of the temple at Tirumala, in India, when he'd shot the story of the girls who sacrifice their hair to the gods. They would bow their heads and wish him this, even as they wept.

Scott settles his face into the cradle again. With the heat seeping up through his legs and his arm unbound for the first time, Scott tries to quiet his mind and focus only on the sounds of their breathing and the gentle string music. Something unspoken but understood charges the air around them, while a hard, dark part of him still hopes that as much as Jason might pray, there will still be things he won't be able to see.

*

When Jason places the heat pack over Scott's back, Scott takes his deepest breath since he got here. Jason is going to work on those crunchy, tight spots, he knows, so he wants to relax, give him the best shot at finding them and easing them away.

"So, I was sort of surprised to hear you were back at work."

"Work?"

"Last night, in the darkroom. I thought you weren't taking pictures anymore?"

Scott's voice is muffled in the cradle. "I'm not. I just develop my old film."

"Huh, I didn't know there was still such a thing as film." Jason presses down on his good shoulder with a flat hand, softly at first, then a little harder, pushing Scott's chest into the table.

"Jason, that's how cameras work." Scott chuckles, interested to see where this will go.

Jason's first push on Scott's bad shoulder is nothing more than a warm graze. "No, no, that's not true. I don't know much about photography, but I know I've taken plenty of pictures, and film has never been involved, not once. *Never.*"

"Too bad, you're missing out. I think the best pictures are taken with film," Scott says, waiting for the pressure to get deeper. It doesn't; Jason's hand is a steady, pleasant weight that makes Scott forget his train of thought. He was about to say something, about how...*how the film...has...a texture*...but the pressure begins to move back and forth through the heat, causing the muscle there to shift. It rolls and spasms a bit, making the shoulder twitch up toward Scott's cheek.

What was I thinking about? Film? Cameras? Yes, cameras. What comes to mind is one specific camera on the shelf of his cupboard, and it makes Scott wince. He can see the cupboard door, looming huge and spiteful in his small flat, but he can't reach out to properly look inside.

Scott remembers the day in the hospital when he had asked Olivia for the camera. He was woozy, drugged up, and half-blind, but he had to see it and hold it in his hands. The things they were telling him, they just couldn't be true; his camera was the only real proof that the day had even happened. That was the last day he'd touched it, holding its cracked body on his lap in the bed, trying to fit the zoom lens on one-handed. It was like a child's toy that had been smashed in a tantrum, and he had cried until Olivia went to fetch someone to give him a shot so he could rest.

On the awful day Olivia helped get him settled back into his flat, she'd held the case out to him, asking where to put it. He turned away, pretending to busy himself with the washing, and told her he didn't care. "I'll just put it up here for now," she'd said lightly, placing it out of the way on the cupboard shelf.

It had once been Scott's best friend, who'd travelled everywhere with him, whom he felt naked without. But then they had a falling out, and now it's a high-maintenance, stand-offish roommate who never talks and requires a wide berth of privacy. They hold a grudge neither side can forgive.

"Feel anything there? Any pain right now?" Jason asks, his hand still warm on the blade of Scott's shoulder.

"No," Scott answers, glad Jason can't see his face. "Nothing."

Jason is still for a moment, then sighs quietly. "All right. We'll leave that bit alone for now."

*

Some time later, after Scott has turned over, Jason leans on the edge of the table next to his chest.

"We're going to try a stretch," Jason says, pulling Scott's injured arm up toward his own shoulder as if to rest Scott's hand on it. Jason catches his eye and must see the worry there. "Don't forget to breathe, okay? This won't hurt."

Scott looks up at the ceiling fan, which seems to look back down on him with its one naked, unblinking eye; he wills his arm to relax even as he's got Jason in a strange half-embrace. The tickle is back in his throat, but he clears it and swallows. "All right, ready."

The heel of Jason's palm presses on Scott's shoulder, while his other hand holds Scott's forearm and pulls upward gently. "Is that okay?"

Strangely, it is; Scott's body eases into the stretch instead of tensing up. "Yeah, it's okay." Scott closes his eyes as Jason pulls again, this time rotating his arm outward a bit. After a few repeats, Jason grasps Scott's wrist and moves the arm around freely, loose as a cooked noodle.

It feels good, but something about the motion on that side of his body brings the tickle back, and soon Scott's throat clearing turns into raspy huffs and then a full-blown barky cough.

"Ugh, can I have some water?" he asks, propping himself up on his good elbow.

Jason retrieves a bottle, and Scott drinks half of it down in three gulps.

"Where is it—here?" Jason's hands hover over Scott's heart. Jason must feel the throb of it, the way it's banging against Scott's ribs.

Scott grunts and shakes his head, pointing to his throat.

Jason moves his hands up to float over Scott's neck, never touching his skin.

Scott wheezes a bit, but tries to hold still. *This is it. He'll finally see it, and he'll figure out what to do,* which Scott thinks might be wonderful and also terrible.

"How are we going to get you out?" Jason asks, squinting as he addresses the thing directly.

"Hey, what about your feather? We could try to sweep it out." Scott believes it's possible, no matter how strange it sounds. *But still. Sweep what out? And where will it go?*

"No, we can't."

"Why not?"

"It's wedged in. It has hooks."

Hooks. Jesus, of course it has hooks—hooks that tether him down all the way back to that day, fix him there, making sure he can't forget. *Good.* If Jason can't get to it, he can hang onto it a little longer.

"You know," Jason says, his eyes still focused on Scott's neck. "I think I've been seeing this all wrong. What if...we stop thinking of it as something you have to get rid of? Maybe it's something you need to say. It's stuck in your throat."

Scott's heartbeat quickens as he watches Jason move to the counter. A moment later, he hears the *plink plink* of the crystals in the bowl. "Uh...what are you..." he begins nervously.

"Aquamarine, blue lace agate, and...lapis." Jason returns with three blue crystals in his hand. One is light and cloudy, another has irregular stripes of sky-blue, grey, and white, and the last is dark-navy with flecks of silver. They look as if Jason just got them out of the ocean, shiny and clean.

"What are those for?"

"Lay back, will you? I'm going to put these on your throat, here?" He places two stones low on Scott's neck. The last one goes in the dip between his collarbones. "That feel all right?"

Scott swallows, wondering if they will somehow act like magnets, pulling the heavy thing out of him for Jason to finally see. His heart is beating fast, and a prickle of sweat breaks on his forehead and under his arms. "Fine, I guess."

"Good. They aren't too heavy there? Or too buzzy or anything?"

Buzzy? "No. They're all right." Scott breathes in and out carefully so they don't slip off, and he finds that concentrating on staying completely still calms his nerves.

"I'm going to turn off the music so we can hear you better."

Wait. Wait Jason, hear what? The music fades, and soon they are alone in the silence.

"Okay now, here's your part. I want you to hum, okay? Like this. *Hummmmm.*" Jason's lips are closed, and the sound is a soft but strong monotone.

The heat in Scott's palms flares up. "What now?"

"The vibration of it will loosen things up in there, get the blood flowing. Try it. *Hummmmm,*" Jason repeats. He is eying Scott with that look, the one that says Scott's going to get on board whether he wants to or not.

Scott's throat feels scratchy inside, and a hum would probably come out sounding more like crackly static. He scrambles a bit, trying to come up with an excuse not to because, *seriously, what is this*? His voice is so weird-sounding. It would disturb the peace in here, and not only that, but what if it does loosen things up? What if that locked down, heavy thing breaks free and slips out, what happens then?

"Ugh, Jason, this is..." He almost says *stupid*, but that would be insulting, and also untrue. What he really means is *terrifying. Too hard. Too close.*

"Here, I'll do it with you. It'll be easier. You join in, right?"

"Uh. Right."

Jason hums that same note a third time and brings Scott's hand up to his throat to rest next to the crystals. Scott takes a shaky inhale, and when he begins, the vibration rumbles gently underneath. His hum disappoints, as he knew it would, fragile and full of holes.

Jason puts three fingers on the other side of Scott's neck and presses down gently, perhaps searching for the secret. "Nobody's going to hear you, Scott. It's just me. Try it again. Lower."

Scott doesn't know anything about singing aside from chorus in primary school, but trying for a lower pitch feels like a good idea. It's hard for him to know where to look. He chooses a wrinkle on the shoulder of Jason's shirt and concentrates as they inhale at the same time, with Jason nodding. Scott's throat likes the lower note better, and it starts out strong. There's a little throb of it in his fingers, but it fades quickly into empty air.

"That was better!" Jason says. "Why don't you close your eyes? That might help."

Scott wants to keep looking at Jason's shoulder because it's solid and strong and it helps him focus; he takes one last look and lets his eyes shut.

When it's dark, the task gets simpler. He hears Jason take a breath in, and he does, too, and out comes a sound that's steadier. Jason shifts Scott's hand away from his throat to the area right under Scott's ribs, the place where his breath expands.

"That was the best one yet. One more."

This time he is alone, but it's all right; the simple, steady sound he makes feels like it is starting to fill not only his throat, but his mouth and his cheeks and his sinuses and even the space behind his eyes. He lets it go for as long as he can, liking the feeling of being filled up with it.

"Ooh, that was weird," Scott says, a bit fascinated. The crystals on his throat are getting warm.

Jason smiles. "Good. Let's add a vowel sound now, properly open things up. How about *oooooooo*?"

Scott has a twinge of nerves. His mouth has to be open to make that sound. He giggles tensely, glad his eyes are shut. "Oh God, really?"

"Yes, really. It's either that or 'Disco Inferno.'"

"Ugh. Okay." He takes an unsteady breath.

The sound is timid, and his lips are tense around it, but soon Jason joins in, and Scott is buoyed by the help. It ends stronger than it began. That wasn't so bad; their voices actually blend easily and sound fine in this soft space.

"More?" Scott asks.

"Yes, more."

Scott is getting better at this, fast. It feels good to impress Jason, so he concentrates on getting a good breath to start with that makes his hands rise on his ribs. The next one is louder and has a sturdy sound, like he means it, and the one after has a nice round balance all throughout, and he gets that vibrating feeling in his cheeks and his forehead. When he lets it fade, the darkness he sees breaks up into two distinct shapes: sky and land.

He continues without being told; he knows this will be the way in this time. Making the sound becomes as easy as breathing. He exhales the round note, pauses, and then breathes in, watching the trees form as the sky gets lighter. Again, and the tops of the mountains appear with their peaks dark against the sky. Again, and the sky gets lighter still, the stars for the first time beginning to disappear into a sky no longer deepest black but cobalt-blue, the colour of the hour before dawn.

Does this mean the night is over? Does this mean my time in the valley is almost up?

"I see it, I'm going," Scott says, just before he loses touch with their room. The sound his voice makes floats through the trees, past the bird that is out there watching him, all the way to the sun that sits just beyond his sight. He calls out to the fire, too, as if it might hear him and answer back. When he spots it, he's relieved to see it's as strong and high as ever, taller than he is, so it can envelop him when he walks through.

*

Sounds come to Scott first, before the scents of candle wax and sawdust, before the sight of the walls made of marble and stone. Excited voices, all belonging to men and boys, chatter over one another. There are deep whispers as well as long, drawn-out notes in song that blend, falter, then blend again. The noise may be dissonant, but to Scott it is rich and lovely, and he feels at home inside it.

When he opens his eyes, he and the other choristers sit in a wide stairwell off the nave of the King's Chapel. They sit three or four to a step, with Scott and John at the top, a bit removed from the others. From here, the two of them can survey it all—Choirmaster Wydeville pacing on the landing in his long black robes, and all the choir with their crisply ironed cassocks, fresh-scrubbed faces, and combed hair. Excitement fairly shines all around them; the youngest are fidgety and getting louder while the older ones are calm, although Scott suspects they are putting on a brave face. None of them have sung in King's Chapel for an audience, after all, not even the oldest of them, Robert, who is nearly twenty and has been here ten years.

"The royal procession has been delayed, and we shall wait here until it arrives," Choirmaster Wydeville had told them over an hour ago, an eager cheeriness in his voice. Since then, the choir has gone from warmed up to cold and warmed up again, and most of them have made at least one trip out to the privy behind the gatehouse, on account of their boredom and nerves.

Of course, the king would be delayed; all manner of folk crowd the streets from London to Cambridge to catch a glimpse of the royal entourage as it makes its way to the newly completed chapel at King's College. The last of the stained-glass windows had been fitted two weeks since, capping the construction project begun long before their grandparents were born. Scott doesn't know whether to believe William, the lead tenor and infuriating know-it-all, who says it's been two hundred years in the building.

"Seems fitting we should have to wait a bit longer," John tells Scott with an easy grin that fails to soothe Scott's nerves.

There are many Johns among the choristers, but next to Scott at the top of the stairs is *his* John, and together they are JohnandGeorgie:

"Where are JohnandGeorgie? They will be late for vespers."

"JohnandGeorgie, this room is a proper sty."

"JohnandGeorgie, time for turndown."

Where there is one there is the other, and so it is here and now. His John is ever calm, his brown eyes warm, watching Scott tug restlessly at the prickly lace collar under his cassock.

Scott turns to him, knowing the question is pointless before he asks it. "How much longer?"

"When his majesty sees fit to grace us with his presence, and no sooner." John straightens Scott's collar, which has become bent with his meddling.

Stray notes bob and tangle in the air, and Scott can pick out some basses rehearsing a few measures from their complicated part in the Credo, and the other trebles are practicing the solo for the Sanctus. It makes him wonder about his chances and his competition. Master Wydeville picks the soloists at the last moment to keep everyone focused; the boy who has displayed the best pitch and timing on the day is chosen.

He knots his eyebrows. "Who will Master pick to sing the Sanctus?"

John smiles. "Don't be a dunderhead. 'Course it will be you. You know it best, and anyway, it's you who's got the sweetest voice of all the trebles, and the strongest."

His John is not one to bestow compliments easily, and Scott's chest grows warm. He folds his lips between his teeth to keep from grinning like mad, but he knows it is true. Vanity might well be a grave sin from which he prays every night to be delivered, but Scott cannot pretend he doesn't hear the tone in his own voice that makes it different from the others. It is clear, bell-like, with none of the weak vibrato or trouble with breath or power that afflict the rest, and many have told him he shall go far, though he is only twelve years old and his voice has yet to change.

Still, their audience today will be no less than the king, along with the queen and their courtiers, and the cardinal, too, with his holy retinue.

"What if I forget the words, or flat the *E*?"

"You won't, Georgie. Remember, come down on *top* of the note."

"Yes, that's right. Land on the *E* rather than climb to it." He nods, but looks again to John, still searching for reassurance.

The smile his John gives him eases Scott's worry and makes his heart thump. "Pretend you're singing it to me out in the garden." John chuckles. "Only, um, louder."

Scott finds he can chuckle about it too. "Louder" may not quite describe it; their voices will have to be enough to fill the vast expanse of stone and marble, with its vaulted ceiling so high the boys have to be careful not to fall over backward when they look up. At first, they were timid, used to the close quarters of the tiny side chapel where they could hear one another plain and close, each voice a separate string in the chord. Once they learned to project their voices to the far corners of the hall, Scott decided he had never heard anything so beautiful in his life. The rumbling of the men's basses is like thunder in a cloud, while bright tenors and trebles float in the air making the place, already magnificent with gold and marble, come alive with sound. He wants nothing more than to do this forever with John and Master Wydeville and the rest. That's what they will do, he's decided. He and John will live out their lives here, become full choir and then choirmasters and composers, working for the king and for God.

"Can we not get started, right away?" Scott swipes his sweaty palms against his robes, and John grabs the one closest to him, rubbing it with his thumb.

"Georgie, you will be fine. Better than fine. How can you not? You've practiced it five hundred times."

That is true. Scott practices the Sanctus while they walk to lessons, while they wash dishes in the kitchens, and, of course, at daily practice. He sings it in the privy and their sleeping room after turndown until one of their roommates, Nicholas, who is two years older and a bore, tells them to "Stop your squalling, dullwits!" So they do, unless neither of them are tired, in which case John will pull the coverlet over their heads so they lie with their noses almost touching and their feet entwined, whisper-singing in the darkness. It's usually John who recalls the pitch and timings best, reminding Scott of the harmonies as he sings the lead lines. Scott likes to hear the little rasp in his throat when John sings so softly. It lulls him to sleep more often than not, feeling the slip of John's mouth against his forehead before he turns so they can sleep spoon-fashion.

"One more time?" Scott asks him, and John nods with a little smile.

Scott is about to start when William turns around and knocks on Scott's knee. "You would do best to hope it will not be you, Georgie, for the Sanctus. You would be gone before nightfall."

"Shut it with your stories," John snaps at him, tightening his grip on Scott's hand. John is only twelve as well, but can forget that sometimes, like a spaniel puppy barking at a wolfhound.

William rolls his eyes. "Come now, John, don't be dim. The cardinal can do whatever he pleases, and the king can't stop 'im."

Scott watches colour rise in John's cheeks.

"We belong to the king. No one can take what belongs to the king. Everyone knows that, right Georgie?" John looks at Scott expectantly, but Scott isn't sure; there have been whispers among the boys for weeks about a time before any of them were here, when the cardinal took one of the older boys, the king's favourite singer, to have for his own choir at Christchurch. Where the story came from, Scott doesn't know, and he doesn't want to believe it could be true. Even so, Scott envisions the boy being plucked up from his desk, still wearing his vestments and carrying his music, to be carted away in a gilded carriage driven by the cardinal himself into a dark night, never to be heard from again.

John gives Scott a comforting pat on the thigh. "Don't listen to that rumpface. He just likes to hear himself talk. Now. Tell me what we shall have for dinner. I'm hungry."

John and Scott talk of how they might steal away a pudding to their sleeping room until the noise outside rises to a dull rumble, then to a rousing clamour with drumbeats and cheering. Master Wydeville turns to greet the messenger in the hall as the bells peal above them.

The choristers rise to their feet at once and scramble to the bottom of the stairs to form their lines. Master Wydeville only has to face them with one strong look to settle them; their preparations are over, and it is time to go to work.

"For the glory of God," Master Wydeville declares.

Twenty-six voices respond as one. "For the glory of God."

Their entrance song, "O Splendor Gloriae," sounds just like they've practiced, although they are finished too soon due to the lengthy procession that moves more slowly than they had expected. The cardinal is still approaching the chancel when the last line of the hymn is finished, and they watch in silence as he hobbles up to the elevated altar, using the arm of a younger priest for balance.

Scott does his best to concentrate on praying, but he can't help studying the cardinal as he reaches the celebrant's chair. To hear William tell it, this holiest of men should be hook-nosed and warty, like a witch wearing a black hood and a pack on his back, ready to stuff them inside. But he looks quite harmless with his powdery skin and weepy eyes. He has a thin white beard, and fine silver hair peeks out from under his scarlet cap. He wears a red cassock with a large golden cross that hangs low on his chest and bounces against it as he moves. Scott has never seen a man so old, or so obviously holy; even the king looks plain in comparison, in the first pew with his dotted ermine cape and dark-brown waistcoat draped with gold.

The cardinal offers his blessings in a weak, reedy voice, and the choir punctuates each with song. Then the psalms are read. The Gloria is fine and clear, and the Credo sounds rich and full, better than Scott has ever heard. Master Wydeville mimes with expressive eyes to remind them to keep breathing, stand up straight, and keep their throats and cheeks soft.

After the Kyrie, Scott wants so badly to whisper to John. His questions are piling up, and his John always knows the answers. Did you see the king's crown, John? What kind of gems are those? And what about the cardinal's rings? How they shine! Why is the queen sitting so far from the king? But his questions will have to wait. This is the holy liturgy of course, requiring silent piety, and John is too far away, in the front row with the rest of the altos.

The boys rise as one at their choirmaster's signal. This is it. The Sanctus.

Scott takes a deep breath and looks to Master Wydeville. *Please, pick me.* Scott places his finger on the first note on the page as if it is already decided, and waits. He hears the basses inside his head and uses them to find his own note, pulsing a whispered hum there.

Master Wydeville raises his arms to shoulder height, then turns his gaze to Scott. Their eyes lock for a moment, and Wydeville nods.

John, it's me. He picked me.

A tingle runs down his arms as Scott fixes his eyes on Wydeville's hand. On its downbeat, Scott begins.

"Sanctus." *Holy.* He is careful not to overpronounce the *S* sounds, or bring it up to volume too fast. He has one purpose, to let his voice be driven by the movement of the choirmaster's arm as if being played with an invisible bow, like a cello or a violin.

After a breath, the word repeats. "Sanctus." The timbre of Scott's voice is sweet but solid, and he pushes it more strongly out from his stomach instead of his chest. How good it feels to finally open his throat to set the sound free! The sun is shining through the ruby-reds and rich purples of the stained-glass windows; it is warm in here, safe, and so beautiful. This is surely where God lives, Scott thinks, though he knows his John disagrees. John says God is everywhere, outside and in, air and water and fire, all around them, always. But this is the house the king built for God, that took a hundred years to build, and Scott wants to fit here, become a part of its beauty, weave his voice into the walls and never leave.

Breathe. Plant my feet. Come down on top of the E.

"Sanctus." *Holy.* Goosebumps rise on Scott's legs with the power of the note, extended completely now to the full and true fortissimo his voice can reach. He meets Wydeville's eyes, which smile at him from their edges, and they go on together, two parts of a finely tuned instrument.

"Dominus Deus Sabaoth. Pleni sunt cæli et terra gloria tua." Lord God of hosts. Heaven and earth are full of thy glory.

Now, John. Sing with me.

The altos are the first to join him, and then the basses. Scott is just where he wants to be, their notes winding around one another with his at the centre. *Thy glory* rises over their heads, *thy glory* climbs the high vault above the altar, *thy glory* reaches all the way to the Crucifixion window where the outstretched arms of Jesus embrace them from the cross. His mum had told Scott that he was born for this, that he would make their name, and Scott does believe it; this is serious work, and the power of it makes his eyes water a little.

"*Hosanna in excelsis.*" The phrase ascends to a crest until the last bars, where the notes finally find a common chord. The power of their full harmony is stunning, and Wydeville's eyes shine when he cups his hands and brings the sound to a sudden close. He folds his hands to his chest as he mouths, "Amen."

Relief flows over Scott, the very best feeling of excitement and exhaustion and pride after a difficult job well done. Now he can drift through the Benedictus and their closing hymn, as neither is a challenge for him. His mind can wander again to dinner and celebrating, and then to the future, where he and John and their friends will fill this hall with song after song, beautiful notes and sacred harmonies as far as the eye can see and the ear can hear.

It is as if John can read his mind about it; he turns to face Scott, showing his back to the altar, something he's been reminded over and over never to do.

Scott's eyes go wide. *Face front, John, face front. What are you doing?*

But his John doesn't wear his usual fond smile. In fact, the look on John's face makes Scott feel like he's swallowed a hot rock that is burning its way down to his stomach. John's eyebrows crease, and his mouth is dropped open with worry. Is John...afraid? But that cannot be. His John is never afraid.

John, turn around now! You'll be sent to bed without dinner. But hard clarity rolls over Scott when he looks up to the chancel. The cardinal's eyes are on him as he leans to the priest next to him, pointing a withered finger Scott's way. The priest looks up to find Scott, too, listening to the cardinal's whispers.

Scott wants to hold his John's hand. He wants to pull him close and ask him another question, the most important one of all. His mouth is suddenly dry because the separation between them feels immense and final.

Is he going to take me away?

Scott knows the answer. He can read it on his John's face. There won't be pheasant with pudding tonight, there won't be turndown with his John beside him, there won't be a new song for them to sing together tomorrow or the day after or ever again. They will not walk this hall together as men.

I'm sorry. It's because I'm so proud. But I prayed, John, I promise you I did, not to be so proud, for God to take my pride away. But He didn't. Why didn't He? I wanted to sing beautifully. Mum told me God loves beautiful singing. But wait, don't worry. If I pray, He will take my voice away so I can't sing anymore, and then he'll have to send me back. He will send me back. That's what I'll do. I will pray so hard. You'll see.

The story unfolds all at once, inevitable, as if it is written into the very stones of this place. Scott will sing for the cardinal at Christchurch, and when his prayers are answered and his voice fails, instead of being sent back to Cambridge, he will be sent to Bristol to compose, and then to Canterbury to teach and direct. He will make his name with fame and wealth, as his mother had predicted, blessed by the God who Scott comes to know *is* all around them, everywhere, as John once said.

Still, Scott will look for his John in every face, in every singer, in every audience for the rest of his life, but he will not see him again. Scott will stay loyal to God who took his voice, as he asked. But it will always be his most bitter truth that God the all-powerful—God who parted the sea and resurrected His son after three days' death, who turns autumn to winter year after lonely year—never does answer the simplest and most fervent of Scott's prayers, the one he prays for decades that his John will find him and hold his hand again.

*

"Did you find the fire?" Jason's voice is low and pulls Scott back into the room, where the soft flannel sheets are the first sensation he feels. When his eyes drift open, Jason is looking down at him.

"Yeah. I did."

"Well done. Do you want to talk about it?"

Scott reaches up to his neck to touch the crystals resting there. They clink softly in his hand when he gathers them, and he leans up on his good elbow to study them carefully, as if they might hold the lesson he is supposed to learn. He sits up, a bit of sadness clinging to him, and tucks the blanket around his waist.

"I was just a boy this time. And I...did something that I thought was right. But it wasn't."

"I'm sorry," Jason says. But he doesn't push for information, and Scott is glad. Instead, Jason makes his way toward the counter. "You have a nice voice, you know."

"Hmm?"

"Your voice, it's nice. You *do* sing, don't you?"

Yes, I did, once. I sang with you.

The thought makes Scott's mind snap to attention, and it takes him a moment to catch up. *Wait, was that...did we?*

"Scott?"

The boy who sat next to me on the stairs. My John. The boy who believed in me. My John who I lost, because of my voice and what I did with it.

Scott rubs a hand over his forehead, confused.

"I used to. A little." He clears his throat. It's a bit mad, deciding which of his two pasts to tell Jason about. "Had a bit part in the year ten musical. But then I switched to the school newspaper." His voice sounds lower to his ears, older. Heavy with the weight of a different life.

"Ah, of course. Photographer and all." Jason comes back to the table with a bottle of water. "Let's do your needles now. Ready?"

Scott nods and trades the crystals for the bottle. He takes a few long gulps that run smoothly down his throat, the burning lump nowhere to be found. The wide open, beautiful chapel space is still fresh in his mind, along with his music book, and the faces of his friends, all of which he tries to commit to memory. But more than that, there is a feeling that lingers, a bewildering mix of excitement and pride tinged with what so quickly turned to loneliness and loss.

He looks at Jason curiously, on the off-chance that his half-mad theory might be true, that Jason might show some sign of recognition.

"Jason, do you...sing?"

"I do. Beautifully, in fact." Jason elevates the head of the table, giving Scott a chuckle and a shake of his head. "But only in the shower. Nobody needs to hear me sing."

I needed to. A long time ago.

Jason is oblivious, turning to take the paper envelopes that hold the needles from the counter. "All right, you can lean back now."

After he settles, Jason moves the blanket from his leg and rips open an envelope. They exchange a look that means they are both ready, and Jason taps the first needle into the thin skin at the top of his foot.

Scott finishes his water and takes a deep breath. That's five times he's walked through the fire. Five books with his name on them in the library, five files in the database, his "Akashic record" that he now has come to understand lives in his fire. Scott is still getting used to the vocabulary of this new system; while reading last night, he finally made friends with words that had once made him cringe, like "collective consciousness" and "universal mind." He'd also looked up definitions for a few terms that kept coming up: etheric record, dharma, and auric field.

Jason taps the second needle into the fleshy muscle near Scott's knee. "Doing all right?"

"Yeah, I'm good."

Then there'd been the part in the text that seemed to explain what might be going on in Jason's treatment room, the paragraph that Scott copied into his black notebook. It described the Akashic Records, made up of every lifetime of every being who ever lived, as the energy that holds the entire universe together. It's threaded through every piece of the cosmos, like the connective tissue in the body weaving through every tiny cell.

Hadn't Jason said something like that once, that events or memories could be stored within the body, and could be released so the brain could see them?

The next three needles go into Scott's wrist quickly, each with its own little burning bite, and then a fourth just under his elbow. Scott had thought they looked like antennae last time, and now he looks at them again, how they reach down below his skin to get at what is underneath. Didn't Jason also say that emotions could be held in the body too? That they could cause sickness or disease, but if they could be loosened, they could be free to go somewhere else where they would be useful? That when they were no longer welcome or needed, the feather could sweep them away?

His thoughts are interrupted when Jason takes his chin between his index finger and thumb and tilts Scott's head a bit, to look over the long scar on his cheek.

"That's looking really good. You're treating it?"

"Mm hmm. With Kelo, three times a day."

Jason examines it closely. "Nice," he says quietly and gives Scott another nod.

"How do you do that?"

"Do what?" Jason is focusing on the position for the last needle, the space between Scott's eyebrows. Their faces are close, and Scott notices the way his eyelashes sweep when he blinks.

"That thing you do. Your relentless...*hope*." Scott says it like it's a foreign concept he's never heard of before.

"Relentless," Jason repeats, and it looks like he is testing the word. "Nobody's ever called me that before. I like it."

Jason's smile makes Scott smile, too, and he suddenly knows that he *is* all right, feeling like he's on the cusp of something he's been dancing around for weeks. It's all starting to make the first bit of sense. Could it be that maybe he's not crazy? Maybe he's not sick? His arm is healing. His voice is strong. He's getting better. If Jason can see it, perhaps it's true. Maybe he has come out the other side of this; maybe he really could be ready now, to put that heavy thing down.

Could I?

The last needle goes in easily, with no pain, and Scott keeps his eyes open. His shoulders are relaxed, he's warm, and he can breathe easily, in and out and in again, with nothing compressing his throat. *Could this be it, the moment that changes everything? I could say it. All I would have to do is open my mouth and let it out.* Omran sits next to him in the cab looking out the window. Scott wishes he could see his face, and it makes his heart pound with nervous heat.

"So." Jason leans against the edge of the table next to Scott's leg and folds his arms. He is smiling.

"So." Scott tilts his chin up, trying to hide his nerves.

"How's your throat?"

Scott lets out an anxious chuckle. "Um, is this one of those times when you ask me a question and you already know the answer?"

"Maybe." Jason shrugs, then nods. "Probably."

It feels like I can breathe again. It feels like I might tell you everything. "It feels good."

"No pain? No congestion?"

Maybe it's something you need to say. It's stuck in your throat. Scott flexes his hands and looks down at his lap. "No, not right now."

"I thought so. Good. Keep your eye on it over the weekend, and let me know if anything changes." Jason comes closer and puts his hand up in front of Scott's throat with a questioning glance. "Can I feel here?"

Scott nods, and Jason's hand moves to the side of his neck, where his pulse would be. The fact that Jason must be able to feel his heart yammering makes Scott look away, down to the baseboard under the window. "Why would it change? I mean, didn't the crystals cure me? Or whatever?" Scott shakes his head, feeling a little silly saying it. "It feels fine, now. Truly."

"Cured? Um, no. They can help, but you're the one that has to do the curing." Jason takes a step back.

Damn. Scott doesn't have to ask how that's done. He swallows and bunches up the blanket in his fists. He catches Jason noticing, and he tries to play it off, but it's too late.

"Same rules as always." Jason's voice is reassuring. "Keep your jaw loose, hydrate, keep warm. Things are going to start to shift in there—" He points to Scott's throat. "—and when they do, it might sound funny, or it might be hard to talk or swallow. It might even hurt." He pauses, looking like he's having trouble figuring out how to say something. "Six months is a long time to carry something that heavy."

Scott chooses his words carefully and is deliberate when he speaks them. "I lost my voice once, Jason. It was a long time ago." *I loved someone. And I lost him.* He's thinking about his John, but he's thinking about Omran too. The stories cross over one another, and it's all a jumble of responsibility, guilt, confusion, and fucking bad timing, with his voice and what he does with it somehow in the centre of it all, again. He scrambles for a way to say it. "I don't know if I'll ever get this right."

Jason studies him closely with that curious, direct look, and it seems he somehow understands what Scott didn't say out loud. "But you *are* getting it right. You may not believe that, but it's true. I know you're working hard for this. Hang in there with me a little longer, yeah? We're close now. We're going to see this through."

His tone leaves no room for doubt, and his words carry enough determination that there's plenty for Scott to borrow.

"All right," Scott says. He meets Jason's confident gaze. "Let's see this through."

Chapter Eight

Noise (n.) Unwanted random variation in light or colour present in images, usually produced by image sensor malfunction or inconsistent film grain and likened to visual "static"; unwanted or meaningless data intermixed with relevant information; disturbance in an electric circuit that interferes with reception of a signal; a loud, surprising, irritating, or unwanted sound; any sound.

Scott does lose his voice.

It's a gradual process that starts small; there is a wheezing tickle he first notices when saying thank you to the cashier at the grocery Friday afternoon that gets scratchier as he spends Saturday filling pages in his notebook with drawings of King's College Chapel in Cambridge. His coughing gets more insistent through the day Sunday as he prints photos in the darkroom, and by dinner, his voice is a gravelly croak.

Hi, something's happening. Thought I should let you know

What's up?

My voice is just about gone

Excellent!

?? Yeah, not so much

Don't worry, this is good!

:/ I sound like I ate broken glass and chased it with petrol

Brilliant! Seriously, good news. I've got to hear this. Can I call?

Yes. I might have to talk in morse code though

Scott smiles and shakes his head. Of course Jason would think this is brilliant.

"Hello?" There is excitement in Jason's voice. Scott chuckles uneasily; this whole situation is suddenly terrifying.

"Are you there? Come on, let's hear it."

"Yes, hi." It's barely a whisper. Scott clears his throat again, to no effect. "I'm okay. Just through with dinner. I ate gravel and frogs." The words are half-formed, and they make Scott laugh again.

"Any pain?"

Scott clears his throat and feels the heavy lump. "No, it's just kind of tight."

"Wow, I'm impressed. That didn't take long."

"Three days. Is that good?" Strangely pleased, Scott picks at a stray thread unravelling from the seam of his jeans.

"Perfect. Sounds like things are shifting around in there."

"I guess?"

"So, it's not locked in anymore, yeah? But your throat is tightening up, squeezing down on it. Not quite ready to let it go, I think."

Scott knows that to be true, but he doesn't want to admit it, and he doesn't want to lie. He pivots just far enough away. "I'm worried."

"I'm not."

"What should I do?" It's just a whisper. Scott clears his throat and tries again. "What should I do?"

"A hot shower with some steam might do some good. Tea and other liquids. And keep your jaw relaxed. Sleep."

"But what if..." Scott closes his eyes and swallows. What if I can't fix this? What if I can't ever let this go?

"You'll be fine. Give it some time."

Scott snaps the thread and begins to pull it apart until it frays. "How much time?"

"That's going to depend on you."

Of course it does. Scott wants to say it'll be quick, he'll get right on it. *Don't worry, Jason, you can count on me.* But that means he'll have to—

"You know, this reminds me of something I read a long time ago. It was an article in some science magazine, I think... Anyway, there's this thing that happens, with caterpillars? They completely break down in the chrysalis, did you know that? I mean, *entirely* into mush before they change."

"Um, okay?"

"Just like you. Breaking down before something new can happen."

"Wait—" Scott tries to make his voice sound offended, but fails. "I'm an insect now?"

Jason laughs. "Yes, yes you are. Sorry."

"No, it's uh...weird, but I get it." Scott recalls the prints he's made of the film from the other night that are still drying in the bathroom.

"This is hard work, you know? But your body knows what to do. So. I'm not worried."

Even though Scott has his doubts, it's hard to argue with Jason's confidence. "I'll take your word for it."

"Do. And you're still up for floating tomorrow, yeah?"

A little blip of nerves flares up in Scott's chest. Their field trip. He's looked at the float centre's website four times, checked and double-checked the address and the route to get there, and committed to memory the FAQs, particularly: What effects does floating have on the body? Might I get bored or frightened? and Is floating successful for everyone?

Scott rubs his forehead and then pushes a lock of hair behind his ear. "Yeah. Meet there at one forty-five, right?"

"Right. And remember, probably best not to eat anything the hour before."

"All right. Thanks."

"And Scott, about your voice. If you want to talk? I mean, really *say* things out loud. To me, or...even just to yourself? That would help too."

Say things.

"All right," Scott says again. "Thanks."

"Take care."

Scott takes his calendar that stands propped up on his bedside cabinet, puts it on his lap, and takes the cap off the Sharpie. The marker makes a little squeak against the shiny paper as he marks off the day. His voice is croaky and dark. "You too."

*

In his dream, Scott has two healthy arms.

He looks down at his shirtless self, and his skin is smooth and tan. The sunshine is intense and close, and judging by the palm trees and puffy white clouds, this must be some tropical island.

Scott and Omran sit together in the shallow end of an outdoor swimming pool, the clean blue water up to their waists, talking and laughing and watching the kids that splash around them. Omran tosses them a beach ball as Scott looks over his shoulder to see Jason sitting on the edge of the pool, kicking his feet gently in the water. He leans back on his hands and tilts his face to the sun, drinking in its warmth and light. It's a hot summer day that smells lightly of sunblock and chlorine. The three of them are together, and Scott is happy.

Scott turns to Omran to properly study his face. He had forgotten the strength in Omran's steady gaze, and the way his eyebrows curve down at the edges. Omran's mouth moves, but Scott can't make out what he says. He's leaning in closer when he notices the little girl in front of them getting pulled off balance and falling in up to her chest.

The water feels colder suddenly, like a current has slid in around them, and they aren't in the pool anymore, but in the sea at a rocky beach. A grey wind picks up, bringing with it the menacing odour of the briny underbelly of the ocean. Omran points at a wave surging in the distance. Scott watches it for a moment but looks down when the water pulls so hard around his legs that he has trouble standing. When he looks up, the wave is gaining speed, growing impossibly fast and high, and he realises with cold alarm it is coming for them, and they won't be able to outrun it. He sprints toward land, but soon the rocks shift under his feet and the water slogs around his legs like mud. It's happening too fast. The roar of the wave gets louder and people are starting to scream.

But wait. *Omran.*

Scott left him. He has to go back. And Jason, where is Jason? How could Scott be so careless, so selfish? He turns to face the wall of green water three storeys high, with adults and children suspended inside it, ready to crash over them. Omran is getting ready to dive under, but it's hopeless, there is no time, it's too massive and heavy and there is nowhere to go. *Where is Jason?*

Scott's vision blurs from sea salt wind and crying. He hears himself scream, "No, *no*!" because God fucking *damn* it, not *again*, why, *fucking FUCKING GOD WHY*, and all he can do is close his eyes and brace for the—

*

"No!" Scott wakes with a jerk, his shout echoing in the dim room. "No, no…" he says weakly as he looks around, trying to recognise something. His eyes catch on the framed tree print on the wall, and then his desk with his black notebook and messenger bag hanging from the chair.

He collapses on his back, the dream still alive in his mind, making him shudder. Without turning his head, he reaches to the night table for his phone. Two thirty a.m. This hasn't happened in a while—a nightmare, a screaming, jolt-awake nightmare.

He wheezes out a dry cough and opens WhatsApp, then chooses Omran's name.

I fucked up again.

Scott stares at the screen awhile, wondering if all of this has come rushing back because he put the calendar down in Jason's bag. Maybe he shouldn't have done that.

It was a wave this time.

A huge fucking wave.

I couldn't stop it. I couldn't.

I'm sorry.

As his heartbeat slows, Scott notices for the first time that the flat is eerily quiet, and his ears aren't ringing. He can still hear the screams of the people at the beach, and the echo of his own "no" bouncing against the walls of the room, but beyond them, he can hear the hum of his refrigerator and the low buzz of the lamp. He can hear the rustle of his body against the sheets. He can even hear a lone car on the street beyond his closed window at this early hour.

But he listens for Omran's voice answering him, saying anything at all, and he doesn't hear a word.

*

"Do I have to put your phone number down? You're going to be sitting right here."

Scott and Jason are looking at the float centre's intake form, stopped at Emergency Contact. A few cups of tea this morning have smoothed Scott's voice to a quiet rasp.

"Nah, just put my name. They know me."

Scott nods. In fact, when he'd arrived, Jason had been behind the counter with the handsome, tattooed proprietor, talking animatedly as they gestured to the centre's computer. Scott was distracted from his jitters by a small twinge of jealousy when he saw they were close enough to brush shoulders. They were in their element, talking shop with their heads together, and for a second, Scott felt inexplicably out of place. But then Jason looked up and saw him, stepped around the counter, and said, without turning back, "Here he is, Drew. This is Scott." Jason's smile had warmed Scott from the inside, and the flutter of whatever that was folded up and retreated when they shook hands.

"Are you going to get a burger while I'm in there?" Scott asks, giving in to another layer of nerves.

"Nah, I'll be right here. No burgers for ninety minutes. Let's synchronise our watches." Jason looks up at him with a shrug and a smile. "Oops, I don't have one."

“I’m gonna be fine,” Scott says dismissively, though his hand shakes a bit as he moves on to the next set of questions with Jason looking on over his shoulder.

Do you have a history of, or are you currently experiencing anxiety, depression, PTSD, addiction, panic attacks, eating disorder or other emotional issue? He circles panic attacks, and a moment later, anxiety. He can feel Jason’s agreement, although he doesn’t look up from the sheet. *For fuck’s sake, this better be the last one of these I ever fill out.*

Two women sit across from them, sipping tea. Scott can hear their conversation plainly over the quiet music. One woman, who has an honest face and no-nonsense tone of voice is talking about how her migraines have all but disappeared since she began floating in April.

Scott leans in toward Jason. “Do you think that’s true?”

“I do. But everybody’s experience is different.”

A man comes out of the back hallway into the waiting area, his greyish hair falling in damp pieces over his ears. His cheeks are rosy, and he walks more quickly than his age would suggest, giving Scott a nod as he passes.

Scott signs the release section, agreeing that the float proprietor will in no way be responsible if Scott falls, slips, trips, drowns, faints, blacks out, or suffers a seizure or other medical emergency while on the premises. He had no idea so much could go wrong floating in just twenty-five centimetres of water; his knees wobble a bit as he walks up to the desk with the clipboard.

Jason must notice how he blows the air out of his mouth as he takes his seat again. “A bit nervous now?”

Scott looks around the room—at the ladies who are so at ease and the man at the counter, making another appointment. *If they can do it, it can't be that hard. Right? But.* "I guess I am, a little. It's...a long time."

"You can come out early if you like. Just do what you feel comfortable with. Do that breathing thing, to help you relax. You're good at that. And who knows, you might fall asleep. I do that sometimes. That'd be fine too."

The thought of getting relaxed enough to sleep in the float tank seems preposterous, and the possibility of having a nightmare makes Scott shake his head and pick at his fingernails. He clears his throat and turns to Jason, who looks more real somehow, out here in the world, than he does back at his office. Outside the confines of his treatment rooms, there is still some kind of power that wafts off him, made of muscle and skin that simmers under the shell of his clothes. Scott almost can't believe this is the same Jason who has seen and touched just about every inch of him, who has prayed over him and steered them through storms.

"Can I tell you something?"

"'Course."

Scott takes a breath. "I had this dream last night." Jason is interested in his dreams; maybe he will understand, or interpret it or whatever, and maybe Scott can get some of his nerves out if he says it out loud. Maybe Scott could ask Jason if it's true that, as a part of him suspects, the dream means that Scott is a terrible person.

Scott recounts it like an action sequence from a disaster movie with his weak, whispery voice. Sitting here now, he can see the pages he drew in his notebook of it, but also smell that sinister deep-sea scent and feel the devastating pull of the undertow. His shoulders curve over as if to brace against getting hit with the wave as he tells the last part, about how he turned his back on Omran, and could only wait for impact.

"And then I woke up, just before it hit."

They sit in silence for a minute, Jason making no move to respond, so Scott waits, loosely registering that the ladies are standing up and following Drew down the hall, leaving the two of them alone in the waiting room. The story of Scott's failure sits between them like a dark stone wall. Scott is content to sit behind it for now because he feels naked; he crosses his arms in front of him in an attempt to cover up.

Jason leans forward and puts his elbows on his knees. His voice is gentle, and his eyes are kind. "Something's coming, isn't it? You can feel it. It's big. And you can't run from it."

Wait.

The dream is about...the future? But Scott thought surely it was about the past, one more in a line of nightmares where Scott dropped the ball, was caught unawares, and fucked up royally, left to do nothing but watch Omran pay. Jason's interpretation has him rethinking it, and he rubs his damp palms against his jeans. There *is* something huge, something heavy rising out of his throat to slam him into the sand and leave him for dead or sweep him away, out to sea.

They sit together for only a minute, Jason waiting for Scott to respond, before Drew approaches them.

"We're ready for you now. Come with me."

*

After a stop at the restroom so Scott can have a quick wee ("And blow your nose while you're at it," Jason had suggested, so he does), the three of them meet in Scott's float room. Drew stands in front of them in what seems like a large, dimly lit bathroom with a shower in one corner and the float pod in the other. The pod itself might be something out of a science fiction movie, a bright white egg with water inside, and a lid that folds down on hydraulic hinges. It looks to Scott like a massive smiling clam, ready to eat him.

Scott takes in the instructions as Drew explains them, trying to keep it all straight. *Strip down, put in earplugs, shower, wash hair, no conditioner, rinse well, dry face, float.* He dips his fingers into the water, and it feels warm, but not hot. The humid air feels good in his throat.

"If there are no more questions, we'll leave you to it," Drew says, gesturing to Jason as if to sweep him out as well.

Jason puts up a hand. "I'll be right out."

"Sure." Drew nods, and the door makes a quiet click as he closes it behind him.

Scott smiles nervously, running his hand over the smooth edge of the pod's open lid. Jason moves the folding chair closer to the pod and lays a towel on the seat.

"Let's put this here, yeah? That way it's close by." He puts his hands on his hips. "So. Think you've got it?"

Scott takes a last look around. "Yeah. If you hear screaming, come running."

"Ha. Just breathe, like you do. The water will hold you. Really let your limbs go if you can, all right?"

“Right. Thanks.” They stand, shifting their weight, and it feels to Scott like some kind of send-off, where they might be standing in front of a train and Scott is the only one who will be getting on.

“Remember,” Jason says, uncharacteristically pensive. “You don’t have to stay in there the whole time. You can get out whenever you want to.”

Scott purses his lips and looks at the pod, then turns to Jason with a smile. The challenge rises up in him, as always where Jason is concerned, and now Scott can’t wait to show Jason how good at this he can be. He starts to unbutton his shirt. “See you on the other side.”

Jason smiles back and turns to the door. “I’ll be right out here.”

*

When Scott puts his earplugs in, the world gets farther away; there is still a mild ringing in his ears, but he can also hear his breath against the back of his throat and the click of his teeth as they clamp together. He can even hear the flannel scrubbing his skin in a new way. He is more inside his body than before.

He studies the pod as he steps out of the shower and pats his face dry. It feels strange, suddenly, that he’s going to climb inside and close himself in. He tries to think of the pod as something cool that the hero is born from, like in *Avatar* or *The Matrix*, rather than a coffin where a vampire hides from daylight, like *Bram Stoker’s Dracula*. He takes a few tentative steps toward it, but the open mouth of the pod grins at him in a way that makes him turn back to the changing area to make sure his phone is off and his jeans are hung neatly on the hook instead of getting inside.

The water will hold you.

His second approach is slow but steady. With one hand on the edge, he steps over and squats to sitting, lowering the lid part way as he goes. The water is slippery; he cups it in his hands, and his skin feels soft when it drips onto his thighs. He lies back carefully. When he stretches his legs, his bum rises off the pod floor, and his arms splay out for balance. He looks at his feet, toes bobbing at the surface, and *this is real, it's working*.

The ceiling of the pod is smooth white, and he closes his eyes for a moment. He pushes one heel down so he can touch the bottom, then lets it go to see what will happen. It pops up like a cork.

The button for the light is just a little distance from his hand. Scott can both feel and hear the thump of his heartbeat quickening as he pushes it. When the light disappears, the bright white walls of the pod do, too, and he keeps his hands against them for a minute more. *The water will hold you.* His head tilts back, his legs drift apart, and he closes his eyes. He doesn't have to swim, or tread, or paddle or think or try.

He is weightless.

*

Sometimes Scott feels as if he's drifting on the open ocean; sometimes he feels he's spinning and has to brace himself with his foot on the floor. He notices that his neck is tense, so he focuses there to let it go. When the light from the room that is visible through the open lid of the clamshell gets annoying, he sits up with a rush of water moving around him to shut the lid. This time when he lies back, he can't tell whether his eyes are closed or open. He blinks, and the black that envelops him looks the same either way.

Scott's mind does wander to everything—from the fact that he'll have to pick up more tea later because he's out, to that earworm of a song that came on shuffle on his way here, to how Jason looked at him before the float with excitement and concern. But Scott knows if something is going to happen here, he's got to stay in the moment, so he tries to bring his attention back to his breathing. When he falls into a comfortable rhythm, he adds the hum Jason taught him. It helps him tune in to the other sounds his body makes: the corkscrewy hiss from his hungry belly, the whisper-creak of his shoulder joints, and the steady drum of his heart. He hears the low vibration of his vocal cords, but also the soft, windy *whoosh* of air across them, two distinctly different sounds at the same time.

His new favourite spot is the nowhere-land where he can drift, with no thought to the breath that's gone or the next one that hasn't happened yet. He can live in the middle, limbs floating, throat silent. He has a fleeting hope that dots of starlight will break through the darkness so he can find his fire and cross to the other side, though that only happens when he's with Jason in the treatment room, with the smell of arnica surrounding them.

Scott thinks of the familiar balsam and orange now, in the pod, and he inhales deeply as if to smell it. He can almost feel Jason's warm palm resting on his bad shoulder and easing it gently under the water. Scott turns his head toward that feeling, glad for the company, even if it's just in his mind. The water closes over his scarred skin as Jason tells him about the difference between hearing and listening. Scott hums again as questions drift and bob in his mind. *What am I listening for? What if I don't recognise it when it comes? What if I don't understand?*

"Your body understands," he hears Jason say softly. "Your mind doesn't have to."

That's right. My body understands. That makes perfect sense and reminds Scott of something else he knows, something he recently learned that he can't quite recall. Still, it's a piece of the puzzle that shifts and settles into place.

The heavy warmth of a stone rests on his shoulder, holding it under the water and making his arm loose and relaxed. A not-altogether-rational worry tickles his thoughts, about whether the fire could appear for him even though he's in a pool of water, but fades when he imagines Jason's fingertips tracing his eyebrows, a movement that makes Scott's jaw drop away from his cheeks and his mind blur.

It isn't the night valley that appears in the darkness behind Scott's eyes, but a person. It's a man with short, curling dark hair, dressed in a green coat.

Scott gasps.

"Salaam alaikum."

That voice—that lovely, rich voice Scott has hoped to hear for months—it's right here, not coming in through his ears, but from inside him and all around him somehow, new, and yet so familiar. The sound makes tears sting his eyes.

"*Wa alaikum as-salaam.*" The shapes of the words are flat in his mouth from disuse, but they feel beautiful to Scott all the same. He listens, afraid to breathe.

"Ah, you remember, *rafiq*! But what's wrong with your voice? You're sick?"

Rafiq. Friend.

It's dark in here, blacker than any black Scott has ever seen, but Omran's low, accented voice paints a picture Scott sees brightly, of brown eyes behind glasses and a smart, tilted smile.

Scott scrambles for an answer as tears leak from his eyes. "Omran, I'm..." *My friend, thank you, I miss you, I need you, I'm here, I'm alive.* But. There is a shadowy layer underneath all of that, that Scott needs Omran to understand.

A long outbreath, an open door, and an inhale that shakes. "I'm a fucking mess."

Scott's throat clamps down on the next sentence before it can make its way out. He coughs around the words instead, the ugly sound bouncing off the pod walls. Scott clears his throat and tries again, but the words won't come, the words that he has typed countless times into his phone late at night, screamed drunk in the shower, whispered to Omran in his dreams.

The pod gets quiet again, and Scott can't stand the silence.

Are you still there? Please, don't go.

"We told stories together, didn't we?" Omran's voice is a cloud that fills the pod, and Scott breathes it in; he resists the urge to reach a wet hand up to touch it with his fingers. More tears slip into the water.

"Yes, we did."

"And now you have another story to tell, that's all."

How does he know that? Scott's eyes look blindly out into the dark. He sniffs and clears his throat. "Yes." The word sounds uneven and weak. "But I...I can't tell it."

"We'll do it together, *rafiq*. Just like before. Let's tell a story."

Then they are sitting in a hotel pool on a sunny summer day, a large inflatable ball bouncing off the surface of the water in front of them.

"N-no," Scott stutters, panicked. The sun here is too bright for his eyes, with no time to adjust. He squints and stands up, turning to see the blurry shape that is Jason sitting at the pool's edge, unaware of the danger. They have to leave, right now.

"We can't stay here." Scott's voice rises. "It's not safe. There's a—"

"Wave, I know." Omran is too relaxed, pointing casually to the horizon. "It'll be here soon."

As if on cue, the sky fills with grey clouds and the wind picks up. The clean, shallow pool is gone; Scott looks down to see rough seawater rush around his legs. *No, no, nonono.*

"Omran, stand up. Please, please, we have to go, now, or else—" He turns to Jason and shouts. "Jason, we have to go!"

But there is only an empty shoreline. *Fuck.*

"No, not again. I can't do this again, please." Scott's limbs are clumsy with desperation and adrenaline. When he tries to take Omran by the arm and pull him up, Omran holds his shaking hand still.

"We're going to dive, *rafiq*."

"No, *no*!" Scott's plea is carried away by the wind that smells like salt and dead things. *No, no, it's coming, it's too big, it's too fast*. The ringing in his ears is an urgent alarm. This is his moment, his chance to fix everything, and Omran won't listen. "I'm not going to fucking let you die here!" Scott turns to the horizon where the wave is already swelling. "Fuck, now, now, come on, *please*, come with me!"

"Listen." Omran's hands are on Scott's shoulders, gripping him square and tight like a child. "We're going to go under. Do you hear me?"

Fucking madness fuck no NO *not again I can't I can't wake up again and face it don't you see it's fucking coming!* And it is coming, already three metres tall and climbing. Scott can't catch his breath. *Jason, I can't breathe. Where is Jason?*

"I can't, I can't."

"You can," Omran says. "That's where you'll find it. You'll see."

Scott hears the first scream, a woman's, followed by those of men and children. The rising water is roaring closer, and the wind begins to whip around them. Ears ringing, heart pounding. It's so goddamn *loud*. "No, this is my last chance, please, please!" Scott is full out crying, and his knees are weak from fear.

Omran's hands hold his cheeks, forcing Scott to focus on him. "We've got to get underneath it. We'll dive low." He pauses, his brown eyes fierce. "Surrender to it. We'll let it roll over us, yes?" Omran searches Scott's face and studies his long scar for a moment, his thumbs wet with

Scott's tears. "There is something down there for you. We're going to go get it. Are you ready?"

The magnitude of what is owed hangs between them. The resistance drains out of his shoulders. Omran is asking him for something.

Trust.

They look up at the wall of blue-green water as big as a building, with a frothy white peak just beginning to crest. Bodies are carried like driftwood inside. Fiery red anger rises up in Scott at this monstrous, evil thing, making his fists clench and his legs lock with newfound strength. The noise is deafening, and Scott roars back at it, cursing it out.

His anger burns away the fear, leaving only sharp focus. There is barely enough time to lock eyes with Omran, and they breathe and count together, three, two, one, and *push*; Scott inhales so deeply his lungs burn and he uses every bit of strength in his legs to dive forward and down, clean through the cold face of the wave.

*

It's as if a door has been slammed, leaving the chaos on the other side.

Scott thought it would be rough under here, churning water throwing him around like a rag doll in a washing machine, and he was all set to fight it. But his furious strokes and desperate kicks slow and stop when he realises he doesn't have to work so hard.

Actually, he doesn't have to work at all. The burning in his lungs is gone. The ringing in his ears, the furious pounding of his heart, it's all vanished. The wave has passed right overhead just like Omran said it would, leaving him drifting in peace where the only sound left is his breath.

Breathe, like you do. The water will hold you.

There are no bubbles, no heavy feeling in his lungs, nothing, he's just *breathing*. It's easy, and he feels light as he looks around this new world of beautiful crystal-blue. There is a sandy floor underneath him, and when he looks up, the surface glimmers far in the distance, lovely sunbeams dancing on it. *The storm must be over.*

"Omran?" Scott's voice is strong.

"Nice dive."

"Where are you?"

Scott is alone, but not; Omran is above, and below, inside and out.

"I'd give you a ten for difficulty. And a four for execution."

Scott's heart is buoyant. He made it, and Omran is not only still here, but he's taking the piss. "Bullshit! That was at least an eight. I was terrified." Scott looks around. The crystalline stillness of the place is captivating. He's never seen a blue so beautiful.

"Now the real work begins, *murshid*."

Murshid? Scott rolls the word over in his mind, and can't place its meaning. He tucks it away for later. "What do I need to do?"

"Find your camera. Do you know where it is?"

Scott is surprised by his own answer. "Yes. I buried it." It's there, in the sand up ahead, where beams of sunlight point like a beacon in bright glowing lines.

He moves smoothly through the water, breathing comfortably, straight to the spotlit mound of sand. He thought it would be cold here, and dark. He thought he would suffocate under the terrifying weight of it all. But he's not frightened; he kneels and begins to dig.

The sand is light and grainy, falling away easily when Scott pushes it aside. His hands make shovelling motions to scoop it away when it gets muddy underneath, and it isn't until his forearms disappear into the hole that he starts to worry. What if it's not here? What if his mind is playing tricks on him, and he's buried it so deep he won't be able to find it? A faraway memory sneaks in, of that dream of himself at the bottom of a hole with a shovel in his hands and tears in his eyes, and Jason calling to him from above. He looks up at the surface again, where the sun is shining. He can't go up empty-handed.

"Omran?" Scott says out loud.

"Yes?"

Scott sighs and sits back on his heels. "Am I in the right place?"

"Always." Omran's voice is deep and clear, and Scott can feel the power of the word as well as hear it.

Scott stares at the empty hole. A part of him wants to call bullshit. But he can recall Omran's commanding look, his unspoken demand for trust.

He gets back to it, still doubtful, but re-energised. It takes just a few more rakes of his hands before the tips of his fingers catch on something. His heart kicks inside, and his pulse rushes in his ears. That's the deep brown colour he remembers.

He digs around it almost frantically, as if the thing is suffocating under the sand. He might be saying words, or cursing apologies as he sweeps the sand away and exposes the body of the bag. He pulls on the straps, the sand shifts around it, and with one more strong yank, it's his.

The bag is bigger than he remembers but as familiar as an old shoe. There are nicks and scrapes on the body, and his ID tag hangs off one of the shoulder straps. He runs a shaking finger affectionately over the peeling British Airways sticker. He had forgotten about that, and had forgotten how the zipper on the largest pocket is missing its pull. He traces the edge of a tear in the fabric, suddenly protective of this part of himself that for months he couldn't bear to face.

"I got it." Scott's arms are trembling, but he hugs the bag to his chest, feeling the hard pieces of the camera shift inside. *Safe and sound* in this peaceful place, with Omran watching over them.

"Now, *murshid*, what are you going to do with it?"

Scott looks up to the surface. Sunbeams filter through in shifting patterns that call him. Jason is up there. The pod is up there, too, and his flat, with its makeshift darkroom and framed tree. And there is Jason's place. A soft, warm table. A white feather on a red cloth, a dish of coloured crystals. A plush leather holdall that has a deep, dark mouth and a gold zipper.

"I don't...want to let you go."

There is nothing for a time, only the grainy sound of sand shifting under Scott's knees.

"Did you get what you came for?" Omran's low voice is light.

Scott considers the backpack in his arms. He takes up a handful of sand and lets it fall through his fingers. "Yes, but..." He almost doesn't ask. It's wrong, isn't it, asking Omran to give anything else after all Scott has taken from him?

"Can I sit here awhile with you?"

He knows, right then, in the moment Omran says "yes," that the work he thought was finished has actually just begun.

*

The overcast afternoon light in the float centre's waiting room is too bright for Scott at first, making him squint and look at the floor.

This moment feels like stepping out into a bright summer day after spending two hours lost in the dark cool of the cinema; his movements are cautious and slow, but his brain feels sharp and his senses supercharged. The world he is coming back to seems different than the one he left. The room that was shades of muted sepia now pops in vibrant colour. Chairs and pillows that were soft before are now plush, and the sounds of voices and music are crisp and vivid. Even the air smells sweeter.

He is vaguely aware of Drew behind the reception desk, speaking on the phone, and two other patrons seated on the small couch. A few more steps forward and he finds Jason, in the same chair he'd occupied before the float, only now he's bent over at the waist, head hanging between his shoulders, his elbows resting on his parted knees. He is studying his palms as he rubs them together slowly, pursing his lips.

He'd had no doubt that Jason would be here, but still, the sight of him alone and quiet and curled over himself makes Scott's chest heat with a tender pang of relief. He doesn't know what to say, doesn't know if his voice will work. He walks toward him, clearing his throat.

"Hey," Jason offers, rising. He is just like the rest of the room. Crisper, brighter than before. Scott notices the reddish tint to his stubble and the concern in his eyes.

"Hey."

"You did it."

"Mm hmm." Scott's voice is weak and whispery, nothing like the full voice he had in the pod, and it sounds strange to him now, unlike himself.

Jason tilts his head. "Ninety minutes wasn't too long after all?"

"No, it was just right. But you, you sat here the whole time?"

"Yeah." Jason glances quickly at the chair, then back. "Well, I might have paced a bit." Jason rubs his palms together as if he's nervous or trying to keep them occupied. Scott hopes Jason will do that thing he does during their post-appointment checks where he feels for tension under Scott's jawline and takes his pulse. He takes a small step closer, to make it easy in case Jason wants to, and realises his own hands are hot and tingling.

"How do you feel?"

"Oh my God...incredible." Scott feels like he's had a good workout, a good cry, and a good nap all at the same time, and he knows his face shows it. He's a bit self-conscious about it, and about his hair, still wet and stringy in its bun. But he is strong, too, sturdy in a way he hasn't felt in ages. And a bit proud, if he's honest, for making it back.

"Yeah?"

"Yeah. It was good. I kept bumping against the sides, and feeling for the bottom?"

Jason nods, handing him a water bottle that was stashed on the neighbouring chair.

"And it was so dark, I couldn't even tell whether my eyes were open or closed."

Jason nods again, bright-eyed. "Amazing, right? No signal in, nothing for your brain to work on. Right where you want to be."

"And the water was warm, you know? It held me up." There is hardly any sound coming out of Scott's throat, the words just formed with breath, but they keep coming. He has to gesture with his hands to really get his point across, as if Jason might not understand. "I thought I was relaxed? And then something would let go, and then I thought I was relaxed, and then something else would let go, and..." This isn't about impressing Jason anymore, it's just the truth. "That was good. I feel really good." Staring at Jason's understanding smile, Scott realises it's not the room that has changed. He has.

Jason starts to walk, breaking their gaze long enough to wave and say a quick thank you to Drew.

"Come back, all right?" Drew says, holding his hand over the phone.

"I will," Scott says, nodding, and although it's all but silent, Scott means it sincerely.

They break out into the world together and stand on the pavement, making no move toward the tube.

"You know, it didn't feel like sensory deprivation though? I mean, I could still feel things. And hear?" *And smell, and touch.*

"Like?"

Scott thinks back. "My body is really loud?" He breathes a silent chuckle, and Jason laughs too. "I liked the feel of the water on my skin. And I thought I smelled arnica." He doesn't mention how he could hear Omran's voice. Or how he could feel his camera bag safe in his arms again, feel the straps tight around his shoulders when he put it on to take it with him. Those things he wants to keep for himself. For now.

He changes the subject. "And remember the dream I told you about?"

"The big wave?"

"Right. I got a do-over."

Jason looks pleasantly surprised. "All right then. Did it turn out differently the second time around?"

Scott shakes his head like, even as he's telling it, he can't quite believe it himself. "Yeah, we uh... I figured out what I have to do. At our next appointment." He meets Jason's eyes, which look at him openly and without judgment. Their blue reminds Scott of someplace safe. "I have something to put in your bag."

The moment feels transparent somehow, a hurdle they've been waiting for that they've finally cleared, and Jason's eyes crinkle as he smiles. It seems utterly fitting that Scott's stomach should pick this moment to growl loudly, making them both laugh.

"Oh, you must be starving. It's almost four," Jason says.

Scott still has his unopened water bottle in one hand, but that won't do at all; it's got to be a burger or a big plate of curry, and it's got to be fast. His mind skips ahead, landing on a picture of himself at an actual table and eating with Jason. It would be brilliant. There is so much more Scott wants to tell him, though truthfully, Scott wouldn't mind if they just ate and didn't talk at all. He can feel the timer ticking on their field trip, and he isn't quite ready for it to end.

"Yeah, can we get a bite? Or seven courses? I'm about to eat this lovely shrub."

Jason laughs, tosses his head toward the west end of the street, and starts to point. "Yeah, there's a...nice..." But then his face falls abruptly. His mouth is still open when he turns back to him with a look Scott doesn't recognise.

Evidently the end is closer than Scott thought. "You probably have to go back to work, don't you?"

"No, it's just that..." Jason's mouth twists, and his hands land on his hips.

"Oh, wait, that's right, patients and doctors can't, like, socialise, or whatever?"

"Right." Jason nods, looking at his shoes for a moment. His face is open and direct when he faces Scott again. "There's a line. If I crossed it, it would be wrong."

Scott's cheeks burn along with his throat. "No, I totally get that."

"There's a soup and wrap place I always go to after. They have good coffee too. Just down a block, and turn right on Warwick. You can't miss it."

"Oh. All right, then." Scott starts to back away, jerking a thumb in that direction.

"I'll see you on Thursd—"

"Thanks for coming wi—"

They both talk at the same time, and a new, uneasy energy rattles between them. Scott feels like they've gone off course, and he is the one who led them there. But Jason holds his hand out as usual, ready for their customary goodbye handshake.

Scott can't push down the urge for Jason to touch him any longer. He does take Jason's hand, locking their eyes for a moment, before he pulls Jason into his chest and wraps his other arm around his back. They hug, shuffling a bit, with Scott's chin tucked into the hollow of Jason's neck. Jason feels stiff in his arms, but Scott doesn't mind because it's real, Jason's hair tickling his nose and his chest warm and solid pressing against him. He squeezes a little tighter before he begins to pull away, but Jason holds on.

"So it was good, then?"

"Yeah." Scott releases his breath with a sigh. He remembers the wave, the fear, the crystal-blue world below, the good feeling of his camera releasing from its grave in the sand. He remembers how, when he was ready to come back, he had pushed off the ground and swum up through the water that was not water toward the light. Omran had been all around him and inside too. *I heard him, Jason. And he heard me.* "Thank you."

Jason's fingers press between his shoulder blades, then there is a pat-pat, the signal that they should part. Pulling away feels gentle, and their eyes don't skip past each other but, instead, settle together carefully.

"Thursday," Jason says plainly.

Maybe this is what dawn breaking in the night valley means. He's turning the corner now that he's got his camera again; he can almost feel its phantom straps over both shoulders, the way he used to wear it in the field. The tightness feels good, pulling him up so he stands up tall. He feels fitted out, prepared, ready for what's coming next.

The end of one thing and the beginning of something else.

"Thursday," Scott repeats.

*

That night, when Scott falls into bed, sleep comes easily. He dreams of a country road cutting a swath through pretty green fields, and Scott knows before he looks that Jason is in the passenger seat with his map, navigating them to Land's End.

"How much longer, do you think?" Scott asks.

Jason traces the map with his finger. "We're getting close. It'll be soon."

The sun is still high in the sky, warm on Scott's arm that rests in the open window. When they get there, to the coast, he'll see the rocky beach for the first time, and maybe they'll swim. It's a perfect day.

Jason turns the old Volkswagen's radio on, and twists the tuner knob to find a station. Static channels slip by, with a piece of a song or a newsy voice.

"Where is it?" Jason mumbles.

"What are you looking for?" They're coasting again, Scott notices, with no pedals on the floor and his hand off the wheel.

"You."

That's funny, and Scott chuckles. "I'm right here."

"No, your voice, silly." Jason closes his eyes and tilts his head a little, listening closely as he continues to turn the knob. "It's here somewhere. I'll find it."

Right, of course. Jason will find it. Scott smiles to himself, feeling lucky. Lucky to have a car that drives itself. Lucky that he remembered to bring his camera and a towel. Lucky to be on this trip with Jason, who time after time sits right here, no matter how long the ride, and helps Scott get everything back that he lost.

"Hey, did you ever figure out what that word means?" Jason asks, his eyes still closed.

"What word?"

"That word Omran said, in the float. How do you say it, myr-*sheed*?"

Scott likes hearing Jason's voice say it, with deep vowels and a soft curl on the *R. Murshid.* He smiles. "I did. It means 'teacher.'"

Chapter Nine

> Resolution (n.) The number of pixels, both horizontally and vertically, used to either capture or display an image; the process of resolving something such as a problem or dispute; the disappearance or coming to an end of a medical symptom or condition; the firm decision to do something; the answer to a problem.

Scott looks away from Jason's book and checks his phone again for the time. One oh-eight.

It's Thursday, and he's in Pearl's, a café a few blocks from Jason's office. He'd spent the morning trying to keep occupied with nervous, half-hearted chores in his kitchen and darkroom, but at half eleven, he finally gave up, took his camera bag, and left. That put him in Stratford with over an hour to spare, so he ducked into the place when he spotted an empty table through the window. He'd had to repeat his order to the waitress since his voice was barely there: a bowl of chicken and rice soup and, though their version barely resembles the real thing, a cup of chai to go with it.

The lunch crowd hums as Scott remembers how the flavoured tea was made in Afghanistan, creamy with milk and warming spices. His first sip had been a revelation, and after, Scott thought perhaps he'd be happy drinking only chai for the rest of his life. That was in Mazar-e-Sharif, the day he and Omran first met.

They'd set up a meeting in the busy restaurant next door to their hotel. Omran came highly recommended, with an accomplished and diverse résumé that had Scott more than a bit intimidated. Scott had aced his Rosetta Stone crash course in Pashto, though, which he thought should count for something. His worry faded only slightly when Omran sat across from him, handsome in a slightly rumpled way, wearing jeans and glasses and well-worn shoes. Their small talk went well, buoying Scott's confidence, and when the waiter came, Scott offered to order their first course. He chuckles to himself now, recalling how his brain froze when he opened the menu and couldn't understand a word. It was written in Dari, not Pashto, and there were no pictures to help; Scott cobbled the order together as best he could as Omran nodded encouragingly, though the waiter gave them a strange look. Minutes later, their food arrived, a plate of sliced raw onions alongside a bowl of pickled lemon. Omran ignored Scott's dismay, chatting easily as he swallowed three crunchy bites of onion, tears leaking from his eyes. His kind laughter broke the ice, and over a delicious second course Omran chose of thick lamb stew with naan, garlic yogurt, and chai, Scott realised they might actually become friends.

Scott looks down into his half-drained teacup, wondering what Omran would think of—

"Donkey piss," says Omran's voice in his ear before Scott even finishes his thought.

C'mon, it's not that bad, Scott thinks back to him. The reply is a smile, and Omran's eyebrows lift behind his glasses.

Scott had been sure he'd lost the deep, friendly sound of Omran's voice for good, but now it's with him whenever he needs it. Since Monday, when he'd heard Omran's voice in the float, it's been *what would Omran think of this photograph? What would Omran say about my flat? Or this busy street I live on?* And there'd been answers each time, even if it was just a wink or a few words:

"Nice contrast."

"Cosy."

"I can see why you like it here."

What would Omran think of my notebook? The painter, or the medic? The runner in the woods?

A warm chuckle; "This is, how do you say it? The tip of the iceberg."

Scott felt Omran right there with him when he walked away from the float centre on Monday with his phantom camera bag tight over his shoulders, plans already beginning to form. He thought about the idea with Omran beside him all through his meal and his tube ride home.

And whether it was because of some newfound courage left over from the float or Omran's voice in his head, it wasn't thirty seconds after he arrived at his flat that Scott found himself standing in front of the hall cupboard. His hand trembled a little on the doorknob, but there the camera bag sat, alone and harmless on the shelf. There was no digging this time, no hard work, no doubtful questions. All he had to do was reach up and take it. The hair on his arms pricked with goosebumps when he held it again, the weight of it pleasant and familiar, and he sat on the bed awhile with it on his lap.

Scott keeps looking at the camera bag now, as if to make sure it won't disappear. When he was working, his routine was to put it under the table between his feet. But today, he doesn't want to let it out of his sight, and there is something disrespectful about letting it touch the floor. Twice, he has moved the chair it sits on to be closer to him, and there has been only one close call, when a man in a business suit with a boxy briefcase bumped the chair on his way past, which made Scott spring out to protect it.

The lunch crowd is thinning; Scott checks the time again. One fifteen.

He slides his phone open and taps on the messaging app. The top thread in the list is Ken Browning from the Associated Press, received yesterday afternoon.

> *Haven't heard from you, mate. Job in Brussels, mid-July. NATO Conference. Available?*

Scott had had to take a minute to think before answering.

> *Recovery slower than I thought. (His thumbs had shaken, typing his reply, but more from excitement than fear.) Shouldn't be long now. I'll ring you when I know something.*
>
> *I'll keep you in mind. Cheers.*
>
> *Cheers.*

That's been the plan all along, hasn't it, to get back to the job? A piece of the old exhilaration comes back when Scott thinks of it; he'll be breathing new air, sleeping in different beds, walking on strange pavements in unfamiliar cities.

But it's terrifying too. Making his way to the gate for an aeroplane seems like something only other people do. Brave people. People who can move freely and have nothing to hide. He suddenly feels like an imposter of himself, pretending, sitting here with a camera bag that holds the pieces of his old life inside.

Scott clears his scratchy throat and the tickle turns into a cough. He thinks he can feel Omran, who had just been here with him a second ago, pulling away.

Under Ken's thread is Olivia's, asking him how the float went, and under that is Jason's from Monday evening.

Still feeling good?

Yes, tired now though

Makes sense. You worked hard today.

?? Floating didn't seem too tough. :)

Trust me. It was. So don't forget your water. And get some sleep.

Will do

Thursday, yeah?

Thursday

Goodnight.

Goodnight. Thank you again for coming with me

You're welcome.

Scott takes another sip of his now cold chai. The faint cinnamon and cardamom spice linger in his mouth, tasting better when he thinks of Jason.

Their text exchange had been direct and to the point, thankfully. Scott still felt odd about the way they'd parted after the float. There is one piece of it all that he can't shake. What, if anything, he should feel about the way Jason had held on to him, pressing his fingers into Scott's back, hugging him close for a few extra moments? It was probably nothing. Jason was right when he'd said there is a line that shouldn't be crossed. But still, it had felt good when the initial stiffness in Jason's hug had softened, to be that close to him before they'd gone their separate ways.

One twenty-one.

Scott can see the grassy edge of Forest Lane Park through the window, just down the street. It's the park where Jason had given a gold ring back to the world, where Scott imagined a lucky little brown bird flying away with it in its beak.

He shifts in his chair and stretches his legs; the seat is getting hard, and he needs to get up and walk. Turning away from the window, he begins to gather his things.

*

Jason's treatment room is light with afternoon sun. It smells fresh, like green herbs and warm towels just out of the dryer. Or maybe it's Jason who brings that scent in with him as he shakes Scott's hand and puts his files down on the counter. He's casual, as expected, in a short-sleeved shirt and joggers; his fringe is down, and his beard is two or three days old. It looks to Scott as if he hasn't had much sleep. But Jason's eyes are alert and studying him, the exam starting already.

"How are you, Scott?"

Scott rocks on his feet and folds his arms in front of him, easing into the comfort of Jason's curious gaze sweeping over his face and his neck. He tells the truth in a scratchy voice. "I'm really good today. You?"

"Perfect." Jason nods before his head tilts toward the counter where Scott's camera bag and Jason's holdall sit side by side. He turns back to Scott with his palms up, his gesture that asks if he can touch. "Pain anywhere?"

Scott doesn't have to think, or lie, or conjure up some way to dance around it. That feels good too. "No. None."

Jason's fingers press under Scott's ears and down his neck. "And your throat?"

"Doesn't hurt. But it's, well. You can hear." Scott's voice is uneven, and sometimes the beginnings and ends of his words are just whispers. He clears his throat quietly but doesn't want to dwell on it. "So," he begins. "There was this guy who went to the doctor, right? And he says, 'Hey doc, I think I'm losing my memory.'"

Jason shoots him a wary look and presses his lips together. "Oh, really?" He reaches for Scott's wrist, unfolding it from where it rests.

"Yeah, really. And the doctor says, 'When did that happen?'"

Now there's a real smile, with a bright play in Jason's eye. "And the guy says..."

Scott smiles, too, hoping his voice holds up for the punchline. "When did what happen?"

"Pssh." Jason shakes his head with a chuckle. "Tell Thomas that's a good one." He's still grinning when he turns Scott's hands over, examining his palms and kneading his fingers. "Warm today," he says mostly to himself. "Good."

There's nothing quite like making Jason smile. But the camera bag is taking up a lot of space on the counter, and Ken's text is still on his mind. "Can I ask you something?"

"Of course."

"So...how do we know when I'm better? I mean, do all of you doctors get together and, like, have a committee meeting and decide?" Scott pictures all of them sitting around a conference table comparing notes, then banging a gavel with a vote. But that wouldn't be right; his ophthalmologist already released him, and the burn unit, too, but Brenna told him they'd be working together for at least four more weeks. As far as he's seen, there aren't any X-rays or other machines here at Jason's to measure anything. It makes Scott wonder what kind of notes Jason writes about him in his tablet.

Jason points to the tree picture on the far wall, and Scott looks there. "No, no meetings. It won't be us who says. It'll be you." Scott stares at the tree, seeing for the first time the way its petals go from pink to purple, and how the dotted highlights on the branches look like snow. Jason's thumb is gentle on his cheek, moving his lower eyelid to see underneath. "We can talk about it, and I can give you my opinion, but ultimately it's your call." He takes a step back. "Are you worried? Because I think you're doing well."

"No, no, I'm not worried." Scott finds himself stealing a glance at his camera bag. It looks tired, maybe, beat-up and worn, especially next to the posh of Jason's leather one. But still, it looks at home and safe among Jason's things. *How can I give Ken an answer about work when I don't even have a camera?*

But maybe what happened at the park counts for something. It's worth a shot.

"I took a picture today."

"You did?"

Scott reaches into his back pocket for his phone. It's shit, but Jason won't care; he swipes the screen open before he can overthink it. "In Forest Lane Park. I had some time to kill."

"Wait." Jason's eyes narrow. "I heard from an expert that photos *must* be taken with film."

Scott's chuckle is hoarse. "Quite so. But this'll do in a pinch." He taps the camera roll to bring up the photo, then hands it over, studying the toe of his boot.

"Oh, nice. This is at the stone wall, by the pond?"

"Yeah." Scott had spotted the lone blooming flower just off the footpath, poking its orange head up amongst the tall grass. There was something gutsy about it, and telling—about nature or persistence—that made him feel something. On impulse, he'd reached for his phone and knelt to take a picture of the plucky thing. “The light’s not quite right, but the composition makes up for it, maybe?” Scott finally looks up to see Jason pinching it bigger.

“It’s the only one blooming. See?” Jason says, pointing at the closed buds surrounding it.

They look together for a moment. The tree on Jason’s forearm shifts, its branches swaying with a tendon moving under the skin as Jason slides the photo around with his thumb. It’s odd, Jason studying something that Scott made. Holding it in his hands.

A nervous flutter makes Scott’s legs jumpy. “It’s too dark. A little flat. Would have been better if there were some highlights on the stones.”

Jason is silent for a moment, considering. He pinches the picture back to full size. “Well, I’m no expert. But I think it’s lovely.”

Scott looks again. He can see why Jason might say that. It’s got good balance, and the flower’s shape gives the eye a nice place to land. “It’s solid enough, for a rookie.”

“Congratulations,” Jason says.

“For what?”

Jason offers Scott the phone, meeting his eyes with a little smile. “For letting yourself be a photographer again.”

Scott swallows, his throat tight. The orange flower’s crêpe-papery petals look back up at him from the screen. He swipes it away and slips the phone back in his pocket. “Thanks.”

Jason turns to the counter. “And what’s this, then?”

Scott feels the first pinch of a headache behind his eyes. He’d known the moment would come, but now that it's here, he doesn't know how to explain it. *It's my camera. It's my job, it's my partner, it's my eyes. It took me around the world. It told stories for me, it won awards for me. It's another part of me that broke. It's why I'm here, now, with you. It's the reason Omran died.*

He can think all these things. But saying them is not possible; the words will never make it past his clenched teeth, so he says nothing. As Jason watches, Scott grasps the case carefully by the shoulder strap, then works the zipper. He's done this hundreds of times routinely, thoughtlessly. But not this time. He needs to be careful.

"You don't have to show me if you don't want to," Jason says.

"No. It's all right." The compartments inside are padded and soft, to protect the various components. Scott pulls the camera body out first.

It is heavier than it looks. It doesn't fit in his hand quite right, since the shell around the battery compartment is cracked and loose, but the feel of it is familiar enough to make Scott sigh. He'd held it briefly the other day, when he unpacked it just long enough to do a quick inventory. Camera. Two lenses, flash. Headlamp. Waist belt with a few pouches and extra batteries. His small backup camera had gone missing that day, along with his notebook and all four of his SD cards. What's in this bag now is all that's left, and Scott holds the biggest piece of it, his darkest secret, out to Jason.

"Oh, um, are you sure?" Jason hesitates. There is a lot going on in his face. Sympathy and sadness, and strangely, nerves.

Scott nods.

The cracked pieces of the case shift when Jason takes it with both hands. He holds it close to his body as a veterinarian might hold an injured animal.

"It's heavy," Jason says, surprised. He studies it, turning it over slowly, examining the broken lens and the scratches on the case.

Scott pulls a zoom lens from one of the compartments, to have something in his hand, but its weight makes his tremble more pronounced. It goes back in the bag, and Scott folds his arms, tucking his hands underneath. He fights the urge to turn his back, walk toward the window, regroup. A vacant silence lives where Omran's voice used to be.

"What happened that day?"

Jason's normally crisp voice has softened so much Scott can hardly hear it over the blood suddenly rushing in his ears. He looks everywhere but at Jason. The white feather on its red cloth, the dish of coloured crystal disks, and a soft stack of flannels. There is a sudden clarity about what happens here, what Jason really does. The problem to be worked out doesn't have anything to do with Scott's eyes, or his jaw, the mobility of his shoulder, or the screws in his arm.

It's in his throat. In his voice. It's in what he won't say.

Scott takes the camera back wordlessly. The move is brisk, but not unkind. Jason's caring hands aren't the problem; it's just that the camera has been out in the open long enough, exposed, and it's got to be put away now. Scott tucks it into its compartment and zips the case closed, feeling Jason's eyes on him, and in a smooth motion, lifts it into the open mouth of Jason's holdall and lowers it in.

Then, images come fast like a slideshow set to fast forward.

An elastic bandage. A splint, a sling. An accusing look. A man on the tube with curling black hair and glasses. Thomas's shaking finger, tracing over an angry, S-shaped scar. Knees giving out in the Blues Kitchen loo when the fucking hand dryer starts by surprise.

These are things he's been holding on to desperately, ever since the day Jason first suggested putting them down, the day they fought. Scott takes hold of the zipper as the ringing rises in his ears.

Panic at shrieking car brakes and distant sirens. Stranded at Tesco's storefront, trying to escape cold rain that feels like shards of glass. My bed, in sweet darkness, for days. No one asking, no one talking, no one looking at me.

As he pulls the zipper, Scott watches them fall in, one by one.

The blurry camera shop window. A whining ring in my ears that won't stop no matter how much I claw at them, even in my sleep. The bathroom floor, cool on my skin. Olivia, crying as she pours the last of the Jack Daniels down the sink.

The noise of the zipper is drowned out by the rise of voices, all talking at once; there are doors slamming, and a siren.

Omran laughing about his bad haircut in the back seat of the cab. A pretty brunette with a book on her lap. An obituary. "Blast radius...pressure wave...mortal pulmonary injury." An X-ray. An IV. An eyepatch. Olivia yelling into the hallway for a nurse. "Will someone change his bloody pillow!" I wish I was dead.

Not far to go now. The snapshots pile in, and Scott pulls the zipper fast.

A cold, grey day. A security checkpoint, a tense conversation. A crippling silence. A green coat that explodes. A hot wall of sound. Screaming. Twisted metal, rough concrete. A bloody shoe.

The zipper closes. Pictures and noise go still.

Scott had thought the bag wouldn't be able to hold it all, but Jason was right. There it is, closed up tight with everything inside. Safe. Protected.

Scott braces himself against the counter for a bit; his legs have gone weak. He reaches for his water and takes a drink, only then realising his cheeks are wet. He wipes at his face with his shirtsleeve. He wants to get on the table. Wants to lie down with rocks in his hands.

He turns to Jason. "Can we start?"

It's Jason's turn to have nothing to say. He's stands there, eyes wide, then finally nods when Scott holds the dish filled with glossy crystals toward him.

"With these?"

*

The flannel sheets feel warm as Scott slips between them.

So that's Jason. He's different for a doctor, isn't he?

Scott's been trying for a response from Omran since Jason left to let Scott get ready. He'd sampled a few oils, leaving arnica for last (*This is the best one, yeah?*), and gave a short tour as he undressed. (*Lots of diplomas, right? That feather is for sweeping, and his rocks are in that pot.*)

And still there is nothing.

It feels strange to start face up. When Scott is on his stomach with his face in the cradle, it's good for hiding; he can burrow in with his back to the room and keep his eyes shut. Even when he opens them, the most he can see is the rug underneath the table, and sometimes Jason's feet. Today they are skipping all that, and he'll be facing the room from the start.

Just wait until you see what he does. And he always...knows things. Scott adjusts the pillow under his knees and is met with silence. Again.

Scott can't help but think he did something wrong. Omran was with him at the café, and at the park too. But then he had shut Omran away, put him down in the bag with all the rest, and now whatever channel he'd tuned into that let Scott hear him is gone. Scott is beginning to think he cut it when he closed that zipper. He wonders briefly if he should explain to Jason that putting his camera inside it was a mistake. But that doesn't feel right either.

He lets out a deep sigh, reminding Omran, and himself, that *it's just for now. Just for now.*

There is no answer.

But there is Jason's soft knock at the door.

"Come in."

"You turned off the music," Jason says, surprised.

It had been Scott's, the one with the pretty cello and heartbeat bass drum. But it was in his way. "Yeah, it sounded like...noise to me today." Scott cringes. "That was rude. Sorry."

"It's all right. Quiet's nice too."

Jason stands behind him and takes a long, deep breath. Now that Scott knows this is Jason's praying, tuning-in time, he tries to stay still, to give off an air of wellness and ease. But his arms are restless, and even though the pillow under his knees is positioned exactly right, his feet can't find a comfortable place to rest. His nose is still runny from his little bout of crying earlier, and he sniffles. His eyes dart from the ceiling fan to the potted plant to the window and back, waiting.

"You're nervous."

"Yeah." It's hard for Scott not to crane his head around to check on the holdall. Putting the heavy things down was supposed to be good for him; Jason had said so. But he's attached to that bag and everything in it with a heavy cord. It's too far out of reach, and that distance may make it snap.

They don't talk as Jason makes trips for hot rocks to wrap into each hand and under each foot. The first brings the usual burst of heat, and the second brings balance. But the settled-down feeling Scott expects never comes, even when Jason replaces the blanket around his feet.

"Do you want to close your eyes? Maybe that'll help."

Scott stares up at the naked pupil of the ceiling fan. "No," he says evenly. "I have to stay here."

Jason nods, crystal disks clinking in his cupped hand. "Are you ready for these?"

"Yeah, let's do it."

Jason places three at the base of Scott's throat. When he gets the last one positioned, he takes a step back and folds his arms.

"All right?"

"Mm hmm." Scott had thought perhaps something magical would happen, as if he would be able to feel something lock into place or dissolve and disappear. But his throat feels just the same. His breath is shallow and too fast, and the knocking in his chest won't stop. His hands grip and ungrip the rocks. Their weight is pulling him down suddenly, trying to pin him to the table, and he needs to be free of them.

"Can I—" He slips both arms out from under the blanket and shakes them, dumping hot rocks out onto his stomach. "Sorry." He coughs weakly and kicks out of the towels that hold the rocks to his feet. "I was kind of...trapped."

"It's all right."

Jason gathers them up quickly as Scott reaches up to his throat to touch the crystals. They feel cool against his skin, which is burning with a swollen, scratchy lump underneath. He begins to sweat under his arms.

"See if you can take longer breaths. And the humming worked last time, so do that if you want."

"I don't think I can," Scott answers with another cough. He takes the crystals from his neck, then turns on his side to sit up.

Jason is unconcerned. "This is a push and pull, Scott, that's all. It's pushing, you're pulling. You've got to both get on the same side."

There had been a time when Scott wouldn't have had any clue what that means, or what "it" is. But he knows now. And he has to look at it, today, straight on.

Omran, am I in the right place?

Scott listens, focusing on the disks that look like sweets in his hand. One orange, one navy, one sky-blue. No answer comes.

The table sinks as Jason leans on it. "I want to tell you something, okay? About grief."

At the sound of the word, Scott's eyes fill. He shuts them against whatever Jason is going to say, and the tears hold.

"Your whole body's been holding on to it. You've been gritting your teeth together to hold it in, right? If you open up now, you can say it, and start to let it go. That's all grief is, Scott. Holding on to something that wants to be let go."

The crystals make rattling noises in Scott's trembling hand, and a tear drips onto his towel. The whole room is waiting for him to speak. But *fuck*, his throat hurts like hell. "Oh. That's all, huh?"

It's a dick thing to say, Scott knows, sarcastic and fucking obnoxious. But it feels good to be angry instead of scared. His blood is electricity lighting up his arms, and he sits up straight, swiping at his cheek to dry it. He knows he's crossing a line but can't be arsed. "What do you even know about it?"

The angles in Jason's face turn steely, and his blue eyes are so sharp they could bite. He squares up as if he's considering his options, then takes a harsh breath through his nose, and another. "I know plenty."

Those three words say that this is bigger than a patient who died. Scott turns away, chastened. Jason backs off, too, stalking to the window and leaving a hollow space between them.

Shit. Omran, where the fuck are you?

With Jason's back to him, the treatment room feels cold and unkind, and Scott doesn't want to be here anymore. He has a fleeting thought of getting up, putting on his clothes, and walking out of here, leaving Jason to stand by the window and watch him go. He'll take his camera back to Camden and put it in the hall cupboard where it belongs and draw the curtains and—

Jason has begun to pace, shaking his head a bit with his hands on his hips.

"All right, Scott, it's down to you. You're the one who's got to make up your mind." Scott can tell he's holding back, choosing his words carefully. "We can do this or not. It's your call."

This is it, the real moment. Scott has to choose. All the reasons why he should do it flood his mind: Olivia. Thomas. Ken, and work. His voice. His ears, his eyes. And standing right in front of him, Jason. But.

"I don't know if I should." If he could just ask Omran; if he could just hear him again. More tears well up, and Scott shakes his head. He feels this acutely, and hates breaking it to Jason. "I can't give it up."

Jason takes a step toward him. "I'll hold it for you. It'll be safe."

"It's not that. It's...it's too...ugh, I *hate* it. Why don't you forget about me, let me go back to..." *What? Go back where?* The thing he is running from is stuck in his throat, and he takes it with him wherever he goes. If he ran home to hide in bed, there it would be, right under the fucking duvet with him.

"Whatever it is, can we please just get it out so we can *look* at it?"

The "we" turns over in Scott's mind. He crosses his arms for something to hold on to.

"Scott, your body's fighting for this. We've come so far. I want to fight, too, don't you? Let's do this. Right now."

This is the fight Scott saw in Jason on that very first day, and again the day those massive horses had hunted him down. It felt new then, and so powerful; Scott had ridden the wake of it for weeks, depended on it to keep his head above water. They were going to get Scott better together, and Scott had made a promise to Jason that he would try. Scott remembers how it felt to be standing strong on his feet and fighting back. Today, apparently, is the day that promise is coming due.

Scott is cold, and he shivers. The voice that comes out has no fight in it. There are tears. "I put it all in your bag."

"All of it?"

"Mm hmm." Scott tries to steady his breathing and focus on Jason, but his jaw hurts and there is a hole burning in his chest that's scaring the shit out of him.

Jason inches closer. "Right. Can you tell me about it?"

Scott brushes his wet cheeks with the back of his hand and looks around. Now that Jason is beside him again, he recognises it as his clean place, full of light and soft things and acceptance, and it wouldn't be that anymore if he lets this ugly thing he did run rampant into the room. It's going to ruin it. Ruin them. "It's really...big."

"I know it is, it's all right." Jason pulls the blanket up and wraps it around Scott's shoulders. "We can handle it. I'm sure we can."

"No, no, it's fucking huge." Inside, in the darkness, it's only his; he can ignore it, or feed it every once in a while, like a stray, and no one else will know. If he lets it out, it will swallow him, and he won't recover. Scott feels sick. He might throw up. A clammy tickle moves over his skin in waves. "It'll be so... I can't, it's too much. God, I'm—" His teeth are chattering. It's so cold. Scott reaches for the blanket and pulls it closer around him, but the shaking won't stop. It's suddenly a struggle to keep his eyes open.

"Try. Just try."

"I think I'm going to be sick."

"It's just nerves. Breathe, see? Nice and easy. It'll be all right."

Scott's teeth make a dull clicking sound that Jason can hear, judging by the way his eyes fix on Scott's mouth.

You'll hate me. I don't want you to hate me.

"Not possible," Jason says simply, shaking his head.

"Holy shit, I said that out loud? Fuck." The wave roils in Scott's stomach, and cold sweat breaks out on his lip.

The table is moving, and Jason suddenly tilts strangely off to the left. He's saying "Keep talking, Scott. Get it out. Tell me what's stuck in there," but his voice sounds like it's at the end of a tunnel. Scott reaches out to him for balance, and their arms tangle. His head hurts, and he can't make Jason understand. This is the wave, the thing that's coming for him that he can't run away from anymore. His next step is diving down into it, to find the thing he buried that wants to choke him. And that means speaking. All of it. Out loud.

"Shit, I'm going to be sick."

This time Jason's eyes get wide. "Yeah. You are. Hold on, holdonholdon..."

They leave the table at the same time, Scott toward the bathroom and Jason toward the rubbish bin. When Scott loses his balance and falls to the floor, Jason is there sliding the bin under him just in time for him to curl over it and heave.

Fuck. Scott grips the edge of the bin as his body spasms over it, spilling everything out of his stomach. "Ugh, sorry." Scott moans when Jason holds out a wet flannel and covers him up with the blanket.

"Not quite the 'get it out' I meant, hmm? But that's a good start."

Scott grunts and wipes his eyes and his mouth. His breathing hitches, and he thinks he might go again. But pressing the cold cloth to his cheek feels good, and the moment passes.

"More?" Jason asks.

Scott shakes his head slowly, getting his bearings. "Shit, sorry about your bin."

"It's seen worse. You have excellent aim."

"I've had some practice."

Jason grabs the bin and gives him a sympathetic wince. "I'll get some water. Stay right there."

Scott's not sure he could get back up on the table if he tried. He's tired, properly bone-tired. His hands feel empty, as if he's lost something. The crystals. He must have dropped them. He pats around his knees for a minute, searching, but comes up empty. A knot of sadness swells in his throat. He rests his head on his hand and closes his eyes.

Jesus, Omran, if you could see me now.

Omran would look at him sideways, maybe give him a gentle kick. He'd probably say, "What are you waiting for? Get up, get dressed. Let's go get the story."

Goosebumps rise on Scott's arms.

How am I going to get back out there? How am I going to take pictures of everybody else? How can I tell their stories if I can't tell mine?

All of this, every piece he put into Jason's bag, every heavy, complicated dark thing he's held on to that was protected and secret comes down to this. As simple as it is, it may be the linchpin of everything.

Jason must be able to tell something's happened because he approaches slowly from the loo and doesn't make a sound when he sits. Scott is dimly aware of the water bottle and of Jason's eyes on him, but he can't move his eyes from the blank spot on the wall.

"We told stories together. Omran and me."

"Yes. You wanted him there in Kabul." Jason speaks carefully. "You asked him to come with you."

Scott swallows. "That's not everything."

"All right, what else is there?"

"Ugh, the truth." Scott cringes and takes an unsteady breath.

“Well. You know what they say about the truth.”

Scott sniffles. “Yeah. It hurts.”

“Well, yeah, there’s that. But it can set you free.”

Free. Being free of this is something Scott can’t imagine and doesn’t deserve.

“Deep breath. Look at me. Say it when you exhale.”

Oh. Oh, God. Scott breathes in, and the first try falters; air spills out, shaky and thin.

“You can do it. I know you can.”

“Shit, Jason.” For the first time, Scott is terrified he really might not be able to do it. What if the hooks won’t let go, even though he’s changed his mind?

“You just need to be brave for a second, and then it’ll be all over.”

Ugh. “I’m not brave.”

“You’re so, so brave. You are. Say it on the next one.”

Scott chuckles thinly, borderline losing it. “Do I have to?”

“’Course not. But you already puked, so why turn back now? I reckon you should push on, yeah?”

Scott breathes in through his nose. His arms are shaking. “Right. Right.” One last time. He breathes out and closes his eyes. *All right.* The air makes a raspy noise in his throat as he inhales, as deep as he can, and he dives.

“It was supposed to be me. I shouldn’t be here. I should have died there, and I didn’t. Omran got killed there instead of me.”

Whooosh. The blood rushes in his ears, and he sways, but there’s more, lots more.

"It was my fault. He got like, *ripped* out of the *world*, and I...I was supposed to protect him, and I didn't. It should have been me."

Scott's teeth chatter, and he tries to breathe again, but his lungs feel punched out, and he can't get any air. He sputters while Jason moves in closer with his hand on Scott's back.

"Keep talking. There's more."

"I can't. Can't breathe."

"You're here with me. Just me. You can do it."

A cold day, a silver car. The scene is oceans away yet right under the surface of his skin, lying in wait.

"Omran and I...we were late," Scott whispers. "Streets blocked off everywhere, traffic stopped." He's sweating. He looks at Jason, as if by chance he'll let him stop, but Jason sits wide-eyed and waiting. "We circled around, couldn't get to the embassy. Blockades. Checkpoints. We ditched the cab and..." Scott shuts his eyes so he can fall into it, feel the pavement under his feet, hear the car horns beeping uselessly. "We ran the last few blocks. But there was a...ugh." Jason is doing something to his back, some kind of pulling, or unwinding. It makes him sit up straighter. "A checkpoint, on the corner."

There's a high whistle in his ear. Time stops, and he's back there, standing on the wrong side of orange police tape, looking at the line of security officers standing between them and where they need to be.

Scott's words are weak when they float out into the room. "Omran had nothing to check, just his ID. But I had my camera."

Jason presses lightly on his back.

"He wanted to wait with me, to answer their questions and make sure I got through." He can see the officer now, thin and young-looking in fatigues and a helmet, bulked up with a bulletproof vest. He's got Scott's credentials in his gloved hands and looks Scott up and down as if they've got all the time in the world. He puts Scott's bag on the table and unzips it to examine its contents. Omran pleads their case in brisk Pashto, saying they'd miss their window if they have to wait much longer.

The officer nods and barely glances inside the bag. Scott looks past him down the block, at the curb lined with dignitaries' vehicles. The embassy is set back a good distance from the street, and there are groups of people making their way across the pavements toward the main door. *Good.* Scott sighs with relief. If they go now, they'll make it. He takes his press ID back and loops the lanyard around his neck, already moving to the edge of the table to collect his bag.

But he can only watch as it is pushed down the line to the next officer. Scott's hands fist as he watches him reach inside and pull his camera from its compartment.

"Please," Scott begins, his nerves making him forget the simple words in Pashto. But Omran steps in, his voice rising. Scott can pick out "photographer" and "official press" but not much else. The officer is unmoved. He takes his time, pushing the camera's power button roughly and removing the lens cap, then bringing it up close to his squinting eye to look inside.

Scott presses pause.

Here it is, the moment before everything went wrong, the moment that haunts his dreams and drives him to the darkroom. For a few precious seconds, Omran is right there waiting by his side, so close that their coat sleeves brush against each other and their clouds of breath mingle in the cold. Omran is a whole person, with alert eyes and chewed fingernails and a dark freckle on his cheek. He is thinking and breathing, alive, safe and sound.

But the image moves in slow motion, and Scott watches it unfold like a scene in a play they keep rehearsing but can never get right. The officer places Scott's camera on the table instead of back in his bag. He reaches in again, this time pulling out the zoom lens. Scott tries to guess how much cash he has left in case he has to offer a bribe to get his equipment back.

He reaches to his back pocket for his wallet as he turns to Omran.

One word changes everything. One word that is still stuck in his throat.

Go.

Scott folds over on himself but can't stop watching. "I told him to go." He shivers, and Jason pulls the blanket across him tighter and rubs his arms like he's trying to get him warm. "And then he asked if I was sure, and I...I *pushed* him away. I said, 'Yes, go, just go, I'll be right behind you.'" Now, just as he's done countless times before, Omran nods and jogs away from him toward the embassy.

Scott grits his teeth and tightens his lips to force the tears back. He rocks a little, out of fear or adrenaline, and Jason holds on to his shoulder.

"No, don't tighten up now, keep going. Breathe. Nice and deep."

"I'm scared," Scott whispers. "I don't want to fucking see it again." The pain behind his eyes feels like needles, sharp and bright.

"I know, but we're almost there. So close. Tell me."

Scott tosses the purple and orange bills down on the table. The officers divide them up as he collects his things, stuffing the zoom lens and the camera in their pockets. Omran is already approaching the main entrance, gesturing to the guards there.

A horn blares in the street, a common enough sound in Kabul. But this one is long and loud. Something's wrong.

Shit!

The shiny silver car has flags on its front bumpers like all the other cars at the curb. But an arm waves from the driver's seat window, and the horn won't stop. The guards leave their post at the embassy door with rifles drawn, all moving toward the car, and Omran is in the middle of it all.

Omran, fuck, get out of there!

Scott swings his bag over his shoulder, camera still in his hand. He starts to run.

The hoofbeats are coming for him, right on his heels, and Scott can't stay ahead of them, even though he feels like he's flying, his feet barely touching the ground. Omran seems to get farther away, not closer, and Scott can't shout loud enough, he can't breathe, he can't reach, he can't find a way out for them.

"I couldn't get to him. I screamed and I ran, but I couldn't. I tried."

"I know, I know you did," Jason says softly.

"And then...fuck, it was so loud for a second. I mean, you never heard anything so fucking loud. And there was this wall of heat that was just...the *air* was on fire, you know? It burned. It burned everything."

He is face down on the ground. He tastes blood, and he can't turn over. It's hot. *Where is everybody?* It's getting harder to see, and he can't hear. All that's left is the shattered glass on the pavement and the shoe that Omran should be wearing.

"I couldn't even move, in the end," Scott says. "It was all happening, and I...couldn't..."

Scott sighs heavily, feeling the tail end of everything he'd kept hidden unwind and slip out. He is empty and tired of talking.

Now starts the part of the story that exists only in a handful of pictures in Jason's file. Scott has filled it in as best he can, but can only guess at the details. Surely there must be ambulances and fire trucks, and people shouting as they run. There would be someone to put the fire out. A paramedic would lift Scott onto a gurney; someone else would pick up his camera and make sure it goes with him.

The reporters and photographers here for the summit would turn their horrified lenses to the street. They would take pictures and interview onlookers. And what used to be Omran would lie there, for hours most likely, while official-looking people would "secure the area, record evidence, and recover remains."

Even those imaginary pictures fade to black as if the film is over and the lights have come back up in the theatre. Scott can't make his body move, and his mind wants to do nothing but sit and stare at the blank screen for a while. Jason must want to as well because they sit in silence, shoulder to shoulder, until the trails of Scott's tears are dry and tight on his cheeks.

*

The thought of his camera alone on the counter brings Scott back to himself.

He looks around the room, almost surprised to see that the walls are still standing and the potted plant in the corner with its drooping leaves is still right where it was before. And Jason is still here too.

Scott doesn't know what to say. What he did hangs between them, and he's not sure he's ready for them to look at each other. He glances over and clears his throat, not from pain but from nerves. "Um. Should I get dressed?"

Jason is looking at him the same as always, directly, in the eyes. He stands and offers his hand. "Not yet. We're not done."

Scott's mouth tastes terrible, and his eyes ache. But if Jason says they aren't done, then they aren't. And even if Scott still doesn't understand crystals or a sweeping feather or the fire door, he does understand one thing for sure. *Jason won't hurt me.*

Scott looks at the table. "Face up?"

Jason nods and lifts the sheet in a gear two speeds slower than normal, and Scott is glad for it; they have come out the other side of something massive, and he is tired. He figures this will be a quick balance of his hips or stretch of his shoulders, and then they'll be done. *Just a little while longer, Omran.*

It feels good to be lying down, warm and tucked in. Scott hopes Jason will stand behind him and do that thing where his hands slide underneath Scott's shoulder blades and pull. Or maybe bring out the eye pillow, or trace circles on his forehead. He closes his eyes and feels himself settle heavily into the table, waiting for wherever Jason will touch him.

First, a hand touches his shoulder, then, fingers light at the base of his neck. "How is your throat then?"

"It's uh..." Scott hesitates, then opens one eye. "Wait, is this one of those questions you already know the answer to?"

"Ha-ha, no. I'm genuinely curious."

Scott swallows, feels it out. "It aches."

"Probably will for a while. Want to hear the good news?"

"There's good news?"

"In my professional opinion, yes, there is." Jason walks around behind him. *Yes*. He slides his hands under both sides of Scott's neck, then down under his shoulder blades. *Even better*.

"What is it?"

"I don't think you'll be coughing anymore."

They chuckle softly together. "There's that. Brilliant."

Jason slides his hands further down and uses his forearms on either side of Scott's head to lift him slightly off the table with a gentle pull. "Yes, it was. You did it. I'm proud of you."

"Ugh, I..." Scott loses focus when Jason releases for a moment, then pulls again, and Scott hears a muffled *pop* in the upper part of his spine. *Aaahhh.* There's space and softness, and Scott closes his eyes, forgetting he was about to say *how could you be, I don't deserve it, all my fault.*

Now Jason lifts Scott's left side so his body tilts at the waist. That feels good too. A pull and a twist to the other side, and Scott's head lolls as if it's on a loose hinge.

"But now I want you to tell me something else."

Scott smells the light scent of detergent on Jason's shirtsleeves. So clean. *Clean and good and perfect.*

"Scott."

Scott breathes Jason's voice in, breathes in everything gentle and beautiful about this place. He lets his head sink heavily into the table when Jason lays him down. His head is turned to the side, and soon Jason's warm hand massages the tight tendon in his neck.

"Scott?"

"Hmm?" Jason's faraway voice is an annoying fly that Scott wants to swat away. Through hazy darkness, he can make out:

"Omran..."

"...talk..."

"...reasons..."

"What?" Scott presses his cheek into the soft flannel sheet and squints, confused. He couldn't have heard that right.

"You survived," Jason goes on. "You're still here. You made it through. Let's talk about why."

Fucking what?

Scott's eyes flash open, and his shoulders seize up. "I don't...I don't know what—" *What the fuck is this now?*

He's done everything he was supposed to do. Jason said they should look at it, and they did. That unforgivable thing he did was stuck, but he told, and it's finished. Scott moves to get up, but Jason puts his hands on his shoulders.

"Wait, wait, just think about it. You lived. You seem to think you shouldn't have, but you did."

"It was a mistake, I just told you! I made a huge fucking mistake."

"We're not done," Jason says as Scott sits up and swings his legs over the side of the table.

"*I'm* done." It was supposed to sound fierce. And final. He should get up and storm out of here with his things and slam the door, hurling insults on the way out. *Stupid fucking place never want to come back here and fuck your questions.* But his words sound defeated and small. He walks to the counter in a teary haze, the blanket dragging on the floor behind him.

"Wait."

"I don't want to talk anymore," Scott says quietly.

Jason's voice is low too. "I know."

The blanket drops when Scott reaches for his pants on the door hook. He fumbles to get them faced right and yanks them up his legs. He can picture himself going. He'll sling his camera bag over his shoulder and breeze by a confused Monica with a wave. His jeans are next.

"I'm not going to slap a plaster over this and send you on your way. I can't do that."

He'll make it down the front steps two at a time, and then he'll reach the pavement and start for home. The fresh air will feel good on his face. Scott zips his flies and shoves his arms through his shirtsleeves. He'll get away from Jason and his questions and his eyes that see everything.

Scott's hands tremble when they try to find the first button. The sharp tone of Jason calling his name makes him stop.

"I did what I was supposed to do. I told you. Everything." Scott looks around the room as if something there will help him figure out why Jason is steering them this way. "Didn't you hear what I said?"

"I did." Jason has a hand on his hip, but his eyes are kind. "That was just the beginning. Now you've got to do the rest."

"For what? What rest?" Scott turns back to the counter and pulls the holdall toward him, cradling it against his stomach with his hand on top.

Jason comes closer. "You've got a wound, just like your arm and your cheek. You opened it up. Now we've got to start healing it. Use your voice again."

"By telling you *why I lived*?"

Jason raises an eyebrow but says nothing.

Goddamn it. Scott suddenly does have a lot more to say. He clenches his fists. "Right. I'll play your game. How about this. *Omran* should have lived."

"Omran had his own thing going. That belongs to him."

"Bullshit." Scott's voice steamrolls right over Jason's, the raspy weakness gone. "He's dead. So now it belongs to me." He spits the words out so loudly it surprises them both. "Omran should have lived. You want me to tell you why? Here. How about Omran was smarter. How about Omran had a *wife*. How about Omran *had plans*, all right? He was a good person. He had shit he wanted to do, okay?"

Jason's voice rises along with Scott's. "It's not up to you to figure out why Omran died. It's only up to you to figure out why you didn't."

Scott remembers his surprise when Jason first said Omran's name. Now a fiery protective streak flares up that wants Jason to back off and let Scott have Omran all to himself again. "Ugh, you're... I don't *know*, what kind of question is that anyway? How should I know?"

"Please sit down," Jason says, gesturing at the table.

"No, I'm going home." Scott should put on his socks and boots. He spots them near the door, too many steps away, and he isn't sure how to muster up the strength to get there.

A frustrated sigh. "Would you please sit down before you fall and crack your head open and bleed all over my floor?"

Scott hadn't noticed, but he's not only leaning against the counter, but listing unsteadily, holding himself up with one arm at an odd angle. *Fuck*. If he tried to leave now, he probably wouldn't get any farther than the waiting room sofa.

Jason holds out a hand, waiting.

Scott bumps past him, their eyes hooking together for a short moment. "I'm not staying long," he mumbles, half sliding, half falling onto the table.

Jason offers water, and Scott takes it. It feels good going down his throat, and he drains the whole bottle, then takes a steadying breath. Jason stands in front of him with arms folded and eyebrows knit.

"Would you stop looking at me like that, please?"

"I'm your doctor. I'm supposed to look at you. Especially when I'm evaluating your fitness to leave my office."

Leaving the office sounds like an ending when Jason says it that way. Everything happened here. It's where he found the fire in the night valley under the stars. Where they traded dreams and found Scott again, the real Scott, who could laugh and be strong. This has come to be Scott's place, too, it seems, with its humming energy and soft sounds. Leaving now feels hot-headed and rash.

"I don't know what you want me to do."

"You've been stuck for a while, you know? Someplace between surviving and not really living. Your voice is stuck too. It's been hurt, and you've been neglecting it, maybe even punishing it, for a bit. But it's like a muscle. You have to exercise it, right? Say something with some power behind it. Something real. 'Maybe I lived because...'" Jason gestures as if Scott's supposed to finish the sentence.

Anything Scott can think of to say feels like washing his hands of what he did and leaving Omran behind. But he is tired of fighting. His shoulders slump, and he raises his hand to rub his eye. "Maybe I lived because it was stupid dumb fucking luck. There's your answer."

"I don't think you believe that."

Well, maybe I don't care what you think is on the tip of his tongue, but Scott stops himself from saying it; he sounds like his five-year-old self fighting with Olivia after he stole her Polly Pocket and hid it under his bed. Bratty. And lying.

"I know it's hard. But you gave me a whole list of reasons why Omran should have lived. Now tell me why you did."

Scott says the first thing that comes to mind, and it actually makes him chuckle softly. "Maybe I lived because Olivia would fucking kill me if I died."

Surprisingly, Jason smirks a bit. "I suppose that's true. Good start." But his mouth quickly returns to its serious line.

"I'm trying, but seriously, could you stop staring at me?"

"Right, sorry." Jason looks around, then walks away to disappear behind him. In a second, the table shifts as Jason sits.

Something real. Something I believe.

The sound of Jason's breath is soft behind him, so close his back grows warm with body heat. Jason's solid presence there holds him up, even though they aren't touching. It makes Scott finally able to say it.

"I think I lived because I was selfish."

The heavy echo of the sentence hovers over them for an endless minute, and Scott tears at the cuticle on his thumb.

"Maybe," Jason finally says. "But I wonder..." He hesitates, and Scott hears the smooth sound of his hands rubbing together. "What if you *didn't* make a mistake? What if you did the very best you could at the time?"

It's strange hearing Jason's voice without being able to see his face. It's a vibration Scott feels all around him, through his clothes, and in his ears too.

"What if you couldn't possibly have known what was going to happen? What if what you did was as much or more than anyone else could have done? What if you could start to believe that?"

Scott turns reflexively to the counter, searching for an answer; he bites his lip and looks at the floor when he realises he won't find one there.

What if?

He was a girl once, in the woods. She ran. She flew. She prayed. *Did she do her best?* Scott isn't sure. He shakes his head, caught between sympathy and guilt.

"I was afraid." Scott might be talking about Afghanistan, or the woods, or he might be talking about now; it's all mixed up, and it's all the same.

Jason's heat gets even closer. *There's more, there's more,* his steady breathing seems to say. And there *is* so much more, in pages that Scott can flip through in his mind.

He is a boy living in a world of sound, where tall cathedral walls and a warm bed are always filled with melody and song. He and the boy beside him practice the hymn measure by measure, pointing at the notes and nodding with the sacred rhythm. Their voices blend, then his own rises above the other. It's his voice that makes him lose everything he loves. His voice that dies of a broken heart.

What if?

Colours flare up and glow in the flames. Each one flickers with its own life. *The tip of the iceberg*.

He is a young man in a sunny corner room of a duke's villa. He wears a rough cotton shirt, and his hands are stained. He smiles shyly at a man in a black waistcoat, then looks down into his box of pigments, his cheeks burning. He is afraid, too, but love makes him bold; he puts his heart in a portrait, inscribed on the chest of the man he loves.

What if, what if?

He is a king in a cold stone fortress weighing impossible odds. Responsibility is not new to him, and neither is war, but both are heavy on his shoulders. His choice will have consequences far beyond this table. His name signed to a parchment scroll will buy them precious time, and he can only pray he will keep his people safe. *Was he doing his best too? What if?*

A cog in the wheel.

An idea begins to piece itself together through the flames. It repeats and disappears, dies and lives again.

Not over. Never finished. Another chance.

He is a young soldier sitting on a bed in a farmhouse at the dead end of a country road. He is lost from his army, lost from everything that makes sense, truly, because men keep killing and bleeding and dying. He holds a young woman in his arms, wondering how in the world he got here.

How I got here.

His platoon had been blown off the map. They had scattered without supplies or a radio, bloody and wandering blind.

We weren't supposed to be there at all.

Scott's heart beats faster, the fate of it dawning on him for the first time.

Am I in the right place?

A stern woman in a bloody apron comes to get him. Not Joffre, not Perrault. Him. She pulls him out of the barn into another world where he'll do something that counts. He can look out the farmhouse window as he hears a woman sing a lullaby. He has mud on his pants and blood on his hands, but he is found. If it was true then, what if it can be true now?

I wasn't lost at all. I was right where I needed to be.

A low, rumbling voice. *Always.*

Scott's eyes grow wide. Their connection is back, and a prickle of goosebumps rise on Scott's arms.

Holy shit, Omran. I figured it out.

Omran smiles his usual crooked smile and speaks again. *Tell him.*

Thoughts weave in and out, overlapping one another, past and present. Scott is just getting hold of it.

"Jason."

"Hmm?"

Scott's voice is just above a whisper. "What if I lived because I'm not done yet?" His heart is pounding.

"Say that louder."

Glimpsing the truth makes Scott sit up straighter. He clears his throat. "What if I lived because I'm not done yet?" There is a little more power behind it this time, though it still sounds frayed on the ends.

Jason takes a deep breath. "Say it again."

Scott chuckles a little, feeling silly. "What if I lived because I'm not done yet." This time, it sounds round and strong, and his cheeks get hot. But it's no longer a guess or a question. He can feel the rightness of it in his throat and in his hands. "Maybe I have more to do, or something, you know? Like, maybe there's something out there, a place I have to go. Or maybe it's something Thomas needs me for? Or Olivia? I mean, what if there's something really important I have to do for them? Or what if...there's a picture I haven't taken yet that someone is going to see, and it's going to help them, right?"

Omran sits across the table from him in a restaurant that smells of chai, snapping his fingers that he got it right.

"Mm hmm. What else?"

A knot slips apart between Scott's shoulder blades, and the possibilities keep coming. "Or what if there's something I'm going to learn? Something that other people need to know, too, and what if...*I'm* the person that is going to show them that? With a story I do? What if there is someone I have to meet? I mean, there could be someone out there, right, who I haven't met yet, that I'll be able to make a difference for, you know? I mean, maybe I lived because I have a story to tell, even for just one person."

He needs to see Jason's eyes. Then he'll know for sure.

Scott turns to him. It's Jason, who told him to stop digging, who threw the blinds open to let the light in. Jason who waited for him while he floated, who watched him leap off that cliff and fly. And after all they've done,

Jason has led them right back here, to the table, so they can finish it just where they started.

Scott's heart is pounding so hard he can hear it, the possibility dawning on him all at once.

What if I was supposed to meet you? Again?

"Jason, what if—" But he leaves it. Because it's completely mad; Jason will look at him sideways and laugh.

"Hmm?"

"Um..." He's got to swerve, or else he'll say too much. "Do you think we have time to use your feather?"

*

He's been afraid of it, if he's honest, because it looks too sharp for sweeping. But when Jason brings his feather back to the table, Scott holds it while Jason adjusts the pillow under his knees. Scott is surprised at its light weight; he runs his finger along its soft white edge and notices how the tip of the vane isn't pointed, but gently curved. He hadn't noticed that before. Strange, how such a delicate thing can feel so powerful.

Jason begins under Scott's chin, sweeping down in slow strokes toward Scott's chest. The feather's edge glides against the fabric of his clothes, making a soft brushing sound, like whispers. There is a finality to it, as if this is what they've been building to since day one, the feather sweeping everything away that Scott is finally aware of but doesn't need anymore.

Jason reminds him to breathe. Scott does, softly, and imagines the hooks loosening to let those pieces of darkness float away.

Jason sweeps along his arms, over his torso, and across his hips with steady and deliberate strokes. His back looks square and strong in his plain T-shirt, but if Scott lets his eyes blur, he sees a handmaiden in a simple dress with rolled-up sleeves, buffing her lady's skin with perfumed oil before her wedding night. Scott tilts his head a bit and sees a white-haired, dark-skinned man who doctors a gash on a young man's cheek with herbs and salve. Jason walks around the foot of the table, and Scott sees an old woman, a great-grandmother, whose face is a map of wrinkles. She seems to be reciting a spell, sprinkling water on a feverish child.

In his relaxed state, he isn't afraid or surprised. *How many times, how many ways has Jason done this?* Scott wonders for the first time if Jason has his own fire, and if he does, if he's ever seen it. It isn't long before his thoughts turn to Omran, who must have one too. And the driver of the silver car. *Another chance. Never over.*

"Thank you," Scott says, not knowing who he's properly talking to. Omran. Jason. But also, Lorenzo, John, and Hélène. Littlest Fox. Madame Samuel, Master Wydeville. And Émile. Georgie. Matteo. The Stone King. And Wings-on-the-Wind. All of them. Everywhere.

The feather skims over the fabric of Scott's jeans. Jason smiles but doesn't look up from his work.

Omran and Jason reply at the same time.

You're welcome.

"You're welcome."

*

The Chawri Bazaar is bustling with rickshaws, scooters, and shoppers on foot. Scott winds his way through stalls filled with fruit and nuts, colourful stacks of fabric, and tinkling chimes made of brass and copper. He's looking for a shop that sells SD cards for cameras because he's all out; he thinks there's a place just ahead, across from the card shop.

When he gets there, the place is empty. In fact, all the noise and frenetic movement of the market is gone. He walks through the little booth alone, and sees a dark-haired man behind the counter, arranging a vase of flowers. It's an old friend Scott hasn't seen for years.

"Omran?"

"Scott! I've been waiting for you! They said you'd come. A memory card, correct?"

"Yeah."

Omran's brown eyes glimmer in a way Scott has never seen, with flecks of gold.

"Um. What are you doing here?" Scott puts his camera bag on the counter. It feels too light, as though it might be empty. He must have left his camera at the hotel. Or in his cupboard in Camden. *Damn.*

"Helping," Omran says simply. "Let's see. Sixty-four gig, I think." He turns around to search among the shelves behind him. "Aha, here it is."

Omran slides a small rectangular box across the counter. A battery.

Scott shakes his head. "I don't need this. I need a memory card."

Omran smiles. "Hmm. I don't think so. You've already got one. Take that instead."

Scott is about to put it in his bag when there is a knock at the door behind him. He spins around to see who it is, and opens his eyes.

There is upholstery he doesn't recognise in dark-brown suede. It smells good, outdoorsy, like cedar and sage. He takes a deep breath and remembers it's actually his own skin that smells that way because he took a shower and used Jason's soap and shampoo. His hair is still damp against his shoulders, and it all comes back to him. He's in Jason's office. He fell asleep on his sofa.

There are three more knocks on the door, and then the sound of Jason's trackies as he walks past his desk, across the room. He sits on the sofa's arm, near where Scott's camera bag rests at his feet. "Hey."

"Hey."

"Haven't had that much excitement in my treatment room since somebody set a fire in the sink, so thanks for that."

That makes Scott smile. "Anytime." His stomach is growling, and he turns over. He feels good; his nap and the ibuprofen Jason gave him have taken the edge off his headache, and his body is comfortably loose and warm, though Jason had hardly touched him. His throat feels tender when he swallows, but it isn't painful or raw. "How long was I asleep?"

"My four o'clock just left. It's a quarter past five."

"Oh, shit, I'm sorry." Scott rushes to get up. "I had no idea."

Jason puts out an arm to wave him down. "It's all right, that was my last. I've got notes to do, so. Did you have a good shower?"

“Yeah, was nice. Thanks.” It had felt good to let the water wash over him, to soap off the sweat and tears and sadness of the day. Jason had offered his office sofa, too, in case Scott needed to rest afterward. Scott intended to come in here only to return Jason’s book, but the sofa looked so inviting he couldn’t resist sitting and, soon, lying down. He’d had a dream, too, though he can’t remember it now.

“Here, I thought maybe you’d want these.” Jason places three crystal disks into Scott’s hand. “That’s carnelian, lapis, and aquamarine.”

Scott lets out a surprised sound. He had thought he’d lost them what feels like days ago. He touches the sky-blue one with his finger and wonders what kind of magic might be inside them. It’s a bit silly, how he’d been afraid they would pull what he’d done out of his throat like magnets. They hadn’t. Jason was right, Scott had to let that go himself.

Scott curls his fingers over them. “Thank you.”

Jason nods. But something about his smile looks a bit wistful, and suddenly the crystals seem to confirm something Scott suspects. They might be a parting gift, or a memento. Something to remember this by because it’s almost over.

“I think you did some proper brilliant work today. Well done.”

It’s a bit awkward to receive Jason’s compliments after what happened. But Scott does feel the truth of it. That heavy thing is out in the open, and Jason is still here, still looking at him the same way he always has. The relief of it makes Scott chuckle. “Brilliant, eh? Well, aside from the puking.”

"Truly brilliant. Puking and all."

There is a hesitation before Jason speaks again. Scott knows what he's going to say because he can feel it too.

"So much so that I'd like to suggest you come back one more time, on Monday. We can do your final evaluations and consider your discharge."

The crystals make a squeaking sound in Scott's hand as they rub against one another. "Discharge. Well. That sounds like I'm getting released from prison." Scott laughs lightly, covering up the fact that he hasn't ever thought about how their time here would end, until now.

"Nah, think of it more like...a graduation." Jason gives him a proud smile. "You've been improving bit by bit since your first appointment, and today went even better than I'd hoped. It was a huge step, you know that, right?" Jason runs his hand over the tree tattoo on his arm. "You're on your way."

Scott is disappointed at the thought, but he doesn't disagree. This feels a bit like the float, when he realised he was finished just as his time was up. There, he had felt a mutual pulling away, when the silence grew too quiet and the water too still. His ears itched to hear and his eyes were ready to see his life again. He had found what he'd been looking for, and he was ready to move on to whatever was next.

"So one more appointment then?"

"I think so."

Scott considers it as excitement and a bit of fear flutter in his stomach. "That means I could go back to work."

"Hold on, let's not get ahead of ourselves. You still have to finish with Brenna, and I'd recommend continuing your acupuncture. You could also consider some sessions with a talk therapist."

"The acupuncture wouldn't be with you?"

"No. But I've got an excellent practitioner I'll recommend." Jason stands. "We'll see where you are on Monday. We can talk about all these next steps then, all right?"

Steps that evidently don't include Jason.

Scott loops the strap of his camera bag over his shoulder and follows Jason to his desk, wondering if those next steps will or won't include the night valley, the fire, his beautiful burning colours that remind him of where he's been, and that there is so much to come.

Jason looks over Scott's face and grasps his wrist to find his pulse, his usual post-appointment review.

"Do you feel better?"

Scott takes a deep breath and smiles. This is Jason, who wouldn't let him off easy. Who kept pushing them forward. And who let him rest. "Yes. I do."

"You'll get home all right? I can call you a taxi."

"No, I'll be fine on the bus." He will be. This time when Scott thinks of leaving it's not to escape Jason and his questions, it's about walking out into the light, letting the sun hit his face. He's ready.

Before they walk out together, Scott's eyes catch on one last thing. The framed picture on Jason's desk, where he sits atop his teammates' shoulders, the day he hurt his knee. Smiling to hide his pain.

The end of one thing. The beginning of something else.

Chapter Ten

Depth of field (n.) The amount of distance between the nearest and farthest objects that appear in acceptably sharp focus in a photograph.

7 October 2016

To: drjason.andrews@jahealthcare.co.uk

From: me

Subject: Thank you

Hi Jason,

Do you remember me? It's been a while, but I wanted to thank you. You helped me so much when I didn't want help, and I appreciate it.

I'm back to work. Attached is a recent article in *The Times* that features a photo of mine. It was sort of buried in the back, but I'm not complaining.

Hope everything is going well for you. Thank you again, sincerely.

Scott

8 October 2016

To: me

From: drjason.andrews@jahealthcare.co.uk

Subject: Thank you

Scott, this is brilliant news! Of course I remember you.

So glad to see you're working again. It's an excellent photo!

Are you staying in London for work, or travelling?

And how are you?

To: drjason.andrews@jahealthcare.co.uk

From: me

Subject: Thank you

Cheers! It's sort of strange to see my credit in print again.

I'll be in London for now, but they tentatively have me down for Paris at the end of next month. I'm on probation, I think? Even though they didn't say that. People are tiptoeing around me a bit, which is annoying. But I like the distance, in a way. I suppose I'll see how it goes. In any case, I wouldn't have been able to get back at it if it wasn't for you, so thank you.

I'm good, truly. I finished my PT with Brenna last month. It was rough there in the middle, but we got through it. I kind of miss her though, is that weird? We ended up almost proper friends.

I still float, and I still see Emilia for acupuncture. The tinnitus came back pretty strongly a couple of weeks ago. We've tried some different things that help a bit, but it'll probably take a while.

That reminds me, do you know anything about sound therapy? Emilia knows a place in Waterloo where they do singing bowls and something called gong baths. It sounds interesting, right? But I don't know.

Anyway, this is getting long, so I'll go.

Is everything good there?

Scott

To: me

From: drjason.andrews@jahealthcare.co.uk

Subject: Thank you

Good that you can be close to home for a bit while you get acclimated back to work. Take it slow. I can imagine people there might be nervous or awkward around you, but I'm sure they are happy to have you back. And if I had a part in your healing so you could get there, I'm glad.

I do know the sound therapy place, but only by reputation. I've never tried it myself. I think it's worth exploring. In fact, if you decide to do it, would you consider getting in touch with me after you go? I've heard some varying reactions (none terrible), but I'm curious how you find it, given your history. Only if you'd like to. No obligation at all.

Good for you for floating. I haven't been in ages, and I should go. With the cold weather setting in, my knee tends to act up and floating helps with that.

I think yes, everything is good here, except I proceed to continually embarrass myself in my footie league. I guess I'm getting old.

Take care.

Jason

26 October 2016

Good day, you have reached the office of Dr Jason Andrews. Our office hours are—beep

"Hi Jason, it's Scott. Okay, so you asked if I'd let you know about Luke's, you know, the sound therapy place? Well, I went, and...whoa. I'm kind of overwhelmed? There was a lot about frequencies and therapeutic percussion, or something—that bit went over my head, really, but it was good. He calls it a sound bath, and it really is like that, strangely. Like, you're immersed in the sounds. Gongs and bells and singing bowls and I don't know what else. Anyway, you can call me back if you want. I'm here. All right. Thanks. I mean goodbye."

You have two new messages. First message received Wednesday, October 26th at 8:15 p.m.

"Hi, Scott, I'm sorry I missed your call. So you went! Sounds like it was good. Was it a group of people, or did you have a one-on-one session? I've heard he does both there. And I was reading about voice frequency therapy on his website. I'm not sure what that is. Any case, I'm interested in the details, and how you're feeling now, so, maybe I'll try you back in a bit. Or you should have my mobile number. You could call that. Thanks, Scott. Take care."

Next message received Wednesday, October 26th at 8:19 p.m.

"Hi Scott, it's Jason again. I wanted to, uh, remind you, I guess, that you're not under any obligation to talk to me about what's going on with your treatments now. I think my message may have sounded a bit doctorish, asking you for the details and such. I didn't mean it like that, I'm just curious, I suppose. The doctor is hard to turn off sometimes. But no worries. So if you feel like calling me back, do. Thanks."

27 October 2016

Describing the mechanics of the sound therapy session to Jason feels brilliant; actually, it's the talking to him again, about anything, even the weather or what he had for lunch, that feels brilliant. Something about the way Jason listens makes Scott choose his words carefully.

"No, it was more like...a wall of sound. Like, no specific notes you can pick out? Just solid tones that hold for a long time and keep overlapping one another."

"Oh, right, I get what you mean. Not a melody, just vibrations?"

"Right. And after a while, it felt like I was completely surrounded by it. It was everywhere, and I could ...get lost in it. I couldn't think about anything. And, huh, now that I'm thinking about it, I couldn't move my arms either."

"Were you sitting? Or lying down?"

"I was sitting, but most everyone else was lying down."

"So you tried to lift your arms, and you couldn't?" There is understanding in Jason's voice but also a note of wonder.

"Yeah. But it wasn't scary. It was comforting, I guess. And safe? That sounds weird. But..."

"No, that makes sense. The sound frequencies sort of overwhelm the thinking part of the brain, in a way? Really interesting. It's, like, the exact opposite of the quiet of floating, but the same result. Hmm. And how about your ears? Any change there? Even temporarily?"

"Well, they—"

"Oh sorry, sorry," Jason says. "This sounds like an interrogation. You don't have to—"

"No, it's okay, I don't mind. There was no change in the ringing after. But that's all right. I'm still going to go back." Scott is sure of this, and though the thought of lying down through it, where the possibility of being completely paralyzed is a bit terrifying, he can't resist the appeal of it.

"It might take a while. Could be a cumulative effect, you know? A sort of retraining of your nervous system over time."

"Right. I hope so." Scott can feel the conversation winding down and searches for a way to keep Jason with him a bit longer. "So, do you have any more questions for me?"

"Um, no, I guess that was it. I appreciate you calling."

"No problem." Scott shakes his head and squints. He's going there, and once he opens the door, it won't just be an idea in his head, it will be out there in the world. "But I wanted to ask you something too."

"What is it?"

"You told me a story once, about a person's wedding ring. They put it in your bag and didn't want it back. You, um, gave it back to the world, I think you said?"

"Right, yeah. I took it to the park."

"Yeah. So. I'm wondering if...um..." There is a pause filled with a long-ago feeling of being understood, a feeling Scott has missed terribly.

"Is this about your camera?" Jason asks.

"Yeah, but... I don't know. I'm just thinking about it. I don't really want to do anything with it yet, I don't think. I guess I want to know...how you do it. In case. Can you tell me how that works?"

"Sure, I can tell you how that works."

3 November 2016

Scott's phone hums just after he's put down his work bag and hung up his coat in the front cupboard. He fishes it out of his back pocket as he walks toward the kitchen.

"Open House—Sound—Friday 7 p.m."

A thought comes to him as he puts the kettle on, and he finds Jason's name in his contacts.

> *There's a sound therapy demo tomorrow night at Luke's. Free and open to the public. Just in case you want to try it*

> *Let's see. Supposed to go to my sister's tomorrow. Some other time though?*

Scott frowns at his phone, then chuckles.

> *Don't be scared. 'Light refreshments will be served'*

> *Ha! I wish I could. But I can't this time.*

> *OK More veg and hummus for me then*

> *I'm sorry to miss it. Let me know if anything interesting happens? (If you want)*

Something interesting always happens at Luke's, Scott thinks, though it's just a bunch of people in a room for an hour with nothing but gongs and bells. And he's sure Jason would think so too. He puts his tea bag in his cup and pinches his lip between his thumb and forefinger.

> *Will do. Have a good weekend*

> *You too*

14 November 2016

Good day, you have reached the office of Dr Jason Andrews. Our—beep

> "Hi Jason, it's Scott. I didn't want to call your mobile and wake you up. I'm taking an early train to Paris, and I'm here waiting at the station. I'm only going to be gone for three days, so no big deal, but... I guess I'm nervous or something. I've been to Paris lots of times, but...I don't know. It feels different this time. I never noticed there are armed police here. Anyway. I just wanted to tell you I was on my way. My first trip away for work. I mean, not first, but you know, first since—" *beep* "—ugh, damn it."

Good day, you—beep

"Yeah. So. It feels kind of important? And don't worry about me or anything. I do want to go, but I didn't realise how weird it would be to have my passport and equipment and...all of that. I have to get used to it again. Anyway, I'll be back on Thursday. All right. Thanks. Ha, I mean, see you."

You have two new messages. First message received Monday, November 14th at 6:40 a.m.

"Hey, Scott. You're probably on the train now, but congratulations! Brilliant that you're on your way. I think it's normal to be nervous. You're going to do just fine. If you need to talk, give me a call. I'll be in and out of appointments today until five. Call me on my mobile, all right? Right. Bye."

Next message received Monday, November 14th at 6:51 a.m.

"Just thought of something—I don't know how much time you'll have, but maybe you'll get to enjoy a bit of the city? There's a lovely bakery in the...tenth, I think? *Pain et Idées*, something like that. Might be something to look forward to. All right, I'll talk with you soon. You'll be fine, Scott. You can do it."

16 November 2016

To: drjason.andrews@jahealthcare.co.uk

From: me

Subject: Paris

Two press conferences down, one to go. Yesterday was rocky but today is smoother, so I'm calling it good.

Thank you for the recommendation. Du Pain et Des Idées was excellent, long line, but entirely worth it. How do they do that with flour and milk? Massive amounts of butter, I suppose. Very close to Place de la République and the Canal Saint-Martin, both very photogenic as well.

Someday, I'd like to visit the countryside too. No time now though, coming home tomorrow. With three two bags of croissants.

We could get together if you're around? If not, that's cool too. I know you're busy.

To: me

From: drjason.andrews@jahealthcare.co.uk

Subject: Paris

Sounds good! How about lunch Friday? We can meet at Pearl's at noon if you want. It's close to my office. Does that work?

18 November 2016

Scott hasn't been in Jason's area of the city in six months, but the bus route to Stratford feels like a reunion with an old friend. The familiar intersections, the way the road curves and bumps, and the names of the shops as they pass by all remind him of last spring. He was still sick then. But now, even though it's cool and cloudy, the streets feel warm, as if they are inviting him back.

Scott's heart beats faster as the bus approaches his stop. He gathers his bags and moves his way to the front, eager to get out and walk the rest of the way to Pearl's. He checks the time. Early, as he'd planned, 11:45.

He smiles to himself as he walks, with his computer bag over one shoulder and the wax bag of croissants, all the way from Paris, in the other hand. He imagines how it will be, what he and Jason will talk about, what it might be like sitting across from him after so long. He wonders, nervously, if there will be—

"Scott, hey!"

He turns, and there is Jason, smiling wide in a windbreaker and joggers.

"Hey, hi!" Scott says as they meet, his arms outstretched as if to hug, and Jason with his hand out to shake. They fumble for a minute, chuckling, and end up in a messy half embrace, patting each other on the back with their free hands. "You're early!"

"So are you," Jason says, pulling back. He points to the bakery bag, a bit awestruck. "And what's this?"

Scott holds the bag out to him. "They're a few days old now, but...I thought you might enjoy them. They're from *Du Pain et Des Idées*."

"For me?" Jason's face lights up, and when their eyes meet, Scott thrills that he is the same as he remembered. Hands warm, blue eyes bright. Jason opens the bag and peeks in at the croissants, taking an exaggerated sniff that makes Scott laugh. "Heavenly. Thank you, this is... incredible."

"You're welcome."

Jason moves toward the café door and holds it open. "Let's go in before all the window seats get taken."

Scott leads them through the tables to a spot for two. As they settle in, he can feel Jason's eyes on him, but when he looks up, Jason turns to the large chalkboard over the bar where the specials are written.

"I have the same thing every time I come—lentil and avocado salad." Jason laughs when Scott makes a face. "But, uh, the mixed grill is good too. And I'll even share my croissants."

"Mixed grill it is," Scott says. It's a strange feeling at first, sitting across from Jason. What they'd gone through together in Jason's treatment room was so heavy and dark Scott hadn't been sure he'd make it through, but that time is gone, and now they are friends out in the world having a simple lunch in a corner café. After the waiter comes to take their order, their conversation starts straightaway.

"So," Jason begins, with the same curious look Scott remembers. "You look good. Your face, I mean."

"Thanks. You look good too. Well, I mean, you look the same." He shrugs because it's all the truth.

"Well, thanks, I think?" Jason takes a sip of his water. "So, what was Paris like?"

"Paris was...busy. A fleabag hotel, I must say, but hey, it's the City of Lights, right? And the bakery made up for the dodgy accommodations."

Jason squints a bit. "And the work part? Your email said it was rocky."

"Eh, it was...fine." It was. It was fine. It will be fine.

"Fine?"

Scott takes a breath, debating how much to say. "Well, I had a bit of an issue at the press conference the first day. Lots of people, small space, that kind of thing? But it was all right. I got out of there, took a walk. Oh, and it was weird. I think one of the junior ministers was hitting on me."

"Oh?" Jason seems surprised at the turn in the conversation. "That's exciting? Maybe?"

Scott recalls the slim politician, who was scruffy and dishevelled in an effortlessly sexy, distinctively French way. "Nah. He was...well, you know when someone's a close talker? And you take a step back and they come closer? And you keep stepping back and they just keep coming? He was that."

Jason chuckles. "But that can be kind of good, can't it?" He leans back in his chair and takes another sip of water.

"Nah, not this time. His breath was stinky."

"Ha! So what did you do about this stinky close talker?"

"I told him the truth, that I wasn't interested." Scott turns to the window and bites his lip. He thought the funny story would be a good way to pivot away from the trouble at the press conference, but it isn't; he recalls the way his hands shook in the crowded press room, how he had to push through the crowd like a salmon swimming upstream to the fresh air of the courtyard. How the man kept coming closer, even though Scott kept moving away. "To be honest, I don't know if I'll ever be interested, you know? It's... I don't know."

Jason studies him for a moment, then speaks quietly. "Don't worry about that now. You don't have to judge it or make any sweeping decisions. Just take your time."

"Yeah. Yeah, all right."

"And anyway, I'm proud of you. Your first work trip, done. Maybe it wasn't perfect, but you did it. Right?" Jason holds up his water glass as if to make a toast.

"Right," Scott agrees, clinking. It feels good, as if they are making a pact or a promise. "To Paris."

Jason raises an eyebrow. "Yes. To Paris."

"Speaking of which, I brought some pictures I took. Do you want to see them?" Scott asks after they drink. He reaches for his computer.

"Absolutely," Jason says, pulling the bakery bag onto his lap with a look over his shoulder. He whispers conspiratorially. "You don't think they'd mind if I had one of these, do you?" He reaches in and breaks off a piece. "I can't resist."

Scott shakes his head, then looks around for the waiter, who is nowhere to be found. He smiles. "You'd better give me a piece of that."

22 November 2016

Scott is standing in the grocer's line when he checks his phone and sees his notifications filled with Instagram likes, all from the same person. Jaandr3ws. That has to be Jason, and he texts him to be sure.

Ha

What?

You followed me on Instagram

Yes. Why is that funny?

Because you liked every post I think

Scott steps out of the line and puts his basket on the floor between his feet. He has a sudden thought.

Wait, are you feeling sorry for me? Because I had trouble in Paris?

No! I followed some wedding photographers. And you came up as a suggestion. So I clicked on you and I got sucked in.

There's a hot thud in Scott's chest as he stares at the screen for a moment. The photo of Jason and his partner from Jason's office flips across Scott's mind, and he takes a breath.

Are you getting married?

Me? God no. My sister is.

Scott is enthused at this news, more than he should be, and he can't help but type:

Congrats! OK I'll follow you back

My Instagram is mostly sports stuff. But you could follow me on Facebook.

OK, I'll find you.

Though there are several Jason Andrews, only two are doctors, and only one has a football as his icon.

This is weird

Sorry!? :/

No, it's OK, ha. Your sister is pretty. Is that weird to say?

She looks like Jason, only in a more delicate package, and with longer hair. Their smiles are just the same.

Katie? No, not weird. She's a stunner, everybody thinks so. That's an amazing picture of the water blessing. Bangkok looks incredible!

Thanks. I like that one too.

And the one of the people praying at the Ganges. Amazing.

I got wet for that one, ha!

Scott scrolls through Jason's Facebook feed, and it's a mix of his family and friends, healthy recipes, yoga, and football. Several photos show him with his teammates, both on the sidelines and in action. In one, he's got his hands on his hips and a brace covering his knee, looking sweaty and tired.

Omg footie pics. Nice. You're quite serious

Oh no. You're liking my pics now. What have I done?

*

Later that night, as he's about to shower, their conversation picks up again.

Are you going to sound on Friday? Thought I'd try it.

Yes! Starts at 7

Anything I need to know?

Wear comfortable clothes, layers. They keep the room on the cold side. They have blankets and mats

How long is it?

An hour. But if you want to stay for the gong bath too it's another half hour or so

Should I?

I'd recommend it. Reserve ahead of time on the web

OK, I will. Thanks for the info.

You're brave! Good on you!

Ha.

See you Fri

See you then.

Scott turns on the water and unbuttons his shirt, humming to himself. He's got something to look forward to.

25 November 2016

Scott guides Jason through the lobby at Luke's, pointing out where they'll sign in, where the mats are stashed, and how to find the water fountain and the restrooms. Men and women mill around quietly, hanging up coats and exchanging greetings. There is soft music that reminds Scott of the kind Jason plays in his office, and on the shelves are books, CDs, and bells to buy.

"Here you are," the woman behind the counter says to Jason when it's his turn to register. "Fill this out and return it to me before the session starts. Make sure to sign the bottom." On the clipboard she holds out is a waiver, with all of the familiar medical questions Scott had been so frustrated by last spring. Jason gives Scott a knowing grin as he picks up a pen.

"You're not going to go get a burger while I'm doing the sound session, are you?" Jason asks.

"Nope, I'll be right here. No burgers. No takeaway, no pizza. Maybe after."

Jason nods. "All right, maybe after."

After they finish registration, they each take a mat and a pillow and enter the sound room, where people have already staked out areas on the floor.

"Let's go over there, in the corner," Scott says. On the way, Scott notices Emilia, his acupuncturist, chatting with one of her friends. He waves and realises when Jason says hello, too, that they know each other as well.

"This is kind of like my yoga class," Jason says, spreading out his mat next to Scott's. "Everybody has a spot." He sits cross-legged, a few nerves visible in the deep breaths he takes as he looks around.

Scott sits as well and points to the large table at the front of the room. Luke stands behind it, checking the various gongs, bells, cymbals, and drums he will be using. "Want to go up and see?" Scott asks, thinking Jason might welcome the distraction.

"No, I think I'll wait here. You can go if you want to."

Scott shakes his head. "Do you want to sit this time, or lie down?"

"You think lying down is better, right?"

"That's what I do. I can relax more that way."

As Jason arranges his pillow, Scott thinks this may be the first time he's ever seen him not in complete control of a situation. Jason's confidence is usually an energy all around him, and although he's perfectly game for whatever might happen here, there's a caution underneath that Scott finds endearing. He feels a surge of pride, being the one who can finally steer the ship for them, the one who knows the ropes and who will be here in case Jason needs him. They lie down, a few feet apart, in silence.

Three bells ring to call the room to attention. Luke greets the participants warmly and wishes them a good session. An air of quiet anticipation fills the room, and Jason and Scott turn to face each other, to check in one last time before they go.

Scott mouths, *Are you ready?*

Jason's eyebrows lift, and he mouths back, *Yes, you?*

Scott gives him a thumbs up as if they're astronauts signing through a window that they're a go for launch. Jason turns away, closing his eyes, and Scott focuses on the tile pattern on the ceiling.

The first sound is a low drum, struck so softly that Scott can't hear the beat, only the tone that fills the air around them. Then there is another overlapping it, also low and long. His breathing lengthens and his shoulders drop away from his ears. The two notes are the only sounds in the room for a while, and Scott knows this is the foundation for what will grow to be a multilayered symphony of vibrations. He turns his head slowly to check in on Jason, who lies still with his palms up, face focused and intent.

Scott closes his eyes and takes a deep breath, ready to submit to the sounds and where they may take him.

Later, in the restaurant down the block, Jason types notes into his phone as Scott listens to him ponder how it all works.

"And there was that one bell, you know the one I mean? The one that sounded sharp at first, then got mellower? I swear, that one made my scalp tingle," Jason says.

"Really? I didn't feel anything on that one. But that cymbal, toward the end, *that* made me grit my teeth."

"Ugh, I know the one. I didn't like it either. Made me fidgety." Jason types that, too, and takes a bite of his salmon salad and barely swallows before he starts to talk. "Now I know why they call it a sound bath. You're completely enveloped in the sound, like you said. The whole brain is submerged in it, right? I didn't get that until now."

Scott puts down his sandwich and wipes his hands on his napkin. "So, do you think you'd come back? I mean, would you want to do it again?"

"Hell, yes, I want to do it again! You said each time is different, right? So now I need to find out about the chimes. He didn't use those tonight. And I'd like to know if each instrument affects the same part of the body in the same way each time, or does it depend on the day? Or the frequency of the note? Or the temperature in the room?" He takes another bite, then turns to his phone again, thumbs typing furiously. "I'm curious, too, about injuries. I mean, we've both had injuries, right?"

Scott nods.

"So, do injured parts of the body react the same to certain frequencies as whole parts do? Would a person with an injury react differently to the same sound profile as a person without an injury? And what about speed of healing? The implications are...fascinating. I'd like to talk to Luke about that, see what he thinks."

Scott nods again, smiling.

"What?" Jason asks around another mouthful of food.

"I forgot how you are."

Jason's face falls. "How am I?"

"Persistent."

"That's me." Jason shrugs, smiling, and puts his phone down. "And I do want to go back. Can you make it next Friday?"

"If I'm in town, absolutely. There's a chance I'll go to Glasgow." Scott's stomach tightens at the thought.

"And is that all right with you?"

"Yeah, I think so," Scott says. "It's just for a day or two. I've got to get back in the saddle, right?" Though the thought of the airport, a new city, and the crunch of a press corps makes his heart beat faster. He picks up his mug of coffee, letting its warmth heat his hands.

"No," Jason says simply. "Not if you don't want to."

They sit in silence, Scott turning the words over and over in his mind. What he wants and what he's able to do may not be the same thing. "No" doesn't feel like an option at the moment, but hearing Jason say it feels like a door cracking open.

"I'll let you know," Scott says.

Jason nods, taking another bite of salad. “Perfect.”

1 December 2016

Hello, you’ve reached Dr Jason Andrews’s mobile. I’m sorry I’m unavailable at the moment. Please leave me a message, and I’ll get right back to you. If this is an emergency, please call 020 8586 5000.

> “Hi, Jason. It’s Scott. I’ve had kind of a shit day. My trip to Glasgow got cancelled. Well, not so much cancelled, I suppose, as they decided to send someone else. David, the suck-up from Bristol, to be specific. So, it turns out I’m going to be in town. I’m planning on going to the group sound thing tomorrow at seven. So just let me know if you’ll be there. All right. Talk to you soon.”

You have one new message. Received Thursday, December 1st at 9:32 p.m.

> “Hi Scott. I suppose it’s been a shit day all around, then. My, um, my cat Bitsy died today, and I’m...well, I’m falling apart a bit, actually. She was very, very old and sick, too, and today was just... I couldn’t bear to see her that way any longer. Didn’t know it would hit me this hard, really? Made a proper fool of myself at the vet’s. I thought I’d be relieved that it was over, you know? But it’s so strange, being in the house without her. Um...yeah. Well. Uh, I had to reschedule some patients, so I have to work late tomorrow. But thanks though. Next week, I think?”

Hello, you've reached Dr Jason Andrews's mobile. I'm sorry I'm—beep

> "Shit, Jason, I was in the shower. Damn. I'm really sorry to hear that. We had cats growing up, and I know how hard it is to lose them. Sounds like she had a good home with you. I think I saw a picture of her in your office. Was she grey with a bell? Anyway, I'm sorry. I hope you have a good weekend. Or, I mean, um, take care, I guess. Ugh, I guess I'm just really sorry. Goodnight."

7 December 2016

Scott sits on his bed with his back against the wall, his computer open on his lap. Jason's talk about his yoga class has Scott intrigued, and what started out as a simple Google search for "sun salutation" landed Scott in a rabbit hole of yoga clothes, recipes, and a new, colourful language about heat and energy. He curls his legs under him and waits for Jason to answer the phone.

"Hello?"

"I need your opinion on my, how do you say it, '*dosha*'? Because an internet quiz on Dr Oz's site seems legit."

"Ha! You can do yoga without getting into all that other stuff. But what did it say?"

"I got *pitta*, but I'm not sure I answered everything right. I mean, how am I supposed to know if I have a penetrating gaze? Or whether my joints are well-knit, or whatever?"

Jason chuckles. "*Pitta* sounds right for you, actually. Because, you know, fiery."

"Ugh. Very funny."

"Ha...too soon?"

"So, what are you, anyway?"

"I'm—" Jason begins, but Scott wants to guess.

"No, wait, don't tell me. You're *vata*. Right?"

"Hmm. Why do you say that?"

Scott's tree photograph stares back at him from above his desk, its low branch beckoning. "Jason, you're textbook *vata*, all about rest and staying warm. I'm right, aren't I?"

"Pssh. Take one quiz on Dr Oz and you think you're an expert."

Scott's cheeks burn. "Ha! I *am* right!"

"Quite so."

Although Jason has played along, Scott notices his voice is tired and has none of its usual crispness. "But that's...not really why I called."

"What's up, then?"

Scott pauses, debating about how to bring it up. But he remembers how it felt to have Jason say Omran's name, the day of their first appointment. "I was just wanting to see how you were doing, with Bitsy passing on."

"Oh, uh, well, it's been a rough few days, I'll say that."

"I'm so sorry. Cats are, well, they're perfect, aren't they? And they live a long time, and keep us company, and I'm just, really sorry." Scott chews on his lip, wondering if he's being helpful at all, or if Jason can't wait to hang up the phone.

"Yeah, thanks. It'll take time, I think, to get used to not having her here. She was more than a pet, you know? She was, well, Bitsy was my mum's cat, and I, uh, I adopted her. When my mum died. So we've, uh, kind of been through a lot together."

Scott gasps quietly. "Oh, I didn't realise. I'm so sorry. I...I had no idea." The news brings to mind their fight over grief in the treatment room, and Scott sees Jason's pained expression all over again, how he tamped down everything he knew about loss. For a moment, he can't imagine the pain of what Jason's been through, the compounded hurt of losing someone twice. But it dawns on him that *he can* imagine it; he's got his broken camera packed up and ready to be given back to the world, as Jason explained, but he hasn't given any real thought to actually *doing* it. Because of how much it will hurt to lose Omran again.

"I know, it's all right. My mum's been gone awhile, six years ago now. It's one of those things where I think I'm over it, you know, going along fine, but... It's still hard, sometimes, and this..." Jason trails off, and the silence leaves a hole that Scott understands.

"Brings it all back," Scott finishes for him.

"Yeah."

"I get that."

"I figured you probably would." After a moment, Jason clears his throat. "So I'm going to miss sound again. I feel like being alone for a few days, outside of work. I think I'll float instead."

"Yeah, that makes sense," Scott says, hiding his disappointment by answering too quickly. "We'll aim for the week after if I'm in town."

"Right, sounds good."

"Take care of yourself, all right? Drink your water, and uh...get some rest." Jason knows this, of course, but Scott wants to remind him anyway.

A faint chuckle makes Scott smile a little. "Will do. Thanks for checking in on me."

"You're welcome. Talk to you soon."

"Right. Bye."

After Scott ends the call, he crawls down to the foot of the bed and looks over to where his old camera bag sits. What would it mean, to give it back to the world? He touches the strap and opens the zipper, then reaches in to feel the hard body of the camera inside, knowing he'll keep it for a while longer.

13 December 2016

You have one new message. Received Tuesday, December 13th at 10:02 a.m.

> "Morning, Scott. Something interesting to tell you. Call me back if you're around."

You have one new message. Received Tuesday, December 13th at 2:41 p.m.

> "Hi, it's me, Jason. Just thought I'd try again. Call me sometime if you can. Thanks."

You have one new message. Received Tuesday, December 13th at 5:14 p.m.

> "Okay, this is a little strange, but I thought it was good, so I'm going to tell you. I had this dream, right? Last night. It was you and me, and uh...Omran was with us. We were in primary together. I could tell it was you and him with me. He had dark hair and glasses like you said, and, well, I *knew* that way you know in dreams, right? We were making paper aeroplanes together out of newspaper, for science. So then we were in Paris, adults, like we are now, standing on the Pont Neuf with our aeroplanes. We were nervous that they wouldn't fly. But when we let go of them, they flew up into the sky so far away we couldn't see them anymore. And we were really happy about it. It was good. I thought it was anyway. So, call me back if you want."

You have one new message and one saved message. New message received Tuesday, December 13th at 5:49 p.m.

> "Hey, it's Jason again. I remembered something else about the dream—we were all speaking Pashto. I mean, I think it was Pashto. Isn't that strange? But it was brilliant. It felt really good to speak a different language so easily and be understood, you know? Hmm. Anyway. Oh, and does this mean you owe me a dream now? Right. I think so. Talk to you soon."

You have one new message and two saved messages. New message received Tuesday, December 13th at 7:26 p.m.

> "Scott, hi. I'm...so, so sorry. I didn't realise what day it was until just now, I swear. Shit. Seriously, I am...I am *so sorry*. If what I said upset you, I mean, even more than you must already be upset, I didn't...ugh, I didn't mean it to. Please call me, anytime, if you need to talk or something. All right? Shit. Well, ugh. I'm sorry. Truly."

14 December 2016

Scott's thumbs hover over the keys. His only reply to Jason yesterday was a short "Thank you for telling me" and "No need to apologise. I'm OK" by text. That had been partially true. There was too much to explain—the vague haze of sadness, the sight of his scars, now a smoother web of coral and pink in the mirror, the old wish to get lost in the darkroom.

The letters make a soft *pock* as they appear.

> *I'm going to sound Friday*
>
> *Good. So am I.*
>
> *OK. See you.*
>
> *See you.*

16 December 2016

It's true that no two nights at sound are the same.

Some nights are soft and bright, with an almost lyrical mix of bells and sweet-sounding gongs. Those nights tend to be mood lifters, where the time moves fast and Scott leaves feeling lighter. Others are grounding, where long, heavy notes resonate through Scott's limbs and draw him into a deep state of rest. Many fall somewhere in between. Scott wonders what tonight will bring as he and Jason wade through pockets of other sounders to find a spot where they can lie side by side. It may be a low, deep night, judging by the set of large hand bells Luke sets out.

Scott gets comfortable as the first notes fill the room. The full bass tones lull him into that lovely place where his arms grow heavy and he can't feel his legs anymore. The chatter in his mind stills and he can breathe deeply for a time. But the notes get louder, and something about the mix of them makes Scott's eyes water.

It could be because he's tired; he hasn't been sleeping as well as usual, since the anniversary. Work helps push the memories aside, and he'd found film to keep him busy in the darkroom until he couldn't keep his eyes open. But then his sleep was full of restless dreams, where he'd see Omran speeding on a motorbike over cobblestone streets, or they'd be hiking on a cold mountain ledge with no gear. Another dream had resurfaced, too, of Scott and Jason riding in Scott's dad's old Volkswagen, driving on the winding road to Land's End.

Scott is able to stay quiet at first, but it gets worse as the notes layer and build. Soon, a simple three-note harmony pierces through a thin barrier he didn't even know was there, and his face is wet, and he can't hide the need to sniffle and wipe his nose.

He opens his eyes briefly, to snap out of the moment and gather himself, and he instinctively checks on Jason, who is lying still with his palms up. But the notes must have hit the same chord in him, too, because his lips press together in a tense line and a tear rolls down the side of this face into his hair.

Scott wipes his eyes and inches a bit closer, silently, to care for him somehow, to let him know they are in it together, even if Jason never notices.

Jason has no animated questions that night when they sit together at the coffee shop after the session. There is no flurry of ideas typed into his phone, and no musings on the science of sound frequencies. He doesn't say much at all, in fact, but neither does Scott; instead, they sit in a comfortable silence, processing where the session has taken them with only a few words.

When their food arrives, it's as if a spell is broken, and Jason is ready to talk. "It's amazing, isn't it?"

"How do you mean?"

Jason's eyes are slightly bloodshot, but he's smiling anyway. "How can I have such a bad headache but feel so good at the same time?"

Scott laughs softly. "I know the feeling. In fact, I used to feel that way in your office sometimes."

"Oh really? Well. Perhaps that's a compliment? I'm not sure."

"I think yes. Yes, it is." Scott looks down at his food, trying to gather his thoughts into something that makes sense. "It felt good to be there, and let it happen. You know? The sound gets to a place inside that kind of, breaks open? I guess? It actually made me cry tonight."

"Me too," Jason says quietly.

"But it feels good. To let it go. Whatever it is. I...I needed that tonight."

"After Omran's anniversary."

"And after Bitsy died," Scott offers.

They let this sit between them for a long moment, until Scott's stomach growls loudly, which makes them chuckle. Scott picks up his sandwich. "You know, I know what I'm talking about with that whole crying-is-a-good-way-to-let-things-go stuff. It was a doctor who told me that."

"Oh?" Jason says, tucking into his salad, eyes shining. "Well, if a doctor told you that, it must be true."

Chapter Eleven

Focus (n.) The point at which an object must be situated with respect to a photographic lens for an image of it to be well defined; a device on a lens which can be adjusted to produce a clear image; a centre of activity, attention, or attraction. (v.) adapt to the prevailing level of light and become able to see clearly.

31 December 2016

Hello, you've reached Dr Jason Andrews's—beep

"Hi Jason, it's Scott. Just wanted to wish you a Happy New Year. Have fun with your sister. People from work are going on a pub crawl. Meh. Olivia invited me to hers for Thai food, and maybe fireworks on the telly. So I'm off too. Have a good one. Be safe. I mean. Have fun. Is what I meant. All right. G'bye."

1 January 2017

You have one new message and three saved messages. Received Sunday, January 1st at 12:06 a.m.

> "Scott! Happy New Year! Are you already in bed? I'm shouting! I guess! I'm sorry! I'm not sure where we are, but Katie's inside, and...I see fireworks out here and! I think we'll stay a bit longer! Happy New Year! Right! All right, it's loud so I'll hang up now! All right! Hanging up! Scott! Happy New Year, all right? Hanging up now!"

Hello, you've reached Dr Jason Andrews's mobile. I'm sorry—beep

> "Good morning. Ha. Sounds like last night was a real banger. Don't forget to drink your water."

You have one new message and three saved messages. Received Sunday, January 1st at 11:40 a.m.

> "Ugh. Ugghh. Scott. Please. In future. Don't ever let me. Go out. Ugh. Drinking. With my sister. And her fiancé. I'm never. Getting. Out. Of this. Mmm. Bed."

4 January 2017

Scott tries to find a quiet corner in the busy airport terminal where he can calm down and hear himself think. He spots an empty seat farthest from the gate door and pulls out his phone to text Jason.

I'm waiting at the gate. Flight to Bern delayed for weather. And I'm sweating like a madman. People are going to think I'm plotting something

OK, take a deep breath.

I'm tryimg. Ugh trying. A little old lady just asked me if I was all right. What am I doing?

Scott you can do this, everything is going to be fine. People fly all the time. Every day, even.

OK I know

That pilot is probably the very best pilot in the whole company.

Uh. OK

And all the mechanics, they're sharp and talented at mechanical type things. This is the stuff I tell myself when I fly. Is it helping?

Not really

OK then, how about some music? Hold please.

Music?

The next message is a Spotify link, with no label or explanation. Scott taps it, then has to laugh at what he sees.

?? What is this??

It's a playlist.

Whose playlist? Linkin Park? System of a Down?? Wait what

Ha!

Are you serious?

Why? What do you mean?

I thought. I don't know what I thought. Godsmack? Incubus? I don't know what to do with this information

Just listen to it!

OK. Jason?

?

I feel better.

Good.

16 January 2017

To: me

From: drjason.andrews@jahealthcare.co.uk

Subject: Photographers?

I think you're still in Poland. Or are you in Turkey already?

I hate to bother you while you're working. But I've got a question, and it's kind of an emergency. You know my sister's getting married in May. We don't have a lot to spend, so most of the budget went to the little place in Greenwich for the reception. She skimped on other things to pay for it, like fewer flowers and a fucking idiot photographer who evidently DOESN'T KEEP A CALENDAR BECAUSE HE DOUBLE-BOOKED HER DAY AND NOW HE'S CANCELLED HER.

You can probably tell where this is going.

Everybody's booked, and she's panicking, as jilted brides do. We're scrambling, and I thought maybe you'd have an idea of someone who could step in. I've got to try to come through for her, so any names you could throw at me? Wouldn't have to be anyone superfamous or special, just someone you trust who's reliable and can take good pictures. We'd owe you big.

Massive thank you for anything you might be able to do.

To: me

From: drjason.andrews@jahealthcare.co.uk

Subject: Photographers?

I didn't even ask after your trip. Charming.

It must be freezing there. Is the coffee good? I feel like I've heard something somewhere about excellent Polish coffee.

And I wanted to give you my personal email address: drj14andrews@gmail.com, so these don't get mixed up with my work messages.

17 January 2017

Fwd to: drj14andrews@gmail.com

From: me

Subject: Photographers?

In Warsaw until Thursday, then Ankara. Back in London on Monday, as it stands now, if all these meetings go as planned. Got here fine. I'm staying in the tiniest hotel room ever, not even like a room, more like a cupboard. Yes, it is freezing-my-balls-off cold. But the coffee is indeed excellent. Thank you for asking.

As for the emergency, what's the wedding date? I'd do it myself, but I'm not sure where I'll be. I've got someone in mind—Jess, a friend from Golds who works for The Resident, last I knew. She takes posh pictures all the time for work. If she can't do it, she'll probably know someone who can.

Tell Katie not to worry, poor thing. Let me know the date, and between Jess and me, we'll get it sorted.

Off the subject: I thought I found a place to give my camera back, but I changed my mind again. Had a weird dream about it, so I think I'll wait on it for now.

How's Monica's daughter doing? Has she had the baby yet?

And is your knee any better?

To: me

From: drj14andrews@gmail.com

Subject: Photographers?

Brilliant, Scott, that's great news!

The wedding is May 13 (Sat).

Seriously, you may have saved the day. I told Katie and she cried, she was so relieved. I can't stand to see her so stressed. This has been tough on her, missing our mum through all this. But I keep telling her it will turn out all right (I think I'm telling myself too). She and Cory are disagreeing about what kind of tuxes for the guys, and I joked with her that I could wear my trackies. She didn't take it well. But maybe this will get me back on her good side.

I appreciate it, mate.

You'll know when the time is right for the camera thing. There's no rush. (Are you carrying it with you on these trips? Is that OK with you?)

No, Hannah hasn't had her baby—any day now. Monica might burst before Hannah does.

I think you owe me a dream, so you could tell me about the weird one you had? Or not.

Scored one at the weekend match! Long overdue. Knee feels better. I think it's the yoga. I know you keep saying you have no time, but I wonder if there would be something in it that would help your ears at all? Couldn't hurt.

P.S. One of my patients has a litter of kittens that need homes. I'm going to say no. Seriously. I'm going to say no.

18 January 2017

To: drj14andrews@gmail.com

From: me

Subject: Photographers?

Congrats on the goal! See? Show those youngsters how it's done.

I like this saving the day thing! It feels good! I'm sorry that you and Katie are sad sometimes about your mum. It's great that you have each other, though, really. Even if you don't get along all the time. There were times Olivia and I didn't speak for one reason or another. But we're more careful about that now.

If there's anything else I can do to help, I'd like to, so let me know.

As for the dream, Omran and I were together on a train, or maybe it was a bus. We were about to get off and Omran said, "You forgot this," and he handed me my camera, which I thought I had over my shoulder, but turns out it was under the seat, and I was about to walk off without it.

And yes, I am carrying my camera with me. I thought it would be good to give it back far from home. Is that bad? Anyway, I'll be hanging on to it a while longer.

I'll call you when I get home about another thing I've been thinking about—too complicated to type out.

P.S. I'd like to float when I get back, but I checked the web, and they have no appointments for two weeks out! Busy!

P.P.S. My vote is an emphatic yes on the kitten(s).

20 January 2017

Scott and Jason aren't able to get a window table at Pearl's since Jason's last appointment went a few minutes long. But the table near the bar is fine, and Jason is halfway through his lentil and avocado salad when he offers Scott his float appointment.

"No, Jason, you don't need to do that." Sure, Scott wants to float, badly, but not so much so that Jason should give up his spot.

"Seriously," Jason says, "it's no problem at all. Perks of being friends with the owner. What night do you want to go?"

Arguing with Jason seems pointless, and Scott hasn't floated in months. "Um, Tuesday or Wednesday, I guess? Is that too soon?"

"I'll call and see. It will be late, though, remember. Nine or so. Friends get spots after business hours."

"That's fine. Perfect, really. Float, then straight home to bed."

"All right. I'll let you know when."

"Thanks."

"Sure. I told you, I owe you for Jess." Jason looks at Scott curiously, then down at Scott's bowl of soup, three-quarters full and getting cold. "Why aren't you eating?"

"Eh, not hungry just now, I guess."

Jason looks sideways at him for a moment, sizing him up. He leans back and takes a sip of his tea. "What was the other thing you wanted to talk to me about?"

When Scott had been far from home, jockeying for a cab on the crowded, noisy street in Warsaw city centre, it had seemed overwhelming. The ringing had grown louder in his ears, and he'd started to sweat; he'd thought for a thrilling second about telling the cab to go to the airport instead of Triple Cross Square. But now, with two more assignments done, a night's sleep with his heated blanket warming his bed, and Jason sitting across from him, the whole thing feels dramatic and overblown.

"Oh, it turned out to be nothing. Just some nerves getting the better of me. It's fine."

Jason doesn't look convinced. "You sure? You've been travelling so much lately. Maybe you could take some time off?"

"Nah, I like to stay busy. It helps." Scott searches for a way to steer the topic away from himself. "How's Katie?"

Jason tilts his head as if to say "nice try," but when Scott raises his eyebrows, Jason doesn't push it. "Er... She's trying to figure out bridesmaid's dresses, I think, which are clearly beyond my scope of expertise. Evidently, there's a difference between baby-pink and ballet slipper–pink. Or maybe she's changed her mind to carnation-pink. I've lost track." His voice slows, and he looks down at his plate. "I thought things were better after the whole asshole photographer situation got solved, but..."

"But what?"

"I, uh, I'm just not very good at this." Jason seems at loose ends. It's oddly disconcerting.

"At wedding planning?"

"No, at being the brother she needs. Or the mum she needs, or whatever. I don't know. When mum died, I was...well, I left for a while. Not literally, but. I was gone in every way that mattered. Katie needed me. But I couldn't do it, and it was a while before I got it together. A long while. So there are...issues."

"Oh. Wow, Jason. I'm so sorry."

Jason pushes up his sleeves as if he's getting ready to work, or maybe because he needs to have something to do with his hands. "Well. It's a lot better now. I've been working on it."

"I'm sure Katie can tell you are. She knows you're doing your best, yeah?"

"I don't know, maybe. I hope so?"

Scott hasn't ever seen Jason lost like this before. His voice doesn't even sound like him. "Anyway, she knows you can't be your mum. She knows you can only be yourself. Right?"

"Um, well. Huh."

"What?

Jason sighs, then laughs a bit. "No, she probably doesn't know. Because I didn't know it myself until you said it just now."

"Okay then," Scott says and picks up his spoon.

Jason watches him take a bite, and then another. "Thanks," he says, and Scott smiles, though his soup is nearly cold.

14 February 2017

Scott picks up his phone to text Jason but sees a notification from him already there.

> *How's Gothenburg?*
>
> *Big day tomorrow, and I'm wired. Nervous. Been pacing around this hotel room for an hour*
>
> *Take a shower. Or have a sit down with a cuppa.*
>
> *Emilia taught me some pressure points. They're not working either*

How about yoga? We did a whole stress class a couple of weeks ago. It can help.

It's getting late, but anything is worth a try.

Ugh. Link me please. I'm desperate

He's got to be kidding. The link Jason sends is a balance on one foot called half-moon.

Nice try, but that pose is not possible

You just said you'd try anything! That's the best one for stress.

But how do I get sideways and stay there? I'll fall right over

Keep your chest open and your neck neutral. Keep your foot pointing forward. Use all your toes.

OK that's weird of you to say "All my toes"

Follow the steps. Do it against the wall first.

Scott brings the phone to the largest open space in the room, in front of the window, and studies the pose again. *Like a starfish.* He balances on one foot, then leans over and puts the tip of his fingers on the floor in front of him. *Starfish, starfish*, but then when he raises his leg, he crumples to the side, painfully.

Scott? You still there?

OK I smacked my ankle on the desk and almost broke this lovely hotel lamp, so thanks for that

Shit, don't hurt yourself. Or their nice things!

I'll stick with that other one you gave me, child's pose or whatever

Try it once on the other side though, so you're balanced.

Um, K. Hold please

Best of luck.

The other try is a bit better; he can at least hold his leg up for a few seconds before he tilts wildly, barely avoiding a collision with another piece of furniture.

Ugh. No. Toes don't help one bit. I have weak toes, I suppose. Ha!

Oh my God.

Right. I'll just have a sit down with some tea I think

Excellent idea. Safer for all the furniture. And body parts.

23 February 2017

Hello, you've reached Dr Jason—beep

"Hi, Jason. Just got home from Emilia's. Good news—the ringing in my left ear is down, way down, unnoticeable most of the time. Something else is going on with the right, maybe a holdover from the injuries, and it still flares up when I'm stressed. But it's so much better. She's actually going to use me in an article she's putting together. A collection of case studies, she said, that she's going to try to get published. I'm kind of proud, I guess? Oh, the Rome trip is back on, I leave the twenty-seventh. All right. Talk to you soon."

You have one new message. Received Friday, February 24th at 5:35 p.m.

"Rome, huh? Nice. So suck-up David is staying home this time, then? Good for you. And good on you for the acupuncture! Ow! Ugh, sorry, speaking of—Robbie's claws are like tiny needles. I'll put you right here, babe, now stay. Right, sorry about that. Yeah, Emilia's told me a bit about what she's working on. It's some fascinating stuff she's got. I'm glad you'll be a part of it. All right, got to get these little guys fed. Jimmy is about to chew my finger off. I'm not going to sound. I'm knackered. Talk to you soon."

28 February 2017

To: drj14andrews@gmail.com

From: me

Subject: Rome

It's 01:00 and I can't sleep.

I thought this would be the place where I could give my camera back. I thought I could leave it on one of these street corners. I could leave it in a pew in the church that's around the corner from the hotel. Or I could go to the Colosseum and leave it there with the ruins. Nobody would know or care, and it would seem kind of logical, you know? But I can't.

I lie in bed, and I stare at the ceiling, thinking about it. A street cleaner would sweep it up, wouldn't he? Or a tourist would find it and throw it in the bin. That's not right.

And I think about my dreams. I had another one, where Omran was telling me not to forget it. We were in a rickshaw in India this time, and I got out and walked away without it. (I don't know why I dream about him in India so much. He was never there with me. But that happens a lot.) He called me back and handed it to me. It was under the seat again.

These dreams are really fucking with me. Why do I keep having them? It's maddening, trying to walk away, move on, or whatever, and to keep getting pulled back in.

Does he think I'd forget? That doesn't even make any sense. I could never.

And then I remember what you told me, that giving my camera back isn't forgetting or pretending that it never was, it's letting it go to make space for something else. I get that, I really do. And I want to do that. But I can't yet.

Sorry to dump this on you.

I'll be home on Friday, early. I'll probably go to sound.

1 March 2017

To: me

From: drj14andrews@gmail.com

Subject: Rome

Damn, I wish I'd seen this last night.

You can call me whenever you want. Don't worry about waking me.

I can't tell you what to do about this one. I do know one thing though, and that's when you give your camera back, it's going to feel good, not bad. It's not going to feel like something you're forced to do, or something that makes you feel guilty or confused. It's going to feel right when you do it, like the next logical step. If you don't feel like that now, which you obviously don't, that means you're not ready. And that's fine.

Maybe your dreams are your mind's way of telling you that. And it's brilliant that it's Omran who's telling you in your dreams. He's your friend. Listen to him. There's nothing to worry about here. It's all going to unfold how it should. That's not doctor me talking, that's just Jason.

And off the subject, how's the food? I had the best pizza in Rome a few years ago, had an egg and pesto on top. (Don't forget to eat, OK?)

And another off the subject, it's been a rumour in my family there was some line of ancestry that comes from Italy. My mum always loved that and said it made total sense because it would explain why she talked with her hands so much. Even though nobody ever tried to trace us there, I still like to believe it because of her.

I'll see you at sound?

(And now I guess I owe you another dream?)

2 March 2017

To: drj14andrews@gmail.com

From: me

Subject: Rome

Thanks.

What you said about my camera makes sense. I'm relieved to hear it. I knew it, I think, but I still worry. It still feels massive to me. But I'll try to put it on the back burner for now.

Not surprisingly, the food is excellent. The spaghetti in the AP canteen is ten times better than any fancy pasta dish I've had at home. Simple tomato sauce with it, and a little red wine, and somehow, it's heavenly.

That's a sweet story about your mum. I feel connected to Italy too. They have all sorts of websites now where you can do your family trees and stuff—you could find out once and for all if the rumour is true. Are your grandparents on her side still alive?

Anyway, thank you again. See you tomorrow.

(And yes, you do)

To: me

From: drj14andrews@gmail.com

Subject: Rome

OK here's one:

I'm with Katie at our house where we grew up. I'm probably twelve years old. We're racing around in the garden, running in circles, laughing. My stomach actually hurts in the dream because I'm laughing so hard, and I'm making funny faces at

> her, and she's squealing and tripping and stuff. I slow down so she can catch up to me, and my mum is watching out of the kitchen window, and she waves. Then my legs get really heavy, and I realise I can't run anymore. Then I can't walk because it's so hard to pull my feet up from the ground to keep going. I look down at my feet, and they get stuck, actually cemented into the ground, and I can't move. And there's a familiar feeling about it, like, "oh not again" because it's happened a lot.
>
> I guess I have that dream probably once every couple of weeks.
>
> Now we're even, I think?

3 March 2017

More often than not, the personality of the sound sessions on Friday nights seem to match what Scott needs on any given week. When he's exhausted and needs rest, it will be a night of large bells and bass drums. When he's anxious or has something on his mind, the tones will be gentle and even a little playful, to pull him out of his thoughts and lift his mood. Tonight's session was like that.

The conversation over dinner afterward is light and relaxed, with Scott happy to leave the issue of his camera off the table. Instead, Jason pulls out his phone and shows Scott a picture of a chiselled male model in a tuxedo.

"Here, take a look at this for me. I need your opinion. Cummerbunds, or no?"

"Yes to the guy. Meh on the suit. Why?"

Jason pulls his camera back and swipes the screen. "Because none of us agrees. Katie thinks morning suits." He shows Scott a new picture, a different man, this time with a classic morning coat, waistcoat, and striped trousers.

"Nice."

"Hold on," Jason says and swipes again. "My stepdad thinks velvet jackets. Ew. I'm not even going to show you that one. And Cory thinks slim fit, four button."

"Very nice." Scott looks at the model in a suit that's sleek and modern, but more appropriate for a music video than a wedding.

"Now I—" Jason pauses dramatically to swipe again. "—think bow ties and braces."

This makes Scott snort before he ever sees the picture.

"What? What's funny?" Jason says incredulously as they bend their heads together over his phone.

"You can't be serious," Scott says, laughing, although the man in the photo is quite handsome, with tattooed forearms showing underneath his rolled-up sleeves.

"Well, clearly you have an opinion." Jason rolls his eyes and puts away his phone.

"Yes, I do. The bride gets what she wants."

Jason shuts his eyes with a deep sigh. "Quite so. Thank you. And Katie thanks you."

"You're both welcome."

"I think you'll be hearing from her soon, actually," Jason says after swallowing a bite of his salad.

"Katie?"

"She'd like you to come to the rehearsal dinner. As a thank you for the photographer fiasco. I gave her your number. I hope that's okay."

The thought of meeting Jason's sister and the rest of his family makes Scott want to stand up and pace, but Jason is oblivious, poking around on his plate for croutons.

"Sure, it's fine, but...she doesn't have to invite me."

"You should come! It'll be pretty simple, dinner and pints. And my family. A little nutty, but harmless, I promise."

Jason continues to eat, not realising that Scott has put his own fork down with a nervous rattle. It's not the occasion that makes him anxious, or meeting Jason's sister, but Jason will be there, too, with his boyfriend. Scott will be able to put a real human to the image of Jason's partner that he's worked up in his head. He's handsome, of course; Scott clearly remembers that from the picture of them on Jason's shelf. But he must be smart, and funny, too, and open-minded, and strong enough to hold all the powerful ideas Jason thinks and talks about. What will it be like to see them so close, to watch them together? Scott wipes his damp hands on his napkin. *Jesus, this could really happen.*

He takes a sip of water. "So, your boyfriend will be there, too, right? I'll get a chance to meet him, finally?"

"My boyfriend?" Jason asks with a confused look that makes his eyebrows crease.

"The guy in the picture with you at your office, on the bookshelf."

"Who...oh, uh, Ian? Wow, that was..." It's Jason's turn to put down his fork. He shakes his head with a little grunt and wipes his mouth with his napkin. "Uh, no, we're not together anymore. We broke up a long time ago. Last summer."

Scott cringes. "Oh, I'm sorry. I didn't realise." *Shit. Last summer?*

Jason doesn't look at him but seems to be studying woodgrain on the table instead. He stumbles over his words, which is very much unlike him. "That's all right, he...well, I was...you know, he did things, but really it wasn't all his fault, I mean. It just...didn't work out."

"Oh. I thought, this whole time, that you were with him. I guess. Sorry," Scott says again, this time meaning *sorry that he hurt you*. But underneath it, he can't help but feel a tiny flutter of relief that he's not sure what to do with. He takes another sip of water. "And you've been single since then?"

"Eh, I've had a few dates here and there." A small smile comes back to Jason's face. "There was one very sympathetic but very needy veterinarian."

"Oh my God, *the* veterinarian? The one with Bitsy?"

"Yeah. That one was over quick. There is one guy I met at yoga though. Seems promising. He's a doctor too."

"Oh. Nice." Scott picks up his fork and pokes a few chips around his plate.

"But you know, I'm busy, with work and the footie league and my family, so."

"Yeah. You've got a lot on your plate, don't you? Me too," Scott says slowly. He's agreeing, though it feels like some of that isn't all the way true. He doesn't know how to do this, really, how to be friends with someone who used to be his doctor, but who isn't anymore. Actually, the friends part seems to be working well. It's whatever the other feelings are that tend to sneak up on him—attraction, excitement, intimacy—that Scott isn't sure how to handle.

Their footing feels slippery suddenly, and Scott looks to change the subject back to something more solid. Like Jason's terrible taste in clothes.

"Bow tie and braces. How dare you?" he says, shaking his head, and Jason chuckles, pulling out his phone again.

"No seriously, take a look at this one. Purple polka dots. Subtle. I bet you'll change your mind."

They ease back into their light conversation, and Scott can forget all the rest for a bit. Jason is here with him, and that is enough.

17 March 2017

Two weeks and two business trips later, Scott looks at the digital images on his computer as his editor looks over his shoulder. They say nothing, but the air is prickly with stress and frustration. When Rich takes a break, Scott picks up his phone.

"Sorry, Jason. I can't make it to Luke's. Have to work late."

"Uh-oh."

"Yeah, all night, most likely. It's not looking good."

"What happened?"

Scott sighs and rubs his eyes. Leave it to Jason to ask

the simple, excellent questions.

Scott could say it was all his interpreter's fault, but that would be a lie. She'd been focused, efficient, and quite helpful. He swallows. "I thought I had the shots. But I rushed, didn't listen, said it would be fine. I just wanted to get out of there, and now Rich and I have to cobble something together out of this stinking shitpile. Have to submit by midnight tomorrow."

"Damn. I'm sorry."

"My own fault."

"Are you all right?"

"Will be." Scott scrolls through the images again, each picture worse than the last, already determined he'll make up for this, if they give him another chance.

"Well. If there's anything I can do, just—"

"Nah, thanks though."

"Uh, okay, well, maybe next week then."

"Next week." Scott bites his lip so he doesn't say any more.

22 March 2017

3:05 p.m.

Scott is hanging up the call with his boss when his phone buzzes with a text notification. It's Jason.

> *I just saw the news. Are you going to Westminster?*

Yes

Damn.

I'm on my way now.

I'm sorry. Call me if you need to.

It's too hard, Jason, he thought. It's too hard to talk to you when I'm on the job. Especially this kind of job.

Scott's ringtone makes him jump. He taps the speakerphone. "Hey, Liv, just a second."

OK. Have to go. Olivia's calling

Even if it's late or whatever, OK?

10:40 p.m.

To: drj14andrews@gmail.com

From: me

Subject: Westminster

I know you said I could call you, even if it was late, but it's easier to write this down than say it.

I don't know what to do. I work, going where they tell me to go, taking pictures of what I'm supposed to take pictures of. But today it was our very own city. I was on the bridge, but I wasn't. I don't know any other way to describe it.

I watch myself from the outside, looking at these places as composition problems. How to fit this rubble into the frame, how to get that twisted piece of rebar with the police tape across it in the same shot as a crashed car so I end up with a good photo. Lighting. F-stop. Depth of field. There are people in uniforms wandering around, marking up the place with chalk. Cleaning up. And I'm trying to find an expressive enough face or a scene that tells the story of what and how. And why. And I can't, it's impossible.

What the fuck am I doing?

My press tags feel so heavy. Every morning I dread putting them on. I wait until the last possible second before someone checks me. Tonight when I took them off I felt free. Like myself again.

I don't think I want to do this anymore.

To: me

From: drj14andrews@gmail.com

Subject: Westminster

Please call me.

You don't have to do it anymore. You don't. You can quit if you want. You don't owe anybody anything.

Call me please.

23 March 2017

To: me

From: drj14andrews@gmail.com

Subject: Westminster

Maybe it's easier for me to write this than say it too.

I can't imagine how hard it must be for you, being there.

You're probably seeing all the same sights and hearing the same sounds that you did in Kabul.

You went through that once, and I don't think you should do it again. That's just me. It's your call. It always is. Taking pictures is what you do. And you can still do that, somewhere else, for someone else, couldn't you? You want to tell a story. But I think a part of you might also think you have to make up for something, or even some score, or be brave or something. Or keep telling stories for Omran because he can't anymore?

It's not wrong to turn away from all of that now, Scott. The story will get told. It doesn't have to be you who tells it.

You're going to say I'm biased. Yes, I am.

You said you feel like yourself when you take your press tags off. What if you could take pictures and feel like yourself at the same time? What kinds of pictures would those be? Would they be like the water blessing? Or the kids at school in New Delhi? You took an excellent photo of an orange flower once, without even trying. And the pictures you took of the gongs at sound are beautiful. And I know you loved taking them.

Just think about it, please.

I'll talk to you tomorrow.

24 March 2017

Scott unlocks his flat door. He shuffles to the bed—jacket, camera bag and all—and falls into it with his shoes on. He loves the arnica smell of his sheets; he closes his eyes and turns his face into the mattress so he can breathe deep. *Home.*

He might fall asleep for a minute, though it's four in the afternoon. There is a wisp of a dream where Omran and Scott are sitting in the library at Scott's primary school, in small chairs meant for kids. Omran slides Scott's broken camera across the table to him.

When he opens his eyes, he's sweating a bit, and thirsty. He eases his feet out of his boots and takes off his jacket. He feels for his phone in his back pocket and calls Jason.

"Hey, Scott."

"Hey."

"You're home?"

"Yeah."

"Are you all right?"

"It was like you said. The sounds and...the sights. But this time, it was right here at home."

"I'm sorry."

They are silent for long moments. With Jason listening, there is no need to add on or fix, nothing to defend or explain.

"I want to quit." It is what it is. He's not sad anymore. It's just a fact.

"All right. When?"

Scott looks at his calendar, for no reason really, because he knows the answer already. "Monday." *The end of one thing. The beginning of something else.*

"Okay then. A good decision, well made. This calls for a celebration, yeah?"

"Nah, I'm knackered."

"I mean tomorrow. Get some rest tonight, and we can meet up for brunch?"

Scott runs his hand through his hair. It feels strange and wrong to celebrate after what's happened. He says nothing but a noncommittal groan.

"Come on. I'll come to Camden. Do you have a favourite spot?"

"Always with the persistence," Scott says, but he can't say no. It's been too long since they've seen each other, and he knows a meal with Jason will help set his mind right. "Okay, I know a good place. I'll send you the address."

25 March 2017

It had taken Scott a long while after the accident to want to come to Blues Kitchen again; the energy of the night-time bar crowd along with the loud wails of blues music kept him away. But on the weekends, it's relaxed, but not sleepy, and the music's festive, but not loud. It's the perfect place for Scott to introduce Jason to his neighbourhood. And he can't wait to see what Jason thinks of the cornbread.

They walk through the crowded front room to a corner table by the bar, and after they've ordered an enormous-but-still-polite quantity of food, Scott notices that Jason's body hasn't stopped moving. He sways sometimes, his shoulders rocking to the music, and his thigh rises up and down as if he's tapping his foot on the floor.

"You like this music, huh?" Scott asks.

"Absolutely! You know what would be the best job of all time?"

"What?"

"Background singer."

Now, Jason adds a finger snap to the mix, and Scott is charmed.

"A background singer. Why?"

"Think about it. You get to travel all over. You get to listen to excellent music every night, from the stage, sing a few *oooh oooh oooh's* every once in a while, and get paid. And if it's a proper band, you'd have it all—huge horn section, a couple guitars, piano, the whole bit. And you're right there, part of it, but not the main attraction, right? No heavy lifting."

"And you get to dance too," Scott suggests, moving his arms like he's seen background singers do.

"That's right. My dream gig," Jason says, staring off wistfully.

Scott remembers the lifetime of singing that still lives inside him somewhere, where he and his best friend sang for royalty. That day in the treatment room, he'd felt the closeness of those boys, and there'd been a hint of feeling after that Jason somehow *was* that boy, his Georgie's John. Scott had been confused and tired, but he'd felt it.

He looks at Jason, dancing a little clumsily and humming off-key. "But you can't sing."

"Quite so. That's why it's called a *dream* gig. And anyway, don't burst my bubble."

Scott laughs. "Fine. Keep the dream alive."

"Let's talk about *your* dream job." Jason squares up in his seat and leans in, clinks his glass brightly against Scott's. "Since you're going to be looking."

"Hold on, give me a minute. I haven't even quit yet." But Scott smiles anyway, anticipating the thought of putting his press pass down and being free.

Jason looks at him, a bit of the playfulness still in his eyes, but his tone utterly serious. "It doesn't hurt to dream. Does it?"

"No, it doesn't."

"So what'll it be? What would you do if you could do anything?"

"My dream gig?"

"Dream gig."

Scott knows what it is already. "You're going to laugh."

"No, I won't. I promise." Jason leans closer.

"Okay." Scott takes a breath. "So...I want to be a photographer."

Jason's eyes get wide, but as promised, he doesn't laugh. "A photographer, huh?"

"Yeah."

"Wow, I hear that's a hard job. You have to have a lot of talent. Some people are so good at it that they actually get awards."

Scott looks down with a smile. "So they say."

Jason's voice gets softer. "So, what kind of pictures are you going to take?"

"Beautiful ones. Complicated ones. Pictures that don't hurt to look at. I did that already. I've had enough of it."

Jason nods. Everything else fades into the background. The music, the restaurant, the other people, the bustle of the Camden Saturday morning. For this moment, it's just the two of them, still doing what they've done since the beginning: trusting each other with their dreams.

Chapter Twelve

Perspective (n.) The sense of depth or spatial relationships between objects in a photograph, along with their dimensions with respect to the camera or the viewer; a picture drawn in perspective, especially one appearing to enlarge or extend the actual space, or give the effect of distance; true understanding of the relative importance of things; a sense of proportion.

11 April 2017

As soon as Scott hangs up with the Human Resources Department, he texts Jason.

Hey! I got the interview with the magazine!

That's great! When is it?

The 24th. My portfolio looks good. But they may not think I'm right for it

How could they not? They'd be insane to pass you over

They said set aside two hours. To tour the offices and tech. And meet the assignment editor

That sounds promising!

I want it.

Sounds like they want you too.

There will be travel. But it would be outdoorsy and lifestyle stuff. Instead of politics and dangerous current events

Dream gig!

What if I don't get it?

You will.

What if I don't?

Then you'll look for something else.

Have you ever wanted something so bad but you had no control over it

Yes.

It sucks

Yes.

Shit. :/

Patience. And hope. :)

16 April 2017

Scott lifts the frying pan off the hob and flips it lightly with his wrist, making the sliced mushrooms jump and sizzle. Jason is cooking, too, on the other end of the phone, a salad made with grains Scott can't pronounce. After a quick comparison of recipes, he figures now is as good a time to ask as any.

"Did I see you at Broadway Market yesterday, around eleven? I thought you saw me, but then you were gone."

"Oh, um, yeah, that was me."

"How come you didn't stop and say hi?"

"Eh, dunno, I saw you were with somebody, so I didn't want to intrude."

"Well, shit, you should have. That's a guy Olivia's been trying to fix me up with for ages, one of her friends' older brothers. *Hugh.*" Scott makes a face when he says the name. "He deals in antiques. Asked if we could take a Saturday morning stroll through the market. I figured how bad could it be, you know? Street food, crafty stuff, more food..."

"Looks like Olivia's got good taste."

Scott moves the mushrooms to the side of the pan with a wooden spoon and picks an egg out of the carton. "Eh. I guess. But he's a snob. Twenty minutes in and I swear I was looking for an excuse to go home."

"Maybe he was nervous. First impressions can be... awkward."

"Jason. I'd pet the dogs and he'd scrunch up his nose and look at my hands like I was dirty. We smelled the candles, you know, the ones from that place that sells the baskets and wooden bowls? He turned his nose up at all of them. I bought six just to spite him." Scott cringes, cracking the egg into the pan. The yolk spreads in an irregular shape, broken.

"Oh my God, you didn't." Jason's shocked laughter is ripply and light, and it makes Scott smile a bit.

"Hell yes, I did! And don't even get me started on his taste in music." Scott remembers Hugh in the record store, flipping through the vinyl LPs with his creepy, pale fingers in a way that seemed precious and fake. "I'm rolling my eyes. Aggressively, if you can't tell."

"I guess I should have rescued you. I will next time."

"No. No next time."

"Aw, don't throw in the towel just yet. Someone special will come along when you least expect."

"Ugh. I'm rolling my eyes again." Of course Jason would say that. He can strike up a relationship with anyone, even in the vet's office or his yoga class. "Hey, speaking of, how's Dr Yoga?"

"Eh. All right, I guess. Remember what I told you about doctors and their egos? Well, yeah. But he's interesting. He does organ work."

"Organ work?"

"Right. Mostly transplants."

“Oh. Wow,” Scott says. *Shit. A surgeon.* He’d hoped Dr Yoga would be something a bit less glamourous. Like a podiatrist.

“He’s on call a lot of the time. Makes it tough to get together. He’s not even sure he can come to the wedding.”

“Oh, that’s too bad.” Scott slides the spatula under the egg, but it’s too soon, and the flip is more like a fold. He tries to straighten it so it will cook evenly, but it splits apart and ends up scrambled instead of fried.

“He’s going to call in a few favours with some of his colleagues though. He said they should be able to trade days.”

“Good, well, that will be good,” Scott says inanely and tosses the spatula into the sink. He turns off the hob, not hungry anymore.

“Yeah, we’ll see how it goes,” Jason says.

“Yeah, we’ll see how it goes.”

9 May 2017

Tuesday is surprisingly sunny and warm; when Scott rounds the corner to Pearl’s he’s surprised to see they’ve put some tables outside, and Jason is seated at one. Scott slides into the chair across from him.

“Wow, gorgeous,” Scott says, the warmth already brightening his mood.

“Have you heard anything?”

“Nope, not yet. They said they’d let me know by the sixth. I didn’t get it.”

"Something probably came up, that's all."

Scott shakes his head and opens the menu, though he orders the same thing every time. "They probably got someone else."

"No, Scott, look at your resume. Look at all your experience, and your awards. I mean, damn, they'd be mad not to hire you."

"I thought I smashed the interview, truly. I thought we clicked. He kept me there for, like, two and a half hours? And showed me the offices and everything. I really want it."

"I know, and I'm telling you, it's a no-brainer."

Scott rubs his forehead and runs his fingers through his hair. "You're biased."

"True. Doesn't mean I'm wrong."

"Ugh, let's change the subject. How's Katie? The wedding's finally here."

"Saturday. The big day." Jason heaves a sigh and looks away.

"Is everything ready?"

"Flowers, food, DJ, yes. But uh...I'll be a mess."

"Your sister's getting married. Of course you'll be a mess. But it's going to be a happy day. Really."

There is a long silence, and then Jason clears his throat. "I know. But there'll be times when I'm going to have to hold it together, and...it's going to be tough."

Scott watches Jason's face blush and his eyes blink back tears. "Wait, hold on a second." He reaches out his hand to touch Jason's folded arm. "Maybe you don't have to hold it together, you know? No one should try to pretend that they don't miss your mum."

"And Katie wants me to dance with her." Jason sniffs, then laughs. "I can't dance."

"You'll be fine. Just hold her tight. But don't squish her dress. Or step on her toes. Or turn her too fast, or—"

Jason swipes at his cheeks. "Anyway, don't forget the rehearsal dinner."

Scott pulls his hand away as a hot swoop in his chest plunges down to his stomach. *Holy. Shit.* "Right, The Old Brewery in Greenwich."

"At seven."

"Seven. I'll be there." A calming idea takes shape, and Scott scratches at his temple. "Hey, do you think Katie would like some pictures of the rehearsal? Or the dinner? I could bring my camera, take some shots. If she wants me to."

"Are you joking? She would love that. But you don't have to. It's supposed to be for fun. She didn't mean for you to work."

"It *will* be fun. I want to. It's a big night. She should have pictures."

"Yes, yes, she should, shouldn't she?" Jason smiles. "If you're offering, I'm accepting. She'll be over the moon when I tell her."

A brilliant feeling wakes up in Scott; he'll have something to do, something he does well. "Then it's settled."

"Seriously, thank you. This means...everything."

Jason's words are soft, and Scott's voice sounds soft too.

"You're welcome."

12 May 2017

Jason's family is small but boisterous, and Scott finds it impossible to fade into the background as he usually would on assignment. Aunt Jane chats him up, wanting to know about his work and his travels, and a cousin, Dale, helps Scott tell knock-knock jokes to the shy flower girl so she'll smile. Katie is even prettier in real life than in the pictures he's seen, and she absolutely glows when she thanks him, again, for saving her wedding. He'll enjoy processing the images tomorrow; he knows of one shot she'll love, of her and Cory laughing at the bawdy toast her best friend made.

Scott likes the way Jason keeps checking on him from near and far. At first, it's a sort of life preserver, to make sure Scott doesn't drown in the group of strangers, but later, it becomes more of a touchstone, where Scott can look for him and there Jason will be, looking back with a smile or a funny face. When a few romantic songs play after the speeches, Scott watches as Jason dances with Katie, and then with his granny. The flower girl pokes Scott on the knee and points to the dance floor too; soon, he finds himself waltzing with her, catching Jason's eye with a grin. Jason doesn't ever look him over critically the way he used to, studying his posture or investigating his scars for signs of healing, and Scott is glad; they're proper friends now, and those scars might as well be invisible. Tonight, though, Jason's expression is different, a bit wistful and starry-eyed. Scott chalks it up to Jason being slightly drunk, or slightly nervous. Maybe both.

The party winds down after the cake is served, and Jason slips into the empty seat beside Scott, just vacated by one of Katie's bridesmaids, who'd spent the last few minutes trying to chat Scott up.

"You let her down easy, I hope. She's been staring at you all night." Jason picks up Scott's fork and takes a big bite of his cake. He looks happy, and a bit flushed with a beer buzz. He doesn't give Scott a chance to answer, gesturing to the cameras that hang around Scott's neck. "I should have known you'd bring two cameras. Let me guess. One's digital and one's for film."

"Well, you're almost right. *Two* are digital," Scott answers, pulling a third camera, his tiny backup Nikon, from his back pocket. "Want to see some of the shots?"

They lean in, and Scott swipes through the images slowly so Jason can see. In one group shot, Jason points to the way Cory and Katie are holding hands behind her back.

"That's a good one. She'll like that," he says, touching the edge of the frame fondly, then wiping at his lip with Scott's napkin. "Thank you."

"For the cake?" Scott chuckles.

"No. Well, yes. But..."

Scott turns the small camera over in his hands, waiting for him to finish. Jason shakes his head, then shrugs and looks across the room at his sister, who's hugging a tearful Aunt Jane. His face changes as he watches her, and Scott sees the heavy thing Jason carries sometimes.

When Jason finally speaks, Scott hangs on every careful word.

"Thank you for bringing three cameras to my sister's party."

Scott smiles, a bit at a loss for what to say. Jason's praise makes his chest pound. "You're welcome. And thank you."

"For the cake?" Jason asks, taking another bite.

Thank you for trusting me.

"Yes. For the cake."

13 May 2017

A notification ding stirs Scott from his light sleep. He feels for his phone on his bedside cabinet without fully turning over.

SUCCESS!

He smiles to himself and rubs one eye with a yawn.

Are you home? Is it over? Is she married?

Yes yus adn yes! I'm proper drunk

Congratulations!! On the married sister part. Not the drunk part

I only cried three times I think. A solid victory!

Scott sits up, now fully awake. It takes a long moment to think of what he should say.

Ha, good on you. Crying is just fine. Somebody told me that once

That was me Scott ME

A good way to let go of things

I don't want to let go of her. I jist got her back. Just a bit ago. I guess I'm crying again.

You don't have to let her go. You can be sad for a while. It's OK (I'm not helping am I)

Yes you are. You help.

Scott smiles, folding his legs underneath him.

Good, hope so

Teribl date.

Oh?

I don't like him. Ive decided

Suddenly, Scott needs to get up and pace.

Dr Yoga?

I want him to leave.

He's still there?

He's not as n ice to Katie as you are. I knew youd be lovely to her. I KNEW that.

Scott walks a path along the side of his bed and back, the glow of his phone the only light in the flat.

If you want him to leave tell him!

I'm going to. Hold please.

OK

STAYYY THERE.

OK

Long minutes pass with no update, and Scott lays back on the bed with his legs hanging over.

Jason are you still there?

The Uber took him. What a git! He didn't eat cake ON PURPOSE !!

Scott runs a hand through his hair with a chuckle, then types:

SAD

What kind of persn doesn't have CKE dumb

Fifteen kinds of wrong

Was white w pink roses v good. M tired

Scott can picture Jason loosening his tie, unbuttoning his collar, stripping off the formalities of the day. He feels his teeth bite into his lip.

Do you think you should go to bed now?

Yes bed. You go to bed too.

Ha, I'm already in bed.

K goodnight.

Night.

You still there?

Still here

Youre a good friend mate.

Scott rolls to his side and hugs a pillow to his chest. He turns his face to the mattress for a long second, then types.

You too.

Night.

Night.

16 May 2017

Hello, you've reached Dr Jason Andrews's mobile. I'm sorry—beep

"Hey, I got it! I got the job! They called to let me know this morning, and they want me to start

Monday! Shit, Jason, you can't believe how fucking *relieved* I am. The HR person was on vacation and that's why they were late calling. Can you believe this? I wanted this job so fucking bad, and I got it. I thought you should be the first to know, since you suggested it and everything. Anyway, maybe you could call me back after work. Okay. Thanks. Whew. Bye."

You have one new message. Received May 16th at 6:12 p.m.

"Brilliant news! I knew you would get it. Excellent! You must be out celebrating. Have fun! I myself shall be going home to sit alone in my tub in a funk because we've been eliminated from the playoffs. It was a proper routing. Personal record for penalties and spent the last bit out with my knee stuck in the cool box. So. Yay me. Seriously, congrats. This is going to be brilliant. I'm happy for you. Later."

Just got your voicemail! Yes we're out. Olivia and some people. At the Black Heart in Camden. You could come

Nah mate, can't tonight. Knee. Thanks though.

Is it OK?

It will be. Ego's a bit bruised.

Aww Sorry!!

Have fun. And congratulations! I'm happy for you!

Thanks! Me too! See you Friday at sound?

See you then!

2 June 2017

Scott and Jason arrive early at Luke's, so they can stake out their favourite corner spot during the increasingly crowded Friday night session. They place their mats with fifteen minutes to spare, and as they settle in, Jason mentions how much Katie adores the photos Scott took at the rehearsal dinner.

"Aww, I'm glad. Yeah, she called to tell me."

"I don't even think she cares if she ever gets the pictures Jess took at the wedding! She's picked out all the ones you took that she wants to blow up and frame. She's going to include some with her thank-you notes, I think, however that works. The one you got of her and Cory during the toast."

"Oh yeah, that was a good one. Honestly, have you ever seen such massive heart eyes?"

"I know, it's gross, ha," Jason says, but the fond curve in his voice says he thinks it's the exact opposite.

"They make a brilliant couple. Lucky." Scott remembers their easy closeness, Katie's hand on Cory's back as they mingled or Cory leaning in as they talked.

"So, Wyoming, is it? When do you leave?"

"Actually, Wyoming and Montana. Yellowstone first, then the Tetons. The project is all about hiking through the national parks. I leave on Thursday."

"Wait. Are you actually going to be hiking?" Jason looks vaguely horrified.

"Yes, as a matter of fact. You sound like that's a bad thing."

"No! No, not at all. Just watch for bears, I guess?"

"Ha. Yeah, I'm a bit jealous of whoever got the Hawaii leg of this gig. But actually, there's this huge hot spring at Yellowstone. It's one of the biggest in the country. Should be excellent."

"Be careful, please."

"Right...you do realise I survived a large explosion in Kabul, don't you?"

Jason's eyes are sharp. "Yes. I hadn't forgotten."

"Well, then. A big puddle of hot water and some bears can't hurt me, all right?" Scott laughs, but the real gravity of the year's turn of events catches up to him, as well as the realisation that Jason might actually be worried. He takes a quiet breath. "I'll keep in touch."

"Do. Are you going to bring your camera?"

"I am." Scott carved out a space in his bag for it ever since he started travelling again. His old, broken camera goes with him everywhere, in case the stars ever align, or perhaps he'd be told in a dream that the time is right to let it go. Maybe this time there will be a cliff he can leave it on or a spot under a tree deep in the woods he can give it to.

"All right then. Good luck."

Scott wants to say more, maybe thank you for worrying, it will be hard to be gone for so long, you're my best friend. But instead, he says, "Thanks."

13 June 2017

Guess how much it costs to send a plush toy bison from Cooke City, Montana, to London

Aw, you shouldn't have!

Idiot, it's for Thomas! ? No guesses?

Where have you been? I was starting to worry that you'd been eaten by a grizzly. Or a vulture.

Hiking. Photographing. No grizzlies. Plenty of wolves though

Wolves?? It's going well, I hope?

Brilliant. Team is ace. And holy shit. More stars than you can believe

Take a picture for me!

Already did, ha. They added a few more days on. Won't be home until the 22nd

Wow, that's a while.

I'll email you soon with pics. It's $443.72 to ship the buffalo by the way

Better smuggle him home in your luggage, then!

Right. See you

See you.

26 June 2017

When Scott arrives at Jason's office Monday afternoon, Monica is hanging up the phone. She brightens as she walks toward him, then comes in for a full hug. He puts down the large package he's brought so he can hug her back.

"Scott, you're a sight for sore eyes," she says, looking him up and down. "So tan!"

"I was gone for a while, in the States."

"Yes, our world traveller. We're glad to have you back."

"Thanks, it's good to be back." And it is, not only to be back in London, but back in Jason's office. The music, the smell, even the rug under Scott's feet are parts of himself he's been missing. "Jason said he'd be between appointments at three thirty. I have something for him."

"Sure, I'll walk you back."

Jason must hear them coming because when Scott reaches his door, he's already rounding the corner of his desk and closing the space between them with his hand extended. "Hey!" he says, and Scott can only take in a glimpse of his bright eyes and a shadow of stubble on his jaw before he's pulled in for a half hug, the package shifting under their arms.

Scott's mind registers Monica's retreat and Jason's warm chest bumping against his and the smell of arnica and green leaves and clean linens; he manages a soft "hey" in return before Jason pulls away.

"Are you taller? Or something?" Jason asks.

"Maybe it's the tan?"

"Yeah, that must be it." Jason studies him for a moment longer and smiles. "All the way from across the pond."

Scott can study him too, now. Sleeves rolled up to his elbows, hair brushing the top of his collar, a bit of copper in his beard.

Jason looks down at the flat parcel wrapped in brown paper. "And what's this?"

"It's a present."

"What's the occasion?"

Scott thinks for a bit. "Dream gig."

Jason smiles bigger, taking the package and laying it on his desk. He pulls open the string and unfolds the wrapping. He's speechless for a minute, leaning over to see the details of the framed photograph.

"It's Montana, in a valley outside Yellowstone. I took a whole roll, trying to get the view just right."

"I'd say you did. It's incredible. Scott, this is...really something. Look at the shape of the trees against the sky. Beautiful. And a proper lot of stars."

"Astounding, isn't it?" Scott couldn't believe it either, when he first saw it, halfway across the world. It is his night valley, complete with the borderline of trees standing watch. This is where he found his fire, found his lives, and found himself again.

"And this is for me? Why?"

"You asked me what would happen if I took pictures that make me feel like myself. Well, this picture makes me feel like myself." *It is myself.* "You helped me get there, truly. So I wanted you to have it."

"I'm just...I... This is amazing, Scott, thank you."

"You're welcome."

"I'm not sure if you meant for me to hang it here in my office, but..." Jason picks up the photo with both hands and holds it at arm's length. "I'd rather hang it at home if you don't mind? I have an idea where it should go."

"It's yours, you can put it anywhere you want." The thought is thrilling—that Jason would want to have the picture close by, to look at every day. "I'm so glad you like it."

"I love it. It means so much to me." He takes a last look, then turns to Scott and hugs him quickly, like before, just long enough for one squeeze and a clap on the shoulder before he breaks away.

"You're welcome." Scott whispers it as his fingers let go of Jason's sleeve. When Jason is fully three steps away, Scott comes back to himself. "I'm going to go. You have another patient coming in, right?

"I do. But it's been great to see you. I'll send you a picture after I hang it tonight."

"All right, and I'll see you at sound, then?"

"Right. Friday."

Scott turns to go, and takes the familiar short trip down the hallway past Monica's desk. He smiles as he opens the door and steps out. Jason is going to take a piece of him home.

29 June 2017

Scott swipes a thin layer of dust from the cover of his black notebook. There are a few more pages filled in now, as well as clippings and cut-outs poking out from between the pages. He's caught a glimpse of the fire only a handful of times since leaving Jason's, twice while he floated, and once while he almost fell asleep at sound.

There is a page with notes about a happy, warm life that was entirely snowbound, as well as one that was fraught with danger, spent alone in a cabin on the edge of a windy plain. He flips through those now, catching glimpses of choirboys and soldiers, war-painted horses and a stone fortress near the ocean. It gives his hands, nervous with energy, something to do as he talks to Jason on the phone.

"I mean, it's been a year and a half since Omran died. I'm not the same person I was."

"I know you aren't."

"So why can't I *do* this? I mean, I took it up to this lovely cliff, where there was this little altar of rocks. It was dusk, breezy and getting cool. Perfect. Beautiful. Like that was where it was supposed to be. All that, and I still couldn't walk away." Scott cringes as he listens to himself talk. But Jason is the only person who could possibly understand. "God. I'm sorry to bring this up again." He snaps the book shut.

"Don't apologise."

"Will we ever *not* talk about this? Ugh."

"We can talk about it all you want. Look, there's something you need from that camera. There's a reason you can't give it up."

"I don't know what it is."

"Maybe Omran is trying to tell you something. Wait, this is gonna sound weird, but..."

Scott chuckles softly, his hand resting protectively on his notebook's cover. "We're way past weird."

"True. So...have you ever asked Omran to *tell* you what he wants?"

Scott swallows. "Ask him?"

"Yeah. Next time you see him. Ask him."

Scott almost laughs, not because it sounds absurd, but because it absolutely doesn't. Perhaps it can be as easy as that.

"All right," he says, "I will."

19 July 2017

To: drj14andrews@gmail.com

From: me

Subject: Do you want a PTSD contact in California?

Wanted to send you this photo. These are the float guys I was telling you about, in front of their place. They have the float tanks downstairs, and upstairs, they have the yoga studio and rehab centre. The bearded guy on the left is Dr Kevin Pena. He's the one who's doing the research on floating and PTSD. Do you want me to give him your contact information?

Turns out I'm going to San Francisco after this, to do a portrait of the Governor at his vacation home. (They contacted me specifically! What? I know?) Then home. I'm a bit nervous to do a political portrait again, but I may have an extra day there, and it's within driving distance of some huge sequoias, so I told them I'd do it. Thomas told me the oldest tree *in the world* is a sequoia, 2100 years old, named General Sherman. So I have to send him a postcard.

I'll send you one, too, to add to your tree collection.

P.S. Robbie and Jimmy are huge. How did that happen?

P.P.S. I haven't seen Omran lately, to ask.

20 July 2017

To: me

From: drj14andrews@gmail.com

Subject: Do you want a PTSD contact in California?

Absolutely, yes, please do give him my numbers.

An interesting development: I found a company that makes singing bowls out of crystal and minerals instead of metals. Brilliant! So I've been talking to Ilsa, the woman who makes them (a very intense—might be in her 70s?—woman of few words), and she said I could come see her place in Stuttgart. She makes tuning forks too. Incredible. Can you imagine a lapis or aquamarine tuning fork?

Here's where it gets interesting. Emilia has been going to sound, right? And Luke's been going to acupuncture, and they're both floating at Drew's. Emilia suggested we start experimenting with combinations of it all, to see what kind of effect it has. Sound bath during acupuncture session, acupuncture while floating, singing bowl during either one, etc. So I'm going to Stuttgart (Luke might go too) and we'll see what we find. I ordered a tourmaline bowl for the office, and it should get here next week.

I can see so many possibilities. All of this works on its own, but what happens when it's put together? We're even talking about testing and control groups and how it might expand on Emilia's study. We haven't cemented the dates yet, but it will probably be at the end of the month.

I'm not sure I'll be playing football this year. With all the rest going on, I might not have time. Actually, that might be an excuse I tell myself because, truly, I'm not sure my knee can take it.

Good on you for California. At this rate, you'll come home with an American accent. Are you definitely on for the river rafting story then? And that'll be another few weeks gone, right? In August?

P.S. My guess is that Robbie and Jimmy are, in fact, leopards, which George neglected to mention when he gave them to me. Monica says Bettina, who was the smallest, is huge now too!

31 July 2017

To: drj14andrews@gmail.com

From: me

Subject: Canyon pics (again)

I hope you don't mind me absolutely inundating your inbox with these. I guess I'm a little excited. They are wanting number two or number four for the cover shot. What do you think?

I saw some plants today that grow nowhere else in the world, only in the canyon. I might send you pics of those later. Or not. I can't say I've perfected my botanical photography quite yet. I'm much better with the portraits of the rock climbers.

Obviously that last one isn't a cover possibility—it's me after we climbed this tiny bunny hill of a butte. I must say, I felt quite pleased with myself (except for the poison ivy). Next to me is our reporter, Tanisha. She's fierce. I'm hoping she'll ask me to come back to cover the bike race in September. Three hundred miles from the canyon to Route 66. (We get to follow in a camper van.)

And that's our guide, Brandon. He's been excellent. Kind of a goofball, but in a good way.

It smells unbelievable here. I wish I could bottle it and bring it home. It's a sagebrushy/nutty/sunshiny smell. And it's so, so dry. I had a massive headache the first day, but now I'm being more careful about the water. It is so fucking hot here! Brandon said 106F (41C!) today, will be the same tomorrow!

As it stands now, I'll be home on the sixth, I think, late.

1 August 2017

To: me

From: drj14andrews@gmail.com

Subject: Canyon pics (again)

Congratulations! Top news! When does the issue come out? Do you get early ones? Never was the kind of office to have magazines in the waiting room, but I suppose I could start.

I like both two and four. But I like one very much as well. And what's wrong with three? Nothing, that's what. Forget it, I like them all. Biased, I guess. Truly, this is top news, and you should be so proud.

Thank you for getting me hooked up with Kevin. He told me he enjoyed talking to you when you were there. He's got some interesting data he's letting me see, and there's a conference in Baltimore, Maryland (!), next spring, where he'll give a paper. I'm thinking about going.

Say hello to the canyon for me. And Vegas. Don't spend all your money in one place. That's what my mum used to say.

P.S. I thought you didn't take selfies?

P.P.S. You cut your hair!

8 August 2017

Are you around?

Working until 5.

Could I come by? I'd like to see your bowl. That sounded weird

Easily amused, ha.

Sorry

Yes, come by at 5:30 so I can finish my notes.

Will do

I'd love to show you my bowls, ha. I have three now, actually. You can try them out.

Great, see you then. Will you have time to talk too?

Everything OK?

I think so. I asked Omran. It would be good if you could tell me again that I can keep my camera a bit longer.

Come at 5.

K thx

*

The singing bowl in Jason's office is larger than Scott had expected, a beautiful warm shade of coral, with a mallet that's heavy in Scott's hand. He's nervous he'll break the bowl if he doesn't hit it just right.

"You can't hurt it, seriously. Just try it," Jason says, stepping back to give Scott room.

"Right." But Scott hesitates again, then tries a few more practice motions that don't make contact. He's seen Luke do this lots of times, and Jason demonstrated a minute ago, filling the room with a rich, strong tone. But now that it's Scott's turn, he's sure it won't sing.

Jason closes his eyes and folds his arms, not with impatience, but with expectation.

Scott sighs and draws the mallet back, then strikes the bowl at its fattest part, where Jason did. The note rings out, so strong that the vibration hums in his chest and cheeks.

The story of Scott's dream is in the room with them, floating around with the long fading note. Scott and Omran stood in the checkout line at Tesco's, waiting to pay. When it was his turn, Scott looked down into his cart filled with dozens of other customers' cameras. Omran pointed to Scott's broken Canon, looking forlorn among the shiny new models, and said, "You need that one."

"Why?" Scott asked.

Omran's answer was "You'll see." But when Scott had tried to put it on the belt, it was too heavy to lift.

"Beautiful, see? You did it," Jason says, opening his eyes. "Do it again."

This time it's purposeful, almost like making a wish before blowing out candles on a birthday cake. *Help me understand. Tell me what you want me to do.*

Scott strikes the bowl again. The sound sings out loud and pure, and he hopes Omran can hear it.

1 September 2017

> To: drj14andrews@gmail.com
>
> From: me
>
> Subject: Route 66?
>
> OK, remember how I told you how brilliant it would be to follow the bicycle race in a camper van?
>
> Right. Not so much.

But the good news is the magazine liked the portraits of the climbers so much they want to do another portrait series, elite bicyclists this time. That'll be in Colorado. These guys train in high altitude, so when they do mountain stages in the tours in France and Italy, they won't have any trouble.

They're a strange lot. Most of them are on the small side, like jockeys, but with massive legs and bums (!!) and arms like twigs. But they are proper *fearless*, speeding down a mountain headfirst on a skinny piece of titanium. The climbers had a kind of thoughtful quality to them—a calm efficiency that (I hope) people could see in the portraits. These dudes are balls-to-the-wall speed demons who despise sitting still. Will make for interesting photos, I hope.

Anyway, I'll be gone longer than I thought. Brandon suggested I stay with him in between, which makes sense.

How are things there? What do your patients think of the bowls?

And how are you?

2 September 2017

To: me

From: drj14andrews@gmail.com

Subject: Route 66?

Congrats on the Colorado job!

And are congrats in order on Brandon as well?

Does that mean you'll be home before the end of the month?

Bowls are good. In fact, we're taking another trip to Stuttgart in a few weeks. Emilia's coming with, to buy a few, and I'd like to get at least one more. I'd like to see what the largest ones are like, whether they'll work the way I think they might. We're going to see if we can drag Drew with us this time too.

I'm well, thanks. Busy with work, excited about the study Kevin is doing. And I found a new yoga class with no flirty doctors, which is brilliant. I miss footie.

3 September 2017

To: drj14andrews@gmail.com

From: me

Subject: Route 66?

Re: job: thank you! Things are good.

Re: Brandon: not sure, but I'll keep you posted

Re: schedule: not sure, but I'll keep you posted

Re: Stuttgart: should be beautiful this time of year. Does a bigger bowl mean lower sound, or does it depend on what it's made of? I'd imagine the big ones might blow the patient right out of the room. Is Luke going?

Internet says there are seven places to float in Denver. Seven! And one has huge tanks so you can really drift? What?! I'll let you know how it goes.

P.S. I'm sorry about footie. Seems wrong that you should have to quit it twice. Can you coach?

24 September 2017

You have one new message. Received September 24th at 5:07 p.m.

"Hi, Scott, how was Denver? Or Sun Valley, was it? I guess I was confused about your schedule. I thought you were coming back a few days ago, but I saw on Instagram you're in Texas somewhere? And with Brandon, too, so I guess it worked out? Anyway, sorry I missed you if you were home. Right, just give me a shout when you're around. I wanted to update you on the synergy project—that's what we're calling the Emilia Luke Jason Drew Kevin Ilsa partnership study—it's getting good. All right, see you."

5 October 2017

To: me

From: drj14andrews@gmail.com

Subject: Where are you?

Do me a favour and send me a quick reply so I know nothing terrible has happened. I don't want to think you're stranded with your arm pinned between two rocks in some canyon somewhere.

Last I saw on Instagram, you and Brandon were alive and kicking outside a burger shop in Boulder. But that's been a while ago. (Do people really eat burgers that big in the States? Or was that for two?)

I'll be gone to Stuttgart for a few days with Luke and Emilia. Will be home Sunday night.

Take care, be safe.

9 October 2017

To: drj14andrews@gmail.com

From: me

Subject: Where are you?

Hi Jason,

I'm sorry I haven't been in touch. I didn't mean for you to worry.

We were in Tuba City, AZ, then Denver, then Boulder, then we went to Austin, Texas, for a bit, and back to Boulder for another job. We're back in Tuba now.

It's been good. And not so good.

Wow, I keep typing and deleting.

> I had another dream about my camera. Omran and I were sitting in this art museum gallery, and it had just one framed picture on the wall, blown up huge, of my camera on my desk. We were sitting on a bench together, right in front of it. There were spotlights on it, like some masterpiece or something, and people were stopping to point at it and stare. I asked him again what he wanted me to know. He said, "Look at it. You'll find it." Same thing he said last time.
>
> I don't get it. What am I supposed to see?
>
> I'll call you when I get home, and we'll talk then if that's all right. I've got one more job at the end of the week, and then I leave on the fourteenth.
>
> I really want to go to sound. I miss it.

15 October 2017

The flat is smaller than Scott remembers. Everything in London seems smaller, in fact; the streets are narrow, the cars cramped and tiny compared to Brandon's big pickup truck, which Scott got used to riding in (and even driving) on the endless open roads of Arizona. Scott's cosy room is comfortable and still smells like him even though he's been gone for over a month. A few clean dishes are in the drainer next to the sink, and his desk holds his books and tools, same as always, as well as his enlargement of the night valley outside of Yellowstone.

Scott had called Jason as soon as he'd dried and dressed after his shower. He'd slipped on his softest pair of flannel bottoms and dialled him with the towel still in his other hand, dabbing at his wet hair. Right away, Jason wanted to know all about his trip, but Scott swerved, encouraging Jason to tell him all the useful German phrases he'd learned. When Jason asked again, Scott changed the subject and let Jason brag about the new yoga poses he's close to perfecting, just to relax into Jason's voice a bit longer. He guesses when Jason quizzes him on how much airline tickets to Baltimore cost, and laughs when Jason tells him he could send three stuffed bison from Wyoming to London for less.

"I missed this," Scott says suddenly as he sorts his dirty laundry into piles. "I missed being here."

"A bit homesick? Well, you were gone for what, six weeks?"

"About six, yeah," Scott says slowly, looking for a way to elaborate. How can he explain how he missed not only his Camden flat, or the London streets, or voices of people who sound like him, but he missed his life, the person he is when he's here?

It was like he had slipped into someone else's skin for those weeks. He'd met Brandon on the canyon job and, at first, hadn't given him a second thought. But Brandon had a way of looking at the landscape that made little treasures appear everywhere. There was a rare plant here, a striated rock there, a seedling, a constellation, a view. Scott was annoyed at first, then a bit charmed; he began to look for these things himself, and find them. His eyes seemed to focus differently, and his pictures took on a new style that felt loose and free.

Scott felt different too. With Brandon, he was spontaneous and unfettered. He was a person who didn't have to study the map or memorise the directions. He could fly wherever the wind blew, and he never looked backward. Together, they only saw what was up ahead, the next bright, unknown place.

It had been so lovely. Until he'd begun to lose himself.

Scott picks up a pair of jeans that are permanently stained with truck dust. "It was a long time away," he says. "A bit too long."

"I was worried there, for a bit, when I didn't hear from you. Thought I might have to send out a search party. But then I saw your Instagram posts, and you seemed happy, so."

"Oh, I was, for a while." Scott rubs the fabric between his fingers, remembering how Brandon had hooked his thumb through Scott's belt loop to pull him close the first time. The kiss was a doorway that Scott walked through to a place where he could do things for fun, and because they felt good.

"For a while?" Jason asks.

"Well, as far as the job goes, it might have been the best work I've ever done. But the, uh, the Brandon part..." Scott sighs, remembering. "He was really young. I mean, not in an age way, but in a life way? Does that make sense?"

"Yeah, I think so."

There were drunken nights spent in the bed of the pickup, lazy mornings in bed playing silly kissing games and eating dry cereal out of the box. Long drives, loud music, laughter. And of course, photographs. But Scott remembers the moment when the door began to shut. Stepping out of the shower together, Brandon's eyes had skipped over Scott's arm. When Scott started to explain the raised mesh of scar tissue, Brandon had handed him a towel with an oddly stiff smile, interrupting with words that repeat now in Scott's mind. "*Don't worry. It's not a big deal.*" The subject was dismissed, and never reopened.

"Let me put it this way," Scott says with a sigh that still holds some fondness. "He was really smart with the outdoorsy stuff. Not so much with what happens on the inside."

"Ah, got it. That's too bad," Jason says. "He could have had himself a keeper."

Scott chuckles. "Maybe. He just wasn't..." Scott tosses his jeans into the laundry pile and lets himself trail off. *He wasn't anything like you.*

"Hey, I have an idea," Jason says.

"What?"

"Why don't you come with us the next time we go to Stuttgart? Meet Ilsa, try out some bowls? You can be an officially unofficial member of the synergy team."

Scott laughs again. He's less than twelve hours back in his flat, and already he's making plans to leave again. "Sure, I'd love to if I'm free."

"Good. I'll let you know when."

"Excellent."

"Oh, and I owe you a dream, don't I?"

At that, Scott's eyes water inexplicably, and he turns away from the hill of dirty laundry on the bed. "No, you don't owe me a thing."

"Too bad, you're getting one anyway. Are you ready?"

Scott pulls the phone away from his face for a moment, to make sure Jason won't hear him sniffling. "Uh, yeah, go ahead."

"Brace yourself. Because this is good."

Now Scott laughs. He paces to the window with a little adrenaline burst, and the lights of the street look colourful and pretty. With the lilt of Jason's soft, sometimes scratchy voice comfortable in his ear, he's home. "Wait, don't tell me. You flew. And crash-landed spectacularly in a fiery ball of flames."

"No! Better! Remember the one where I was on the lift? Where the buttons weren't right?"

Scott dips his forehead so it touches the cool window, and smiles. It was forever ago, in the treatment room. There were three dreams that day, and this one had made Scott sad. "Oh God. You were dressed up, and kept getting lost."

"Yes! So listen. There I am, back in the lift. Dressed to the nines, shiny shoes, even flowers in my hands. The whole bit."

"Oh no."

"Oh yes. And there are the buttons, all lit up, labelled for, like, thirty floors or something. Plus the roof, ballroom, lobby, all of it."

Scott is nervous for him and bites his lip. "Here it comes."

"But this time, people come in, all dressed up too. Ladies and gents, posh tuxes, elegant dresses. And we're all going to the same place, right? I know we are, even though they don't tell me. And they're waiting for me to press the button."

“Shit, no.”

“Yes! So the pressure’s on. And I know, even in my dream, that I’ve done this, like, fifty times, and it *never* works. I’m sweating it, big time. I press the button for the ballroom. And guess what?”

“You made it?”

“We made it! To the ballroom! On the first try! The door opens, and everybody files out, snooty as you please. The stuffy music’s playing, there’s a waiter with a silver tray, people are dancing...”

It feels like a victory for both of them, somehow, and Scott feels like giving him a fist-bump. Or a hug. He’s left tracing a shape on the window with his finger, a spiral that turns into a question mark. “That’s amazing! Good on you!”

“Thanks,” Jason says, laughing a bit. “I’m pretty proud of myself, I must say. It felt so good to finally get there, you know? Where I was supposed to be.”

“Yeah, I do.” It does feel good, wonderful, even, after so long. Scott takes a breath. “Thanks for telling me. I...missed...I missed talking to you while I was gone.”

Jason waits a beat before he answers, but then Scott hears his soft puff of breath, and it’s all right. “Me too. I’m glad you’re back.”

“I am too,” Scott says, and when he closes his eyes, he can see Jason’s smile.

23 October 2017

It didn't sound like he had plans for Sat. But I think he has to leave Sun for Oslo

Who

Oh shit. Wrong chat!

Who are you talking about me to? Never mind, you don't have to answer ha

No one :/ Where's the I Fucked Up I Take It Back button? Honestly

Is this a secret? About my birthday?

No, nothing to see here—Go about your business.

Ha

Birthday. What birthday? Whose, when? I don't know anything. I can't hear you

OK I have dinner with Liv Sat night at 7. But nothing else all day. I do leave Sun for Oslo

OK, thanks. I mean, I don't know what you're talking about. Birthdays? Whatever.

26 October 2017

Scott's "surprise" birthday dinner on Thursday at Blues Kitchen is a festive, multi-course affair. Luke, Drew, Emilia, Jason, and Scott have occupied their cosy table for nearly two hours, sampling Scott's favourite dishes, a few pitchers of sweet sangria, and many, many side dishes of cornbread. The group gives Scott a gift certificate for a float they've pitched in for, as well as a keychain with a tiny plastic camera labelled "London," which has a photo of Big Ben inside the viewfinder.

When the little party breaks up and the others say their goodbyes, Jason stays behind.

Scott's head is delightfully buzzy and his stomach is pleasantly full; he thinks they could stay awhile, enjoying the mellow music and chatting alone. But they both have to work tomorrow, and Scott has research to do for his trip. "It's getting late. I'll walk you to the tube?"

"All right, but I've got something to give you first." Jason reaches into his jacket pocket and comes up with a dark-green drawstring bag that fits neatly in his palm.

"You already set up this dinner. And the float..."

Jason shrugs and holds it out to him across the table. "It's just a little something."

Scott's heart pounds. A gift? He swallows and reaches out. "What is this, why did you..." He feels the weight of it, surprisingly heavy for such a small thing. He unties the ribbon drawstring and carefully shakes out a smooth gemstone, walnut sized, with striations of yellow, transparent orange, and cloudy white. It's strikingly beautiful.

"It's citrine. Do you like it?"

"I...I do. It's amazing." Scott cradles it gently, looking at the waves and starbursts on its surface up-close. It feels good in his hand.

"All the way from Stuttgart," Jason says proudly. "Ilsa has all sorts of wonderful pieces."

"I'm glad you picked this one." Scott holds it up to the light, seeing the delicate structures inside.

"It's for clear sight."

Scott blinks quickly, feeling his nose burn.

"I mean, I know you already have clear sight. You're a photographer, after all. And you can see other things, too, you know? Like the fire, and all your dreams? Anyway. It felt perfect."

"It is, it really is," Scott says. "I love it. Thank you."

"You're welcome. Happy birthday."

Scott doesn't want to put it away, so holds it in his hand as they leave the table. He carries it as they walk the few blocks to the tube and still holds it as they briefly hug goodbye. He folds his arms to ward off the chill of the evening as he walks back to his flat, still with the stone tucked in his hand. When he gets home, he lays the drawstring bag on his bedside cabinet and puts the citrine on top, along with the others from Jason's treatment room, and when he closes his eyes to sleep, it is the last thing he sees.

6 November 2017

To: me

From: drj14andrews@gmail.com

Subject: Plans

As an unofficially official (officially unofficial?) member of Team Synergy, please be aware that a trip to Stuttgart is being planned for December 1–3. Do you know your schedule that far in advance? Can you request time off? I hope you can make it. Luke can't, but Drew can.

How's Milan? Are the skiers there as friendly as the ones in Norway?

Everything OK?

Coaching footie is just as fun as playing. No, not really, but if I tell myself that often enough, it might turn out to be true. Much easier on the knees anyway. And we're 5–1 so far, so I can't be complete rubbish, now can I? (I use the term "coaching" loosely—it's more like shouting into the void from the edge of the pitch and paying for pints after.)

P.S. Had dinner with Katie and Cory Saturday. Baby on the way! (She didn't have a drop to drink, so I guessed.)

To: drj14andrews@gmail.com

From: me

Subject: Plans

Top news about Katie! Tell her congrats for me? Being an uncle is fun. Highly recommend.

Congrats on the footie record too! Well done to you and your mates.

Milan is a) cold b) beautiful, and c) delicious. Got everything I need today, so I'm coming home early.

Don't know about Stuttgart yet. Will know better next week. I know I've got Paris coming up, then Bern. I'll let you know.

16 November 2017

Hello, you've reached Dr—beep

"Hi. I found something. It's huge, and I'm coming home. Call me, yeah? It's important. It's about Omran, and my camera. Shit, Jason, there was an SD card in my camera. Omran was telling me to look *inside it* this whole time. Call me, please, as soon as you can, all right? I might be on the train when you call, but I'm coming home, I'll be there tonight. Train leaves Bern at eleven. Talk to you soon. Thanks."

Chapter Thirteen

Transparency (n.) The proportion of the light that is passed through the emulsion on an area of a photographic image; a positive photographic image on a transparent material that can be viewed when light is shone through it; the quality or state of being transparent, i.e., allowing light to pass through with little or no interruption; the quality or state of being clearly recognizable, open, or honest.

The familiar groan of his stubborn shirt drawer makes Scott stir in his sleep.

Someone's here, who...?

It's all Scott can do to open his eyes and peer through the half-light. Beside his bed, the dim outline of a shirtless man comes into soft focus.

Scott blinks. It can't be, but it's Jason, opening Scott's shirt drawer and looking over his shoulder with a wince.

"Sorry," Jason whispers, and holds up a white T-shirt. "May I?"

Scott can't piece together why Jason is here, and why he has no shirt on, while he himself is dressed but so comfortable and pleasantly exhausted, tucked under the covers in his warm bed in Camden. He can only smile and nod before his eyes close again, hoping he'll remember this later because, although it's just a dream, it feels so warm and lovely.

*

Scott arrives at Pearl's before the Saturday lunch crowd, so he can take his pick of tables near the window. Jason's last text a half hour ago had said footie practice had gone long, but he'd still be able to run home to shower and make it here by noon. A few people stride by briskly, though the pavement in Jason's direction is empty. Scott has time to order for them before he boots up his laptop, leaving the SD card, for now, tucked safely in the inside pocket of his camera bag.

He pulls out his phone to check the time and swipes open a Snapchat notification. It's Olivia and Thomas, long-lashed and rosy-cheeked, smiling big with fluffy grey bunny ears sprouting out of their hair. The caption says "Hoppy Saturday Uncle Scott." He chuckles, flipping over to his selfie screen to thumb through the filters. He tries the rainbow tongue first, and then the flower crown, but ultimately chooses the bunny, too, and makes a silly face at them. He captions it "Bad hare day?"

"But grandmother, what long ears you have," a voice from behind him says. Its close, lilting sound makes Scott's shoulders jump.

Jason's hair, cut shorter since Scott last saw him, is still damp; his nose is pink with cold, and his cheeks are dewy, like they've very recently been shaved.

Scott rises to step into Jason's outstretched arms.

“Am I late?” Jason asks as they hug quickly, touching chests and ending with a pat on the back. He smells faintly of cedar and cinnamon.

“No no, right on time. I ordered your usual. Hope that’s all right. Tea’s hot.”

Jason shrugs off his coat and hangs it over the back of his chair, the one next to Scott instead of the one across the table. “Aw, thanks, mate. I’m absolutely starved. And tea too! Brilliant.” He sits, his gaze holding on the laptop for an extra second. He takes a deep breath and sinks more comfortably in his chair. Finally, his eyes rise to meet Scott’s. “Hello,” he says with a smile.

“Hello.” Jason’s newly cut hair is swept off his forehead and at the back makes a straight, neat line against the nape of his neck. Scott has to look away for fear he’s staring. “I’m sorry I took you away from your mates. After practice pints, and all.”

Jason pours himself a cup of tea. “You’re kidding, right? It’s no contest. Wouldn’t miss this.” He throws his chin toward the laptop. “Can we have a look?”

Scott retrieves the card from his bag as Jason scoots his chair closer. The background photograph on his laptop is a picture they both know well, of the night valley near Yellowstone, where the black silhouettes of the trees look noble and kind against the dark-purple sky strewn with a thousand stars.

“Nervous?” Jason asks, possibly seeing the slight shake in Scott’s hand as he inserts the card into its slot.

“Nah.” It’s the truth, mostly. Scott’s ears had rung, and there’d been the familiar sick feeling in his stomach when he found the card; he’d actually taken the first look at its contents with his fingers halfway covering his eyes. But that was yesterday. He isn't afraid anymore. Scott's about to tell him as much when Jason's head tilts, causing a piece of his damp fringe to fall against his forehead. Scott watches him sweep it back, and he realises that, yes, he might be a bit nervous, but not for the reason Jason must think. "I'm just excited. It's good."

"Good."

Scott taps the screen to select the drive. Next to him, Jason's knee is bouncing, making a rustling noise under the table. Jason rubs his hands against the thighs of his trackies as if his palms are sweating.

"Nervous?" Scott asks Jason the exact same question, with a little smile to soften the word.

Jason smiles back, caught out. "Uh, yes. Yes, I am."

"Don't be. It's all right."

It's more than all right. It's a miracle, actually, a proper miracle in so many ways that Scott hasn't fully wrapped his mind around it. A miracle that on the day Omran died, someone found Scott's camera on the pavement and sent it along with him in the ambulance. A miracle the police didn't confiscate it as evidence. A miracle it was never lost through all of Scott's transfers, packings, and plane rides. A miracle he never drunkenly chucked it out his flat window or sent it down the rubbish chute. A miracle he didn't leave it among the ruins in Rome, offer it up on the rocks in Arizona, or lay it to rest under the trees at Yellowstone. A miracle Omran kept after him in his sleep when Scott didn't understand, telling him in every way he could to look, look again, and look again.

Just yesterday morning had been the last one of these dreams—when Omran had shown Scott the cameras in a shop window. He pointed at Scott's, which sat on a pedestal among all the rest, and told him to take a closer look. But of course, the cameras were inside, and the shop was locked up tight.

"Open the door," Omran told Scott simply. That one sentence broke through Scott's sleep and made him sit up so quickly he was dizzy and saw sparkles of light behind his eyes.

Open the door.

Scott threw back the heavy hotel blackout curtains and squinted hard against the morning light. He took the camera from the cushioned corner of his bag and flipped it sideways, examining its damaged body. Blinking fast against bright light and tears, he ran his thumb along the edge of the memory slot door.

Omran.

He closed his eyes.

Am I in the right place?

Always, murshid.

Scott gave the door a little push, and *click*, felt it give and flip open, revealing the black edge of the card. Blood rushed in his ears as he pressed on it gently. It held fast, stuck. "Please, please," he whispered as he pushed harder, wiggling the card slightly back and forth in the slot. Scott gasped out loud as he felt the little hooks inside give it up; the card popped up a bit, enough for his trembling fingers to grasp it and slide it out.

And then there was the last miracle—when he had fumbled the card into his reader, and his laptop had purred as usual before displaying a window of over three hundred files, as if nothing was out of the ordinary at all.

It's the same window Scott and Jason see now.

Jason leans in, resting his elbows on the table. "What is this? Is that New York?"

"Yeah, and here's India," Scott says, pinching the thumbnails bigger.

"Whoa." Jason inches even closer, his arm brushing Scott's. "There's a ton of stuff on here."

They watch the cold-silver and police-blue frames of New York give way to the bright yellows and purples of the streets of New Delhi. Scott scrolls to the end of the list, where the palette turns to slate-greys and rich browns.

"Okay, here's Kabul."

The pictures are dated with yellow numbers on the bottom right of each photo: 11 Dec 2015, the day before the attack. Several photos show blown-out skeleton buildings lining streets five lanes deep with vehicles. The next few show a central city roundabout with a monument in the middle; it's jammed with cars, trucks, and groups of men dressed in calf-length wool tunics and headscarves or caps. Scott slowly slides past ramshackle storefronts, vibrant billboards, and groups of women in blue burqas crossing a busy street. He could skip to the end, but he wants to give Jason some context, to give Omran a sense of place.

He stops and enlarges a frame that shows a marbled structure with towers on each side and a great dome at the top, dwarfing all of the nearby buildings. Its caramel colour shines against a wintry grey sky.

"This is the mosque we visited."

"Wow, it's massive," Jason says, impressed.

"It's the largest in the country, the Grand Mosque. It holds ten thousand people. And the call to prayer is—"

Their waitress arrives and places dishes of soup and sandwiches at the far end of the table. They thank her, but Jason turns back to Scott and makes no move to touch his food.

"The call to prayer is gorgeous. Ancient. Gave me goosebumps. It would ring out over the streets, and everything stopped for a few minutes."

Jason's eyes squint as if he's trying to picture it.

"They have a garden too." Scott flips through another few pictures, showing the gated area behind the mosque that takes up the rest of the city block. He takes a breath and shifts in his chair when he comes to the photograph he wants.

"And here's the park at Massoud Square, that afternoon."

A massive flock of charcoal-grey, white, and brown pigeons gathers among bowls on the ground as men in brightly coloured garb toss seeds to them. Two birds are silhouetted against the sky in the upper right of the frame, their wings outstretched in a blur.

"Beautiful," Jason says, even though the light is all wrong and the balance feels off.

He's right, it does feel beautiful. Scott can still hear Omran chatting with the men, sharing small talk and a little bag of dried fruit and nuts bought from a street vendor. He pulls his hand away from the screen and tilts the laptop toward Jason.

"This one? He's here?" Jason asks as Scott leans back in his chair.

"Mm hmm."

Scott watches Jason study it, and has to smile with a bit of pride when Jason points to a slender, broad-shouldered man in Western clothes and glasses, standing among a group of men in the background.

"Is that Omran?" Jason asks.

"Yeah." The new fact of having a picture of him strikes Scott again, and he sighs with how good it feels. "That's Omran."

Omran is listening intently to an elderly man with a stooped back and a serious look, who's gesturing with both hands as if he's explaining something intricate and important. Omran did that a lot; as much as he liked to talk and tell stories, this picture reminds Scott of how good he was at listening.

"Jesus, Scott, I can't...I can't believe it. He's right here."

"Incredible, yeah?"

"My God. Can we make this bigger?"

"Yeah, just..." Scott makes a pinching motion with his hand.

Jason zooms in, focusing on Omran's head and shoulders. His face gets bigger and closer, showing the colour in his cheeks and the friendly, open expression on his face. Omran is real, a young man in a green coat having a conversation on a chilly Friday afternoon.

"And there's another one?"

Scott swipes the screen once more and the next photo appears, another angle of the same scene. This time, Omran is laughing with his head tilted up and his eyes closed. The old man grips his forearm, mouth wide in a smile.

Jason looks at him, shaking his head. “Oh my God. Scott. That’s amazing. Look at him.”

They gaze together at Omran for a long moment, then Jason enlarges this photo too.

“That man must have told him a joke or something. Look at how he’s laughing.”

“I know.” Scott chuckles softly, and the sound opens the door for the tears to come. They aren’t sad tears, but relieved, and grateful. He blinks them back and sniffles. “Can you even...believe these were here, in my camera, the whole time? I was so scared I was going to forget him, you know? But looking at these, I can remember so much about him.”

“Hmm. Like?”

“Like...how his wedding ring was silver, not gold. Or how he’s standing, do you see that? He used to always stand like that, very formal and straight. And how he always wore his shirts untucked. And he’d sometimes take his glasses off and clean them with the hem, to help him think.”

“Scott, is this what he was trying to tell you? Is this what he wanted you to see?”

“I don’t know. I think so?” Scott takes a deep breath and studies the photo. He can almost hear the bubbly cooing of the pigeons and the soft snap of their wings. He can taste the sweetness of dates and smell the cold city wind of the winter day. He can touch the sleeve of Omran's jacket, catch the deep brown of his eyes. "I think he's telling me...that this is how he wants to be remembered. Happy. Or at least, that's what I *hope* he wants, you know?" Scott's voice sounds a bit thick, and his chin is trembling. But he is smiling too.

"Are *you* all right?"

Scott swipes wetness from his cheek. "I am. It feels really good to see him."

Jason nods, his eyes glistening too. "It does, doesn't it?"

"I've been telling him how sorry I am for so long, Jason. I mean, I said it over and over, for months. And now all I want to say is thank you, thank you for staying with me. Thank you for what you taught me. Thank you for showing me this. And..." Scott shakes his head and wipes his eyes with the back of his hand. "I'm so grateful, I can't even..."

Jason nods again, and the shape of his mouth is a thin line with his lips pressed together. "I am too," he says, so quietly Scott barely hears him. "Thank you."

*

They let the laptop fall asleep as they talk and eat lukewarm soup, and Scott can't think of a better meal he's eaten, ever.

It's because Omran is here with them in a very real way, finally found. But it's also because he's comfortably tired and quite relieved to be home again, with Jason, where their conversation easily goes from Omran and Kabul to travel and funny stories about aeroplane rides to

Katie's honeymoon and how Cory called the baby "Ned" when he saw the ultrasound.

It's partially because Jason hasn't moved his chair, so they sit on the same side of the table with their thighs almost touching and a bit of sun shining through the window on them.

With Jason so close, Scott's skin hums.

It isn't the closest they've been, of course; there were the weeks Scott spent in Jason's treatment room and on his table, with the words "doctor" and "patient" between them. Those days were so long ago, and yet here they are side by side again, right and proper because today is the day. Scott's legs are jumpy with energy that wants to move forward to carry out the last piece of his and Omran's story together.

"After we eat, do you want to go for a walk?"

Jason makes a face. "A walk? It's a bit cold for a walk, yeah?"

"I have something I want to do at the park. And you could come."

At first Jason is confused and gives Scott a squinty side-eye. But Scott looks back at him plainly, with a hint of a smile. *It's time, Jason, it's finally time.*

Jason shakes his head, then seems to suspect. "Your camera?"

"Mm hmm."

They take their next breath together, deeply in and out. *The next logical step.*

"You're going to give it back?"

"Yes."

Jason's face changes, making Scott's heart jump. He's actually beaming.

"Come on then," Jason says, rubbing his hands together. "Enough dawdling. Eat up."

*

Scott and Jason approach the gravel path to the pond without speaking.

Their conversation had been as full and animated as when they first left the café, walking briskly and crossing their arms against the chill. But it had gone quiet as soon as they crossed the entrance to the park.

It hasn't been for lack of things to say; there might never be an end to the string of stories Scott wants to tell Jason. It's not because they are sad either. In fact, Scott has noticed the gentle smile on Jason's face even when he's looking down at the pavement. What Scott has to do is important, almost sacred, and they both know it. It's as if they are pilgrims, and there is a thoughtful respect in their silence.

When they reach the edge of the knee-high stone wall, Scott slows and grips the camera bag's strap at his shoulder.

"I thought this would be a good place." He swings his arm out, pointing at the spot where the orange flower poked its head up out of the tall grass two Junes ago. That was the day Scott put the camera in Jason's bag. The day he finally spoke.

"I like it," Jason says, looking up at the trees, then down toward the water.

In his head, Scott had pictured ducks at the pond, tall green grass, and warm sunbeams glinting off the stones. But it's almost winter now, and cold; any flowers have long since died, and the long, dry stalks of brown grass are bent over. Fallen leaves are strewn across the path and collect in damp piles at the base of the wall. But still, the trees that form a cove around the pond feel like witnesses, and the stone wall is a memorial that will weather the years.

Jason turns, noticing something at the edge of the pond. He takes the few steps to get there and bends down to retrieve a small rock, then brushes it off, revealing its dark maroon and tan markings. "I'll be right back there." He thumbs toward a wooden bench a short distance away and walks backward a few steps, giving the rock a small toss in the air and catching it as he speaks. "Are you good?"

"Yeah, I am. I won't be long."

"No hurry." Jason gives him one last smile. He turns away, tucking his hands in his pockets. Then Scott is alone, listening to Jason's footsteps receding along the path.

*

"Omran."

Scott speaks quietly, even though there is no one around to hear him and think strangely of him talking to himself. The moment feels reverent, for soft voices. *And Omran isn't hearing with his ears anyway.*

He lifts his camera out of the padded compartment, listening for a response. There is no voice, just a whisper of a breeze rustling the tree branches nearby. And that's all right.

The camera looks small when Scott sets it on the wall. It's empty now, the memory card back in the pocket of his camera bag, so it's only a shell of a thing. It doesn't hold photographs anymore, or light, or stories. Scott wonders if it will be too exposed here, out in the open. It will be rained on, surely, and maybe there will be snow. There won't be many children around until spring, but still. The wind will blow. The camera could fall. But that all seems just as it should be.

Scott looks up at the afternoon clouds that hide the sun.

"Omran?"

Again, there is no answer, only the gentle lap of water making *shush, shush* sounds against the bank.

"I'm giving my camera back," he says gently, speaking to the cold air all around. He had thought this moment would feel heavy and that he should say something insightful, like a eulogy. But it doesn't feel that way. This isn't Omran he's putting to rest. He knows that now.

"It's not so I can forget what happened, or walk away and leave it behind. I can't do that. I don't want to. It's more, um..." Scott looks back at Jason, as if for help.

He's sitting on the bench, shoulders slumped a bit, elbows on his knees. He stares down at the rock he passes from one hand to the other.

"It's letting go of something that wants to be let go. And making room. For something new. And it took me a long time to understand that, but I do now. You've moved on to your paradise." Scott smiles at the thought. "And I know that letting go doesn't mean forgetting."

Scott turns back to his camera and kneels in front of it. The eye of the lens looks back at him, cracked, but round and waiting. It's no longer accusing him of anything, staring him down, or pulling at him with an invisible cord. It's a piece of equipment whose job is done. It's as if, Scott thinks with wonder, the camera has let Scott go too.

Perhaps there should be tears. But there is only an opened-up feeling, and a smile. "Thank you. For everything you gave me. And for letting me let you go."

The breeze rustles the grass, and Scott sweeps away a few wayward leaves from the wall. The camera looks right here, somehow, like this is where it was meant to be all the while.

"All right. I'm going to leave now," Scott says softly.

There is no answer; there are only the rhythms of life all around him. There is the bird hiding in the branches, puffing up his feathers to keep warm, the grass all around Scott's feet, and the seeds that will rest over winter and break through the ground in the spring. Life is everywhere, in the rustle of leaves in the trees across the pond, and the wind that makes them move. Even in the cloud that changes shape to reveal the sun again.

Scott lifts his chin and closes his eyes. "Goodbye, *murshid*."

His empty camera bag feels light on his shoulder as he turns away from the wall, heart pounding. He can't wait to tell Jason he finally *got* it; it's all as it should be, and it feels good, like Jason said it would. He walks slowly at first, but when he looks up to see Jason already standing and waiting for him, his body feels light and starts to move quickly. Jason is smiling and wide-eyed, and Scott wants to laugh and shout at him because this feels *brilliant*, and he actually breaks into a jog with his arms opening as they get close. For a split second, he can see Jason's face change to a bit of shock, but he doesn't let himself care as he fairly crashes into him, folding him up tight in a hug.

"It was perfect, Jason, did you see how...*perfect*?" Scott says into the collar of Jason's coat. Scott presses his cheek into Jason's hair, and Jason hugs him back, even letting himself be lifted a bit off his heels, which, *strange*, but Scott can't help it. He feels strong.

"Yeah, brilliant. It was." Jason chuckles and pats his back as they sway, still holding on.

Scott takes a deep breath. Through Jason's coat he can feel the solid jut of his shoulder blade and the flat, wide surface of his back. He tilts his head and nuzzles his cheek against Jason's ear. "It was easy. It felt good."

In his arms Jason breathes deeply, too, and for a second, Scott feels him loosen, like all of his muscles go slack at the same time, and Scott is left holding him up. Jason melts against him for a moment, but Scott must have imagined it because just as quickly, Jason's body tenses, and he begins to pull away. Scott's hands, his arms, his whole body moves to keep him close, and Jason relents, letting himself be folded in again.

"You're happy?" Jason's voice is low.

The heat in Scott's chest blooms, so much so he's sure Jason must feel it through their jackets. "Yeah. I am."

One more breath together, and Jason's arm drags down his back until his hand touches Scott's side. There is a little push there as Jason moves away. A shock of cold air fills the space between them, and Jason glances at him in a new way, his eyes unsettled, darting from Scott's face to the ground and back again.

"Good. That's good." Jason rubs his palms together as if trying to keep them warm. They shuffle awkwardly until Jason takes another backward step, leaving Scott to watch the distance grow between them.

It's too far.

The barrier that held them apart is gone now. Scott only feels the breathless relief of freedom as his body moves him forward, truly and purposely forward for what feels like the first time. The step closes the gap, and he reaches for Jason's hand. The tables are turned, and he cradles Jason's palm, studying it, tracing the fine lines there with his thumbs. His heart pounds as he tries to think of what to say. It feels like they are embarking on something, taking off from a new spot, and Scott is going to be the one to steer them there this time. He takes Jason's other hand, too, and gives them both a squeeze, as if to strengthen his resolve.

"Let me hold on to these for a bit? I don't want to let you go just yet." He lets out a whispery chuckle and finally looks up to see that Jason's jitters are gone; he is looking at Scott with that direct gaze, where he's not only looking, but actually seeing. Scott sighs with relief.

Jason licks his lips and swallows, looking down at their hands. "I thought...I thought you were in love with him."

"Him *who*?" Scott is suddenly wobbly on his feet. "Do you mean Omran?"

"Omran..." Jason shrugs, staring down at their hands. "Luke? Brandon? Or Hugh?" He says that last name haughtily, the expression on his face saying he can't stand its sound.

Scott shakes his head because it's so unimaginable. "Shit, Jason, no. What? God, I'm—" The safe refuge of Jason's face is beautiful, just inches away. Scott wants to touch it, to smooth away the new worried lines. He pushes their fingers together tighter, and Jason lets him. "I'm not." Scott could laugh with the absolute madness of the idea. But Jason's eyebrows are questioning, waiting, and this is no joke. "I'm not in love with any of them."

Jason sighs, and Scott watches his face soften. "You're not?"

Scott pulls him in gently by the hand even though he'd like to crush him to his chest. Their thighs and knees bump together, and Scott reaches under Jason's jacket collar, his thumb stroking Jason's jaw. He pulls Jason's face toward him so their cold noses touch first, then their foreheads.

"No, no," Scott whispers as Jason's eyes close; Jason's warm hand covers his, fitting their fingers together against his cheek.

"Thank God, Scott. I was praying." Jason tilts his face into their hands. "You don't know how much I prayed that you weren't."

Scott's heart jumps in his chest. He pulls back, just far enough to see. Jason's eyes have opened again, too, and yes, it's there, Scott can read it in a look that pulls him in and keeps him safe, full of wanting and relief.

The first kiss is a chaste one that presses the corner of Jason's mouth, barely tasting that last word; the second one and the third, too, are slips of kisses that are gentle and make no sound. They make their way across Jason's lips before Scott can stop himself.

"How could I be, Jason? When you're..." *who you are.* Scott shakes his head with the absolute inability to explain, then Jason is shifting, yielding.

His lips are softer than Scott had imagined, and warmer, and *God, this is Jason,* real and moving and smiling softly against his lips. Jason who taught him how to breathe again, to speak again, who kept him warm, is taking Scott in his arms, both of them strong and holding each other up, mouths finding their way together to finally taste.

"I want us to go back to mine. Do you want to?" Scott asks against Jason's mouth, in between kisses he places there. He feels Jason nod, and Scott hugs him tighter, fighting the urge to slide his arm under Jason's jacket to be a layer closer to his skin.

"Let's go." Jason pulls back far enough to look properly into Scott's eyes. He's got one hand on Scott's jaw, his touch decidedly different than it had been all those times back in his office. It's deeper, cradling, and Scott could sob with how good it feels to finally, finally have this.

"Bus? Tube?" Scott asks shakily, and he can't believe it because, apparently, they are going back to his flat in Camden right now, today, he and Jason together, his best friend, and they are kissing and properly touching with their fingers entwined again.

Jason laughs, then whispers like they are sharing a secret. "Black cab. It's faster."

*

When the door to his flat swings open, Scott has a frantic moment of *clean sheets? Washing in the sink? Fuck what if pants dirty laundry towels smelly boots*, but Jason's arms around his waist and lips on his jaw distract him from the particular hazards of surprise guests.

"This is..." Scott says, chuckling, "...home." He yanks the keys out of the lock and tosses them toward the little table next to the door. He misses, and they go clinking to the floor.

"It's lovely," Jason says without looking, letting go of Scott's hip long enough to peel off his jacket and let it drop. They are a tangle of arms slipping out of sleeves and legs shuffling and knees bumping together as they flip off their shoes. Lips find each other again, opening and tasting, and Scott can't believe they are at last just feet from his bed where they can lie down together.

The gentle pine smell of arnica surrounds them, and Scott opens one eye to check for piles of yesterday's travelling clothes; there are none, thank Christ, but it doesn't seem Jason would care, the way he hooks his leg over Scott's and pulls his face in for a kiss with both hands, then pulls them both down onto the bed.

Scott's head is a mess of what are we, where can I put my hands, eyelashes, skin, ear, kiss, can I, so beautiful that beautiful blue, thighs heavy what are we doing? But his body knows, the muscles taut and humming with adrenaline, ready to push and pull. Jason is pulling, too, grabbing him by the hips and rolling him over so he—

"Ow, shit," Jason hisses as *whoops*, Scott crushes Jason's thigh underneath him.

"Ugh sorry—"

They chuckle as they kiss and readjust, Jason whispering, "Here, let me..." and Scott lifting his weight, so when Jason shimmies a bit and they reconnect it's *ahhh*, perfectly aligned with Scott's thighs on the inside, cradled in heat, so good he has to drop his head against Jason's shoulder and catch his breath.

The methodical, practiced doctor's touch is nowhere to be found; these are hands that pull hard at him. They slip under Scott's shirt, wrap around his waist, climb up his back with fingertips kneading, making Scott roll his hips.

Then Jason has Scott's earlobe between his lips and a hand on the nape of his neck, his hips rising up to meet where Scott is pushing over him. Scott slips a hand under Jason's body so he can help, lifting and pressing Jason against him in a glorious, slow grind. Jason's light moaning hums in his ear, which somehow makes Scott's thighs spread out to get more leverage. Jason is strong against him, and Scott can't tell if he's trying to pull him in closer or push him away; he braces up on his hands to get a proper, breathless look. Jason grabs and fumbles with Scott's shirt buttons, and *yes, yes*, Scott wants to rip Jason's shirt off, too, *skin, soft, warm*, but there's no time.

"Jason, let's..." Scott shakes his head, and Jason understands, forgetting his shirt and shifting to Scott's flies.

"Kiss me, kiss me," Jason says, pulling the front lip of his trackies down with one hand and working Scott's button and zipper with the other. They're free, and Jason lets Scott arch against him, smooth and hot. Jason's hand cups the curve of his arse cheek; *shit, it's almost over,* though it's just begun, and Scott can't help but let his hips go where they want, yearning, pressing, not enough skin touching, but Jason's tongue in his mouth is wet, sweet friction. The freckles on Jason's cheek are mesmerizing; he can't close his eyes, can't shut off from this moment because *blue, my sweet, I missed you, let me see you*, and the energy and heat of his whole body is concentrated on the hard heat between their legs.

They reach and reach, Jason forming half words of pleasure with his eyes intense and searching, and at last, Jason's warm hand moves between them, strong, purposeful, exquisite; everything Jason taught Scott about breathing is forgotten as Scott trembles with the racking explosion of it. There is a faraway ring in his ears as Jason tightens up around him, legs twisting and crushing, and they gasp for air together, wetness spilling over Jason's shirt.

Scott can finally gaze at Jason with no care about how long he's been staring. But Jason must find it funny because, after a few breaths, he's chuckling with his hand over his mouth.

"What...what the fuck," Scott asks him, laughing himself because he can't help it; Jason's flushed cheeks and crinkling eyes are magical, thrilling after what they've done.

"Well then," Jason begins with a snicker.

"Yeah, that, uh, didn't take long," Scott says, shaking his head, which makes Jason full out laugh. He rests his hand on Scott's chest, right over his pounding heart, and tries to catch his breath.

"Didn't take long my arse, it's been a year and a half." The last of the afternoon light is bending in Jason's eyes as he laughs warmly. He strokes a gentle caress up Scott's arm. Their noses brush against each other, and Jason's smile nuzzles into Scott's lips. The kiss is gentle, no longer searching, but knowing. His tongue licks out, catching Scott's lip, teasing it closer until it's taken lazily into Jason's mouth. They sigh.

Scott can't hold himself up anymore; the events of the day, his camera, and the sated-sleepy feeling of coming down are taking their toll. He rolls onto the bed, and—

How long?

Scott's thumb rubs over Jason's palm as he does the figuring, counting back eighteen months. *November, October, September...May*?

"Wait, it's been a year and a half since what?"

Jason's hand burrows under Scott's. Their fingers lace together, and Jason studies them as if seeing the past there. "It was before your first float. You were losing your voice. And I thought I'd do anything just to hear it again. I was in love. With you."

Scott can't breathe. He remembers. He was so scared then, scared he might never come back to himself, scared down to his soul that he didn't deserve to. So scared he couldn't even speak.

Jason swallows and turns his face to the ceiling. "So I waited."

Scott feels a warm pinch in his chest as memories bend in his tired mind—a snapshot of a happy couple on Jason's office shelf, three crystals in Scott's hand that he knew were a goodbye, a long-ago phone conversation about blind dates and boyfriends and finding love. And Jason's voice, hesitating, about Ian. *"It just didn't work out."*

"You waited?" Scott gathers Jason's fingers, warm and real, inside his. "For me, all this time?"

Jason looks at Scott straight on. There is no humour in his voice, no trace of laughter anymore, only tenderness. "Had to. There are the rules, right? But more than that... I had to wait until you were free. *Truly* free."

This revelation settles in deep, making Scott's arms feel heavy; he's so tired, but he's desperate to keep his eyes open, to stay here now. "But Jason, Jesus. All this time...the wedding, and sound, and all my trips? And—" *And Brandon.* Scott doesn't say it, just nestles his leg between Jason's so their feet overlap.

"Was worth it," Jason whispers.

It's getting harder and harder for Scott to stay awake. His body and his brain feel so utterly spent, and his bed has never felt so soft; this place of nightmares is now the place where Jason loved him.

He's walking on a dirt path through a forest, the canopy of green leaves a fluttering ceiling above him.

"So," Scott whispers with the last of his energy, "we're in love."

"Yes. We are."

The leaves are ideas, and one falls from above, dancing downward to land on the path in front of him.

Scott picks up the leaf and studies its vibrant green colour and webbed veins. This leaf is the truth that Jason has said out loud. Scott smiles. He'll tell the truth too.

"I'll always find you," he says to the leaf, to the forest, to Jason.

Jason's slow kisses on his eyebrow tell him he can rest, and Scott falls fully into that place, his words carried away on the wind.

*

The familiar groan of his stubborn shirt drawer makes Scott stir.

Someone's here, who...?

It's all Scott can do to open his eyes and peer through the half-light. Beside his bed, the dim outline of a shirtless man comes into soft focus.

Scott blinks. It can't be, but it's Jason, opening Scott's shirt drawer and looking over his shoulder with a wince.

"Sorry," Jason whispers, and holds up a white T-shirt with an expression of "can I?"

Scott can't piece together why Jason is here, and why he has no shirt on, while he himself is dressed but so comfortable and pleasantly exhausted, tucked under the covers in his warm bed in Camden. He can only smile and nod before his eyes close again, hoping he'll remember this later because, although it's just a dream, it feels so warm and lovely.

*

Scott flexes his ankles and stretches his legs. His thigh muscles are pleasantly achy with the satisfying soreness that comes with strenuous exercise. *Or sex*, he thinks happily, opening his eyes.

Jason sits in Scott's desk chair with his knees bent and his feet on the bed. It's full dark, but the kitchen light is on as well as the lamp that shines over Jason's shoulder to the coffee-table book he's reading. He looks soft and young in Scott's T-shirt and brushed cotton bottoms. He gives the entire room a soft feel, actually, and Scott is glad he doesn't appear to be leaving any time soon.

Jason's foot is within reach, the cuff of the bottoms rolled up high enough to reveal a small tattoo on his calf. A triangle. It jogs a hazy memory that Scott can't quite place, and he tries to remember where he's seen one like it recently. He inventories the many portraits he's taken but comes up empty.

He takes a deep, waking breath, and reaches out to squeeze Jason's big toe. "Hello."

"Hello." The bottom half of Jason's face is invisible behind *In Focus: Innovations in Photojournalism*, but Scott sees the shimmer of fondness in his eyes.

"What time is it?"

"Half six, give or take."

"Jesus, sorry I slept so long."

"'S'all right. Rough day." Jason gives him a wink. "Anyway, it gave me a chance to get comfy. I looked around a bit since you skipped right over the tour."

Scott's eyes go straight to his desk, but there his black notebook sits, closed alongside his books and printouts, just where he left it. "Yeah, ha, how rude of me."

Jason has a look in his eye that Scott hasn't ever seen. Contentment. "Well. It was kind of my fault too."

"Yes, yes it was." Scott's heart flutters at the memory.

Jason rises from the chair with the big book still in his hand and slides next to Scott on the bed. He gives Scott a kiss before rolling over on his back, propping the book up on his stomach and letting it lean on his thighs. They share Scott's pillow.

"Your photographs are better than the ones in this book, you know."

"You're biased."

"Very."

Scott has to chuckle. "Actually, my photographs *are* in that book."

Jason lets out a little gasp. "Where?" He flips to the index and runs his fingers down the listings. "Holy shit, they are."

Scott stretches and half yawns as Jason finds the page.

"God, Scott. How the hell did you do that?" Jason points to the book, where Scott's photo of the devastation of a seaside town in the Philippines by Typhoon Haiyan takes up the better part of the spread.

"Do what?"

Jason traces the sunlight that falls in beams through the brightening sky, the few brightly coloured rooftops left standing among the debris, and the silhouettes of proud palm trees that frame the coast. "Tell a whole story with one picture."

Scott doesn't answer as Jason takes up his hand and kisses it, then kisses it again, and places it on his chest over his heart, with his hand on top. They lie like that, looking at the photograph, and Scott thinks again of the pictures in his notebook, the pictures he's drawn from memory and those he's printed and collected from books and magazines, to tell the stories of his own lives.

"It's the way you see," Jason murmurs, turning toward him. "Your eyes, the way you can create a feeling. I love that."

Scott's heart lifts. He lets his eyes linger on the intricate details of Jason's face that he's always had to turn away from too soon. The triangle of freckles on his cheek, the lashes that make his eyes look delicate. It's the face he'll tell all his secrets to, and they will be safe.

He could sit up right now, take his notebook off the desk, and bring it right back here. He could hand it over to Jason, no question.

"I have some more stories for you," Scott says, Jason's heart warm under his hand.

"Oh?" Jason comes closer and rubs their noses together. "I want to hear them. While we eat maybe?" A kiss. "I'm hungry, are you?"

With that, the moment is gone and the notebook forgotten; Scott can't think of a thing he'd rather do than sit across from Jason and watch him eat prawn masala and tandoori chicken with naan from the takeaway down the street. "I am. Let's eat."

*

Scott does tell stories over dinner; if there is a picture on the wall or a figurine on the shelf, it has a story, and Jason asks about them all, down to the framed photograph of the students in New Delhi and the ten-gallon-hat salt and pepper shakers from Austin. They make quick work of the food but linger over a bottle of wine.

Jason tells stories too. There is one about his disastrous gap year backpacking in Australia, and one about how his mum had a wish to swim with dolphins that went unfulfilled. The straight edges of Jason's voice melt when he talks about her. The candle Scott had lit for their date casts soft shadows on Jason's face, and Scott tells him how much he's sorry.

When it's time to clean up, Scott is the first to stand, not knowing what their next move should be. Jason may want to go home; he's got the cats there, after all, who've been alone all day, as well as clean clothes, and his own bed that he may want to get back to. Scott collects their plates, and Jason rises to help, gathering the cardboard takeaway boxes.

"Where's your bin?"

"Under the sink, here," Scott says. They brush past each other in a silence loaded with uncertainty.

Scott turns on the tap to fill the sink and squeezes the soap over their dishes. He watches the bubbles grow, going over some possibilities. *You can stay if you want. You don't have to go. I'd like you to stay. Do you want to stay?*

Then Jason's chest presses against Scott's back, and he reaches around to turn off the water. "We could leave those."

"Yeah?" Scott turns his head and is somehow dumbstruck that Jason is right beside him, to be kissed at will. The tree on Jason's forearm pins him gently against the counter, and Scott lets out a relieved sigh.

"Yeah. Let's go back to bed, hmm?" Jason turns him, and they sway a bit like two teenagers dancing awkwardly at their first disco.

Scott nods and tastes the faint trace of wine on Jason's lips. He's half hard already, but Jason is, too, underneath the cotton fabric of his borrowed bottoms, and that makes Scott bold.

"Can I?" he asks softly, sliding his hands under the hem of Jason's shirt. The step changes as Jason raises his arms, letting Scott tug it up and off. His chest is slightly muscular, with sparse hair and small nipples. Scott lets the shirt drop to the floor as his fingertips graze over the naked skin he's never seen before. He ducks down to taste and smell the crook of Jason's neck, pulling him close.

Now Scott tastes smoky spices and the gentle saltiness that is Jason underneath. He lets his lips drag across the hollow between Jason's collarbones where a crystal would sit, but a black shape catches his eye.

Masts, hull, and sails cover Jason's bicep in fine detail, plain and strong on his skin.

Scott swallows. "That's a ship," he says out loud.

Jason is panting a bit, clinging to Scott's waist. "Yeah, a beauty, right? That's my girl."

A beauty. Stately. Regal. A jade and gold pin at his brother's neck, glinting at him from across the room long ago.

Scott raises a hand to touch it, his heart pounding now for a different reason. "She is. Beautiful."

"She's old. My first tattoo. She reminds me to keep exploring, you know?" Jason smiles, and Scott smiles, too, blinking quickly as he ducks down to press his lips against Jason's shoulder.

"Your turn now, hmm?" Jason whispers, pulling at the hem of Scott's shirt. Scott lifts his arms to let himself be undressed.

*

Scott offered Jason the bathroom first.

Jason was impressed with Scott's array of travel-sized toiletries collected from hotels and aeroplanes, and Scott had to fairly push himself out to give Jason some privacy. But as soon as the door shut, he made his way to his desk for his notebook and opened to the page marked "Monday, 23 May 2016."

It's a page he'd looked at often over the many months since he created it, and he knew the feeling of the place beyond the words and drawings. The smell of salt wind and incense. A signet ring and an anchor bracelet. A stone fortress that felt heavy with responsibility. A man, his brother, who had wise eyes and a ship pin at his collar. And the simple, vivid words: allies, ocean, stone, trust.

That's been ten minutes ago; the notebook has been tucked away, Scott has taken his turn in the bathroom, and now Jason, fresh-faced and shirtless, waits for him in his bed. Scott walks across the room feeling much like a jittery groom on a long-ago wedding night, when newlyweds still had secrets to discover about each other.

The little lamp on Scott's bedside cabinet is on, so Jason is lit up, looking as if he might be a bit nervous too. As he sweeps the duvet aside to invite Scott in, one of his knees peeks out from under the blanket. That's where Scott's hand goes first.

He has seen the scar before, in footie photographs on Jason's Facebook page, where it's usually covered with a brace or wrapped with an elastic bandage. But in a few pictures of Jason on the sideline or crouching in the front row in the team photo, the scar was visible, a long, pale-pink line down the middle of his kneecap. Scott remembers enlarging the pictures on his phone, and then looking at them on his laptop, too, to see them better. He even traced the scar with his finger once, before he caught himself being creepy. It was thrilling, seeing it; it made Jason vulnerable, more human somehow. It felt like a badge of something, too, evidence of pain and recovery. They are both wearing a sign of what's been endured on their skin.

The line is faded, just visible under a sparse layer of hair. Scott runs his fingers over it for real, and his touch makes Jason sigh, goosebumps rising on his legs.

Jason traces Scott's S-shaped scar, still raised against a mottled background of discoloured and uneven skin. It has very much settled down from where it had been six months ago. Even Thomas, who used to ask to see it just for the gross factor, has grown unimpressed and bored with it.

Jason's head tilts, silent for a minute. His voice is tender when he speaks. "Your body is..."

Nerves drum in Scott's chest. "What?" he whispers, looking down. *Scarred. Damaged. "Not a big deal."*

Jason gazes at the skin, tracing the lightest of the dark lines. "Special to me."

Now the drum is from relief rather than nerves, and Scott leans forward to kiss him, gently, to say thank you.

"And your scars are prettier than mine," Jason says.

Scott chuckles. "Thomas thinks it looks like a map. With roads and things, and a river running down the middle?"

Jason considers, then grins. "I see it! There's the Thames," he says, pointing. "And this must be the Tower Bridge." He traces a ridge of silvery tissue, sweeping his light touch up toward Scott's shoulder. "And here's Whitehall Gardens. And Buckingham Gate." Scott takes an unsteady breath as Jason leans in. "And way out here, this must be St. Albans." Jason presses his lips to the tiny misshapen crater. "And Chelmsford." His kisses are dry and soft, but make Scott gasp when they reach his collarbone and linger there.

Scott licks his lips, the body edges of Jason's knee still bumping against his palm. "Jason?"

Jason's tongue trails a path up Scott's neck. "Hmm?"

"I'm glad you became a doctor instead of, like, an accountant."

Jason lets out a little snort but doesn't forget the task at hand. "What?" he mumbles, kissing Scott's jaw.

"Or a stockbroker or something."

Their lips connect, but Jason's eyes are open. "And why is that?"

Scott still can't wrap his mind around how it all worked, even though he watched it unfold with his own eyes, everything that had to happen for their paths to cross. This time.

"Because I never would have met you."

Jason stops mid-kiss, and he looks at Scott sideways. "Hmm. How do you know? Maybe you would need someone to manage your many millions of pounds, right? When you're hanging in galleries all over the world?"

"Right," Scott says, gesturing to the tiny flat. "You can see how well that's going so far."

They chuckle together for a moment, but soon Jason sighs and fixes Scott with a serious look.

"What?"

"There was a time when I...I wanted to forget all the anatomy and the physics and the biology and *the rules* so I could just...kiss you better." Jason's hand is on Scott's heart, caressing the skin there. "Hold you better. Love you better. I knew it doesn't work that way, but still." Jason shakes his head a bit. "I wanted to try."

Scott thinks of the office, the table, Jason's hands on him, his eyes on him, seeing down into everything Scott had been trying to hide. "I would have let you."

"No," Jason murmurs, "couldn't." He kisses Scott's jaw tenderly, like a blessing, along the path of the pale-pink scar.

"You can do that now if you still want to."

He trails down Scott's arm lightly with his fingertips. "But you're better now."

Scott puts on a pout and points to the first scar he sees, a tiny tan crevice above his right nipple. He murmurs, "Well, this one hurts a bit."

There is a world passing between them, full of patience and longing, of history.

"No, it doesn't."

Full of giving and taking, and of asking permission and allowing. Of touching, and of trust.

"You're right, it doesn't. But I still want you to. If you still do."

And finally, desire.

"I want to."

Jason's low, nearly desperate whisper makes Scott want to lie down. He tips his chin slightly and leans in.

"Go on then."

*

Later, when Scott's muscles are wrung out and trembling, he takes Jason's face between his hands and touches his lips with his thumb. He thinks of all the sounds he made and didn't make on Jason's table across town forever ago, and how lovely their voices sound now, layering over each other, one low and one high. This is how they will sing together this time. This is how they will sound. One is loud where the other is soft, one gasps while the other moans. Even their breaths are a harmony, finding a rhythm of humming and blending, held and released.

Jason whispers into his ear. "I like that sound."

Scott whispers back. "I like you making us make that sound."

For every one of Jason's sharp edges there is a soft curve, and Scott wants to memorise them all. The jut of his collarbone next to the muscled round of his shoulder. The slant of his forearm where it's connected to his wrist, resting on the smooth, supple rise of his abdomen. The line of his jaw inches away from the delicate curl of his eyelashes.

What's even better are the surprises. Scott has already discovered the details of Jason's widow's peak and the dark-walnut birthmark on the inside of his thigh. The latest are faint trails of stretch marks along his hips. Scott traces them tenderly with his tongue, pleased that he's the one who gets to see them, taste them.

Their hands find each other, and Jason's shoulders crimp together as he turns his face toward the pillow.

"Does that feel good?"

"Yes, ugh. Please. Do that again." Jason, who reminded Scott how to breathe so long ago, now seems to have forgotten how; he pants with shallow gasps and grips Scott's arms as if to fix him in place. Scott will gladly be trapped here with him, watching the muscles of his back stretch and release with pleasure.

I thought about you in Paris, Jason. I thought about you in Bern, in Warsaw, in Rome. I felt you with me in the night valley; you don't know that, but you're there with me. I can't tell you how I know it, but I do, and I missed you. I missed you right here at home. I missed you.

Scott says all of this with his tongue and his lips and his fingers and his mouth over and inside the hidden parts of him, and when Jason's legs begin to quiver and his breath dips and his movements get urgent and choppy and his voice rises with driving groans that are music the words become *I love you, let go, yes, it's me, let go with me, I love you, I've loved you for so long. So much longer than you know.*

Jason seeks out Scott's mouth. When Scott's lips brush near, Jason's tongue darts out to catch them, and Scott tastes sweat and the ocean; when Jason shivers, Scott pulls the duvet up over them, and they settle in, foreheads together and arms entwined.

Jason's voice drifts between them, soft as feathers.

"You're not going anywhere, are you?"

"What—now?" Scott asks, chuckling softly, mesmerised by Jason's flushed cheeks and lips that have gone deep pink.

“Yes, now.”

“Nah, I think I’ll stay a while. This is my flat, after all.”

“Good. Just checking. I’m not great at watching you leave.” Jason closes his eyes.

“What do you mean?”

“You were always going away. I could never keep you. You were always walking out, and I had to keep letting you go. I don’t want to do that anymore.”

“I’m not going anywhere,” Scott says, letting his eyes close for a moment too. “I like it here. Where you are.”

“All right. Me too.”

Scott tucks the duvet around Jason’s shoulder. “Warm enough?”

“Mm hmm. It’s cosy in here.” Jason tucks his chin, and Scott watches as the lines of his face go slack. He turns off the lamp, draping them in darkness.

*

“Scott?”

Jason’s breath is soft on his neck, but Scott doesn’t answer. He’s losing his grip on consciousness again, tucked in with Jason curving around his back like a spoon.

“I think you’re sleeping, right?” There is a drag of lips on Scott’s shoulder, and a sigh. “I want to tell you something anyway.”

Scott’s breathing is soft and even, floating on Jason’s words.

“You said something to me. A long time ago. You said, ‘What if I lived because I’m not done yet?’ Remember that?" It might be Jason's cheek against his shoulder now, or his forehead. "You said there might be someone out there that you hadn't met yet. That maybe you'd help that person. Make a difference for them. You said they might...need you."

Scott does remember. He remembers every second on that table, on the floor, every word his throat could speak.

"Well. I think that person is me." Jason stays quiet for a minute, his stomach rising and falling softly against Scott's back. "And I have this feeling that...doctor, stockbroker, dustman, chef, professional footie player? Whatever. I would have found a way to meet you. No matter what."

In the clarity of this hazy place between awake and asleep, Scott knows it's true.

I'll always find you; I'll always find you.

Lips brush Scott's shoulder. "Goodnight."

*

Scott dreams of his stepdad's little Volkswagen again.

This time, Scott and Jason are pulling up to the paved parking area at the seashore at Land's End. Stray pebbles crunch under their tires, and the brakes squeak as the car comes to a stop. Salt air breezes through their open windows; a gull cries overhead and joins its mates on the sand. Their timing is perfect. It's golden hour, and the sunlight drips off the rocks like caramel.

"Finally here," Scott says as he turns the motor off.

Jason hums, focusing on the horizon. "Was worth it though, right?"

Scott isn't sure yet. They look out at the water and the rocks, and at the sky with its sparse cotton clouds. Maybe they aren't supposed to get out. What would it mean if they did, if they actually opened the doors and walked out together onto the rocky beach? Touched the water with their feet?

"Come on," Jason urges lightly. "We can always go back if you don't like it."

Scott watches Jason pull the lever on his door, knowing in his heart it isn't true. They can't go back. The only way is forward, and as if to carry home the point, Jason walks on ahead, down through the dunes like he knows this place, like there is something out there he needs. He turns and holds out his arm, hand up. "Come on!" He beckons again. His fringe is blowing in the sea breeze, and he squints against the sun with a radiant smile. Scott wants to take his picture. He reaches into the back seat for his camera bag and loops it over his shoulder as he steps out.

They walk down the wooden plank stairs to the beach hand in hand, in silence.

The beach is beautiful in an otherworldly sort of way, with its clear green water and tall rock formations that jut up like hills in the sea. Waves lap up to the shoreline in small swells that break with a bit of hissing foam. The word "cove" may have been invented for this place; Scott feels protected, cared for, even though they are alone, walking on the very edge of the continent.

"I like it here," he says, closing his eyes for a moment. He feels silly that he was ever scared.

"Good. It's mine." Jason reaches down to scoop up a handful of small rocks that make up the pebbly beach. He studies them for a moment and drops all but one back to the ground.

"What do you mean it's yours?"

Jason rubs the little grey stone between his fingers. It shines like a marble, laced through with glints of jasper and mica.

"Your place is the night valley, right? Where you find the fire? This is my place. These are mine."

Scott looks down. There are hundreds of stones, maybe thousands, in shades of grey, brown, and black. Are they...all of Jason's lives? The thought is baffling. "Jason, all of these are...?"

Jason chuckles. "No, not all of them. I know them when I see them though." He takes Scott's hand and places the stone in his palm. It is exquisite, cool and heavy, and holds a world; it makes perfect sense that Jason's lives would look like this, precious and eternal.

"Tell me about this one?" Scott asks. He senses it will be rough. A flipbook of snapshots flickers in his imagination where Jason is a dark-eyed, copper-skinned girl, waiting alone in a carpeted desert tent while the night wind blows outside.

"Okay. Let's walk."

And they do. Jason tells the story slowly, like an interpreter, feeling around for the right words to express what he sees. It's a tale of a long life lived bravely, not without hardship, full of both cruel heartbreak and enduring love. Jason's voice is content and matter of fact, and when the story ends, he slips the stone in his pocket.

Scott thinks of his own black notebook, his own sacred fire that he's kept secret all this while. "Why didn't you tell me about what you found here?"

They stop walking. Jason looks down at the stony surface of the ground, then turns to the horizon again. "Because I don't know about it yet. You're going to teach me."

Scott's heart plumps. But Jason is distracted, tilting his head, listening. "Do you hear that?"

There is the faraway splashing of the waves on the shore and the gentle cawing of seabirds. Behind it is the sound of water running, like the misty spray of a hose.

Scott looks up the beach, trying to place the sound. "Is it raining somewhere?"

"Nah. That's me in the shower." Jason's eyes are playful, and his smile hides a secret.

*

Scott turns away from him, rolling out of the dream and back into his bed.

It *is* the shower.

He is alone. He squints across the dim flat and sees the strip of light that spills out from under the bathroom door. The sound of the shower spray hitting the tile walls sounds strange to him from out here, but comforting all the same. Scott rubs his eyes, the image of Jason looking out to the edge of the world still behind them. How many lives are there? How many stories are hidden in the sand, waiting to be picked up and told?

Scott sits up, suddenly fully awake. Could there be a stone on Jason's beach that holds the story of two boys who sang together in a great cathedral? Or one about a loyal warrior in a stone fortress who showed his brother how to be patient, and how to trust?

There would be, wouldn't there, if what Scott suspects is true?

He turns to his desk. The black spine of his notebook is visible under a stack of books and photography magazines. There could be a stone that tells the story of a blue-eyed young woman in a farmhouse who hid her secret from soldiers. And another that tells about a young Italian duke, caught between duty and love. And couldn't there be one about a special child dressed in fox furs—

What if, oh my God, what if?

The runner in falcon colours lifts the rust-red pelt away from the child's face, and the puzzle piece slides into place. The stone would keep the life of a child with a triangle on her chin who was destined for great things among her people. A child who slipped from Scott's grasp in a tallgrass prairie at the edge of a forest.

The sound of the shower stops abruptly. Jason must be stepping out, dripping, searching for a towel. Scott rubs his thighs so he has something to do with his hands, wondering what they will do next, and what on earth he'll say about any of this.

Long moments later the door opens, and it is another while before Jason steps out. He is a vision, damp, holding Scott's towel closed around his waist with one hand. He carries something in the other that Scott can't see.

"Morning," Scott says with a nervous smile. "You're up early."

Jason doesn't answer. His hair hangs in dark, shiny strings across his forehead. The showery clean scent wafts in with him and sweeps away the remnants of all of Scott's questions. Jason nudges Scott's knees apart to stand between them. One hand rests on Scott's neck as he bends down for a kiss, the other he hides behind his back.

"Good morning. I'm sorry if I woke you."

A wave of heat rises up Scott's arms. This could be the moment, in the quiet early morning of his flat, with Jason standing warm and clean between his legs. Scott could tell him.

"I dreamt about you," he says, reaching around Jason's waist, searching for his hand. Jason lets his fingers go, and Scott feels the flat foil package with the circle in the middle. "What's this?"

"I wasn't snooping, swear. I was looking for some mouthwash in your medicine cabinet. But I thought..."

Scott presses his lips to the soft, dewy skin of Jason's stomach, then takes him by the waist and pulls him down on the mattress.

"Ooh, smooth." Jason laughs as the towel slips apart where Scott moves over him. Scott wants to press his lips, his fingers, his own pounding heart against every part of him. But first things first.

"You're not going anywhere, are you?" Scott asks, pulling up.

"Uh, no. I'm naked."

"Good. I'm going to go for a wee, brush my teeth, and get us some water. Stay right here, yeah?"

"I like your breath."

"But you're all minty." He glances at the condom still in Jason's hand, and smiles. "Don't move. I'll be right back. God, you smell good," he says as he gets up and jogs toward the loo. He spies his Leica on his desk on the way and almost shrugs off the idea, but in a second, he backs up and opens its hard leather case.

"Mind if I snap your picture?"

Jason rests his head on his outstretched arm. "Snap away. Just be quick about it, for fuck's sake," he says, laughing. "How's my hair?"

Scott focuses him in the field, adjusting the angle to get the tiny bit of light that is just starting to open up the room. "It's perfect." The towel is crumpled in a strange shape, there isn't enough contrast, and Jason's face is half in shadow. But Scott wants to keep this moment, where Jason is so beautiful and unguarded looking back at him. The moment that describes how completely everything has changed. The moment that marks the end of one thing and the beginning of something else.

*

Jason in the office is precise, focused, and methodical; Jason in bed is unstructured, with none of his practiced attention to symmetry, balance, or order. He might kiss and nip at one of Scott's nipples and forget about the other. He could press one of Scott's shoulders roughly into the mattress one minute, then gently stroke the inside of his forearm the next. It is moment by moment, breath by breath, spontaneous in a way Scott would never have guessed. It feels like a dance they discover together for the first time, especially for each other.

But still, Scott catches a glimpse of the doctor when Jason looks down from where he's straddled across Scott's hips. His eyes go from downy soft to sharp when he notices that Scott's jaw is tight.

Relax this, Jason's tongue says as he licks gently at Scott's mouth, beckoning it to open. *Let your teeth go*, Jason's thumb says, tracing against his bottom lip. He opens the condom with smooth efficiency and rolls it down Scott's length as they kiss, their mouths teasing around breaths they let go of together.

They lie on their sides, legs interwoven, curled into an egg shape so Scott can hold Jason close the way he likes. Jason leans his head back.

"That feels good," he whispers, and the air rushes out of his lungs as Scott's fingers draw over the hottest part of him, where his thighs ease open.

It's me, Jason, it's me, Scott tells him silently as they rock gently away and back, painstakingly slow, so each can attune to the other.

Do you remember me?

Each breath Scott takes seems to fill Jason, too, the shallow swell of Jason's stomach rising under Scott's hot hand. This isn't so much Scott pushing forward, breaking through, as much as Jason yielding, unfolding, taking him in.

I carried you. I held you.

That was then, back in those other worlds when it was a matter of life and death. It is so this time around, too, only it was Jason's turn to carry him and pull them through. Scott laces kisses across his shoulders, traces a path with a light touch of his finger. He tastes wine and salt and caramel sun on rocks.

You sang with me. You held my hand.

Jason presses closer and turns his head to face him, grasping the back of Scott's thigh. Scott hears his own soft groan, then Jason's delicate, silvery sigh. Still, they are hardly moving, only a slow shift of a leg, a tensing and releasing of a forearm where it holds fast.

She's going to take you places.

Jason's ship lies over the map of scars on Scott's arm, and he thinks of their travels, everywhere they've been in time and place. Both on the table and out in the world, Scott would go, and Jason would bring him back. Here in bed, they are everywhere and always, holding each other open, helping each other breathe, finding the way together.

Do you remember me? I remember you.

Scott's breath catches as he presses a kiss to the sails.

"Are you okay?" Jason asks.

Jason will surely hear the thickness in his voice; Scott hides his face in his neck. "Yeah, I'm...afraid I'm going to say something stupid."

Jason's lips are pink and damp, and there is a sheen of sweat on his forehead. His voice sounds smooth, like pearls. "Why don't you whisper it then?"

His lips brush Jason's ear, and Scott holds him tighter. "I heard what you said last night. When you thought I was sleeping."

Jason rounds his hips, opening more so Scott can press further inside him.

"It's you," Scott whispers, letting his body be the strong, stable support Jason can lean against and be held by. "I know it's you. I'm always going to find you. Every time. Always."

Scott loses the words when he slants up inside Jason, holding his hips in place. All that was gentle now rushes forward; their breathing is fierce, their kisses chasing and catching. Each muscle finds a way to tangle, tighten, and let go. There will be no better love for him than this, no one who could know him more completely, even down to the darkest parts of him. No one who can say he's seen Scott this way. He wants to push deeper into that acceptance, test it, push against the walls of it, be held by it. Every fibre in him pushes out, opening from the inside, and Jason is the only person in the world strong enough to absorb it, heart ready to meet him.

"Let's be together, you and me, every time," Scott says between soft groans. He's trying not to growl in Jason's ear, but it's getting harder with Jason pressing back on him, their rhythm building.

"Yes," Jason whispers as Scott closes his eyes. "Yes, you and me."

Jason turns so he can pull Scott over him; Scott's hips press forward as Jason guides him inside again with a sighing breath. They lift up and pull back on a current until Jason's thighs tremble, and Scott folds them against his body, warm in his arms. Jason's shining eyes are the colour of quiet, safe crystal waters that looked so familiar in a new mother's face. Scott has to gasp and cry out, and cushion his lips across Jason's sweaty forehead because they are coming, arching and pulsing and open, so deep and so free.

Hands search each other out while hot cheeks brush together, and once urgent kisses turn lazy and slow. Scott watches Jason smile and sigh, and he thinks of how many of his faces there still are to see. He wants to see Jason take his first bite of papaya salad in the Bang Rak marketplace; he wants to see how his fringe blows in the wind when they reach the top of Fourmile Creek in Boulder. He wants to take his picture standing on the sand, swimming in the ocean, and sitting under a shady tree with bits of sunlight dappling his face. He wants Jason's voice to be the sound that speaks all the words of their love story.

But for now, they are in a space all their own, where nothing exists but the spell they whisper over each other to bind their hearts together.

*

The full light of day colours the room now, and muted street sounds filter through the windows. Jason's head rests on Scott's chest, and his fingers walk from scar to scar on the flushed skin there.

"I think I may have left a mark," Jason says, and they both look down at Scott's torso and giggle.

Jason eyes the bedside cabinet. Scott has a new calendar there now, marked up with birthdays and travel notes; the crystals are there, too, aquamarine, lapis, carnelian, and citrine. He leans up and picks his way through until he finds what he wants. "Can I borrow your Sharpie?"

"What are you going to do with it?"

Jason pulls off the cap as he straddles Scott's lap, the sheets wrinkling between them. He pulls Scott's hand from where it rests to place it on his own thigh with a little pat. "You'll see. Ready?"

As ever. Scott bites his lip. "Yes."

Jason's eyes twinkle, and his hair falls over his forehead in soft lines. The tip of the marker touches down just above Scott's wrist, and makes him jump.

"Steady now. This says 'permanent marking pen' right here on the label, see?" Jason brings the marker well up to Scott's eyes with a smile. Scott grips his thighs.

"Okay, I'll try."

"Right. Here we go." One of Jason's hands lies flat on Scott's chest, while the other draws two long vertical lines pointing down to his wrist. A tree trunk? A skyscraper? No, because at the bottom, Jason draws a curve with a pointed tail on the end. The words "permanent" and "steady" roll over and over in Scott's mind as the felt tip touches his skin, sharp and soft at the same time.

Oh...oh my God.

Their smiles are gone, their playful teasing replaced by quiet breath. Jason draws an arching line that makes the second side a mirror of the first.

"Are you making me a bracelet?"

Jason adds a crossbar at the top. "I'm making you an anchor, for when you go away. The anchor for my ship, yeah? To tie us together. Bring us back home." Jason thinks a minute, tilting his head and smoothing his fringe. "Do you like it?"

There is a lovely pricking in Scott's eyes. "I do."

Jason adds the ring at the top, where a chain or rope would go. "You were gone for a while."

Scott nods, suspecting Jason isn't talking about being gone abroad; he means before that, gone from the world, from his own life, gone from himself. "You helped me get back."

Jason smiles as he draws a little *J* underneath, as a signature, and blows a cool puff of air over it to make sure it's dry. "There. What do you think?"

"I think I could love it." Scott reaches for Jason's hand, squeezes for a moment, and then he pulls the marker from between his fingers. "And I think it's my turn." He rises up, meeting Jason above him, and they sit for a minute with their foreheads pressed together and their eyes closing. He knows just what he'll do.

"Get comfortable. This might take a while."

Jason's thighs tighten around him. "Don't make it too long," he says, low in his throat.

"Hush now. An artist mustn't be rushed." This time, Scott reaches for Jason's hand as if asking him to dance. Jason chuckles but offers it, and Scott sets to work.

It shouldn't be a straight line, but rather one that curves and crosses over in a knot. The rope will be woven of threads from here and from the past—Hélène, Émile, JohnandGeorgie, the brothers on the sea, Littlest Fox, Wings-on-the-Wind, Matteo, Lorenzo—twisted together to make the cord that will connect them. Over land, over sea, over time.

He begins the design at the top of Jason's wrist, drawing strands as they wind and turn in a figure eight. As the rope gets longer, he begins to realise that the others are woven in, too—Mme Samuel and Master Wydeville. Lorenzo's bride. Even the enemy warriors with their war bonnets. The driver of the silver car.

And, of course, Omran.

Jason's eyes study him. There is a fond turn in his voice. "Are you making me a bracelet?"

Scott turns his wrist over gently, to bring the rope around to the back where he'll leave the ends open. They will be together, even if they are apart. "I'm making you a rope. Do you like it?"

Jason takes a deep breath. "I do."

Now, murshid. Tell him now.

Omran's smiling voice is strong, and Scott agrees. Yes, this is the moment, now, in the full light of day.

"We've been together for a long time." Scott overlaps their hands so their drawings meet.

"I know," Jason smiles, then kisses each of Scott's fingers slowly—index, middle, ring, pinkie, and thumb. "Almost twenty-four hours."

"No, there's more." Scott looks to his desk where his notebook is hidden.

Ages. Centuries. Longer than I can remember.

He smiles when he sees Jason's questioning look. His heartbeat quickens, he takes one big breath, and then...he dives.

"I have a story to tell you."

Epilogue

Golden hour (n.) The period shortly after sunrise and shortly before sunset, varying by season, in which the sun is low in the sky producing a soft, diffuse light that adds texture and depth to an image. Also referred to as "magic hour."

2 February 2019

Scott has transformed Jason's office into a temporary photography studio, complete with lights and a small flash umbrella. It's taken them a while to get Jason posed, and now he's situated in front of his bookshelf at just the right height. With the lighting perfect and his subject seated comfortably, Scott should be having an easy time of it, but Jason is fidgeting and making faces, acting as if no one has ever taken a picture of him before.

"Would you sit still please? And look professional, or...smart."

Jason pouts. "Why can't we use that picture you took of me in Bangkok? That was a good one."

Scott drops his camera from his face and rolls his eyes. He knows exactly what picture Jason is talking about, where he stood on the hotel balcony with the dusky night behind him. The picture sits on Scott's bedside cabinet, right next to the picture of the two of them that Olivia took at their flat-warming party. The last of the sun gave off warm reddish light, and Jason seemed to glow.

"Because you had no shirt on in that picture. And you were sunburned."

"You're quite picky," Jason gripes, adjusting his fringe again.

"Well, Jesus, this is a big conference. There'll be lots of bigwigs there. Can't have a racy picture of you in the program, can we? Honestly, this will take two seconds." Scott raises his camera and finds Jason in the frame. The book Jason contributed a chapter to is just over his shoulder on the shelf, along with Jason's favourite Buddha and the pretty painted tile they found in Florence.

"Right, right." Jason takes a breath and shakes his arms out, trying to loosen up. He puts on a pleasant, professional smile.

"There. That's it. Lift your chin a bit. Not that much. Yes." Scott clicks the shutter, advances the film, and takes another. Jason's mouth stays still, but his eyes soften as though he can look right into Scott's heart through the camera. Scott clicks again. *That's it. That's the one.*

Jason crosses his eyes before Scott can take a fourth. "Did you get it?"

"Yeah."

"Good." Jason slides off the chair and shrugs his shoulders as if shaking off a costume. "Do you know what I want to do?"

I want to marry you. "What?"

He steps closer, looking Scott up and down, then takes the camera from him and places it on his desk. "I want to go home."

His cheeks are suddenly beautifully flushed. He traces up the line of buttons on Scott's shirt, then slides his hand beneath the collar. "I want to get under the covers and make love, hmm?" Jason leans in and brushes their cheeks together. He smells of orange and pine and the sea, and his breath is soft in Scott's ear.

"Love, love, love. And more love."

Acknowledgements

Writing this book been a journey full of curves, hills, and even a dead end or two. Many smart and passionate people traveled all or part of this book's roads with me, and I'm grateful.

Nic, I appreciate your early cheerleading and valuable feedback. You helped me find the fun in writing again.

Heather, thank you for your help with British-English edits through many drafts. Your help and humor were priceless, and I'm grateful.

Anitra, thank you so much for your energetic and steadfast support. From gentle encouragement to keyboard smashes and everything in between, you've been my champion from the start and I appreciate the hell out of you.

Meg, your special attention to the medical aspects of this story gave me a foundation to build from. Thank you for the reads and re-reads, the diagrams and definitions. Your patients are so fortunate to have you on their side.

My Wednesday night group, Beth, Brenda, and Melissa, and now Beth Junior, you are magnificent mentors in all things heart, soul, body, and mind. Thank you for reminding me to put my swords down every now and again. I love you.

Erin at Salt & Sage Books, thank you for organizing the sensitivity edit services with patience and expertise. Heba, your sensitivity read was insightful and your suggestions improved the manuscript in important ways. Thank you.

Thank you to my team at NineStar Press. Raevyn, I appreciate your organizational expertise in managing our journey. Natasha, thank you so much for putting your extraordinary talent toward creating the cover. I am awestruck by the gorgeous face you created for the story that lived only inside my mind for years. And Elisabetta, your editorial skill is nothing short of epic. I picture you sitting at your desk, striking out unnecessary words and errant punctuation while surrounded by reference books, superhero cape on your shoulders and red marker behind your ear. You also asked important questions and made sure the story flowed with ease and accessibility. I am beyond thrilled that this novel led me to you. Thank you. (And I promise I'll go easy on the emails and text messages in the next one.)

Amanda, our sphere is where the magic happens. Thank you for the hours, the attention, the photography experience, the humor, the red and blue pencils, the nudging, the suggestions, the patience, and the belief. And of course, thank you for the friendship, which is best of all.

And lastly, thank you to my little family, Greg and Erin. You are the heart inside my heart.

About Cynthia Hamill

Cynthia's love of romance began in eighth grade when she chose to read *Jane Eyre* instead of *Huckleberry Finn*. Charlotte Brontë, Emily Brontë, and Daphne du Maurier shaped her passion for love stories that feature mysterious plots and unforgettable characters. At thirteen, she couldn't have imagined a world where books appear on screens at the touch of a button, but decades later, romances of all genres fill her (digital) shelves while her dog-eared, well-loved copy of *Jane Eyre* still lives on her bedside table.

Cynthia's art history degree landed her a museum job in New York, but she left the Big Apple when her own love story took her to the prairies of the Midwest. She now lives a stone's throw from the Mississippi River, and you can find her poring over art books, reading tarot cards, taking nature walks with her family, and reading and writing love stories.

Email

cynthia.w.hamill@gmail.com

Facebook

@cynthiahamillromance

Twitter

@cynthiawhamill

Website

cynthiahamill.com

Connect with NineStar Press

www.ninestarpress.com

www.facebook.com/ninestarpress

www.facebook.com/groups/NineStarNiche

www.twitter.com/ninestarpress

www.instagram.com/ninestarpress

www.ingramcontent.com/pod-product-compliance
Lightning Source LLC
LaVergne TN
LVHW050911080826
845145LV00001B/56

* 9 7 8 1 6 4 8 9 0 3 2 0 5 *